MW01633468

DAVID HAZARD

LOST LAKE
THE SOLITUDES WILDERNESS
MOHAWK CAVES
LOST MOUNTAIN
MOHAWK CAVES
FLOW LANDS

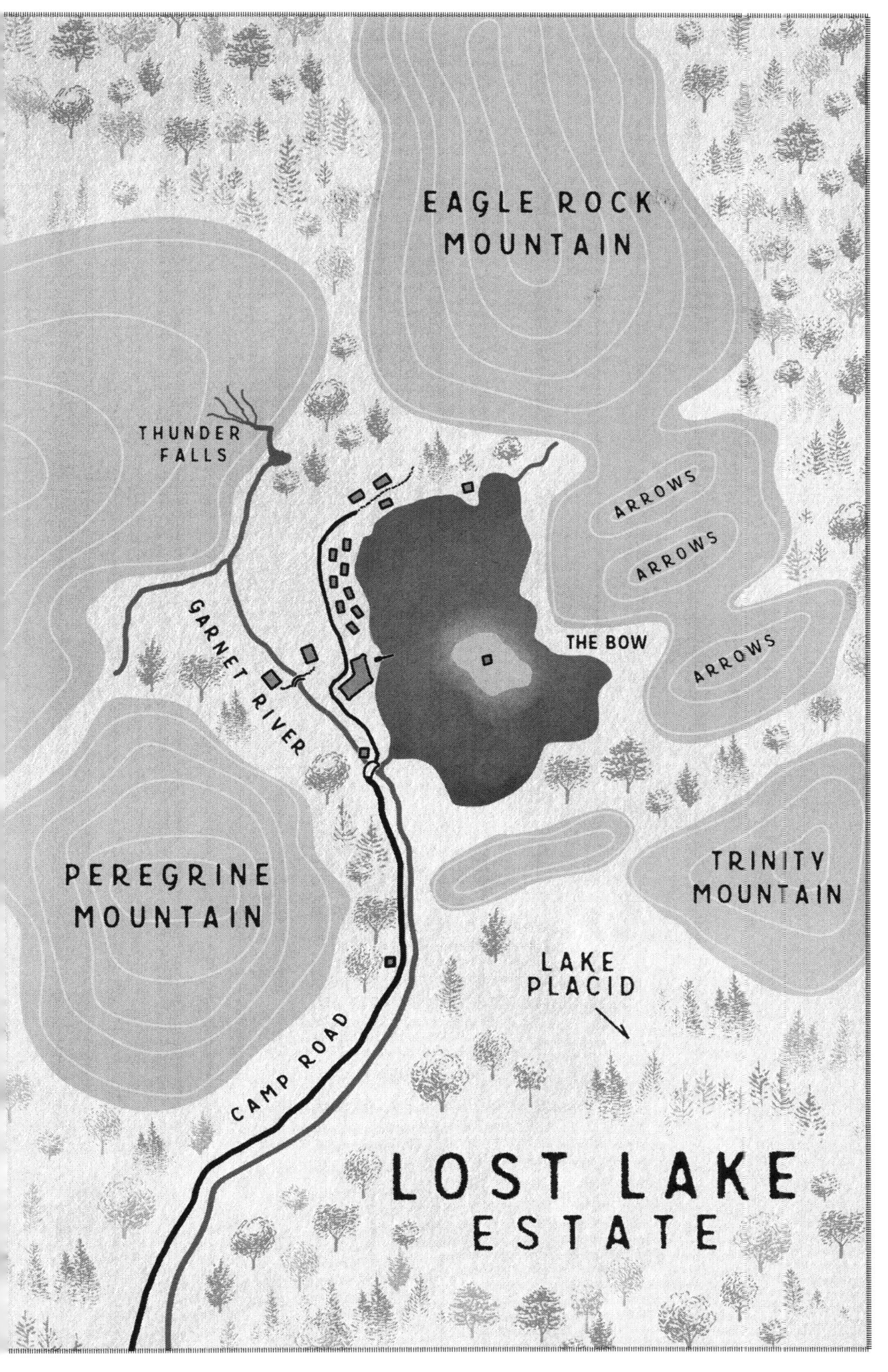
EAGLE ROCK
MOUNTAIN
THUNDER
FALLS
GARNET RIVER
ARROWS
ARROWS
ARROWS
THE BOW
PEREGRINE
MOUNTAIN
TRINITY
MOUNTAIN
LAKE
PLACID
CAMP ROAD
LOST LAKE
ESTATE

Powers Rising

Published by ASCENT, 2021, First Edition

For permission to quote or reproduce, contact:
info@lostlakeseries.com

Follow David Hazard and LostLake:
LostLakeSeries | AscentPublishing

ISBN 978-1-7356825-2-5

Artist: Mark Ivan Cole. Find Mark online at:
markivancole.wordpress.com
Facebook: MarkIvanColeArtist / Instagram: @markivancole

For images of the people,
places and wildlife of Lost Lake
visit:

LostLakeSeries.com/sketchbook

PROLOGUE

TASHI NYIMA
AUSPICIOUS DAY FOR OFFERINGS TO ANIMAL SPIRITS

DECEMBER

30TH

"*Cetan*," Dhani murmured, as if he were a thousand miles away. Or twelve thousand.

The loud crash of a pan hitting a wooden table brought him instantly back to the hard, cedar wood chair where he was seated in Sahm's kitchen.

Sahm stared at him over the hot, Tibetan flatbreads he had just dropped. Most of the dozen small loaves were strewn across the table, but three had rolled off onto the wooden floor where they lay steaming, folded, and ruined.

He had been thinking about the flatbreads that were taken a few days ago, on Christmas night, by an intruder—a bear, he had thought.

Since then, though, he felt subtle but distinct sensations lingering on the cabin's atmosphere, like fingerprints, letting him know a human being had entered here, or maybe more than one. But who? The ability to sense this was brand new; the wonders of another *siddhi* starting to make itself known.

Dhani said again, absently, "Cetan"—and Sahm forgot the bread and stared at him.

"What word did you say?"

"I. . . ," Dhani hesitated, feeling nervous. "I said *eagle*."

"Yes, but you said it in Tibetan. Where did you learn that word? I did not teach it to you."

"I don't know. It just came to me."

Sahm's eyes did not leave Dhani's bewildered face as he stooped to pick up the loaves from the floor. "It came to you how?"

Dhani stared out through the frost fingers on the kitchen window at the morning sunlight sparking on the late December snow. On the shore of Lost Lake, a gust of cold wind sent a small mound of ice crystals spiraling upward in a tiny cyclone of white.

"I guess I was starting to daydream. I was in these really high, snowy mountains."

"Climbing?"

"No, flying."

"Today is *Tashi Nyima*, an important day for making offerings to animal spirits," Sahm said. "It is no surprise you are thinking like an animal spirit." He brushed dust off the three ruined flatbreads. "These and three more I will take into the woods today as gifts for the hungry creatures. Tell me more about your daydream."

Dhani stared at the clear sky outside. When he had come in from the icy morning, Sahm had given him a cup of the hot sassafras tea he usually liked, but he had not touched it while his mind was soaring far away. Now the golden liquid was cool.

"I was circling around and around in the air over this beautiful lake. The water was so many colors—aqua, green, yellow, and red. I was rising higher and higher. I wish I really could fly. I was this big huge bird, with huge wings, and my feathers were gold and black."

Sahm's mouth fell open. "You were flying over *Danzengcuo,* the Five Color Lake, it seems. In the form of a *lammergeyer.*"

"*Where* was I? *What* was I?"

"The Five Color Lake is not far from my home in Tibet. And the bird you speak of is sometimes called the Himalayan eagle. This is important. What were you doing?"

"Sahm, I don't know anything about where you come from or about Himalayan birds. I was just circling around."

"But you used the word *cetan,* which is very special to me. Think, please. Why did you say it?"

"I was rising higher and circling over that lake you said. And another bird—a regular old eagle—started to come up from beneath me. It was perfect and amazing, the way it flew. But. . . ." He stopped.

"But what?"

Dhani felt a pressure weighing on him now, as if Sahm were pushing too deeply into his mind. Having to keep certain things he had done in the past secret made it uncomfortable when people pressed him with questions.

"When the eagle was far away from me that was okay. When it got too close, I felt really, really uneasy. Then I panicked. So I shouted at it."

"And the word you shouted to keep the eagle from getting too close, that word was *cetan.*"

"If you say so. I just thought I said eagle."

Sahm grew quiet, and now he had a look of disappointment.

"Why do you look unhappy?" Dhani asked quickly, feeling anxious. "What do you think that means?" He had only come to ask if Sahm would go exploring with him on new show shoes Kate Holman had purchased for the Lost Lake program. Now, he wished he had kept his mouth shut. "It was just a daydream. It's not a big deal."

Sahm was pacing. "As I told you, today is very auspicious where animals and animal omens are concerned. Dreams of any kind are a language and always have something to tell us. Most certainly this one does."

"Then what do you think it means?"

"First, I believe it means that *I* must be more patient and wait. I must not place pressure on you. People awaken to the truth of who they are slowly, only as they are able." Sahm thought, but did not say, *The vision also says that you possess great and powerful* siddhis*—but these abilities must be allowed to arise on their own.*

Dhani was confused. Why was Sahm now talking about himself? He skipped over that.

"It's kinda weird you used that word—'awaken'," Dhani responded, looking thoughtful. "A few nights ago—late on Christmas night—I had another, I guess you'd call it, daydream. Sometimes I think I get day-dreams and reality confused. They get mixed up in my head."

"Please tell me more about this."

"I was in the aviary late that night. I went there because I felt sort of like someone had called me. I didn't hear anything—I just felt it. Then suddenly this really bright blue light filled the whole barn and the eagle that won't fly began acting weird and I thought voices were saying things to me."

"You saw a blue light and voices spoke. What did they tell you?"

The brilliant light filled Dhani's mind again, he recalled the mid-night snow tapping on the barn's dark windows, and the words. . . .

"It is time to let yourself arise."

"Yes, awaken soon. You are the one we have waited for."

But who was the *we* that waited for him? How was he supposed to arise? What did that even mean? These questions had circled around his mind since that strange encounter. The whole thing made him feel psycho, and he decided to hide these events carefully from Claire so she didn't pull away.

He hated lying to Sahm, but said, "I can't remember what they told me." Completely untrue, because he had written down the message on a scrap of paper in his room.

Sahm pressed his lips together. "So, again, it is clear that you are not yet ready."

Dhani wanted to be done with all this. He pushed his chair back from the table and stood. "Actually, Sahm, it's probably too cold outside to go snowshoeing. I saw Grady on my way over here. He said it's only five degrees above zero right now but that it's gonna be warmer tomorrow. Maybe we can go after morning chores."

"Yes. If I can finish all my work for Jo in the clinic."

"Can I ask you for a favor?"

"Certainly."

"Can you forget what we were just talking about? I know I sort of brought it up, but talking about this stuff makes me feel strange."

"It is unlikely I will forget it, but I will not speak of such things unless you do."

"Thanks, man. You're the best."

When Dhani had gone out the front door, Sahm turned to washing the pans—and startled when the kitchen filled with brilliant blue light.

The shining figure from which the light radiated held up one hand in a gesture of blessing when Sahm began to prostrate himself.

"Sahmdup, there is no need for this."

Sahm looked into eyes of deep compassion that shone from the smiling face of the Great One. He wanted to speak, but felt tongue-tied.

"I have come to tell you not to trouble yourself about the boy. The battles he chose to face before he entered this lifetime will strengthen him for what is soon to come."

Sahm thought immediately of Dhani's many fears—of Steve Tanner, of others in the program, even his fears about the girl, Claire. "The boy's mind turns so many things into obstacles, and his abilities are buried beneath those many fears. He resists knowing the truth. I know that I am here to help him, and I wish to, but—"

"If you try to help him too much, he will not find his strength and great gifts. Without those things, he will not be able to do the work he is here to do. You must be at his side to train and urge him on. As for the work of freeing himself, that he must do on his own. It will tax your patience—observe yourself, Sahmdup, now that you have reentered the path of your training, as well."

Sahm bowed his head and pressed his hands together in front of his heart center. In his mind's eye, he saw Dhani cringing in the presence of Tanner, and doubt came. Surely, any great gifts Dhani might have must manifest soon—though that seemed so unlikely—and he remembered the dire warning his grandfather had issued months ago:

"It no longer matters where you are in this world. What is coming upon us all, you cannot escape. No one can. Wherever you believe you can hide, it will find you. There is no more hiding. Everyone who cares about life on this earth is needed now."

In response to Sahm's doubts, *Dzes-Sa* told him, *"Hold steady, Sahmdup. If you are anxious and hurried, you will be unsteady, and you will not be able to fulfill the purpose for which you were brought here. The young one will find his own way through doubt and resistance. His spirit will awaken."*

"But will it be in time to help face what is coming upon us all—whatever that darkness is?"

"The good karma accumulated in past lifetimes can help him overcome the terrible obstacles that have fallen in his path during this lifetime. Let us hope it does."

When Dhani pulled the door of Sahm's cabin closed behind him and turned to go down the steps, the sight that met him made his stomach flip—and he stepped into the daydream that had almost bloomed in his mind in Sahm's kitchen. . . .

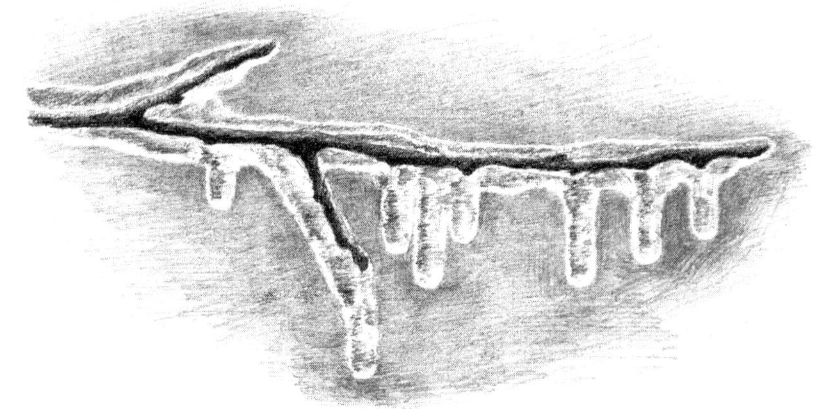

. . .Before him were many old, stone and mud-roofed buildings arranged around a village square. Hundreds of people were watching dancers in bright red, blue, green, and yellow costumes and wearing huge masks. The masks reminded him of the fanged visage of Vajrapani, the Buddha of fierce compassion he had seen in a small picture on Sahm's meditation altar. Men in saffron colored robes were chanting, clanging cymbals, and blowing into ten-foot long, deep-sounding horns, their ear-splitting blast echoing from high, snow-covered mountain peaks that ringed the village. In the center of the square, a juniper and sandalwood scented bonfire sent sparks up into the brisk, Himalayan air.

For an instant, he remembered hearing the sound of cymbals and horns like these many months before, during a strange encounter with a great fish out on Lost Lake. And he remembered the spark of recognition or welcome in the Great Northern Pike's eye the first day he arrived at Lost Lake, as if it had known him and rejoiced at his presence.

In the distance, Dhani could see Danzengcuo, the Five Colored Lake, its shores surrounded by the tallest evergreen trees he had ever seen.

This village is near where Sahm is from, he thought.

One of the men in saffron robes crashed his cymbals loudly and shouted above the noise.

"He has come! The One we have waited for has come!"

All across the open square, hundreds of heads turned toward Dhani, smiling and cheering.

Stunned, he stepped back, and the bright blue robe embroidered with gold symbols he was wearing fluttered on a slight breeze coming down the mountain slopes. For a split-second, he caught sight of the symbols on his robe—words in Tibetan—but he was too focused on the joyful ceremony at hand to read them.

"Let us offer gifts to our great helpers, the animal spirits," he heard himself call out.

He walked into the throng of people, brushing the shoulders of chanters, musicians, and dancers who were now still and silent as he passed. Beyond the wall of people, at the center of the square, currents of mountain air made the bonfire leap and roar.

Stopping just within the aura of the fire's intense heat, he waited as two young men brought a huge silver tray filled with sweet cakes made with barley flour, yak butter, and honey. He reached for one and did not recognize his own hands, which were old and wrinkled.

As he lifted an offering from the platter, he felt the warm butter and honey sag and start to run from the cakes down his wrists—and thought, This all happened to me a long, long time ago.

"On this auspicious day," he cried out, "we offer songs, dances, gifts, and our deepest gratitude to the spirits of good animals everywhere that are sent to help us."

Horns blasted, cymbals crashed, and the crowd shouted.

He was too focused on placing the first offering into the bonfire's leaping flames to hear what they were saying, and movement far overhead caught his attention.

An eagle was circling above him. Higher still, one lone, gold and black lammergeyer was soaring on cold drafts surging up the mountains. . . .

. . .like the smaller gusts kicking up swirls of ice crystals here on the shore along Lost Lake.

Dhani blinked hard and the blue flash that had blinded him

dissolved, and he could see again. He found himself standing flat-footed and stupefied, holding out cold hands as if he were making an offering to the roaring bonfire that had just vanished, along with the whole scene, from his mind. But not before the old man he was in the vision turned his head as they separated and became two people again. . . and a look in the Old One's eyes shot through him like an arrow, along with a message.

"It is true. You are the one they have been waiting for. Feel the gift that lies dormant in you. You hold within you what is needed to do the work that must be done in the world."

He reached out to touch Dhani's chest, but Dhani felt a surge of terror. . . .

"No!" Dhani shouted at the air, stuffing his hands over his ears. His whole body was shaking. "Whatever it is *they* want from me, whoever *they* are, I can't do it. I'm just a doofus. Just a kid."

He stumbled and slipped his way over ice hunks along the frozen lakefront toward his cabin. This was exactly the kind of weird daydreaming his mother had begged him to stop. He could hear her voice now. "You're too old for this crap. Go find kids to play soccer with, or better yet get a girlfriend. At least stop talking about your little imaginary things when *he's* around. It makes him think he needs to toughen you up, and you know what happens then." *He* was her boyfriend, the one Dhani secretly called The Monster.

Unconsciously, Dhani rubbed his arms and torso at the memory of the man. If even the slightest thing set him off, there was severe hell to pay. Sometimes, even for his mother, for not "straightening the whiny, little sissy out" sooner.

Why, when he was trying so hard to stop these crazy, wild imaginings, were they only getting stronger? Just a moment ago the scene in his mind was so strong he felt like he had actually stepped through a doorway into another time and place.

He had thrust his hands in the pocket of his black hoody to keep them warm but, slipping again, he pulled them out to catch himself if he fell. Something small and round was inside his closed right fist.

He opened it, and in his palm was the seer stone from Sahm's altar. He had no memory of picking up; in fact, he knew for certain he had not taken it.

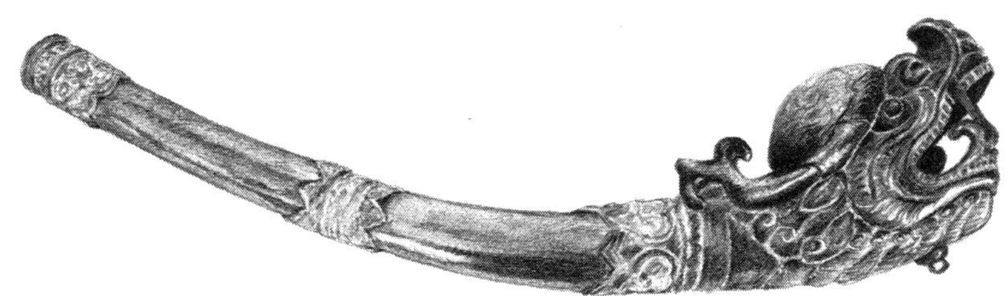

POWERS RISING

1

January

4th

"So, you have no idea where she works now?"

The man on the other end of the line in DC sounded kind enough, but also like he was busy and needed to go.

"My restaurant opens for lunch in a half-hour—Dhani? that's your name, right?"

"Yeah."

He was in Kate's office, staring out the back windows at the snow-wrapped peak of Lost Mountain. The sky had been gray for days, and this morning, wind high up blew white clouds of snow off the loftiest crags, making the tiny, charcoal stick-figures of trees vanish and reappear in ghostly fashion. In the after-Christmas desolation of Adirondack winter, and in the aftermath of his unsettling daydreams, the intense desire to locate his mother had come roaring back.

"A whole crowd is gonna pour out of these federal offices all around me, Dhani, and I need to be sure my kitchen staff is prepping."

"I don't know where my mom is, though." He stopped himself from talking about needing to protect her from the Monster, pretty sure the guy would just hang up on him. "A judge came up with your number somehow and gave it to me. He said she was working there."

"*Was*. I'd like to find her, too. She walked out one night with a bunch of meat and groceries from my cooler."

And then he did hang up.

Dhani turned to Kate and Tom, who were seated at their desks.

"Judge Sewell said he wasn't sure about the number," said Kate. Seeing Dhani's crestfallen look, she spoke softly. "Did you learn anything?"

He didn't want to say the full truth. "I guess she got a job somewhere else."

4TH

Grady's boot slipped on the frozen mud, nearly causing him to slide off the narrow path along the south side of Lost Mountain. He was walking with his right shoulder to the high, rock wall along a native trail his old Abanake Indian friend had shown him, still there from ancient times, but barely detectible unless you knew it was there among the scrub pines and glacier-thrown boulders. Today, he had decided, was a good clear day—icy air but strong sun—to check for signs of winter poachers and forbidden trappers who sometimes slipped onto Kate Holman's posted lands.

As he regained his footing, he caught sight of a symbol etched into the frozen dirt, probably with someone's boot heel. The last few days had brought a deep-freeze, but with the sun's warmth amplified by the rock wall, spots of bare ground had melted and refrozen.

"A dot and a dash," he said out loud. Morse code for the letter *A*. He had learned the symbols during his few days at church camp when he was twelve, before he got kicked out for swearing in chapel.

Who would have left this symbol, and why?

He watched his footing more carefully now, not only for icy patches but to see if there were more symbols. Past a long stretch of crusted snow, another short patch of frozen mud appeared, and a couple more letters in code.

"Two dots, *I*. . . Dot and dash. . .another *A*," he read, his breath dissipating in a plume on the cold air. Then a blank stretch, and two more letters. "Two dashes, *M*. . .another *I*."

He rubbed his ears, which had begun to sting with the cold. "I AM," he said, "Or MIAM. And the letters ran together in his head into a word.

Miami. He grinned. Was the trespasser who was out here during the last few days of mixed deep-freeze and thaw wishing they were on a beach far south of here, lying in the warm sand? He was, and thought about tequila and beach cabanas.

A large hawk called from the forest far below the narrow path then, distracting him. Whatever fool had hiked way out here in the harsh winter temperatures was almost forgotten.

Almost, because something not quite right about the coded letters stuck with him for another hour—until the thought was buried when he recalled the avalanche of tasks and repairs shouting for his attention back at Kate's lodge.

5TH

The ten days following such a wonderful Christmas had turned on a dime and a series of small events had left Kate's mind uneasy, unsettled and churning with conflict.

Emmalyn had complained that Dhani was acting strangely. "Sometimes he walks right past people like he's weirded-out in a trance. He scares me." Dhani was down about his errant mother. Mike Yazzie had kicked Garrett out of his class two days in a row. Grady mentioned that someone might have trespassed through the estate on a back trail and he was keeping an eye out. Steve Tanner was skipping staff meetings and Eric Trovert reported he was holing up on Osprey Island, "And when I went out to check on him, he shut the door in my face." Bay

Trovert had corrected and softened the picture of that event, saying, "Tanner did tell you it wasn't a good time and you asked him if you could come in anyway," and Eric had glared at her.

Her breathing felt shallow and she made an effort to slow and deepen it.

My life was so peaceful here in these beautiful mountains. Why was I so naïve to think everyone would happily pull together toward the same goals, get along great, and everything would just. . .flow?

Tom was a steadying, balancing influence, but the program pressures occasionally broke through her coping skills, especially in the middle of the night. This morning, her mind felt like a raging torrent, as she tried to push back against the deluge of troubling thoughts and the undercurrent of discouragement that came with them.

I *need to have more inner resources to handle all these complaints, conflicts, and stresses.*

In the small mammal's area in one of Jo Rondeau's rehabilitation barns, Sahm was about to change the filter on the huge, aquatic tank where three young otters were dashing after each other in wild, playful abandon.

He smiled at them—and then out of nowhere felt a jolt of tension, and thought of Kate. Unbidden, the Bodhisattva prayer flew through his mind.

May you be free of suffering and the root of suffering.

Dear Kate. What was troubling her? The jolt he'd felt was not for nothing.

And he prayed again. *May you be free from suffering. . .* feeling energy go out from himself.

The eruption of stressful thoughts made Kate feel like she could crawl out of her skin. She wanted to throw on cross country skis or bear paw snowshoes and just. . . escape this office. No, escape this program.

Be out in the air where she could breathe.

But you don't want to escape. Not really. You just don't want to feel the way you're feeling.

For no reason she could think of, she pushed aside a stack of papers on her desk and picked up a book Sahm recommended, written by a Tibetan master teacher. Opening it at random, her eyes fell on a passage—what were the chances?—all about dealing with a tumultuous thought-flow:

"It's essential to start by repeatedly placing our mind on the breath."

She took long, slow deep breaths.

"Recognize each thought, acknowledge it. . . ."

Steve Tanner came to mind. The island cabin where he'd taken refuge was meant to be a place of rejuvenation. A U.S. Senator, a friend of her late husband, had found it very refreshing after the tensions of Washington, staying there when he'd come to Lost Lake several years ago on a highly secretive fact-finding trip. Was Steve just out there isolating himself, amplifying the remnants of pain and grief he'd brought with him?

". . . let the thought resolve, and return to focusing on the breath."

She imagined thoughts of Steve dissolving in the stream of her thought-flow. . . and took a few more deep breaths.

"This breaks up the river of discursiveness."

It was true. By allowing thoughts to arise, letting them pass through without engaging them too much but refocusing on her breath instead, she could feel the onslaught of troubling thoughts start to break up a little.

"This practice takes us to the innermost circle of peaceful abiding, where we become aware of thoughts arising in our stillness."

Yes, that's what she felt. A central place inside her that was still, calm.

"It's like standing next to an iced-over mountain stream; we hear water popping and bubbles."

She imagined the sound of the Garnet River just beyond the first barn that housed Jo's clinic with its current chuckling along under the ice.

"As long as we stay focused on the breath, we can just let thoughts arise and fall. The subtle energy that comes with each thought will naturally dissolve as we let the thought pass. Indulging these subtle movements of the mind at all tends to strengthen them and actually create disturbance in our mind."

She had been trained, of course, to take on problems head-on, powering her way through to a usually exhausted finish. If she was going to direct this program, she needed another skill—this one, which the teacher called "peaceful abiding"—learning how to remain in a calm, even blissful state, in the midst of a whole list of challenges.

". . .we build another kind of strength by relaxing into our breathing. This allows the natural stillness of mind to develop. Experiencing the stability and joy of our mind becomes much more appealing than listening to our mental chatter."

From the open doorway of her office suite, someone cleared their throat.

Kate put the book down and turned to see Ivy, her cook, standing there.

"I hate to disturb you, Kate. You look so calm and peaceful. Grady just came by and said the ice broke off a huge branch from a tree next to your greenhouse and it smashed through two big panes of glass."

Kate took in three deep breaths, then a fourth. "I assume he's on it, getting it fixed."

"Yes, he just wanted you to know, in case you go out there. He's got a repair crew coming out with replacement panes in three hours."

When Ivy was gone, Kate took more deep breaths. It was just broken glass. Not a young person going off the rails or being injured. Not Steve Tanner walking out on the program midyear, a thought that lay behind her concern for him personally.

She felt calm. *Score one... this time.*

Then she busied herself, to keep her mind from re-engaging with the conflicts and full-on stresses of the first semester which, in reality, would very likely boil up again. She reread the Tibetan teacher's words, to make sure she had a firm grip on the practice of peaceful abiding.

Ivy came back in with a steaming cup of mint tea. "Are you at all worried about Tanner? He's been awfully reclusive out on that island."

A ripple of anxiety tried to return, but Kate let out a breath and let it go.

"Worrying doesn't help or change things. He's probably just resting up after all those strenuous hikes and campouts he led last year. I'm guessing he's fine."

Steve pulled the bottle of whiskey from the pantry. The amber liquid inside was down to less than a splash in a shot glass. Reaching deeper on the shelf, he pulled out another bottle, still unopened, twisted the cap off, and took a big swig.

Looking out in the cabin's main room, he saw Pal lying beside the morning fire, watching.

What Steve thought he saw in those eyes was a reproach.

You've been day drinking again.

He clenched the bottle tighter. "You got a problem with this, you can go back to that owner who dumped you in the woods. Remember how you almost drowned in that pond?" He took another drink.

Pal rose to a sitting position and his lip curled in a silent growl.

Steve's head hurt this morning and he swore. "What's wrong with you? I'm good to you. I feed you. Growl at me again, and I'll kick your head."

Pal continued to stare, unblinking.

Steve saw in the black lab's intense gaze a direct, male-to-male challenge. In Afghanistan, he had encountered stray dogs whose crazed and deadly stare made his blood go cold. In Kabul, one had locked eyes with him just before baring its fangs and attacking. That warning growl gave him the seconds he needed to follow instinct, whip out his side arm, and fire the two rounds that blew the lunging creature back four feet, dead.

Now he realized this was a different look. Just as penetrating, but full of something like sorrow and compassion mixed.

He set the bottle down on the counter, and when he did, Pal's eyes followed. The lab continued to stare at the bottle—and growled again.

"Well, isn't this a cheesy scene from a TV movie," Steve said, trying to make light of it. "Guy drinks a little too much. Dog growls at whiskey bottle."

In the next moment, though, he felt a twinge in his chest—of guilt and deep sadness. What the hell was he doing?

Silencing the voices and shutting out the strange things he'd seen—or trying to.

"I should give you back to Jo," he said, agitated, sad. "Or drop you off at a shelter. I don't need another conscience. One's bad enough. And you should have a better master than me."

The look of sadness did not leave Pal's eyes, and Steve had the sense that he himself was coming close to a dangerous edge again, just as he had at Christmas when thoughts of oblivion had almost driven him over it. Was that what the lab was doing now—trying to keep him away from that place again?

And you just threatened to kick the sweetest dog on earth. What's wrong with you?

He picked up the liquor bottle and waved it at Pal, trying to play off his angry words as if he had just been joking, though he was not ready to fully give in.

"All right, all right. I'll pour it in a glass with ice or a splash of water. How's that—more civilized for you?"

The lab did not leave him all morning, even following outside in the icy wind when Steve went to bring in more split oak for the fire—dark thoughts and memories like ghosts now mercifully driven away by the freshness of the winter air.

Sahm stood beside the otters' tank, his tasks here finished, feeling acutely aware.

Beyond the musical murmur of the circulating water lay a silence—one deeper than any in this world. From that vast space came a great weight, as if the air pressure had risen, and along with that a sense of certainty.

Something was shifting. The dark stain on the sky that he had witnessed months before was moving closer. And the powers needed to face it had better arise soon.

A half-hour later, the sharp rap on the cabin door did not startle Sahm. He had come back to rest after his morning round of chores, but only a moment before this urgent knock, a voice in his head had sounded—

"He is here. With his friend."

—along with the sense that there were not one but two people standing outside on his porch.

Vajra, sprawled and sleeping by the woodstove, raised his head and growled. The limp he had sustained two months ago was finally, completely gone.

Sahm ushered in Dhani and Ray-Ray from the frigid morning air, a small blast of cold invading the cabin with them. "You have exams later today," he said.

"I really need to talk to you," Dhani replied, stripping off his coat and kicking his snowy boots onto the mat by the door. He began pacing. "I can't focus my mind. Ray-Ray just wanted to come and hang out."

"You can 'hang out' by the wood stove with Vajra," Sahm nodded to Ray-Ray who was hooking his coat on a wall peg. "And you can help me make hot drinks, Dhani. I was about to make a remedy for Randy Wolfmoon's grandfather, who has chest congestion. For us—strong, black tea."

Dhani looked at Ray-Ray, who was staring at Sahm's meditation altar. "What?"

"'Hey, it's the altar boys. You here to get altered?'," said Ray-Ray, sounding theatrical.

Dhani's face was blank.

"It's a quote from a movie, 'The Dangerous Lives of Altar Boys'. I'm joking, to keep from peeing my pants looking at Sahm's demon gods."

"They're not demons. Sahm already told you, they're fierce, protector Buddhas."

Ray-Ray shook his head. "Look like demons to me."

In the kitchen, Dhani rummaged for spoons. "Do you have sugar or honey?"

Inwardly, Sahm was reaching out to Dhani's mind, which felt like roiling torrents of water.

"No need for that," Sahm replied, pouring hot water from a kettle through a strainer full of dried green leaf clippings. "Too sweet. Clear green tea is better. This will calm you." He handed Dhani a steaming cup. "Now why did you come when you should be studying?"

"A whole bunch of stuff is bothering me. My mind is like, crammed with all these worries."

"That is true."

Dhani missed that. "Mostly, it's about my mom. I can't stop thinking that she's in real trouble." He rethought that. "She gets herself in trouble. I should be there for her."

Sahm blew across the surface of the steaming tea. At least he was not obsessing about the girl this time. That was good.

In his meditations for each student in the program, whenever Sahm came to Claire, a fierce *dakini*—a female, protector Buddha—had appeared. At Christmas, she had opened a door and made the first step onto a new path, her own path, and right now she needed no interference or distractions from boys or anyone. Something lay ahead for her of greatest importance and it would resolve her inner turmoil about her parents in prison—that was the sense he got in meditation.

Dzes-Sa's voice spoke into Sahm's mind.

"Sever these cords of worry. Open his mind wider."

Without forethought, Sahm raised one hand above his head and brought it down in a swift, cutting motion—imagining he was using his grandfather's *phurba*.

"Separate from your mother. *Now.*"

Dhani stared at him, mouth open.

Then Sahm reached out and, with the first finger of his right hand, tapped Dhani's forehead just above and between his eyes. He felt a wave of energy pass through and out of himself into Dhani.

"Tell me what you felt and saw just now," said Sahm.

"I—I don't know. First, it was kinda like, I didn't get rid of my mom. It was like, something pushed her away from me. A little ways anyway."

Sahm felt a bit of frustration. As a complete severing of crippling soul-ties, he sensed it had not done very much. The tie was strong and deep. Clutching. But maybe it was a first small step toward releasing Dhani's trapped spirit—the first flicker of a greater force that needed to burst from within the young man to push him free.

"There is much training ahead for you, Sahmdup," said Dzes-Sa, "on this part of your life's path. You have been brought here so that, as you teach this boy, he will be your teacher also. That is in keeping with the way of things."

"Then when you touched my forehead, for a second I kinda saw the whole sky inside my mind."

"And now you feel more space inside you?"

Dhani had a faint smile. "Yeah. Like my head isn't *crowded* or something. And like there's this big open space in there somewhere."

All his life, he had felt concern for his mother because of her wild behavior. It had taken over almost every waking minute. Now, it was as if that concern was beginning to leave him. For the first time, he wasn't thinking about what he did wrong to deserve her boyfriends' abuse. A new thought occurred. Why did she always choose men who were bad to them. Or at least bad to *him*?

The few moments of open space within him receded, and he was aware only of Sahm and the cabin again.

"I don't feel as scared for my mom, but I still wish I knew where she was."

So, a small step forward. Sahm handed Dhani a cup and picked up the other two. "Your friend is waiting for his tea. He is quite agitated."

Dhani stared at him. "I don't think so. He was pretty cool when we left him."

Sahm smiled, feeling the energy coming from the cabin's front room. Yes, *agitated.*

Out in the cabin's open room, Ray-Ray was standing at Sahm's altar table. He had picked up a small gray stick, no longer than an inch, and was looking at it closely.

Sahm offered him a cup. "That is a small bone from the little finger of an ancient teacher. I was keeping it in a small wooden box in my pack, but he deserves a place of honor. I should have placed him there before."

"*Ohmygod.*" Ray-Ray nearly dropped it on the table and took a step back from Sahm without accepting the cup. "Why do you have that?"

"It reminds me that in this form I am temporary. That I have been here in this world before. And after I leave this body and pass through the *Bardo,* I may return here again. It also reminds me that many men and women have passed down to me very important knowledge."

Dhani picked up the bone between a thumb and forefinger—then looked at Sahm, surprised. "Whoa. Why does it feel like it's humming a little?—like it has batteries in it or something." He looked at Ray-Ray. "Did you feel that?"

Ray-Ray was staring at the altar, wiping his hand on his pants. "I touched a dead guy's finger joint. So gross.—My father would say you're worshipping false gods. And that this is a gateway to let in evil."

"How does your father know so much about evil?"

"My father wouldn't want me touching anything on this table—or even to be talking to you."

Sahm was wide-eyed with surprise. "Why?"

"Because something evil could jump off that stuff and get inside us."

"That is not possible."

"Yes it is. Evil is everywhere. It's already in every one of us."

"Where did you hear this?"

"My dad. The people in our church."

"What you call God," Sahm responded in a gentle tone, "is already in every one of us waiting to be discovered and made stronger, like a fire that has been covered with ashes. Remove the ashes—God is there. Evil cannot stay."

Ray-Ray vehemently shook his head. "No. We're sinful and evil. The whole world. All of us."

"I don't think I am," said Dhani.

Ray-Ray almost said, *"Didn't you try to kill your mom's boyfriend?"* but checked himself.

Sahm was shaking his head. "'The world is evil. Everyone is evil. I am evil.' That is bad religion."

"Why would you say that?" Ray-Ray resisted.

"You are believers in Jesus, is that true?"

"Yeah."

"Jesus told you, 'Remove the log from your eye," and 'If your eye is full of darkness, how great that darkness is.'"

"What are you saying?"

"Our teachers say Jesus meant that you can notice the human failings of other people and yourself and if you have a *dark* mind—one that is full of judgment and negativity—you will see only the failings and miss the full truth. But if you have a mind full of light—compassion and kindness—you will see the truth about us all. Your Jesus also said, 'You are the light of the world. Do not hide your light.' See?—he taught that we already have the light in us, just as the Buddha taught, and it only needs to be revealed. If you say you believe in Jesus, why do you not accept his teaching?"

Ray-Ray looked upset and sounded resistant. "No. You don't get it. I'm a bad person. I am."

"No, you're not," Dhani said. "You're a good friend. You should stop saying that."

"I think someone has told you a wrong thing," Sahm concluded, "and you are young and believed them. I also think you should drink your tea before it gets cold. And consider what we have talked about here."

When they were gone, Sahm returned to the kitchen to make the medicinal tea for Randy Wolfmoon's grandfather. Before leaving India with Kate, he had bought small packs of Ayurvedic medicines which he had stored on a shelf by the stove.

Reaching for the small red tin of dried *vasaka* leaves, good for clearing congestion, he pried the tight lid off.

The container was empty. So were the tins next to it, which had held dried golden root—also good for congestion—and sedum leaves—good for reducing pain and inflammation.

He felt again an energy fingerprint, left by one of the people who had snuck in here.

7TH

"Can I come in?" Dugan asked, knocking lightly on Kate's open office door.

Kate turned toward him, holding a phone receiver to one ear and nodding.

"I was wondering something," he said, when they were seated in comfortable armchairs in front of the fireplace with its small blaze. "It's kind of personal. Hope you don't mind."

"You can ask, and if I think it's too personal, I'll tell you."

Ivy brought in drinks—hot coffee for Kate, orange juice for Dugan.

"It's about that guy you went with before you met the guy you married. The Black guy."

"Ephraim. What about him?"

"Well, it's really about you."

Her eyebrows went up.

"Did you take him as a lover because you really liked him or because you thought Black men were exotic? You know—the whole White woman attracted to Black males thing."

"A legitimate question. Derek Owusu raises it in his book."

"You read Owusu's book, *Safe*?"

"*On Black British Men Reclaiming Space*—yes."

Dugan drummed his fingers on his thighs. "Wow. What do you think?"

"Did I see myself in his claim that White women love to dominate Black men and we oppress Black men into doing what we want? Dugan, I'm certain there are women who 'exoticize' Black men, as Owusu and the other essayists in his book say. I've heard some of them talk, and it's horrifying."

"Why do they do that? Is it a racist thing?"

"Humans have their fantasies and humans love to wield power over those they think of as weaker or inferior. In the case of Black men, I can only accept as true the stories told by men who were pressured to perform intimate acts with their bosses or landlords or lose their jobs or homes. How terrible is that?"

"So. . . ?"

"You're asking did I exoticize Ephraim? No. Ephraim was stunning in every way, though—his intellect, his physique, his spirituality and, yes, as a lover. He utterly captured my heart. As I told you before, when his parents insisted he break it off because they were afraid of White supremacist reprisals, I was devastated. I didn't go out with anyone else for almost two years. No one ever matched Ephraim."

Dugan drained the glass before he spoke again. "But do you believe what one guy says in the book—Courttia Newland—'If I didn't submit to being exoticized by White women I was punished?'"

Kate looked at him closely, and replied in a quiet voice. "Yes, I believe them. And it makes me sick."

When Tom entered the office a half-hour later, he stopped and studied Kate's face.

"You have a very enigmatic smile. What's going on?"

"I just had a lively conversation with one of the smartest young men in this program—Dugan. He's deep-thinking, intense, challenging, boldly honest, and reads voraciously. I couldn't be happier."

Tom saw her mood flicker.

"What?"

"I just hope his thinking leads him in a positive direction. There are so many strong influences on young people in this world. I hope he meets the right ones."

She brightened again. "*But*—do you remember us saying we hoped to see miracles here? At Christmas I felt hopeful because I saw a few happening that night. And I'm going to believe that, even if it takes Dugan to some dark places first, his intellectual questing is his own pathway to one."

Makayla stared out the window of the upstairs study room in Kate's lodge. The cold blue of the sky, the stark white angles of the winter mountains, the barren expanse of the iced-over lake—all of it made her thin body shudder. She pulled the collar of her heavy sweater up.

"Could you stop singing and drumming your fingers?" she snapped at Jalil, who was seated across the table. "I'm trying to study for finals and it's hard enough trying to concentrate on algebra."

"What—you don't like Watsky?" He kept singing.

I don't care where you've been,
how many miles, I still love you.
Show me someone who says they got no baggage
I'll show you somebody who's got no story
Nothing gory means no glory, but baby please don't bore me.
Every single person got a couple skeletons—

"I like Watsky," she interrupted, "but I'm not a fan of you trying to act like him. Especially when algebra is kicking my butt."

"Sorry, music's just like, in my blood."

Makayla laughed.

"What?"

"You're not really a drummer like you told everyone."

"Yeah, I am. Why would you say that?"

"Because you're not any good at it." She started thumping her hands on the table, out of rhythm. "This is you."

His face fell.

She reached over and, with her pen, quickly drew the Salamander Tribe sigil on the back of his hand.

"Why'd you do that?"

"I like what Claire came up with for us. And I just think it looks good on you. Also it made you stop drumming."

A smile spread across his face. "Or is it because you like me?"

She looked down at her notes. "Did you hear Jo say she can't get an answer out of the state lab in Albany where she sent the dead frogs and deformed salamanders? She's pretty pissed."

"What's she gonna do?"

"She didn't say. But she told me if we find more in the spring we're supposed to bring 'em to her."

"You haven't talked to me very much before. Are you just flirting with me now because you realized Rocco definitely isn't into you?"

Shoving her chair back, Makayla leapt to her feet—then pushed his notebook on the floor and walked out, her heels striking hard on the wood floor.

He called after her. "I know you're taking the salamanders to your room, the ones you found after the first ones died, because you like them, and you're not supposed to"—realizing as the words came out how childish he sounded.

In the lodge's great room, Claire's pencil flicked the fine lines of Ray-Ray's eyebrows onto a sheet in her sketchbook as across from her he flipped through his notes.

"I can't study French if you're staring at me," he said, not looking up.

"You should have taken Spanish. I think it's easy. Stop studying for a few minutes and look at me."

He put down his notes. "Four days of exams ahead. You ready?"

"Ready as I'm going to be.—Smile. Your whole face lights up when you do."

He made a pouting face, but couldn't hold it and broke into a wide grin.

"Much better. Stay like that."

"This feels weird. Can I talk?"

"If it helps you keep smiling."

"I'm almost ready for exams to start tomorrow, but I don't know about this winter campout in a few weeks."

"Gee, thanks for reminding me about that," she frowned. "I hope Tanner doesn't expect us to jump in a frozen lake like that stupid thing he did back in November, making people jump in that ice-cold pool at the base of Thunder Falls. That better not be required."

"If it is, *this* guy's outa there."

Claire's pencil paused midway through sketching Ray-Ray's broad smile. She was amazed that somehow he was almost always smiling. Only occasionally in the past few weeks, for fleeting moments, did it look as if something was troubling him.

"Speaking of that day, do you think Dhani threw Tanner's hat in the fire?"

"I honestly don't think so," he answered.

"But you don't know so."

He got a serious look. "Why do you care about him so much? You say you don't want anyone to be close to you because you don't trust anybody. But with Dhani, it's like you're his big sister. You watch out for him and wanna be sure he's okay."

"But do you think he did it?" she pressed, sounding defensive. Then backed off. "I'm not sure why I'm like that with Dhani. He just wants to be liked and that's kinda touching. And there's something about him no one understands. Maybe I'm just curious what he's all about."

"Like, is he really a nice guy or is he an arsonist with murderous tendencies?"

"Is that the vibe you get?"

"No. You're right. There is something strange going on with him."

"Unusual."

"Yeah. Unusual is better. Especially when he's around birds."

She set her sketchbook down. "Two days ago, you were helping Jo inventory new medical supplies and Dhani and I went to clean the aviary. The young blue jay had one of its claws stuck in the wire mesh and we went into the clinic to get Ron to help. Ron had a hawk that was brought in the day before. He was trying to treat it for mites, spraying it with garlic juice."

"Garlic juice?"

"Yeah, that's how they get rid of mites, I guess, and it stunk. But that's not the point. The hawk was shrieking and flapping so hard its wings kept getting loose from Ron's grip. He told us to leave because he said we were making it agitated and it would injure itself.

"I turned to go, but Dhani walked straight up to the table and reached out his hand. He did it too quick for Ron to stop him. Or anyway, he didn't stop him. He let Dhani stroke the hawk's head and it just... it instantly got totally quiet and still."

"So, he's like a bird whisperer or something?"

"Or something."

"I think Sahm's teaching him this weird Tibetan magical stuff. He shouldn't do that."

"Why?"

"I don't know. Maybe it'll summon demons and they'll take Dhani over."

Claire laughed. "Do you really think that—I mean, seeing how good Sahm is to everyone? No self-respecting demon would bother with him. He's way too nice."

Ray-Ray still looked serious. "The way I was brought up, other religions are always suspect."

"Maybe what your religion taught you is wrong. Did you ever think about that?"

He stared at her and a thought flickered. What if that was true? He dismissed it.

Claire bit the end of her pencil. "Your smile went away."

"Sorry." He flashed a big, goofy, toothy grin.

"Stop it. That's weird." She shifted directions. "I worry a lot more about Dhani being around Tanner. They haven't liked each other from the very beginning. I thought things were better the morning they went for coffee. But after the burned hat thing, they're a lot worse. And if you notice, the other kids are also staying way away from Dhani now. Even more than before."

"Most of them did already. But hey, he's got you and me. And Sahm."

The black line of her pencil created his jawline. "That's true. He does have us.—Where *is* Dhani?"

"Beats me. When I came over here, I thought he might be studying with you."

Close to dusk, nearing his cabin, Ray-Ray saw deer tracks leading out toward the open meadow between the camp road and the mountains and Thunder Falls. There were other tracks, too—boots. He shook his head.

Dhani, Dhani, Dhani. You can't be following wild animals when you need to hit the books.

From the distant, blue shadowed slopes of Eagle Rock Mountain came the call of a coyote, and he hoped Dhani would be safe out in winter fields alone.

He raised his head and scented the air, flicking his tail. The coyotes were not near, but he would keep his guard up. The small horns on his head would provide defense.

Looking back across the meadow, he saw the young human dressed in black just standing, staring after him as he walked toward the tree line.

His mind flickered: for an instant, he was the young human, watching a deer cross a snow field; now he was the young buck, looking back at the human.

He was *the buck.*

He continued north across the meadow, his sharp, narrow hoofs breaking through the crust of a thin covering of snow. Around him, the last brown sheaves of meadow growth rattled in the icy, moving air.

With his sharp front teeth, he sliced off the remnants of gray-dead mint and yarrow, what little there was, grinding the bitter mass for a long time in his back teeth. This place had been well browsed and he would have to search along the tree line, stretching up on his hind legs to sheer whatever greenery he could still reach on the tangy cedars around the perimeter of the meadow. After that, inside the forest in places where the snow was not too deep, he would paw the frozen mounds open in search of more browse—matted ferns and the twisted wands of raspberry bushes—that had been buried during the heavy snows.

If he found ample to eat, he would search and find her and lead her back to it; winter meant hunger and the constant need to forage. He would find her, because she belonged with him and he with her, and he wanted with all his might and his soul for her to survive these harsh months and see spring with him again. Their second.

His mind flickered once more: he saw the face of a young human—a female, with sweet-scented hair and deep brown eyes; then he saw a lithe, young doe—russet and tan, also with brown eyes.

He wanted to fall into those eyes and stay wherever she was.

The coyote howled again, his heart skipped, and he jolted alert. Where was she? Where he'd last seen her—in a thicket by the river... or inside one of the human places. He felt confused. Why wasn't he with her, to protect her and fight for her if necessary? He should be.

His heart began to pound, stronger and louder, as if it would come out of his body.

During the last year, his heart had already moved outside his body and joined itself with the loveliest creature, and he longed for her....

Dhani clenched his eyes shut, and when he opened them, the buck had disappeared inside the distant tree line. He flexed his hands, which were burning with the cold. He shivered, and his lips were numb. He had been standing here too long, letting the icy air seep through his hoody, and he turned for the cabin.

Yes, the buck was gone, but as he trudged back what remained was a deep and shared longing. For a faithful and true companion. Someone to be with and walk with through the wilderness of this world, to fend off its challenges together.

In the cabin's welcomed warmth, he held his tingling hands up close to his face in wonder. There was black grit under his nails and his fingers were dirty and smelled of mint and field yarrow.

9TH

It was midnight, and Imani and Makayla slipped into the pitch-darkness inside Kate's greenhouse.

By flashlight, they picked their way carefully between wood and wire racks that were covered in empty flats pressed out of brown peat waiting to be filled with soil and seeds. The cool air smelled of moist humus and a sweet smell, like flowers blooming somewhere further off in the dark greenhouse. At the back, farthest away from the camp road, the potting room was all night shadows except for a faint glow.

"Glad you made it," said Garrett, when they slid open the glass door and stepped inside.

He and Dugan were seated on big plastic sacks, with a small flashlight lying on the gravel floor. It gave off just enough light to prevent stumbling and to faintly make out faces. Behind them was a wall of glass, and the wood line outside was obscured by the black, moonless night.

"Pull up a big bag of—" he looked between his knees and read, "—*peat*. And sit down. Anyone see you?"

"No. The instructors' cabin was totally dark," said Imani. "But we slid out her window just in case."

"I was watching the whole way here," Makayla added, "so we could avoid Grady if he was out checking the grounds like he does sometimes. No sign of him. It's all good."

"It's about to get a whole lot better," Dugan grinned.

He handed Imani a glass pipe with a glowing tip. "Time to celebrate. Exams are bull crap."

Imani sniffed at the pipe's small plume of gray smoke. "Are you kidding me? What did you cut this with? It smells medicine-y."

"We'll find out. I have a *vah-rah-ih-tay* for us to try."

The door slid open quietly, and in the dim light Emmalyn and Tia Leesha appeared, along with Jalil.

"More ladies," Dugan smiled broadly. "Like the Black-Eyed Peas said," and he started singing, "'tonight's gonna be a good good ni-i-i-ght.'"

Emmalyn and Tia Leesha sat as far from Garrett as possible. Jalil ignored Makayla and sat by himself. "I brought the tunes," he said, pulling an iPod from his coat pocket.

"You probably can't get Radio Garden on that, can you?" Imani asked. "I've been listening to Skyrock Algeria on the computer in the study room. Really cool hip-hop with African and Saharan rhythms."

Jalil shook his head. "Can't get on the net with this. Did you get permission to go online?"

Imani smiled.

"So—a bit of a rebel," Garrett laughed. He lit another pipe and passed it. "Did Trovert ever ask you again about where you really got that?"

"Nope," Jalil replied. "Guess he bought the 'street vendor' line." He sounded proud.

"That's good. But you gotta hide stuff better or you're gonna blow up and the whole damn thing goes down."

Imani took a hit from a pipe. "This is bitter. You need to crack a window or Kate's gonna smell it when she comes in here.—What whole damn thing are we talking about?"

Dugan leaned closer until his shoulder touched hers. "You and me gotta get closer first before my man and I divulge our secrets."

She slid away, almost knocking Makayla off their shared peat bag. "So that's not happening." She turned to Garrett. "What's in those two flasks?"

He reached down and picked up one in each hand. "Jack."

"Where'd you get Jack?"

"From Grady."

She looked incredulous. "Grady *gave* you Jack?"

"Sure."

"You're lying. How'd you really get it?"

Tia Leesha looked up at the doorway and let out a small, sharp scream.

A shadowy form in the darkness stepped closer. . . and became Carter. In the dim light, her eyes looked empty.

"Don't do that!" Tia Leesha, shouted. "Why you always sneakin' around? You gave me a heart attack."

Garrett had jumped to his feet and looked angry. "Why'd you hafta yell? Stuff a sock in it. You wanna give away our best party spot?"

Then he pulled another bag of peat over beside his own, and looked at Carter. "Got a seat for you right here next to me. And some refreshments." He stuck out one of the flasks.

Carter took it and swigged, and swigged again. Then handed it back and sat down on the bag of peat Garrett had offered—after shoving it with her boot three feet away from him.

In the mellowing mood, talk circled around music, courses, instructors.

Imani took another hit from the pipe. "Is this stuff doing anything for anyone? I'm not getting a buzz and it tastes weird.—Now Mike Yazzie. That is one fine man."

"Ron is a total babe," said Makayla.

"Too wiry from all that running. Yazzie's got the body—a real man's body," Imani replied, and looked at Garrett, Dugan, and Jalil. "You boys should take note."

Carter laughed.

Garrett glanced from Carter to Imani and sounded tweaked. "Yeah, well, Jo is smokin'. I'd do her any day and she would love it."

"Any day she'd give you the time of day," Imani laughed. "Which would be *neh-ver.*"

"Hey, you were just drooling all over Yazzie."

"I didn't brag 'and he would love it'."

"How about you," Garrett looked to Carter. "Who do you think is hot?"

"Kurt Cobain."

Garrett snorted. "Okay, but he's dead."

"I like the dead."

The only sound was low music from Jalil's iPod.

Dugan had been moody and mostly quiet since Imani's brush-off. He stretched. "I'm kinda tired, and I think this party's running down."

"We're just getting started," Garrett beamed. He handed a pipe to Carter again. "Come on. Take another hit."

Carter hesitated, then took the pipe from him and stared at it. "A hit of what? Whoever sold you this crap stole your money."

She flung the pipe back at him.

He stuck up his hand to catch it but missed, and the pipe flew past him into the dark, where they heard it strike something metal and break.

Garrett kept smiling. "I can get you high without herb."

Carter stood up to leave. "I seriously don't think so."

Rocco unlocked the storage cabinet and took out the cub's medicine. The little black bear he had cradled in one arm let out a faint bawl, and a movement made him look over his shoulder.

"Dhani—hey. What're you doing here in the clinic so late?"

"I was worried that I forgot to close one of the bird enclosures real good. Thought I'd check, and I saw the lights on. What are you doing here?"

"This little guy—," Rocco nodded at the cub he was rocking, "—he needs this med every eight hours. I volunteered for the midnight dose."

The little cub grabbed Rocco's free hand in both paws, sniffing at the medicine bottle then trying to chew it. Otherwise, he remained docile, not like his brother, who was pacing his enclosure, pawing at the wires. The blond slash on the bigger cub's shoulder—which had earned him the nickname "The Flash" from Rocco—was more pronounced now that he had grown. In comparison to his younger litter mate, the larger cub was bigger now by half, making it clear something was preventing the smaller one from thriving.

"This guy had a rough start," Rocco said, wresting the bottle away from the little cub. "Kind of like a lot of people. I never thought about that much until I got into this program."

"Yeah," Dhani said absently, and turned to go.

"Hey," Rocco stopped him. "I never talked with you about this last year, but that was pretty amazing—you knowing about that storm coming up on Peregrine Mountain out of a clear blue sky. Emmalyn keeps saying it was Satanic. How did you do that?"

"Emmalyn says everything is Satanic because she's kind of obsessed. I don't know how I knew. I just did."

He stared at a tiny lump in the center of Rocco's chest beneath his sweatshirt. "Does that bear claw ever scratch you? Where'd you get it?"

Rocco opened the medicine bottle, pulled the dropper partway out and watched till the clear liquid filled it to the right level. "This guy's big brother over there. He tore it partway off trying to climb his cage. Jo had to cut it free from the wires. I drilled a small hole and hung it on this leather cord.—But wait a minute."

The medicine dropper was still poised in his hand, and he stopped rocking the little cub. "You can't see it through this sweatshirt. How do you know what I'm wearing?"

As soon as the words had spilled out, unexpectedly, Dhani wished he hadn't opened his mouth. Hadn't he just vowed that he wouldn't say weird things and bring on ridicule for being the strange kid? He tried to play it off.

"Lucky guess."

"I don't believe that. You've got some kind of ability. Come on, tell me how you do it."

"I really don't know. I wish it didn't happen."

Rocco slid the dropper back in the bottle, and put one hand on Dhani's shoulder.

"Hey, it's okay with me. My old, Italian great-grandma, she's right from Sicily and she says some people have the gift of second sight. The church was against people who had it, but she said, 'The church isn't always right—especially if they think someone has a power they can't control. Actually, my mom said that last part."

He reached for the leather cord that hung around his neck and pulled something up out of his sweatshirt—a bear claw that was dangling in the center of it—and slid it off over his head.

"Here. Take this."

"Why?" Dhani balked, stepping back.

"I just think you're supposed to have it."

"But you like these bear cubs. They're like, your special friends."

"Jo keeps saying I shouldn't get attached, but it's kinda too late. I love these guys." His face relaxed and he smiled. "We can be friends. You and me. Maybe you'll tell me how you do what you do once you figure it out."

"But you're cool and popular."

"Garrett and Dugan treat me like crap. How popular is that?"

"They're jealous because the girls like you."

"Not the one I want to."

He hung the bear claw around Dhani's neck. "You're the magic man. You should have this. Now I gotta give this little guy his meds, then go back and dive back under those warm covers. It's hella cold out tonight."

When Dhani was gone, he pulled the little cub up to against his cheek and rocked him. He didn't care about the smell of its thin coat, which was sickly and sour.

"Please get better. Please."

"Why are you stuck on her?" Dugan said in a low voice and pulled his collar up against the freezing night air. In the cold dark, he and Garrett walked quietly along the dirt road back to their cabin. "She's a freakin' zombie. Who says, 'I like the dead'?"

"She said 'maybe'. Maybe she'd let me get her high. That means Carter wants me. We just got off on the wrong foot because of stupid muscle head Rocco. But that's okay. I'm gonna hurt him bad. Just biding my time."

Dugan started to laugh. "Carter wants you? Looks to me she wants to eat your head off like a praying mantis. What's with you and this girl? Sure, she's hot and all but—"

"Hot and nasty. The way I like 'em."

"I see the nasty. But I also see the bizarre. You know what they say, bro. 'Never do crazy.'"

"Oh, I'll do her. Before spring. Wanna bet? And even if she is totally crazy, I'll find a use for her."

"That how you look at everyone—for how you can use them? That how you look at me?"

"You're kidding me, right?" Garrett stopped walking. In the pitch-dark, he tried to scan the road to be sure they were completely alone. No one could hear this. "You and me are in business together. Who let you keep all the money from those GPS's we sold?"

"Yeah, well just don't give *me* the business."

"Bro. That seriously hurts me."

"You tried to put one over on everyone tonight, passing fake weed with swigs of Jack to cover up the no-buzz. But see, no one bought it."

"I can't help it the smoke was really mild." He slapped Dugan on the shoulder.

Dugan snorted. "I'm surprised no one knocked you on the head to get their money back. Prolly just didn't wanna get into it with you 'cause you're a fast-talker and you're slick. But they ain't stupid and I'm not either."

"Oh, come on, bro. I'd never try to put anything over on you. Like I said, we're partners."

"Right, right. But I'm still keepin' both eyes on you—*bro*."

10TH

Claire knocked at Sahm's door and it slid open a little.

"Are you home?" When he didn't answer her third call, she gave up and started down the front porch steps.

At the bottom, she noticed something she had missed coming here from the path along the lake—footprints leading away from the cabin into the woods. The prints were widely spaced, as if someone had run or jogged. Why had he rushed out in such a hurry that he hadn't even pulled the door closed?

Following the trail around to the far side, she could see the prints led between the outdoor shed where Sahm stacked his heating wood and a large boulder next to the huge white pine that spread its gangly branches in all directions. The prints led into a stand of bushy, green firs and bare gray hardwoods on the eastern mountain slopes beside the lake.

She hesitated, but only for a moment. Where had he gone? The questions that had grown in her mind were pressing for answers, and she decided to follow his tracks in under the trees.

Here, the snow lay unevenly over half-buried windfallen branches, downed trunks, stones, and ice-flattened undergrowth. Under the trees, where the sun hadn't reached in to melt the snow cover, she had to trudge through some small drifts. Sahm had already pushed through them, making her going a little easier, but snow got under the cuffs of her pants and fell inside the tops of her boots, making her ankles cold. The rest of her was quickly growing warm inside her coat, and she took off her hat and gloves. Small threads of steam rose from her hands into the cold air.

Hopefully, Sahm hadn't gone too far.

On a steep rise, she nearly lost her footing, but caught herself. Up ahead where Sahm's footprints led, she noticed a place where the snow was churned up. Pushing on, breath coming harder, she came to the spot. The trees opened up a little here, and there were signs of a small but intense struggle—and it occurred to Claire that she had come upon a small, woodland drama etched in snow.

Directly in front were two streaks in the white powder. A large bird—maybe an owl—had swooped in from the right, its talons slicing two clean lines into the layer of white powder. The predator had swooped in low after something.

A few steps beyond that there were brown tufts of fur and blood stains—the point of impact. The snow was chaotically thrown in all directions by beating wings and kicking legs. The prey had fought hard against the predator.

A little further still and there was a wider blood-streaked trough in the snow. On either side of it every few inches were light depressions where the bird's wings had beat hard against the snow to lift up from the ground. The predator had been stronger and more determined and dragged away its prize.

In a few feet, the trough became shallower and the blood streaks lighter—and clearly predator and prey had risen into the air.

Beyond, there were only Sahm's prints in the snow again.

Claire stood there, moved by the drama she imagined unfolding here in the wild. One that must happen a hundred times a day in the forests and mountains of Kate's estate and countless times in the great wilderness around her. She felt at odds—sad for the small, furry creature that lost, happy for the hungry, winged assailant that won. Both wanted just to live, and she could not decide which side to come down on.

A small, distant sound pulled her out of her thoughts. Up ahead, not far but on the back side of the rise she'd been climbing, someone was talking. More like saying a single phrase over and over quickly. It sounded both intense and clear on the still forest air.

The closer she listened, the more she was sure the voice was Sahm's.

Continuing on past the signs of bloody scuffle, she reached the top of the rise and stopped.

Just below her, Sahm was kneeling in the snow and his back was towards her. She approached slowly, the sound of his voice becoming louder. She could make out that he was chanting in a sing-songy way, probably in Tibetan, and saw him making strange hand gestures. For a second she remembered the times she thought she had almost caught Dhani making gestures behind her back, which he denied—but this sight drew her full attention.

Something small and light brown lay in front of Sahm next to a thorny tangle that may have been berry bushes, in a bed of ferns that were bent and brown.

He turned his head, and stopped chanting. With one hand, he waved her forward to join him. His face, usually bright, now had a more serious look.

When Claire reached him, she saw what he was kneeling beside. A small brown rabbit, with its side torn open in red gashes and blood coming from its nose and mouth. She could see the pink muscle sheath and the white curved ribs beneath that. They were fluttering in and out with the rabbit's rapid, shallow breathing. Occasionally, it would kick or jerk, probably in great pain in its death throes.

"The hawk let her go after all," Sahm said, simply. "I found her here."

"Do you think she has babies in a burrow nearby?"

"No. See." Gently, he parted the rabbit's fur, revealing a smooth, pink underside. "No teats."

"What were you doing?"

"Invoking one of the healing spirits, summoning them with special *mudras*." He made the yogic hand gestures again.

"What are you going to do now?" She looked at the crumpled rabbit and had uneasy visions of Sahm using a rock to humanely knock the small creature unconscious, helping it to die.

"I hope to see why she was allowed to live. Clearly, she is a sign."

"What do you mean?"

"I was in my cabin and I saw her fall from the air to this spot. So there is a message here."

"You were in your cabin way back there and you *saw* her fall here. How?"

He gave her a wondering look. "In my mind."

Claire shook her head. "But that's not possible."

"Then how did I come to be here? And also why are you here?"

"I came to find you."

"That is why you think you came. In the Bön way of understanding, you were brought here to see this."

"No, I went to your cabin to talk to you about—"

She stopped because a thought occurred.

I came talk to you about your practices—and here I am, seeing one.

"I came to talk about what you're teaching Dhani," she said instead.

Sahm rose from his kneeling position. "The prayers have stopped her bleeding for now. I will take her back and learn why this has happened."

"Take her to Jo," Claire insisted. "Jo will help her. Or put her out of her misery."

He had taken off his coat and begun to gently wrap the rabbit in it.

"I will not be cruel and make her live, if it is time for her to pass into the *Bardo*. The small bit of healing energy that I raised has calmed her. At the cabin, I can give her remedies for pain. But I will keep her here and care for her. There is a reason why the hawk dropped her when he could have had a few good meals.

"And," he looked up at Claire, "there is also a reason why I—and you—were led to this spot today. Otherwise we would not both be here to find this portent. Jo will not understand such things and the message being sent will not come through."

Inside the cabin, Claire warmed herself beside the stove as Sahm settled the rabbit in a box near it filled with soft cloths. He had salved and bound her wounds. Now he dipped the tip of another cloth in a tincture he had boiled and cooled, and squeezed drops into the small creature's mouth. She lay still, breathing shallowly, her body making small convulsions at first when she swallowed—then growing more still the more tincture he administered.

"Is she dying?"

"No. Free from pain for now. And sleeping."

Claire looked at Vajra, who was lying across the room by Sahm's armchair, alert, staring at Sahm and his ministrations with the rabbit.

"Aren't you afraid Vajra will go for her when you're not looking? I mean, he is half wolf. He could tear her up in two seconds."

"Vajra is an old soul. A protector. He will not harm her."

He stood, went over to his armchair, then motioned to Claire to sit, as well.

"I'll stay by the fire. It feels good," she said, still warming up. Really, she felt uncomfortable, not about being alone with Sahm but about what she was seeing and hearing.

"What did you mean, you saw her falling from the air?" she challenged him. "How did you know it was something real happening and not just your imagination?"

He stroked Vajra's charcoal black head and ears. "If you have spent your life training and opening the mind, as I have, there is a way you know. Some feel a small vibration. For others, the place where they are standing becomes faint, like a mist, and what they are experiencing in their mind becomes more solid and real. If you practice, you come to know. I left my practice for a time, but now it is coming back."

What he described sounded to Claire more like mental illness. "Do other people where you come from have things like this happen?"

"Only the few who are trained by the masters, and they are becoming fewer and fewer. My grandfather was one. He trained me—not completely, but a little—before I left Tibet."

Claire suddenly found that she wanted to know more about Sahm, where he came from, why he left. It hadn't occurred to her to ask before. Also how he had known exactly where to find the hurt rabbit out in such a huge forest. But she returned to the question she'd asked before and he had not answered. "Is this what you're teaching Dhani?"

"Tell me why you ask that."

"He has this thing with birds. It's like they listen to him. I've seen it. He can touch them and calm them. I think Ron recognizes it, too. He let Dhani touch a wounded hawk that was going crazy. It should have ripped up his hand with its beak, but it settled down and just looked at him."

"Claire, I cannot teach anyone to do that. No one can. These are not tricks. Dhani has a *siddhi*—a skill that has a kind of power with it. In fact, he has many skills that will awaken."

She folded her arms across her chest, holding back her opinion.

"In Tibet, we believe that we have all lived many lifetimes. If we were fortunate, we learned to have skills that we bring from our past into the present. Dhani must have brought his skill from the past to the present."

Claire tensed. "I don't believe in that."

"What do you believe?"

"We die, and that's all."

"Just—die. Body decays and minerals go back into the earth. What happens to the life energy that is you, your spirit?"

"I don't know."

"We know that energy cannot be destroyed. It has to go somewhere."

She hesitated. "Now you sound like a science teacher."

"A knowledgeable science teacher would agree with what I am telling you."

"Probably not all of it."

"No, certainly not. Not here in the west. Everything must be scientifically proven. But think about this, Claire. One hundred years ago, before there was the ability to take x-rays, if someone had said they could take pictures inside your body, you would not have believed that either. But it became possible. What if there is another place—one that we call the *Bardo* and you would call a dimension—where our consciousness and energy go to before they are reborn in another body? What if we just have not found a way to detect that place yet with scientific instruments?"

Claire suddenly wanted the conversation to be over. "I don't believe in life after death and I don't believe Dhani was somebody in another lifetime."

"You don't have to believe something for it to be true. It can be true whether you believe it or not. His soul is a great soul. That much I know. But then there is the young man you and I see in front of us right now. It is difficult for him here and he needs your friendship just as you need his."

"I just want to be sure you're not telling Dhani stuff that will make him do weird things in front of the other kids here. Most of them already think he's a freak."

He thought of *Dzes-Sa* and how he had directed him to begin clearing and opening Dhani's trapped energies and awareness—but decided Claire would not likely understand. If she did not believe that souls existed, how would she accept that they are part of a greater whole? He decided on a simpler response.

"I can only guide what Dhani is already doing on his own. I can explain to him the skills he has and how best to use them.

To be truthful," he turned the conversation, "he is not very interested. He only wants to talk, talk, talk about you."

Claire ignored that.

"He wants to protect you—just as you want to protect him. I think it is interesting that the two of you were brought together here and you feel the same way toward each other, don't you?"

Not exactly the same, she thought, and remained silent.

"But since you are concerned," Sahm continued, "I will tell him to be very careful about who he allows to witness his skills. It is true that most will not understand yet, but hopefully they will awaken, too. Does that put your mind at ease about your friend?"

"I don't get any of this stuff about special skills and the *Bardo* or whatever. But as long I know you're really trying to help him, I guess I'm okay with him being around you."

"Maybe you can convince Dhani's other good friend, Israel, that I am not evil."

"His family is super religious, so I'm not surprised he thinks that way. I can talk to him.—*Wait.* How did you know that his name is Israel, when he always goes by Ray-Ray?"

Sahm only smiled.

"I'm going to leave now," Claire said quickly, "before you start telling me stuff you know about me."

As she pulled on her coat and boots to leave, Vajra rose from beside Sahm's chair, padded into the middle of the cabin's open room and stood watching her every movement. "He follows me, you know," she said, yanking on her hat.

"Are you afraid of him?"

"No. I had a dog when I was little."

"What happened to the dog?"

She was relieved he didn't somehow blurt out her puppy's name. "I don't know.—They took her away from me."

"Now you have this one. Vajra."

"But he's yours."

"He is not the property of anyone. He has lived with me by our mutual agreement. But it seems he wants to be your companion now, too."

"Like I said, I had a dog. It was taken away from me. I don't need another one."

When she was gone, Vajra stood staring after her out the cabin's front windows for a long time. When she disappeared from view, he went back to Sahm's side and settled next to him.

"The door inside her that began to open has closed again," Sahm said to him. "Until she allows it to open again, we must both wait. She is not ready for you to replace her dog, Annie."

Then he stared at the small, wounded rabbit, mildly amazed. Knowing things he had no way of knowing—like the name of Claire's dog that someone had taken from her—was happening more frequently and with greater clarity. The strength of his own *siddhis* seemed to be increasing.

What would be revealed, he wondered, by this small injured creature he had been sent out into the forest to rescue?

15TH

Ray-Ray hit the aviary early, as he liked to do because no one else was around the barns, and he got to be alone with the inmates.

The ravens and songbirds were quiet this morning, even when he filled their feeders and watering dishes. He would clean them in a little while. Right now he had another goal.

Peering into the cage that housed the young blue jay, he studied the small bird, still asleep with its head under one wing—the one that had not been injured by the cat bite. He had come to admire the beautiful creature, a male, with his powder blue feathers, top knot, and his feisty look when the jay focused his black bead eyes to follow Ray-Ray's movements during the months he had cleaned the bird's cage.

"Hey," he said quietly.

The blue jay lifted his head and gave the now familiar greeting—a chirp that Ray-Ray heard as "Hey."

"Hey hey," Ray-Ray said, smiling.

"*Hey.*" Then the jay went into a changing chorus of other calls.

"You can sure deliver some tunes."

He read Jo's notes on the chart. "Says you're getting better again. Two bouts of serious infection. Two long courses of antibiotics. Two close calls. Seems like you keep dodging bullets and pulling through. You earned the street cred, so I say you need a street name. Like Bluey or Bluey McBlue. Haw, that's stupid. We'll come up with something though—right?"

"*Hey,*" the young bird shouted back.

His father's voice invaded. "*God himself has turned his back on you.*"

Just after breakfast and before morning chores, Rocco met Bay on the bridge next to Grady's cottage again. Now, a current of icy air flowed down over the river current as it passed beneath the span, but the fingers of early sunlight promised more warmth today.

Not yet, though, and Rocco blew on his fingers to warm them.

"No gloves?" said Bay.

"I never wear 'em."

She smiled and shook her head. "Are you sure you're going to be ready for the winter campout? It's going to be a challenge."

"We're meeting tomorrow afternoon, after Jo and I take care of the bear cubs. Tanner is issuing stuff we need in our packs."

"They'll give you thermal gloves. Use them.—How are the cubs doing? Jo tells me one isn't thriving."

"He'll be fine," he said, sounding defensive. "I'm taking care of him at least four times a day now." He sounded proud of that.

They left the bridge and started down the road. Grady and his crew had been up early and plowed away the four inches of snow that had fallen during the night. There was no wind, and the branches of every shrub and tree were sleeved in crystalline ice and powdery white.

"I've wanted to ask you, Rocco, before you tell me what's on your mind—why do you want to talk specifically to me and not to Eric?"

"It's okay that I do, right?"

"Sure. But most young men are more comfortable talking to male counselors. I'm fine with talking to you. Just curious."

Rocco cleared his throat. "It's kinda what I want to talk with you about."

Then he fell silent as they strode along the winding road through the gray, winter-bare trees and strewn boulders capped with icy snow. For a while, the only sound was the crunch of their boots on the frozen road. They passed the trailhead leading west along the brook that spilled east out the Flow Lands and heard the low gurgle of water beneath ice. A winter bird—a tan and crimson female cardinal, the only bright spot in the gray woods—trilled again and again, its sound fading behind them the further they walked, until the woods were still again.

"I asked to talk to you," Rocco said finally, "because I was upset about my mom."

"Yes, I remember."

"And I was afraid I might choke up. So I asked to talk to you instead of Eric because I thought if I got weepy he'd be angry or disgusted with me."

"Angry? Why do you think Eric would—"

"But I didn't cry, did I?" he interrupted her.

"No, you didn't."

"I stayed strong, right?"

Bay kept pace and was thoughtful for a long moment. "That's really important to you, isn't it?—that everyone sees you as strong and no one sees you cry or thinks you're weak."

They came around another bend in the road. Off to one side, there were huge tire tracks, as if someone had backed into the woods to turn around. As they got closer, they saw cigarette butts in the snow, and footprints. Sometime after the road was plowed, someone had parked there for a smoke.

"I guess Grady's crew took a really long break here," Bay said, then turned her head when she heard Rocco sniff.

For a fleeting moment, Rocco remembered overhearing Garrett talk about meeting someone who had come out from town, and wondered if this was where they'd met. They had all made a pact not to talk about each others' private doings because that would likely bring on more adult surveillance. And really, the less he knew about Garrett the better.

Now his face became like a small boy's, and his lip trembled—but when he spoke his voice was deep and husky. Masculine in an exaggerated way. "Men don't cry. Babies and girls cry."

"What's making you so sad right now?"

"Lots of things," he managed to get out.

"I think I get it now. You don't want to cry in front of a man, but it's okay to cry in front of me because I'm a woman. Is that it?"

"But I *didn't* cry," he insisted, his fists clenching. "And I'm not crying now."

She wanted to say, "You're on the verge," or "It's okay, let it out." But she waited.

"You probably want me to cry," he said, with an accusing tone.

"No, Rocco. Unless you need to."

"Well, I don't." He wiped his eyes roughly on a coat sleeve.

"Can I speak honestly with you?"

He didn't reply.

"I think it's really important to you to *not* show any kind of weakness. You told me so many really painful things, and you let me see you fight back all the emotions. Like you're doing right now. You're a fighter, Rocco, and you're very strong. I think you want me to see that."

"Being a strong guy is good, right?"

They reached the gate, where the camp road met the narrow, gravel road that wound down from the mountains into town.

Bay was silent for a moment. "I think you'd like me to say 'yes,' but honestly—no, not always. Sometimes you have to let people see where you're hurt or weak. That's how we let other people know something's wrong and we need help."

"My dad would pull me out of this program if he suspected someone was telling me stuff like this," Rocco shot back.

"You said before you have mixed feelings about your father."

Rocco rubbed the stubble on his chin, and blew out a long breath. "I didn't say that. I love my dad."

Then suddenly he stretched, flexed, yawned—and in the brief span of those movements his expression altered completely. He smiled at her.

Bay sensed he wanted to change the subject. "You said before you were concerned about your mom. Do you want to say anything more about her? Or about your experience here so far?"

Rocco turned and looked up the camp road.

"Can we go back now?"

2

New Moon

16th

The snow around where he stood was melted in a circle, and his whole body felt hot. Sweat poured down his temples, sides, and legs. All around him in the night, the huge bowl-shaped valley that cradled Lost Lake was silent and only a slight breeze stirred the forests, and it felt good on his fiery skin.

Sahm had only just pulled the bed covers up to his chin, when in his mind's-eye the gleaming shape of a rabbit had hopped onto his bed and touched a front paw to his forehead. Energy had roared through his body, and he'd had to quit the cabin to make his skin and muscles cool down.

Looking up now, he saw the sky was full of stars but moonless, and it came to him. This was the night of the new moon, auspicious in itself, but also the beginning of the lunar cycle that would usher in a new year on the Tibetan calendar. New energies would prevail, and he shuffled through his still-waking mind to recall which ones.

The earth. . . and the rabbit.

He thought of the wounded creature curled in the box beside the wood stove. Why hadn't he recalled the nature of the upcoming new year when he'd found the poor, torn-up rabbit the hawk had dropped in the woods?

He felt himself caught up in the cycle of a new season that was about to roll out.

"What is unstable must become strong as earth. . . ," said voices, distant and all around him, as if the earth, air, water, and the fire of the stars were speaking from the ethers.

"Who are you?" he called out.

". . .and the timid rabbit must become a bold warrior."

"Tell me. Who are you?" he called out again.

From within the deep night silence, he felt a sense of great powers awakening—or perhaps they had always been awake and he was the one awakening to them.

"I'm done with you guys," the voice on the other end of the call said, with anger. "I'm going to find another team and come up with a different plan."

"We can find Olivia Neri's husband. We think we may finally know his last whereabouts."

"You can't find your head in broad daylight using both hands. The money people are running out of patience. Pretty soon, they're out."

"You're the one dictating that we do everything low-tech, which makes this a hell of a lot harder. So your 'money people' can shut up. This is our cause, too, and we—" The phone went dead.

17TH

"Stack the bags of soil there," Kate said, pointing to the back wall of windows inside the greenhouse potting room.

"Isn't it kinda early to start seed plants?" the younger of the two delivery men said. He appeared to be in his early twenties at most and not very awake. He hadn't bothered to do more than run his fingers through his wild looking, unwashed hair.

It wasn't his look, though; something else about him made her uneasy.

The older one said, in a rebuking tone, "Mrs. Holman grows her own fresh greens all winter."

"You can stop by the office with your invoice and see my administrator, Tom," Kate said in reply. Her attention was on the young man who was struggling with the fifty-pound bags. He was red-eyed and sluggish, as if he might be hungover. "Tom will write you a check."

"Amazing place you got here," said the bleary young man, when they finished stacking the bags. He was now focused out the windows of the greenhouse at the two big outbuildings across the dirt road—one, where the new gym and workout rooms were just completed, the other for storage. "What's in them?"

"When the new hydroponic equipment comes in," Kate said to the head man, ignoring the question, wanting them gone, "let me know."

When they left, she started out the door of the potting room, deciding what to plant first—cresses, arugula, or mustard greens—when a bright object on the floor near the back windows caught her eye and she turned back.

Stooping, she picked up a piece of broken, red- and blue-colored glass—what seemed to be a small, hollow stem. Then noticed another piece behind a bag of peat—a bowl, charred black inside. Next to it was a tiny, round silver screen.

A pipe?

For half a moment, her mind was blank. Then it came to her.

She would call the greenhouse supplier in Lake Placid village and ask them not to send this particular young man the next time she needed a delivery. She didn't need a drug user coming here, checking out her estate and accidentally dropping paraphernalia the students might find.

Dhani avoided the line where Steve Tanner was issuing winter survival gear and looked around the outbuilding's big, open room for Claire. He was glad she hadn't been with him coming out here when his feet went out from under him and he fell and bruised his hip on the icy road. But he missed her. And something felt wrong.

Ten feet away was the line where Randy Wolfmoon was handing Jalil a clear plastic bag with an article of white clothing folded inside it.

"These long johns better keep me from freezing my butt off out there," Jalil said, looking not very happy. "Tanner just said it could get down to zero."

"I hope they keep you warm too, man, because you got no butt to begin with," said Randy. "I should give you two pairs."

"Hey, the workout room's open now, and Yazzie's going to help me bulk up."

Behind Jalil were Emmalyn and Tia Leesha, whispering. They always seemed to be whispering together, Dhani thought, stepping up behind them.

Emmalyn looked over her shoulder at him, with a wary, accusing look. "I'll tell you where later," she said to Tia Leesha.

Dhani was used to being avoided and shunned by now. He didn't care. He was just eager to show Randy what he had brought with him.

Tia Leesha looked down and saw that his right hand was stuffed into the pouch of his hoody. "What you got in there—a gun?"

Emmalyn backed away. "That's not even funny."

Dhani rolled his eyes and started to say, "Leave me alone"—but the words that came out quietly were, "You and your mom can go to prison for tricking with cops."

Emmalyn's face went red with embarrassment and anger.

Tia Leesha hadn't heard—she was saying to Dhani, "I figure you're gonna snap one of these days. I just hope I'm not around when you do."

Dhani rushed away from them, really wishing Claire was here now. When he didn't know how to speak up for himself, she had a way of shutting stupid people up.

Emmalyn glared furiously after him. How he had guessed that her mother was paying her to party with older men—from the assistant D.A. to local cops—she was terrified to think. Probably Sahm's demon gods were revealing hidden things to him.

Tia Leesha looked wary. "You got a scary look. Like you wanna kill psycho boy."

Emmalyn shrugged, reaffixing her mask of charm. "Not really. He's just a weirdo."

But now it's all-out war.

Where did that come from—the mental image of Emmalyn partying with older guys? And how did he know they were men from the legal system?

Dhani felt shaken by what had just happened. He really, *really* didn't want to be the kid who said crazy stuff—especially stuff like what he had just said to Emmalyn. He was kind of surprised she hadn't slapped him for accusing her of tricking with cops.

At the same time, he also felt as if he had stepped into a greater open space inside himself—for just a moment—or it had opened up and allowed him to enter. And in that space, maybe something had been revealed.

He hoped it wouldn't happen again, tried to shake it off. He needed to find Claire—that would help. Unless she was in a bad mood, it always did.

When Dhani spotted her, she was already at one of the tables set up around the perimeter with Makayla and Imani. They were folding sweat-wicking socks, gloves, and glove liners into pouches in the packs Ron Cambric was setting out. He would try to catch her after, to see why she had been avoiding him—again—for a week.

"Remain in the clear, open sky that spreads out within you."

"Stop," Dhani said loudly, putting his hands over his ears. Who had said that? The voice was not his own.

Laurel Wysocki was passing, carrying a box of herbal blister ointments. "Sure. Can I help with something?"

He tried to think how to play it off, but his mind was blank. "It was just. . . uh. . . nothing."

She smiled, watching him closely for a moment, then went on.

Great. So now I'm the kid who walks around yelling at invisible voices.

When he reached the front of the personal supplies line, Randy Wolfmoon held up one hand. "Hang on. I gotta get more t.p. from storage." He stepped inside the door behind him, then returned with small white rolls. "Use it sparingly," he smiled. "This time of year there's no leaves to use out there."

Dhani pulled something out of his hoody pocket and held it up—an eagle's wing feather. It was long, narrow, and black all the way up the thin white shaft to its slender tip. "I'm going to tie this to my pack. I think it's cool."

Randy had a faint smile. "Dude, like I told you when I gave it to you, that's really really old and *very* special. You gotta treat it gently and with great respect. You should leave it in your room. It could get busted up hanging on your pack or it could fall off and you'd lose it."

Dhani looked down. "Yeah, I guess you're right. I won't take it. I just—it just feels right when I hold it."

"Not sure why," Randy said, "but I was already thinking about giving it to you. Then Ron told me how you rescued that owl without it tearing you to shreds. Also, how you got that injured hawk to calm down. Then I knew it was time to pass it along and I was putting it in the right hands."

"Really?" Dhani's face brightened.

"Yep. Certain people have a special connection with the creatures. Grady and I talk about that sometimes. Maybe you're one of them."

His arms loaded with gear, Dhani walked to the tables where backpacks with name tags waited. Eric Trovert was there, strapping small bear-paw snowshoes they had been issued to his own pack. Next to Eric was Rocco's pack, and next to that Dhani found his.

"Nice feather," Eric said. "Hawk?"

"Eagle." Dhani dumped his armful of gear on the table. Eric's remark didn't really sound genuine. More like he was just trying to start a buddy-buddy kind of conversation.

Eric stuck out a hand. "Mind if I look at it?"

Dhani did not extend the feather. He set it down next to his pack.

"Randy Wolfmoon gave it to me. His great-grandfather gave him two of them. He said certain guys in his family were important medicine men for like, generations. This one is a magic feather and it's been in his family for a couple hundred years."

Eric's eyebrows went up. "Well, it's quite an honor for you to have it then. No wonder you want to protect it. What does it do?"

The sense of open space inside him was there again, and Dhani sensed something beneath the bright and friendly tone. Flat disbelief.

"Nothing yet. But Randy says it's supposed to help you know the future. . . and know things about other people."

"Interesting."

Dhani began to slip things into his pack—a small first-aid kit, pairs of heavy socks.

"Yeah, it is. One of his great-great-great-great-grandfathers was medicine man to Joseph Brant during the Revolutionary War. Did you ever hear of him? He was a Mohawk warrior and hero, who helped us win the war. The medicine man from Randy's family did this feather ceremony thing and warned Brant not to trust the Americans. He said they'd use him to fight for their cause, then betray him. He told him that before the war even started."

Dhani was sounding agitated now.

"Brant didn't believe him because he trusted us white people and really wanted all the lands that we promised the Mohawks if they fought for our side. After the war, the Americans accused him of torturing and slaughtering women and children, but he didn't do it. They said that so they could take away the Mohawks' territory. He was betrayed, just as the ceremonial feathers foretold."

"I know a bit about Revolutionary War history," said Eric, "and I believe Brant was rewarded with other lands later."

"Yeah, but not the ones that were promised. They took away the lands that had a lot of game and gave the Mohawks land that was swampy and bad—and then they even took that away."

Eric's mind was moving in another direction.

"In my field, we'd say that believing in things like magic feathers is something for pre-adolescents."

Dhani was pulling the small, white rock Sahm had given him from his jeans pocket. He stopped.

"What's that?" Eric asked.

Dhani felt cornered, and swallowed once before answering.

"Sahm gave me a. . .a stone. He said it helps you see and hear things."

Eric's packing slowed, but he kept his hands moving and tried to sound casual. "I'm sorry—it does *what*?"

Dhani looked around to be sure no one else was close by, and decided to risk. After all, Eric and Bay Trovert were here so you could be honest about things that were secret—and there were secrets he carried that sometimes he wished he didn't.

He said, in a lowered voice, "This is important. I can tell you anything, right, because you're a psychologist, and you won't tell anyone else?"

"Not unless what you tell me has to do with a serious crime, like abuse of a minor or a murder."

"Do you think it's possible to hear what animals are thinking?"

Eric wanted to proceed carefully. Dhani had not opened up in any way, in any sessions or casual talks they'd had to this point. "Tell me about it. A lot of people like to play imagination games—is this yours?"

". . . imagination games. . . ."

"No," Dhani said, backing off a little. "I—I'm just wondering is all."

Eric slid a headlamp into a pouch along with extra batteries. "Let's suppose someone could hear animals talk. What would they say?"

"If it was a flock of birds, they might warn each other that someone's coming, and to fly away. They might thank someone for helping them—like if someone saved an owl from dying."

Eric was on alert now—Dhani was clearly talking about himself—but remained casual. He kept his hands moving, stuffing a silver survival blanket into a second pouch.

"What do you think it would mean," Eric asked, tossing it back to Dhani, "if a person had special abilities like that? Would it mean they were specially chosen to do something or to be someone?" He edged closer to what he was getting at. "Do you think it means he's supposed to accomplish a certain important task. . . or get revenge on someone?"

Dhani shook his head. "I don't have any idea. That's why I decided to ask you. I sometimes—." He stopped.

"Sometimes you—what?"

The first, tentative span of a bridge had been extended from Dhani's side, and Eric was trying hard to keep communication open. What Dhani was saying wasn't just unusual. It was a bit unnerving.

Dhani read the look on Eric's face. "Nothing. Never mind."

"I'd like to talk with you more about this, Dhani. It really interests me. Maybe we can hang out together on the hikes and campouts. You can also come talk to me any time. I'd like that."

Dhani had looked up from packing and saw through the mask that was Eric's smiling face. Inside him was a cloud of wariness that put him off, and he quickly reversed direction.

"You said believing in magic feathers was childish."

Rocco was approaching then, coming across the open room with his armload of gear, and Ron was pointing him to the pack that lay beside Dhani's.

"I didn't say childish."

"But that's what you meant. I feel kinda stupid now."

Eric felt the fragile bridge collapsing and tried to save it.

"Dhani, it concerns me that you haven't opened up to me or Bay or any adult here that I know of. I'd like it if you opened up to me—but I just now blew it by making you feel childish. Bad move on my part. Can we just ignore that? Can I have a do-over?"

Dhani turned back to his pack and was silent for a long time before speaking again.

"It's all good," he finally replied. "I can talk to Sahm. He's cool. And Randy Wolfmoon is pretty great. They both talk with me about stuff."

"Dhani, I really didn't mean it the way I think you took it."

Rocco dumped his armload on the table. "*Whew*—this is gonna be one cold campout. But why are we stuffing our packs now when we're not going into the mountains for another couple weeks?"

Eric replied, "Steve wants to check us out on a short hike in winter gear with full packs before we make the climb."

Then he turned back to Dhani. "How about it—want to talk again sometime soon?"

"It's all good," Dhani said.

This is what he knew would happen if he tried to tell any official kind of person what was happening to him, like the vision he'd seen of himself as an old man in a Tibetan village. Just like his mom, they'd accuse him of playing games for attention or judge him as being really whack.

He pulled up his hood and went on packing in silence.

When Dhani zipped the last pouch closed, Claire was already gone and Ray-Ray had just stepped up to Tanner's table to get his gear. He decided to go back to the cabin or else go to Kate's and see if Ivy had left fig bars out for a snack like she did sometimes. . . or. . . .

His arms and legs felt twitchy with anxious energy and he didn't know what to do with himself. The sense of wide-openness inside was all but gone.

Why was Claire avoiding him *now*? He came back to that. Her mood swings were getting old but—he couldn't escape the feeling that she really did care about him. If she was going to dump him, like everyone else, he wished she would just say so.

Outside, the sun had gone in and the cold air made his cheeks tingle. Emmalyn and Tia Leesha were standing in a huddle with Makayla and Imani, all of them swaddled in coats and scarfs and shuffling their feet to keep warm. At least two of them were talking at once.

"We have to dig snow shelters?" said Makayla, looking upset. "Who told you that? I don't want to sleep in the snow."

As he passed, Emmalyn turned her head, saw him, and stepped away from the others.

Her face was sweet and remorseful. "I'm sorry I acted rude in there. God wouldn't like that."

Dhani was going to say, *"No problem,"* but instead a voice inside compelled him to say, "You can stop being fake any time now."

Her eyes flashed anger, then—knowing others were witnessing this—they got wide and innocent again. She let her lip tremble a little. "Why would you even say that? You're mean."

Dhani felt a wave of confusion, certainty, and uneasiness about the words that had flown out of his mouth.

"I don't know. It just came out."

He wasn't really sorry, though. Something about her didn't feel right. In fact, it felt sneaky and pretend.

He kept walking, knowing now where he needed to go. The one place where he could be alone and quiet and feel settled again.

"Beating yourself up over it won't help," Bay said, as she drove her pickup out the camp road. Eric stared out the passenger side window. "Some people take a long, long time to trust us and open up. You know that."

He shook off the mood.

"Right now, it can't be about me anyway. We have a kid who is hinting that he hears voices. What are we dealing with—onset schizophrenia?"

"He only hinted, he didn't tell you that. And I don't pick up those symptoms from him. I observe him, and I don't see any other signs."

"Then what—overactive imagination?"

"Synesthesia is a possibility. That's when one sensory organ is stimulated as if it was another sense organ—like when people take drugs and think they can smell emotions or taste colors."

"I know what synesthesia is," Eric responded quickly.

"Well that sounded defensive.—He could also be a highly sensitive person. Studies are being done on that. He could be hyperalert to body language, eye movements, facial expressions—even things like voice tonality in birds. He's so sensitive to those cues in humans maybe he's translating that into messages from animals."

Eric relaxed. "I'll have to read some of those studies. I need to keep up with you." Smiling, he reached over and gently squeezed her arm.

"Then there's the possibility. . . ."

He gave her a questioning look.

"What if he *can* hear birds and animals?"

Eric's hand dropped onto the console between them. "You're joking."

"No. As a person of science, I have to stay open to all possibilities."

"Don't go New-Agey on me, Bay."

"And don't patronize me, Eric. Studies are being done by major research institutions on yogis, shamans, and medicine people from all over the world. They can do incredible things with their minds."

Eric opened his mouth to speak, hesitated, then said, "I'm going to work with this *fact*. We have a kid who set someone on fire. He came to us because a judge—a judge, not a psychologist—said he believes in that kid. I *and you* have to be sure that belief was not misplaced. You play good cop and look for signs Dhani has some special ability and I'll play the other cop. The one who wants to be sure he isn't slipping into mental illness, while a friendly climbing instructor and a Tibetan Sherpa both feed into it."

Bay gripped the steering wheel. "Don't do your 'good cop, other cop' thing. We're on the same team. Keep your mind open or you'll miss the cues as to what's going on with this kid. And stop acting like you're more rational than me. I hate that."

20TH

The sliding door to the aviary was open slightly as Claire approached, checking the scribbled, morning feeding list Jo had given her.

snowy owl—small rabbit (chest freezer)
raven—three mice (chest freezer), one small scoop grain/seed mix
blue jay—cracked corn, two scoops
kestrel in the last cage—(Ron will show you its new special diet)

On the list went, through all the current inmates. Right now there were thirteen, from songbirds to birds of prey. Interesting mix, Claire thought. As usual, there was no mention of the young eagle.

"I still hope to release him back into the wild, which means the less human contact the better," Jo said repeatedly—only recently adding, "though that's getting to be more iffy the longer he's here."

"Why?" Claire had asked.

"Eagles and animals can imprint on human beings. They can come to think we're safe. And in the case of bald eagles, they can think the wrong person is safe and swoop in looking to be fed, and it turns out to be some yahoo with a gun who wants to wall-mount a trophy bird in his 'man cave'."

"Aren't eagles protected by law, though?"

"Some idiots only care about bragging rights."

A low voice, barely audible, coming from inside the aviary got Claire's attention. Who was speaking as if they didn't want to be heard?

She slid the huge aviary door open quietly on its track, then carefully closed it behind her. Now she could tell the voice was coming from behind the door to the eagle's enclosure, and realized it was Dhani's voice. The eagle was supposed be in the outside enclosure before they went in to clean and leave food for it. But he was inside the cage talking to the eagle.

She tilted her head near to the door.

"Were you alive before like, in another lifetime?" Dhani was saying. "Were you someone who lived around here? Or did you come from far away?"

Then it grew quiet.

Claire straightened and peered in through the one-way glass—surprised at the sight inside.

For months, the eagle had sat hunched on its low perch, facing the corner. Now it was facing the center of the cage. Dhani was standing there holding out an open hand. As he spoke, the eagle tilted its head from side to side, its black and gold eyes staring, fixated, locked with Dhani's.

Claire felt a wave of apprehension and anger. Her first thought was to pound on the door and get Dhani out of there. If Jo came in, she would be furious and pull him from the eagle tribe. Maybe assign him to hauling crapped-in hay and stinking clinic garbage from now on. Besides that, if the eagle attacked, its razor talons could tear Dhani's skin like tissue paper.

But she didn't intervene—and she didn't know why she didn't.

"He won't be hurt."

The strange thought went through her mind, in a voice that didn't sound like her own, and with it came a deep sense of knowing. Was some connection happening here between Dhani and the eagle?

She pushed the words aside. Where had they come from? And there was still Jo, who could walk in at any moment.

Tapping with her knuckles on the door, she saw Dhani startle and whip his head around.

When he slid the cage door open, just wide enough to slip out into the open walkway, he looked relieved.

"I thought you were Jo. If she caught me, she would—"

"I know what she would do. She'd kick your butt." Claire's voice was intense. "Why did you go in there when she told us a million times not to?"

"I. . . ."

"You what?"

"If I tell you, you'll treat me like everyone else does. You'll treat me weirder than you already do."

"What do you mean? I don't treat you weird."

Dhani's voice was suddenly intense.

"*Yes, you do.* Sometimes you act like you're my friend. Then you totally avoid me. You did it before and you're doing it again. It's so confusing. If you're going to treat me like everyone else here, I wish you'd go ahead make up your mind and tell me to get lost."

She hesitated, knowing he was right. She was nice to him, then distant. But she remembered what Sahm had confided—that Dhani was fixated on her—and she didn't know what to say. She didn't want to encourage that.

"If you don't want me around, just *tell* me," Dhani said, sounding frustrated. "When we're working here, I'll do my list of stuff and stay away from you."

"You won't be hurt."

Again, the other voice in Claire's head startled her.

Dhani paced in a circle, running his hands through his hair, making it stand up wildly. "I just can't deal with 'we're friends, we're not friends.' If it's some kind of girl game you play, I don't like it."

She reached out and grabbed his arm. "Guys play games just like girls. But I'm not playing one with you. I—I'm sorry. I'll try not to be weird with you again. I'm just going through stuff, Dhani."

Her attention was divided now between wanting to reassure Dhani and what was going on inside her head. He was good kid, and didn't deserve to be hurt by anyone. At the same time, she was confused by what the voice had told her and unsettled that she'd heard it at all.

"He needs you and you need him."

She shut the strange voice out of her head.

"Dhani, I like you."

His face lit up, and she knew she had to correct where his mind was probably heading.

"I'm your *friend*," she said, reaching for a safe ending to this conversation. "If I get moody or just need to be alone it's totally not about you."

Not always anyway.

That was her own thought; the other voice had gone silent.

Dhani nodded, his expression settling somewhere between a little disappointed and still hopeful. "Then don't weird-out on me, okay?"

"I won't. I promise."

"So. . . can I show you the magic eagle feather Randy gave me?"

She felt a little lift, seeing he had accepted her answer, and then a small sinking feeling at his last statement about a magic feather. Maybe he really did need her—at the very least, to help him grow up.

She decided to steer him away from Sahm and his strange ways and Randy's talk about magic, and most definitely away from his imagined conversations with birds.

"Can we take care of this first?" She held up Jo's feeding list.

"Deal."

When they finished, Claire was closing the kestrel's enclosure door after filling its tray with the new type of food mixture Ron had left for it—dead mice laced with liquid vitamins.

Dhani tried to stand close to her without being obvious. He wanted just to be near her—to smell the scent of her hair, watch how she moved. He didn't want her as "a friend". He wanted her to feel about him the way he felt about her.

But she didn't. But *could* she?

"I'm going to work on a paper in the computer room upstairs at Kate's lodge," Claire said, lifting the galvanized bucket she'd used to distribute seeds and hunks of suet. "Maybe later, you and Ray-Ray and I can hang out."

Ray-Ray. So he would be the safe wall between them. "Sure," Dhani replied, trying to sound okay with it.

She turned her back and started for the door.

On impulse Dhani raised one hand and—sure that she couldn't see him—made a gesture.

She had just turned her head, though, to check the latch on a cage and caught half a glimpse of the movement, and turned to him.

"What did you just do?"

His hand had dropped back to his side. "Nothing."

"You did something behind my back."

"*No*. Really. I was scratching my face."

She looked wary for another moment. Then, as if she was satisfied with his reply, she said, "Yazzie is lifeguarding and giving lessons at Kate's pool this afternoon. If you want to swim, that's where I'm headed later."

"I don't like to swim."

"Come on. You've seen her indoor pool. It's amazing."

"How about after you swim?"

"Maybe I'll try to find you."

"Maybe?" he thought. *Why not "definitely"?*

And once again, whether she meant to or not, she left him feeling like he was on unsteady ground.

Imani was sitting alone on the edge of the pool, her feet in the warm water. The air was humid and the three huge walls of windows that looked south from the atrium out onto the lake and mountains had fogged up a little – and Mike Yazzie was in the shallow end of the pool showing Tia Leesha how to doggy paddle.

Rocco emerged from the door of the changing room where he'd slipped into his trunks, and made his way around the pool's padded deck, smiling to himself. For once, Makayla wasn't attached to Imani's side and he could talk to her privately and without interference.

"Mind if I sit here?" he asked when he reached her.

"Seat's taken."

Rocco looked around at the otherwise empty atrium. "Is Makayla in the girls' changing room?"

"No. She's got something going on with her head today. I was talking to her and she sort of blanked out for like, a whole minute. I told her she needs to rest. She said she's going to play with the salamanders."

"Jo won't like that. So—actually, no one's sitting here."

"I like my space."

Rocco took a few steps back. Leaving six feet between them, he sat down and slid his feet and lower legs into the pool. "Hey, the water's nice and warm."

Imani remained silent, watching Tia Leesha splash and choke and cough out a little water.

"I can't put my face in the water," she complained. "You're tryna *drown* me."

"No," Yazzie responded, "I'm gonna teach you how to swim so you *don't* drown. Stop inhaling under water."

"Suppose I don't wanna learn?"

"Suppose you stop bellyaching and actually try."

Rocco watched her. "She's afraid. That's why she complains."

"I just think she's too lazy to try," Imani countered. "I cannot figure out why she's in this program."

He saw an opening. "That's kinda harsh. I think Tia Leesha is just scared all the time.—So why are you in the program? You never said."

"Why are *you* in it?" she pushed back.

"One of my cousins and me, we were skimming credit card info at gas stations."

Imani looked over at him. "Is that true or are you lying? That's serious stuff."

"There's ways you can do it that're pretty easy. You just fit a gas pump with a skimmer. You get the card number and the pin. My cousin had a machine to make cards with. I was just buying stuff online. Laptops. TVs. Jeans. Jackets. Cameras. Sunglasses. We both got busted. He went to jail because he's twenty-two. I went to juvenile."

"That's a sophisticated level of criminal activity. For a boy."

He ignored that. "Not really. My dad was pissed because it was 'punk' stuff to him."

Imani faced him fully. "Your dad?—what is he into?"

Rocco looked around. No one else had come in and Yazzie and Tia Leesha were still arguing, so there was no one to hear. Even so, he leaned closer to her.

"My dad has a *business*—okay?"

"I guess it's not a business the law approves of."

"He wants me to take it over eventually. That's why he was pissed when I got caught. He wanted me to stay 'clean' or at least look that way."

"So, you're in this program because if you don't screw up here your record will be permanently sealed. Was that the deal?"

"Yeah."

Claire came in then, wearing her swimsuit and carrying a towel. Seeing Imani and Rocco together, she nodded and sat down at the far end of the pool.

Imani was staring out the windows overlooking the lake. "So, you play the game here. Kiss up to Tanner like you do. Then you leave here in a couple years looking all clean in the eyes of the world and the cops."

"Tanner's okay. He's harsh like my father, but I like him. And yeah—that's what my dad's hoping for. A permanently sealed or eradicated record. He pushed me to say yes to the judge. That's why I'm here."

"Nice. You enjoy this beautiful place, then leave and slide right back into your old life. Lucky you."

"What does that mean—lucky me?"

"Nothing."

"Then why'd you say it?"

She leaned forward and, with a push, propelled herself off the deck into the water. Then swam away from him across the pool.

"How did I know you'd be lurking around, waiting for me," Imani said, emerging in an hour from the changing room into the hallway.

"If you want me to I'll leave."

She didn't answer and started to walk past him.

He stretched out one arm and braced his hand against the wall, stopping her.

"I can duck right under this," she said, in a firm tone.

"Then do it."

She stood still, staring ahead, then looked at him. "What do you want from me? I've told you a bunch of times I have a boyfriend."

"And he's in prison."

"Not forever."

"Why are you here at Lost Lake? I told you why I am."

"I didn't ask you to."

"Tell me—because you know what? I know a lot of girls who are gangbangers and you're not anything like them."

"How do you know gangbangers?"

"My dad works with the gangs in DC and Baltimore. He's got a whole network of them doing stuff for him."

"He has connections with the gangs."

"I know what they're like and you're not like them. You're kind and really smart and sophisticated."

Imani stepped back. "I can't do this. It's a bad idea."

He reached out to touch her arm and missed when she stepped away. "Come on."

"Why you being so aggressive? Back the hell off."

"Women like it when men are aggressive, right?"

"Not grabbing at us like you just did." She backed further away. "Who taught you to do that? Your daddy, the Don?"

He looked remorseful and stared at the floor. "Just tell me—Please."

Now she was the one to look around, though no one else was in the hallway. She had left Claire in the locker room showering and recuperating from swimming laps.

"It's not too cold outside," he said. "Can we walk and talk?"

"What I tell you stays just between us."

"Got it."

They had crossed the bridge, passed behind Jo's barn, and now turned north with the river on their right. Thunder Falls sounded from far ahead. Here, the path was slick in some places, covered in small snowdrifts in others but passable. From their left, a thin draft of cold air moved down through the steep, blue-shadowed woods on the slopes of Lost Mountain.

"You sure you want to hear this?" Imani insisted. "You said your dad has contact with gangs, so I'm not sure. Convince me you're safe."

"My dad—," he kicked a small ice-coated stick off the trail, "—don't worry about him. We don't have any contact right now. None."

"Well, you better *never* pass this on. What I'm going to tell you could get me or people in my family killed." She took a deep breath.

"I'm here because I'm involved with a murder."

He stopped and stared at her.

"I didn't do it. And I wasn't directly involved at all. My guy is in the Black Guerilla Family, and they were involved."

"They're more like a prison kinda gang."

"He got in when he was in Lorton for three years on some stupid marijuana charge. When he came out he was deeper into drug running than before.—There was this guy who was trying to get out of the gang, so he went into hiding and disappeared. But they got his girlfriend as punishment. See, nobody leaves. Ever."

"They killed *her* instead of him."

"Yeah. I was in my guy's apartment one night and his boys were there with their ladies and we were all partying. Most everyone was banged up on something. He got a phone call and went into his bedroom which was right next to the kitchen. He didn't know I was in there getting some food. I overheard him saying what they did to this girl. Cut her up one night and threw her body in the Potomac River way out in Maryland. He even named the spot—Brunswick. He said it was raining a lot and the river was high there. He was laughing that 'she looked like horse meat when my boys finished with her'."

Rocco stopped in the middle of the path. "You had nothing to do with that?"

"*Jerk*—I told you. Listen to me. He came into the kitchen after, looking at me all, 'Did you hear somethin'?' I got all smiles and hugged him up. 'No, baby, why?' I said. He got all humorous sounding and said, 'Never mind. Get me a sangwidge.' And I kissed him and laughed. Inside I was freakin', but I knew I had to go out in that other room and smile and laugh and party it up just like nothing happened. After everybody left, he said, 'Baby, let's go make some love.' I felt sick but I did it."

"I hate hearing that," Rocco said, tightening his fists.

"It was either that or act strange and tip him off, and I was terrified. I had to work hard to keep from shaking."

"I still hate it."

She kept going.

"The next day, I told my mom. She knew something was wrong with me and kept asking. After she was pissed at me for gangbangin', she said, 'You got to go to the police. Now that you know, you're an accessory to murder if you don't turn them in.' I was scared but she read me a description from the internet of the girl's body. They cut up her face and she didn't look human. Then they tied cement blocks to her and dropped her off a bridge. They did all that to her while she was still alive. I threw up."

"Damn."

"That day, I went to a police investigator. He took my statement, exactly what I heard, and told me to play it cool, pretend like nothing was wrong. He said they would put together a case and go after the guys who killed her. I said, 'They'll kill me for telling you this.' He said, 'Don't worry, we'll protect you.'

"Well, it took them three months to put all the pieces together, and then they showed up at a bunch of apartments, kicking in doors and making arrests. They got my boyfriend. Get this—he used his one phone call from jail to call me and ask, 'Did you do this?' I was coming out of my skin. I said, 'No, baby! No!' He said, 'They got me for accessory to murder and I'm goin' back inside for ten to fifteen years. I got to find whoever turned us in and get them to testify to the whole truth. I wasn't in on it the day it happened.' It's a mess."

"You don't think he was directly involved in killing her?"

"Not my guy. I hope not anyway. He's my bae. But just because he knew about it they call him an 'accessory after the fact'. If the guys who did the deed get life in prison, he'll get up to fifteen years in a cage."

Imani's chest was rising and falling fast and she tried to slow her breathing. Her eyes had filled with tears.

Rocco was putting it all together. "You didn't come here from detention. You're in witness protection, aren't you?"

"The Black Guerilla Family is all over DC and Baltimore. If you know the gangs, you know that. The police said, 'You have to get out of town for a long time. We know this judge who's looking for young people for a program that's hundreds of miles from here, hidden up in some mountains.' They said I need to disappear at least until the trials are over, but it could be a couple years before they get to court."

"That's how you wound up here."

"We're trying to figure out where I go next."

"Doesn't your boyfriend wonder why you left town?"

"His friends from the gang have called my house, talked to my mom. Our cover story is someone in my family sent my picture to some modeling agency contest in Europe. He thinks that's where I went and why I can't visit or call him. I'm trying to become a high fashion model now. But he's not stupid either. He's got gang people looking for the rat. I know, because people have been accused and threatened. All it would take is for one dirty cop to leak that information. I had to get out of DC and go into hiding."

"God."

"Tell me. Nothing was done to protect me for six whole months. They said they didn't want it to look like I was running. The gang took out one of their own, one of the killers, because they thought he might have snitched. Beat his head in with a crowbar. I didn't even go out at night or stay at my mom's. Then the judge almost said no. But the investigator kept twisting his arm, and here I am."

"If he hadn't finally said yes," she finished, staring at the river, "who knows."

"*Stop*," said Rocco. His eyes were flashing with anger. "I don't want to think about that."

For a while, he was silent. Then he stepped closer to her.

She backed away.

"Why did you decide to tell me all this?"

"Why do you think?"

"I thought maybe you're trying to get close."

She was direct, her voice even. "I told you because you're trying to fall in love with me—or maybe just trying to get off with me out in one of those barns some night, I don't know. I'm telling you so you understand very clearly why it's better for you to stay away from me. Way far away."

"What if I don't want to?"

Her eyes got a hard look. "Then you're really, really stupid. And you don't stand a chance with me anyway. Because I never hook up with stupid."

The soft plant light in one terrarium was enough to keep Makayla from tripping in the gentle darkness of the amphibious animals room. Little waterfalls Ron had set up in three of the glass tanks made a peaceful, trickling sound. This made her love the space almost as much as she loved the small creatures housed here.

She passed the dark terrarium where Lightning, the damaged box turtle, was pulled into his shell and came to the salamander tank. Lifting three rocks, she found where the smallest one was hiding.

Carefully, she picked up the wriggling creature between thumb and forefinger and set it in the palm of her right hand, admiring its sleek, golden body with its tiny red spots like decorative jewels. Jo had said these spots secreted a toxin and the red color warned off predators. So what had taken off its front left leg and rear right foot similar to the way other salamanders were maimed?

She held the small animal up close to her face, so she could watch the tiniest pulse in its throat. It didn't move, but seemed—though maybe it was just imagination—that it was watching her unafraid.

Maimed. She felt that way.

"You know I could never hurt you," she whispered. "I love you guys."

There was something about these gentle creatures that reached out to her. They were harmless and docile, and yet she sensed the tiny fire of life inside them. A will to survive though severely wounded.

She thought about her mother and father, and how she wanted her own life apart from them, to live her way not theirs. Not trying to impress, not clawing for success. She thought of what a fight it would be when the Lost Lake program was done, to pull away from them—her mother especially.

What was her mother's deal anyway? She always seemed to be hinting rather than saying something outright, about her father.

"Be careful, Makayla. That's all I'm saying."

Setting the salamander back in the soil at the edge of the little stream Ron had created, she placed the flat rock over it carefully, recognizing its need to feel protected.

Every time she walked into this room, she was glad Jo had placed her in the Salamander tribe. It was where she belonged, and she wished she never had to go home again.

25TH

Jalil stood up and flexed in the mirror. He had been moving between the leg-press and bench press machines for an hour before moving on. In the mirror, he saw behind him, seated on a rowing machine, Carter, who was grinning at him. Her eyes looked wild.

He whipped his head around. "What's your deal? Why are you so bizarro world?"

She kept rowing, staring at him, silent.

He felt his stomach tighten, feeling humiliated by the fact that he had never worked out before and his muscles were thin and wiry. The heat of humiliation made him feel irritated—but at the same time, Carter was watching him closely, studying his body. Maybe she really got into slim, wiry guys. He smiled awkwardly at her.

On the other side of the workout room in the free weights area, Rocco was punching and delivering roundhouse kicks to one of the heavy workout bags. A dozen feet away from him, Dugan was drilling taped fists into another bag.

Escaping from Carter, Jalil wiped his face with a towel and made up a reason to talk to Rocco.

"Hey, let me know when you're done," he said, nodding at the bag. "I want to try it."

Rocco was breathing hard and sweating. "Right. You'll break your wrists, little man."

Dugan looked over and laughed.

Jalil felt his stomach tighten more and the heat rise again. "No, I won't."

Rocco kicked the bag again, hard.

"Not if you show me how to do it the right way."

"Go ask Yazzie. I'm not your trainer."

Jalil tensed, then charged at Rocco and shoved him. "You're an idiot. And you treat me like crap."

Rocco turned, his fists clenched. "Push me again and I'll punch your head."

Dugan had stopped swinging at the bag and mocked Rocco. "Ooooo, someone's having her period."

"Shut up," Rocco fired back.

"I'll push you if I want," Jalil yelled at Rocco, who was ignoring him, focused on Dugan.

"You can try to make me," Dugan smirked.

Rocco bulled his way past Jalil, throwing an elbow that hit him in the mouth. When he was a foot from Dugan he leaned into his face. "I'll make you any time I want."

Dugan kept smiling. "We'll see."

"What does that mean?"

"We'll see. That's what it means."

From the doorway, Mike Yazzie shouted, "*You two.* Stacking cords of wood after your little bout in November should have taught you guys something. But I can see you guys are hard heads. Come into my office."

Jalil wiped his lower lip. A streak of red came off on the back of his hand.

When Rocco and Dugan were gone, he walked to the drinking fountain to run cold water on his lip and spit more blood.

Carter had moved to a stair-climbing machine, her eyes following his movements. "Don't spit the blood out," she said. "Swallow it."

"Why?"

"Drink it. I would."

"Sick," he said, smiling. She scared him, but he couldn't show her that. "My kind of woman."

When he had showered and was outside the workout building, Rocco walked slow in hopes of avoiding Dugan. Yazzie had blasted them both, then sent Dugan away first, to walk back to his cabin and cool down. Yazzie's warning had hit home.

"You've been a great sparring partner this month, Rocco. But I'm about to recommend that you be put on probationary status here. Him, too. You keep fighting and you get a one-way ticket back to juvenile detention. This program is for young men and women who want to change. Do you get that?"

"Yes, sir," Rocco had replied.

Dugan had looked somber and nodded.

"Then this bull crap between you two is over. I'm not gonna make you shake hands. You're both still hot. Go shower, and stay away from each other for a couple days. Then figure out how to solve whatever mess you got going on between you. Go see Mr. Trovert if you can't figure it out on your own."

"Yes, sir," Rocco repeated.

He breathed deeply as he walked now, taking in the view of the lake and mountains. He didn't want to go back to DC—not just to detention but in-range of his father. He felt confused about that. How could he love someone and sometimes not love him at the same time?

Still, there was Dugan with his insults and whatever the hell his problem was. From now on, he would just ignore him. If he could.

"Hey."

Dugan stepped out from behind the storage barn up ahead.

Rocco didn't respond, but Dugan walked out into the camp road in front of him, blocking his way.

Rocco tried to sidestep and Dugan met him chest to chest—smiled warmly and stuck out his hand. "Truce."

Rocco stepped back and studied his face. "Really? Simple as that?"

"Yeah. I been a jerk. I let this whole thing between you and me get out of hand. We're gonna be here a long time, so we gotta become friends."

Rocco did not respond. The sudden turn-around seemed too easy, and it put him off.

"Or at least be friend-*ly*. Hey, I don't want Yazzie's one-way bus ticket back to juvie either."

"Right." Rocco stuck out his fist. "You're right. No reason we can't be friend-*ly*."

Dugan fist-bumped.

"Past is the past. It's a new day. Maybe in time you and me can even become good buds."

"Trees begin to prepare for an oncoming winter as early as late summer, when they sense daylight hours declining," said Laurel Wysocki.

"Why do we need to know this?" Garrett asked, chin resting in his palm, making it obvious by his look he was completely bored.

"Because we're talking about *adaptation* as a skill in nature and as a life skill," Bay interjected. "Please pay attention—this is important."

"Trees slowly go into a dormant state all through the fall," Laurel continued, "and reach their adapted tolerance by mid-winter. This part is very cool, I think. Through a combination of cellular changes that involve shrinkage, dehydration, and sugar concentration, the cells harden and become glasslike. This helps prevent freezing and damage to living cells."

"Are you saying they somehow *know* they have to do this to survive? Like, they're *aware*?"

"I'm not saying that exactly—"

"Yes. They *are aware*," said a quiet voice from the back of the classroom.

Heads turned.

It was Dhani who had spoken, and he stared at everyone, eyes wide.

"I. . .I'm not sure why I said that. It just came out." He pulled the hood of his hoody up and sank down in his chair.

Garrett laughed. "Freak boy thinks trees are standing around going, 'Oh crap, winter's coming. Better get my defense on."

Imani glared at him. "You need to keep more thoughts *inside* your head. Because no one wants to hear most of them."

Ray-Ray leaned close to Dhani and whispered. "Did you get that from Sahm? Is that what he believes—that trees are aware, just like us?"

"No," Dhani whispered back. "I just. . . I *know* it's true. I don't care if you don't believe it. I just *know* it. And I don't know why I do. We're not the only beings on this earth that have intelligence."

"Can we stick with today's topic," said Bay, "which is learning to adapt and protect ourselves from harm in order to stay healthy and thrive?

"Laurel and I decided to tag-team this topic because there are important messages in nature, if we pay attention. Sometimes even our survival depends on us knowing when and how to make changes."

Imani caught Rocco looking at her and mouthed, *Don't start with me.*

Laurel stepped in again. "Sometimes trees are planted in the wrong zone, one that pretty much guarantees their growth and survival will be a struggle."

"Like lots of us," Bay remarked.

"For example," Laurel continued, "in climates where winters are extremely cold, trees that can't adapt well can start to freeze. The life-sustaining sap in their capillaries expands, creating inner pressure. When that pressure becomes great enough, the bark breaks, and worse. If you look around the forests in winter and spring, you'll see trees where one side has actually exploded."

Bay picked up. "We're not asking you to share personal information right here in front of everyone. Spilling your guts to a room full of people can be the worst thing to do if those people aren't trained to handle the information.

"What we're asking is that you identify conditions you've lived with that challenge your personal wellbeing and growth. As is true in nature, being fully aware of those conditions—and especially their source—is the first step. Why you've allowed it or been forced to accept those conditions to this point in your life is important to know. What you can do about it is next.

"So just think about these things for now," she concluded, "and reach out to me or Eric or an instructor you feel comfortable with.—Do any of you relate to what we're saying?"

From outside the huge windows of the classroom came the faint screech of a hawk as it circled over Lost Lake, then there was total silence.

Imani stared at her hands, and Rocco sank low in his seat.

Makayla appeared to be miles and miles away. Emmalyn flashed a look of hopelessness, then anger. Ray-Ray's face was an unreadable mask. Dhani had pulled the drawstrings of his hood tight. Others snapped gum or fidgeted in their seats.

"Is that it for today?" said Garrett, with an exaggerated yawn. "Can we go now?"

Claire was engrossed in her sketchbook, where she started to draw the shattered limb of a tree—then erased it and drew a slender twig with a tiny leafbud.

Out in the hallway, Garrett slapped Dugan on the back. "You get anything out of that, my brother? 'Cuz I didn't."

"Yeah, but it's not the kind of 'adapting for survival' they mean."

28TH

Kate pulled off the bear paw snowshoes, straightened, stretched and looked up at the top of Peregrine Mountain. The late-day sun was gleaming red off the ice-covered summit where she had hiked today and now it was easing down behind the peak.

Despite the long vigorous hike now behind her, she felt a great river of energy coursing in her body.

Sahm came across the back deck of her lodge from behind, and a sudden vision of her arose. . . .

Her soul did not fit inside this wooden structure she inhabited. When she was indoors for a long time she was restless as a caged creature—a winged thing that needed openness and the free air. She was a great soul, much more at home hiking, kayaking, snowshoeing. And talking with the young people, she was luminous. Ignited. . . .

"Ivy said I would find you here. You wish to talk with me, Kate."

"It's been a while, Sahm. We've both been busy since the students arrived. I should have reached out to you sooner."

"You want to talk about Dhani."

She stepped back a little. "How did you know?" Then she held up a hand. "Wait—I understand you have a special way of knowing things. And that's what I want to talk with you about—in relation to Dhani Jones."

She brushed snow from one of the benches, sat, and motioned for him to join her.

"This is a delicate matter, Sahm. When you have a gift like yours, people in this part of the world think you're either tricking them somehow or they think you're odd. Not normal."

"Dhani is not normal, in the way western people think. I believe he has a special gift. Many perhaps."

"That's the thing. In the world you come from, such gifted people are honored. Here they're treated with suspicion and fear. They're often shunned. We're not ready for them here."

"I do not understand. Why is that so?"

She skipped over answering that for now. "Dhani told Eric Trovert that he thinks he's hearing birds talk to him."

Sahm smiled—but seeing that Kate did not, he let it fade.

She pressed on. "That's. . . strange, Sahm."

"What if this is the way to make your program succeed?" he said, not sure where this idea came from.

"What do you mean?"

"Every person has gifts they have brought into this life from previous lives. If you could discover those gifts in these young people—"

She held up one hand to stop him, and the white light he had always seen within her dimmed a little.

"I might even be inclined to agree with you, Sahm, that maybe we were all here before. But encouraging these students to believe that is the kind of thing that could bring us down with the institutions that gave us permission to have the Lost Lake program."

He considered. "What is it you want to tell me about Dhani?"

"Are you teaching him about your religion?"

"I did not have to tell him about Bön. He knows our practices already. He brought them here with him."

"Well, I want you to talk with him about *other* things. Don't bring up your religion." She saw his face fall and amended that. "Unless he brings it up. And even then, try to talk with him about his courses, nature, the injured animals—something else."

"Some of the other students are interested in spiritual things, too, Kate. You should know. The boy Jalil and the girl Makayla. They are asking Randy Wolfmoon about his people's ways. You must know, Kate, that people need more than intellectual training. Their spirits hunger for knowledge, too."

She looked in a quandary. "All right. If they ask questions then—alright. Of course you can answer."

Sahm nodded. "If there is nothing else, Jo needs me in the barns. When I came through the kitchen, Ivy told me there will be sleet and freezing rain late this afternoon. Please be very mindful when you drive to town, Kate."

Driving into town later, her mind jumped between her concerns about people—Steve Tanner and Dhani were uppermost on her mind—and the stops she needed to make in Lake Placid. It was already late and she was hurrying.

The first white pellets of sleet tapped the windshield and she touched the brakes to test how slick the road was. Sahm's words raced back.

". . .be very mindful when you drive to town."

She had not told him or anyone that was her plan.

3

February

3rd

"What is it, Tom? You look unsettled."

Tom placed the phone receiver back in its cradle on Kate's desk. "That was Clayton, the young man who works my farm. A snowstorm knocked the power out for a day and his wife, Lissa, went into my farmhouse to check on things.

"When she looked in my office, she saw file and desk drawers left partly opened. Stacks of papers shuffled. And an old laptop I meant to get rid of was missing."

"That's bad news. Someone could have all your personal information."

"No. I had the hard drive taken out when a friend built the one I brought here with me. Keys weren't working on the old one, and a rebuilt one was cheaper than a new one."

"That was frugal—and lucky I guess."

"You make do, when you're on a priest's salary. And yes, lucky. They won't get anything off that computer. It's a shell."

"Do you have any idea what they could have been looking for?"

"No idea whatsoever. But whatever it was, they were disappointed, I'm sure. Lissa keeps all my financial records, so there wasn't even credit card or bank account information in those file drawers."

"What are you going to do about it?"

"A sheriff's deputy showed up, took notes. But since nothing seems to have been taken, he said it's likely his report will just get filed away. They don't have the manpower to chase down every unlawful entry."

Dhani scuffed his tennis shoes in the thin blanket of powdery snow that had fallen overnight. Some fell inside his sneakers, but he didn't feel the cold. His mind felt wide open, and—strangely—the solid world all around him was distant and vague.

He dug his hands in his pockets and thought about the white stone Sahm had given him and the eagle feather from Randy Wolfmoon. He had made his own small meditation altar on top of the cedarwood dresser in his room. This morning, twirling the feather in his fingers and rolling the stone in his palm he had felt—exactly *what,* he wasn't sure.

Different. Not lightheaded exactly but as if solid objects were becoming slightly transparent. The trees, fences, Kate's lodge, and the barns beside the river—everything looked like a pale, blue-tinted negative of itself. It was as if he were in another place, one that was more real, looking in on the world of forms, which had become less real.

He came to the barn where he was headed and reached for the door handle half-expecting it to turn into a talking head.

I'm still in bed asleep and this is all a dream.

In the clinic, Jo ran through the list of chores for him to do in the aviary. Claire already had her list, she said, her lips moving but little sound coming out. He bobble-headed as if he were paying full attention, though she sounded like she was speaking to him from a great distance.

This really is *all a dream*, he fought to convince himself.

When Jo handed him the list, the sting of a small paper cut left a red line on one index finger.

Another part of his mind argued, *No,* this *is real.*

He wanted to shake it off—this pull of a far-off sense of bliss, a letting go and falling upward. And at the same time he liked it. It felt natural, like a place in his mind he knew well.

Making his way to the aviary, he tried to get rid of the wooly numbness and the impression that every floor- and wallboard was etched by a bright-blue pen point—also the sense that the whole interior of the barn was shimmering.

Claire.

He would steady his mind looking for her.

She was not in the aviary, though, where Jo had sent her with the list of early morning duties. It wasn't unlike Claire these days to detour outside alone with her sketchbook before and after chores, tutorials, and everything else really. She seemed caught up and distant again.

No one had turned on the aviary lights yet and he did not reach for the switch, leaving the space in early-morning shadow.

Along the central corridor between the enclosures, pale columns of sunlight poured in through the eastern portals that opened to the outdoor cages. Outside the frosted panes—it was only 12 degrees—crystalline icicles that hung from the outside eaves like jagged teeth caught the sun's early orange-pink rays. Dhani walked the corridor slowly, looking side to side into the cages to see which of the inmates was awake.

Something was very different.

Today, the inmates seemed to be out waiting for him or they quickly emerged from leafy hideaways in the branches as he passed by. Every small, dark, shining eye was on him. And it was unusually quiet. Normally, he was greeted by chirps or shrieks. Today—no bird calls, trills, songs, hoots, or even a single flutter. The usual smell—straw dust, offal, disinfectant, medicines, the scent of blood from torn-apart roadkill—that was missing, too.

He turned in a circle trying to understand what was happening here, agitated. *Am I asleep or awake?* his mind shouted.

"We have waited. You are the ancient one," came a distinct response.

His head snapped around. The voice came from down near the eagle's cage.

I am the one who's supposed to do WHAT?

Part of his own mind commanded. *Stop it. This is weird as crap. Find Claire, and see if she wants to hang out.*

The image of the old, magic eagle feather flashed like lightning through his head, setting his mind ablaze.

From the eagle's cage came a faint *thump.* Immediately, the slanting column of light outside that enclosure filled with a small, swirling cloud of dust motes. Some disturbance was going on inside.

Striding back up the aisle, Dhani eyed the entryway door warily, straining to listen.

No voices, no footsteps. No sound of running water from the janitor's closet or noises in the supply room. He was still alone here, but maybe not for long.

Sliding open the enclosure door, he stepped inside. The floor was covered in shreds of fur and meat that had dried—probably rabbit—and it smelled of sweet, rotting straw and bitter, yellow-gray bird mess.

A flicker of movement above drew his attention to the highest branch.

The eagle stared down at him, unblinking, its talons curled and clutching.

For a split second he saw. . .

. . .the old man in the wheelchair he had met in town, bent fingers tearing helplessly at the soda can. . . .

but the eagle's eyes pulled him back into the moment.

You can *fly!* Dhani thought, with excitement.

The eagle slowly closed its gold and black eyes, and when the lids touched. . . .

Dhani felt electricity shoot through his being—a jolt so powerful his whole body clenched and contorted—arms and legs, diaphragm, spine, facial muscles. His fingers curled into claws. For a second it was like he had stepped on an exposed electric cable and this was its fatal surge.

Then he relaxed, felt all his muscles go loose and his eyes flew open again. . . .

The eagle's gaze clutched him in a powerful grip.

"I am here to set you free."

From what?

The eagle spread his massive wings and held steady in that position—majestic, proud.

"Who were you?" the eagle spoke into his mind.

When?

"Before you became this frightened one."

Dhani blinked and searched his mind, as if he should know the answer.

I don't remember who I was—or what that even means.

"You have forgotten. This frightened boy—this is the person you must shed."

Who am *I?* he pressed.

"You are the one we have waited for."

Stop saying that. What does it even mean?

As if from miles and miles away, he heard the enclosure door behind him slide open and someone stepped inside with him.

"You are the one who is one of us."

A voice from behind startled him. "What are you *doing*?"

He started to turn toward the door to see who spoke, and heard the fluttering of wings from behind. The eagle launched from its perch high up and plunged at him, passing like a cool lightning directly through his torso, shooting out into his bones, muscles and skin as it passed.

Dhani flinched, his whole body jerking from the surge.

Circling, the eagle rose to the top of the cage again, flapped and folded its wings, then settled on the perch—leaving him shocked and starting to awaken.

"Dhani," Claire hissed from the doorway.

The eagle loosed its mind-hold on him and vision wavered. Dhani staggered a little, regained his footing and wheeled around to face her.

Claire was staring at him, her eyes fierce.

"Get out now," she insisted, looking over her shoulder, "before Jo shows up and catches us."

Dhani turned back one last time to look at the eagle.

It was huddled down on its branch in the corner again, where it had been for months.

"What was going on in there?" Claire demanded, when they were back out in the central aisle. "You had this weird, scary kind of smile."

The air was loud with random chirps and whistles. The walls, ceiling, floor, and cages were slowly becoming solid and sliding back to the way they had always been, the same dull browns and tans and steel grays.

"What if I told you the eagle was talking to me?" Dhani said, feeling vague. And in the next second, he wanted to punch himself for telling her what he'd vowed not to.

"The eagle was *not* talking to you. What were you really doing?"

"*. . .this frightened one.*" Is that who he wanted to be? He decided to chance it with her. After all, she'd said she was his friend.

"Claire, really, I think he was talking to me. It happened on Christmas Eve the first time. This morning, after I messed around with the magic feather Randy gave me, I felt like I was supposed to go back into his enclosure. The eagle said stuff to me just now."

Claire stared at him, her mind flipping back to the first trek, up Peregrine Mountain, when Dhani had known lightning was about to strike. Also Christmas Eve when the night sky was clear but he had known it would be snowing in a half-hour.

She wanted to dismiss those incidents as lucky guesses.

"Tell me you were in there collecting more 'magic feathers.' If you want to imagine there's such a thing as magic I'm okay with that, I guess. Sometimes I imagine I have a nice home to go back to. We all have fantasies."

For the first time, he felt really irritated at her and gritted his teeth.

"You've been avoiding me. You think I'm crazy, just like everyone else."

"No, I don't."

"Yes, you do."

"Don't tell me what I think."

"Do you believe me then—that I think the eagle may be trying to tell me something?"

"Yes," she stood her ground. "I think you think that."

"I'm not doing word games with you," he shot back, stronger, frustrated. "You believe me or you don't."

"Okay. I don't."

That rocked him on his heels. He had pushed her, and now that she was being honest he wished he hadn't.

"So, do you think I'm *crazy*? Tell me right now." The gauzy feeling in his head was gone completely and objects were solid and not like shimmering negative-images—and in the face of Claire's adamant refusal to believe him, he doubted himself.

She relaxed. "No. But I don't really understand you or how your head works."

"I guess I'm really asking, do you think I'm going to hurt you? Or set someone else on fire? Are you *afraid* of me. Is that why you're avoiding me?"

"I—," Claire fished for a response.

Now her head was at war with her heart. "I *think* your mind seems to go off into these wild places I don't understand. But if I listen to my *gut—no,* I don't think you're dangerous. That's what's so confusing. What you told everyone about setting your mother's boyfriend on fire doesn't match who *I* think you really are."

He hadn't expected that. "Well. . .I *did* do what I said."

"And that's what I really don't believe, Dhani.—I don't know if a bird can talk to you. Maybe that's even possible, who knows? There's lots we don't know about the world. But I do know I don't believe you can hurt someone. Anyone. It's just not in you."

To his surprise—he hadn't expected this—Claire's belief that he was not dangerous put him on the defensive.

"Well, I did do it. I just told you. But I wouldn't hurt anyone else. Especially not you."

That hung in the air untouched.

"You've got to stay away from the eagle, Dhani," she said in moment. "If it has a lot of human contact, Jo says it'll be in danger when it's freed into the wild again."

Dhani almost said the words that came to mind. *He's not an* it. *And he's not an ordinary eagle.*

Instead he just stared at her.

Claire stared back at him more intensely. "Where's the list Jo gave you. We need to get busy."

Dhani was mopping the floor with disinfectant when Ray-Ray came in with his chore list from Jo. His mouth was moving and he was saying something. In his head, all Dhani could hear was what the eagle had said as it passed through him.

"Who were you before you let other people twist you into who you have become? You must meet that person."

4TH

"Who exactly is this Monica Saint woman," Kate asked. "And why is she so interested in knowing about Sahm?"

She took note of the fact that Judge Sewell had waited to the end of the phone call to bring up the issue. That made it sound casual, but she knew him better.

"She's got this thing about religion," he had said. "According to her, he's promoting his beliefs to some of the students. You did question him about that, as I asked in my last email, didn't you?"

"Where is she getting this information?"

"She won't say.—Did you question him?"

"Sahm cleans the barns for Jo and hauls gear for Steve to help with the wilderness training. He's a simple, kind and wonderful young man who had to escape from Tibet. Let me guess—she wants us to promote her religion instead."

"No. She's pure social scientist and secularist. She's an equal-opportunity hater of all religious beliefs. She's been assigned by social services to review all files pertaining to the young people in your program. Candidly, I believe she's ticked off that I'm in charge and she's not. We can't just blow her off, though, Kate, so don't get your back up. She's got a lot of pull, she reads all the reports Tom sends down, and we need her on our side."

Her mind went to the talk she'd just had with Sahm, voicing Eric Trovert's concern about Dhani pretending to have special powers, probably to impress a girl. As if that would do it. Now this—a woman concerned about someone mentioning their religion. These silly, insignificant matters did not need to grow out of proportion.

"What do you want me to do?"

"Just keep an eye on it. That's all. No need to get alarmed."

She relaxed a little. "We've put so much time and effort into starting this program. Hard to not be alarmed when I know every detail, every conversation is being this scrutinized."

"That's why we need to play it super-smart and squeaky clean. Especially this first year."

"Fine."

"Kate."

"Kate *what*?"

"I'm going to ignore that tone and leave you with a name and message for Steve Tanner. He needs to be in your office at two this afternoon. This woman, a reporter, is going to phone him, and tell him I said it's important he take the call."

She scratched the information on her note pad.

An hour later when Emmalyn came into the office she was clasping her hands, adjusting her hair, and acting nervous.

Kate stopped answering emails. "What is it, Emmalyn?"

"I don't want to sound negative. . . ."

After Judge Sewell's cagey dance around an issue she was not in the mood. "Just come out with it."

"I don't want to say anything bad about Father Baden. My mama says it's not good to point out other people's mistakes. But the computer printer ink and the notebooks we need keep running out of stock. Also, we needed a book for our literature class a week ago and I saw a note on Father Baden's desk that they still need to be ordered. I checked Amazon—I hope you don't mind I used his computer—and I can order all the copies we need *used*, so they'll be a lot cheaper."

Kate smiled at her and felt boosted a bit.

"Tom—which is what he prefers—has been filing a lot of endless reports, scheduling doctors' and other appointments. I'm sure he would appreciate the help."

Emmalyn stopped fidgeting and smiled. "I could handle the ordering and restocking. I used to do that for my mama's place. I just want to be helpful and do a good job."

Kate could imagine what she ordered for her "mama's place", a backcountry strip club.

"You're doing very well. I'll tell Tom to hand the job of ordering over to you. He gets a bit overwhelmed with ordering Jo's pharmaceutical supplies, too. So trust me. He won't mind at all."

She turned back to her computer, feeling satisfaction. Regardless of the qualms of bureaucratic nitpickers, here was proof positive the program was working.

"So how have you been, Thi?" And how did you find me?"

"I couldn't for a long time, Steve. Believe me I tried for over a year. How did you drop off the grid so completely? I just happened to be at a fundraiser with Judge John Sewell. He said he's great friends with your new boss, Kate Holman, and he came up and said, 'Aren't you the reporter who was there that day at National Cathedral?' He'd seen the footage my camera guys captured that my producer wouldn't air, because it was so unsettling for the public to view."

Steve forced to the back of his mind the image of Thi Martin, kneeling on the sidewalk opposite him as they leaned over Olivia as her blood and her life ran out. He looked out the front window of Kate's office across the lake to Osprey Island, his refuge, vaguely wishing he hadn't made this call.

"I've been planning a program for the second anniversary of"—she chose a term carefully—"the event."

His shoulders tightened.

"Why?"

"Because the case has gone cold. I tried to contact the investigator and all I could find out was that he moved to some remote little island off the coast of Florida over a year ago. I made three calls to DC Metro, and they couldn't even tell me who's following up on the case. That's crazy. So I'm dedicating one of my morning talk shows around the event and the fact that the perpetrator is still at-large. Someone out there has to know something, and maybe we can get them to come forward. The station is planning a huge promo leading up to it. The mayor has agreed to be on since she's the one who honored Olivia twice for her work."

"Are you calling for my permission?"

"I need you to be on the show that morning."

A sick, empty feeling gripped his stomach. It was the feeling of his own life draining out, just as it did every time he remembered Olivia's eyes going blank and her hand sagging limp in his. His knees felt weak and he wished for the forgetfulness he felt while fishing alone in Grady's canoe. Since Christmas Eve, he had cut back a bit on the drinking that had amplified his dark despair that night. He was probably lucky that Pal, his black retriever, had found him out on the end of an icy dock, on a far edge of darkness, and with his sweet nature willed peace and life back into him.

"I don't know. Do you really need me there?"

"I want to ask you some background questions about Olivia so viewers can know who she really was, what she loved to do. And mainly how hard she worked for the down-and-out kids of DC. Make her a real person to them, not just a face and a statistic. That's getting hard to do with all these mass shootings now. People just shut down and try to not to think that real human beings just like them are dying."

Steve's head was a jumble of responses. He felt angry the police had dropped the ball, at the same time jolted into action to do something. Also trapped by the request because it meant being in the public eye when he had buried himself here in the wilderness. And he was aggravated by the term "down-and-out". That only fed a "poor me" attitude that was in his face every day, coming from a few of these kids who didn't want to try and instead complained about the Lost Lake program—a pure gift that was being served to them on a silver platter.

He crushed all those responses.

"Okay." Underneath everything else was his drive to find Olivia's killer and see her death avenged. He imagined. . . .

. . .prison guards strapping a useless street thug, crack-head to a table. Needles being stuck into forearm veins. Chemicals sliding down clear tubing, delivering the lethal injection. . .and watching through the glass for the moment when that worthless piece of excrement's body began to jerk and heave.

"When do you need me to be there?"

6TH

Rocco closed the door of his room quietly, tip-toed down the hall and out the cabin door into the cold night. All the cabins were dark. It was moonless, but he knew the paths well enough now to find his way out the camp road to the outbuildings and Kate's greenhouse.

The only sound in the night was the tread of his boots on the frozen dirt.

From behind, a voice whispered, "*Hey.*"

He jumped and almost yelled.

Jalil was coming up silently in the dark.

"*Hat Boy*. Why are you following me?"

"You're going to the greenhouse, right?"

"Why are you tagging along after me?"

"I'm not tagging along. I heard there was a party."

"Well, just don't hang around near me when we get there."

Jalil stopped in the road. "Why do you keep treating me like crap? I asked you before and you didn't answer?"

Rocco kept walking.

"If I talk to you, you ignore me. When I ask if I can sit at your table at any meal, you say there's no room even when there's an empty seat. And you keep calling me Hat Boy. I hate that."

"You always wear hats," Rocco said over his shoulder. "And you should shut up or Grady will hear your big mouth if he's out patrolling."

Dugan handed Rocco a silver hip flask. "Here you go, my man."

Garrett stared at the two of them.

"Nah," Rocco declined. "I gotta get through this program clean as can be. If I don't, my dad'll beat the living crap outa me."

"Just a swig."

"I'm serious. He's not the kinda guy you want to cross or let down, even if you're his kid."

"Come on. Everyone has to. That way, if we ever get caught, no one can say they're innocent."

Rocco took the flask, raised the silver mouthpiece to his lips and tilted his head back once, fast.

"Okay, satisfied?" he said wiping his mouth on his coat sleeve. "Who's got the tunes?"

Jalil had come in after him and was seated across the circle of peat bags, plugging his iPod into a small speaker. "It's almost all country up here. These mountain boys likes them their honky-tonk music and their big trucks. Every other commercial is for a Ford F-150. I need some CDs and a player, Garrett."

Then he looked around the group, his eyes wide and startled looking.

Rocco laughed at him. "What's Garrett—your personal Santa Claus?"

Imani reached for the flask when she came in.

"I believe I need a sip of that."

Dugan shoved a glass pipe at Rocco.

"Want a hit?"

Rocco waved him off.

"No. If we get caught just say I did it, too."

Jalil had made his way through the static to a country station and had the volume turned low.

Makayla leaned close to Rocco. "No drinking, no drugs. I like that." She slid her hand around his upper arm and squeezed. "I can't do substances either. It wrecks my head."

She leaned close to him and whispered. "I—lose time."

"Seriously?" Rocco whispered back. "You said that at Christmas, but I thought you were just being dramatic. Are you?"

She looked hurt, and now he caught sight of Imani.

Imani was staring across at them, looking—*jealous*, Rocco decided. "That's something you should have checked out," he said to Makayla.

Carter slid open the door to the potting room and passed between everyone, making for the seat beside Jalil.

"Hey," she said, laying a hand on his thigh, smiling. Then she flashed a quick look across at Garrett who had a pinched, irritable look.

"What happened to your hand?" Jalil asked, looking down at the gauze bandage on Carter's index finger.

"Cut it on a knife."

Jalil had switched stations and turned the sound up.

"Now *that's* some good music," Imani said. She stood and began to move to it.

My love, he makes me feel like nobody else, nobody else.
But my love, he doesn't love me. . . .

"So," Garrett said quietly to Dugan, whose eyes were running up and down the curves of Imani's body, "when did you and muscle head get to be so buddy-buddy?" His voice had a slight edge to it.

Dugan leaned away from Garrett and closer to Rocco, slapped him on the shoulder and said out loud. "Dude and I are friends now."

Then he spoke up to the rest of the group. "Y'all need to know Rocco and I resolved our differences. Maybe some of you other guys should do the same. Get rid of the petty, catty vibe in this group. We gonna be together a *looong* time."

Rocco was ignoring Makayla now. He was staring at Imani and looked mesmerized.

"Which one of you guys is stronger?" Carter addressed Rocco and Dugan. "You both look strong, but one guy's always stronger than the other guy. I mean Rocco's like a bull and Dugan you're like a stallion."

Imani kept dancing, arms over her head making graceful gestures, as the song moved her.

One, don't pick up the phone.
You know he's only calling 'cause he's drunk and alone. . . .

After Carter's statement, there was an awkward pause in conversation.

"What?" said Carter, looking around the circle.

"Geez," Makayla replied, sounding cautious. "You've been so quiet all year except in class."

"Yeah," said Garrett. "Who knew you could speak."

"I speak to people who are worth talking to."

Garrett's mouth snapped shut.

"This is a party, dudes," Dugan jumped in. "The room may be dark, but the mood should be *light*. See, this is the vibe I mean. Someone's always got a beef with somebody.—Hey, Rocco," he said, changing his tone, "Carter just gave me an idea."

"What you got."

"We're pretty evenly matched, I'd say. What about a little sparring one of these late nights in Yazzie's boxing ring. Just for fun. I know you been sparring with him. Let's show the ladies what our guns can do."

Rocco shrugged. "I don't wanna fight you."

"Just an exhibition, man. Sparring, not fighting." He slapped Rocco on the back again. Then he flexed his right arm. "Also give the ladies a show."

Imani stopped dancing and rolled her eyes. "Why do boys always think we're interested in your 'guns'? Seems to me y'all are more interested in them than we are."

"Because you really are interested," Rocco responded, siding with Dugan, "even when you pretend you're not."

"You'd be surprised how attractive a guy who *reads* is."

"I read."

"What?—Cereal boxes don't count," Imani said, and turned her back on him, continuing to dance.

"Flirt."

"Why d'you think something's about you when it's not? I'm dancing 'cause I like this song."

Rocco's eyes remained stuck on her.

> *. . .Three, don't be his friend.*
> *You know you're gonna wake up in his bed in the mornin'. . . .*

Dugan came back at Rocco. "How about it, buddy? A little sparring match. Just for fun."

Rocco didn't answer. He seemed to be elsewhere.

Dugan winked at Garrett.

“I know—you’re more of a tender guy, getting’ all mushy over sick lil’ baby bears. Tryna seem all sweet and soft for the ladies.”

In the half-dark, no one saw Rocco’s jaw clench. “Sure. Sparring. Just for fun.”

Walking back to his cabin in the dark, Rocco heard his father’s voice in his head. . . .

“He backed down from a fight at school?” his father roared at his mother.

“His teacher said he talked the other boy out of fighting. That’s not backing down, that’s smart.”

His father loomed over him, grabbed his collar and shook him.

“You stand up for yourself and fight—you hear me?”

“Leave him alone,” his mother objected. “He’s only ten.”

The slap knocked her backwards, and when Rocco shouted, “Leave her alone,” the next slap sent him sprawling on the floor.

Bending over him, his father thrust a finger in his face.

“You back down from a fight, ever, you’re no son of mine. Be a man.”

7TH

Ron laid the small, furry body on the stainless steel examining table.

“You found it on the floor next to the tank,” Jo repeated what he’d said.

He nodded and, without thinking, straightened the young otter’s wide tail.

“Yeah. There was some blood coming out of its mouth and nose. Dried. So it must have fallen out of the tank headfirst, I guess. Emmalyn’s going to be really sad. This is the little guy she called Otto.”

“Ron, the lip of that tank is only five feet from the floor. Even if it could climb out—which is impossible given the way the rim curves inward—it might have injured itself. But it wouldn’t have died from that kind of fall.”

"So—brain tumor, thoracic hemorrhage?"

"I'll have to do an autopsy sometime. We've got a new inmate coming in about an hour."

Ron picked up the limp body. "Who are we getting?"

"You're gonna love this.—A small cougar."

"No way. Since when do we have cougars in here in the 'dacks?"

"I don't know. But some guys were telemarking down the back side of Whiteface and saw tracks and a blood trail. Environmental Conservation guys went back in and found it."

"Shot?"

"Probably. They say it's not in bad shape, but couldn't say exactly where the wound is."

"Must have been after someone's pet."

"Doesn't matter. They're endangered and protected. I'm going to put out the word to see if anyone knows who shot it."

"Needle in a haystack, Jo. No one wants to rat on anyone else up here."

"Anyway—we're going to keep the cougar sequestered after the surgery. I don't want word getting out that they may be making a comeback up here. The yahoos will be out hunting them.

"Good call."

"Wrap the otter, get it in the freezer and then disinfect one of the big holding cages in the treatment room. Then scrub up. Emergency surgery is in about—," Jo looked at the wall clock, "—a half-hour. They were driving through Placid fifteen minutes ago. Should be here any minute."

Ron wrapped the small otter's body, noticing one side was flattened, as if its ribs had been crushed by something. On a guess, he slid one of his little fingers in its mouth and pried open the stiffening jaw as gently as possible. Even in death, as far as he was concerned, all living creatures were owed respect.

As he'd suspected, its tongue was swollen and blue. The injury that killed this little guy was from a high-impact trauma, one much more forceful than a five-foot fall from the aquatic tank.

The small cub lay in the crook of Rocco's left arm, listless, not grabbing for the bottle, barely sucking. Rocco squeezed the formula into its pink mouth.

"Come on, buddy, you gotta eat. You need to get strong so you can—"

A short fit of coughing erupted from deep in his chest. When it subsided, he dug a crumbling sugar cookie out of his pocket.

"You finish this bottle and I'll give you one of Ivy's treats."

The cub turned its head and reached out a paw for the cookie.

"Nope. Take the medicine first."

Another short fit of coughing came over him.

Jo had entered the room, brandishing medicine vials and hypodermic needles.

"Rocco, you know the x-rays showed this guy has abnormalities in his lungs. And you're in here, holding him, coughing, when I told you to stay away."

"It's just a little cold. I'm almost over it. And I miss this little guy. I think he misses me, too. Two weeks ago, he was starting to follow me around the room here like a puppy."

"You had him out playing with him?—Rocco."

"Sorry."

"Look. Even a surgical mask may not protect him from germs. And stop bringing cookies to them and acting like they're domestic pets. They'll associate humans with sweet treats and friendliness, and that's a very bad idea once they're released."

She set down the medicines and needles, and took the cub from his arms. "You have a big heart, Rocco. But you can't let it rule over common sense and good medical practice. Humans can think they're helping, when they're actually causing harm. You don't want to be the cause of us losing this guy."

He stepped back quickly from her and the cub, looking crestfallen. "Is that possible? Do you think I could have just given him my cold?"

Choosing her words carefully, Jo replied, "I'm starting him on a course of stronger antibiotics. Let's just give him every chance from this point on, okay?"

Rocco's face clouded with worry.

Seeing that, she squeezed his shoulder. "Look, if good juju counts for anything in medicine—and who knows, maybe it does—this guy may rocket to recovery based on your love for him alone."

He looked at the larger cub, asleep in its pen. It was curled in a ball, its face under one paw, the blond streak on its shoulder moving just slightly as it breathed. "I hope I didn't give The Flash my cold."

"Stop calling him The Flash."

9TH

Dhani stood up suddenly, bumping his plate into his orange juice, spilling it across the table.

"Something bad just happened."

"Damn, dude," Jalil raised his voice, "you dumped juice on my toast."

The others at breakfast stared, forks partway to their lips.

"Oh god," Tia Leesha said, cringing. "I knew he was gonna lose it totally. He got a AR-15 inside that hoody?"

"Stuff it, Tia," Ray-Ray growled. "No one needs your drama this morning."

"Dhani, sit down." Claire grabbed his sleeve and snapped at him. "Nothing bad happened."

"You're wrong," Dhani shot back. "Stop acting like I'm psycho. Something *did* just happen."

Knocking over his chair he went for the door.

In the large barn, Dhani searched among the cages, stopping beside the bear cubs' pen.

"Oh crap, oh crap, oh crap," he said. "I'm really sorry, man."

Others had piled into the area after him—Claire, Ray-Ray, Imani, Tia Leesha and Dugan.

"Oh no."

"Poor little guy."

Before them, Rocco was curled up in the straw, his hand lying gently on the body of the smallest black bear cub. The cub's brown fur was matted, as if it had been sweating hard. Through the matting, the sharp lines of ribs were visible on its emaciated body.

"He was doing okay." Rocco's voice cracked as he struggled to speak. "I was. . .taking good care of him. I did. . . everything Jo said. He wasn't supposed to. . . ."

He couldn't finish and his body began to heave with stifled sobs.

Garrett came in, followed by Emmalyn. He and Dugan locked eyes and grinned.

Imani caught the look and glared at them.

"What happened?" Jo's voice interrupted.

Rocco's face was stained with tears.

"He's dead. I was kind of busy with school stuff for a couple days, plus healing my cold, and didn't come to take care of him. I'm so sorry, buddy."

Emmalynn teared up. "I know how you feel. Otto, my favorite little otter just died." She glared at Carter, whose mouth showed just the faintest trace of a grin. "Died or was killed," Emmalyn added quietly—but everyone was focused on Rocco and the cub.

"*I* was here," Imani insisted. "*I* took care of him."

"Maybe if *I* was here, though. We were so tight."

She had knelt down, and laid her hand on his shoulder. "He wasn't thriving. You watched his chart. You know that. Come out of the pen, Rocco."

"No." He stroked the cubs head. "They'll just throw his body away."

Jo stepped through the line of onlookers, reached out and laid her arm on his shoulder.

"We won't do that. Ron will bury him."

"He's with God," Emmalyn whispered.

Garrett cough-laughed.

Imani was still kneeling by Rocco and glaring at Garrett and Dugan, who were hiding their laughter behind their hands.

Garrett said, "Maybe you gave it your cold man."

"Wouldn't it be tragic," said Dugan, shaking his head, "if you actually killed your little buddy there?"

Imani had a look of rage, and mouthed at both of them. *Get. Out.*

Dugan rubbed one fist on his cheek and mouthed back. *Boo hoo.*

Jo's voice was strong. "We do our best here, Rocco, but the animals we treat don't always make it. Come out of the pen and get yourself together. I'm sorry the cub died, too, but you can't let yourself get this attached. Lesson learned."

"That's harsh," Ray-Ray muttered to Claire.

Claire was staring at Dhani. "How did you know something bad had happened?"

The others were staring at him, too.

"Amazing."

"Cool."

"That's voodoo," Tia Leesha recoiled.

"Amen," Emmalyn said.

On their way back to the breakfast room, Dhani said to Claire "I told you. I just—know things. Sometimes I know about nature stuff. More and more, I know stuff about animals. I don't exactly know how."

Jo said, "It wasn't your fault, Rocco. It wasn't. Whatever you had was viral. The cub had bacterial pneumonia."

"But you told me his immune system was weak. I shouldn't have been in here. Why didn't I listen?"

Jo was about to say something, then hesitated. When she spoke again she was direct, but her voice was kind. "Good question, Rocco. Why didn't you listen?"

His voice was choked. "Because I—because I'm a jerk."

"I don't accept that," Jo pushed back. "Try again."

He cleared his throat. "Because I liked him so much. Because I didn't want him to be sick and all alone."

She nodded. "Rocco, I know you try to hide it, but you have a big heart. That's a good thing. A gift. Don't waste it."

Suddenly Jo found herself fighting an unexpected wave of emotion, and turned away from Rocco to a countertop, where a new shipment of medications was waiting to be checked in and stored.

"And because of you, he didn't die alone. That's a good thing, too."

10TH

"Thanks for taking the time to talk with me," said Claire.

Sitting on the restaurant's veranda on the backside of Mirror Lake, she and the Troverts could see the village of Lake Placid across the frozen expanse. Yesterday, a flood of warm air had poured in through the mountain valleys, and Bay had picked a nice restaurant near the village with outdoor seating.

Claire looked at the icy white expanse of lake, which was starting to melt under the sun—then at the Troverts.

Watch them, she thought. This kind of setting was a typical counselors' trick. Get you relaxed, make you feel special. She would remain on her guard to keep from falling into some clever question-trap.

"No need to thank us, Claire," said Bay, when the waiter brought their steaming soups and left them alone. "Come to Eric and me any time.—Is this about the prosecutor in DC? Kate said he's starting to push again for you to go back there."

"Tom says Judge Sewell is still fighting him and thinks I won't have to. I just want them all to go away and leave me alone."

"Is that what this is about—you're concerned you'll have to go back?"

"Well, I don't want to see my parents. At all. But I'm not worried about testifying if they force me to. I don't know anything about my parents' drug dealing. I was a really little. It's not like they filled me in on their connections."

Eric was thoughtful. "The prosecutor is probably getting ready to run for a big, public office, like Attorney General. And he's probably using the threat of making you testify to pressure your parents into talking."

Claire made a disgusted sound. "They never gave a crap about me then and I'm a thousand percent sure they don't now."

Bay cleared her throat. "You should know that your parents' lawyer asked Judge Sewell to find out if your dad can call you."

"*No,*" Claire said without missing a beat. "You can pass the message back to him that just—*no.* The judge can't force me to talk to him, can he?"

Bay placed her hand lightly on Claire's forearm. "No, Claire. He can't. And no one here will force you to do anything."

Hand on forearm, Claire thought. *Nice touch. Nice try.*

"It may help ease your mind," Eric picked it up, "to hear that Tom and Kate and Judge Sewell are pushing to have you testify from here—online—if you even have to testify at all. Kate will have a good lawyer here to represent you. That way the prosecutor can't bully you. And keep in mind, the judge in DC knows you're a juvenile and will protect you, too."

She had asked for this meeting, but here they were taking over with their agenda—adult-'splaining.

Claire gave a short, bitter laugh.

"Protect me—seriously? Like they did when I was being bullied in foster care and everyone including the courts labelled *me* as the problem? I don't mean to offend you, but you have no freakin' idea what it's really like when you're stuck in the system."

"We do, actually," Eric replied.

The waiter arrived with drink refills, interrupting.

"You're right, Claire," said Bay, when the waiter was gone and with a glance at Eric. "We really don't know the system from the *inside*. We've worked with many young people, but no one who's gone through what you have. But please know that we will do whatever we can, whatever we have to, to help and support you."

Claire raised a spoon to her lips and blew on the steaming soup. So, they had different ways of trying to win her trust. Say they knew what she'd gone through, then grovel and say they didn't. She wasn't playing either game.

"You're both nice. But the truth is, I know I'm on my own and no one's really on my side. Not really. People say they are, but then it's, 'Sorry you don't like it, but these are the rules.' Everyone's there to support the system because that's their job. That's what pays their bills. When you've been in this system long enough, you figure out that the adults who are supposed to be helping you are more worried about getting the paycheck that will buy their kid's next piece of sports equipment. So you lose out to a pair of basketball shoes or a lacrosse stick. If it meant protecting this program in some way, even you guys and Kate would toss me under the bus."

Eric and Bay looked at each other in stunned silence for a long moment.

"Damn," Eric said, finally.

Claire's face was expressionless, and she felt in-charge now. "I'm waiting for you to say some observant, counselor-thing like," her voice dropped in tone, "'You sound very angry, Claire.'"

"No," Eric shook his head. "I was going to say you're very savvy."

Now comes the 'you're a bright young woman' line.

Bay stepped in. "Eric and I wanted to work with Kate and you guys here because we see the same thing you see. A system overwhelmed by young people who shouldn't be in *a system*, but many of them are through no fault of their own. We see counselors, lawyers, and judges who started out eagerly as youth advocates but now they're overwhelmed by the number of cases to handle."

"We're *people* not *cases*," Claire responded quickly, angry.

"I can only say you're not a *case* to Eric and me. You're a person."

"We are on your side, Claire," Eric added. "We really are."

She started to respond, but didn't—or she would have said, *"That is so cliché."*

There was a long silence, and Bay changed the subject. "What is it *you* want to talk about today?"

"It's Dhani," Claire ventured, setting the spoon in the now empty bowl. "He gets into this strange place in his mind. He thinks the old, eagle feather Randy gave him is magical. And he thinks a stone he got from Sahm is a 'seer stone'."

"We're aware of these things," Bay replied, "from something he hinted to Eric. Why does he think that—do you know?"

"He said Sahm is teaching him about Tibetan religion or magic or something. Sahm's got this altar in his cabin and Dhani goes there sometimes to talk to him in private. I think he's encouraging Dhani to believe he can hear animals talk. I like Sahm. He's cool. But I think he believes some very weird things."

"Did Dhani tell you that?"

"No. I went to see Sahm a few weeks ago and I found him out in the woods with a rabbit that had been torn up by a hawk. He told me he was inside his cabin and *saw* the bird drop the rabbit—even though that's totally impossible. He would have had to see through walls and trees. He said he saw it in like, a supernatural vision."

She stopped, waiting for a response.

Eric cleared his throat. "How does this business with Sahm directly concern Dhani? How do you think it affects his behavior?"

"The other day I found him inside the eagle's cage. Please don't tell Jo. She'd be so pissed and he wasn't in there long. I don't think the eagle was exposed to human contact for more than a minute or two. I blasted Dhani for doing it.

"He was spaced-out when I found him. That's why I'm here. He didn't seem to hear me walk in behind him, and when he came-to he said he thinks the eagle was talking to him. That isn't normal. And if the other kids ever heard him say that they'd go nuts. Everyone avoids him except Ray-Ray and me. Possibly Rocco, too, now. I think they all wish he wasn't here. Even Ray-Ray's getting uncomfortable around him and he's Dhani's only close friend."

"Other than you," Bay responded.

"Other than me."

"Jo told me about the incident with the bear cub. That Dhani seemed to know the cub was dead before anyone was told about it."

"That's true. He did."

"What do you think's going on with him?" Eric asked.

Claire settled on an answer. "I think Sahm believes some strange things and Dhani thinks Sahm is cool. And for some reason, Dhani wants to impress me that he's someone important."

"'. . .for some reason.'" Bay repeated. "What would that be?"

"He likes me."

Eric rubbed his chin and summarized. "He has a crush on you and he's trying to impress you in his own way. So he's telling you he has a 'super power.'"

This was more of the diagnostic, counselor-y stuff Claire hated, but she went along. "Something like that, yeah."

With a quick glance toward Eric, Bay took over. "We're not here to speculate about another person. Let's talk about you, Claire. You care about Dhani, but it's getting hard to be his friend because he's asking you to buy into things you don't believe. Is that correct?"

"Yeah. But I do want to be his friend. Just a friend. How do I do that without him getting the wrong idea? I tried telling him I believe he's a good person even though I didn't believe the stuff about the eagle, but I could see he was getting mad."

Clouds had crossed over the sun and a breeze came at them across the melting lake ice, picking up the cold. Bay shivered and pulled her collar up.

"You've given us a lot to think about, Claire. I'd like to talk this over with Eric and evaluate options. Would you mind if we finished lunch inside and then meet with you again in a couple of days?"

Claire smiled and nodded.

My friend is getting sucked into a crazy fantasy. But sure, take all the time you need to evaluate *this.*

"Maybe we should have Dhani observed and studied for psychic tendencies," Bay said, between deep breaths and dodging a puddle.

The flood of warm air had melted the ice on the roads and they were jogging up the long incline along the base of Whiteface Mountain late in the afternoon, with the sound of trickling or rushing water all around them.

"Or psychosis," Eric huffed. "Or just teenaged-boy neurosis around girls."

"There are other possibilities besides the clinical boxes."

"So you think he's psychic. Just because he guessed correctly that a very sickly bear cub died."

"Jo thinks he's jonesing for attention."

Eric slowed their running pace to a jog. "But *you* think he has some kind of special powers."

"You told me your grandfather had unusual experiences you couldn't explain."

"Why are you bringing that up?"

"Because you're resisting looking at possibilities in order to support your foregone conclusion."

"Or you are."

"You said your grandfather was at home across town from you and in his mind's-eye he *saw* you fall from a swing in your backyard. When he sped over, he found you lying there unconscious and with a severely broken arm. Your parents were in the front of the house working and distracted and they didn't even know you were badly injured. That had to register with you somewhere inside your analytically objective head."

"He made a lot of claims. I always thought he was exaggerating. He was an emotional guy. Kind of dramatic."

"So you're saying he was a liar."

"Don't put words in my mouth. He had his own weird reality that he believed in."

"He told you the day and time your dad was going to die."

"Dad was already dying."

"Yes, but he said, 'Go visit him today before twelve'—and you didn't go and the seizure that took him hit just before noon."

"Thanks for the reminder."

"He said your dad came to him in a dream right before the World Series one year and said, 'Tell Eric, this time the Cubs will win the pennant and I'll be there watching with you guys.'"

"Yeah, well that was a hopeful thing to say. The three of us loved baseball."

"Your grandfather told you this right before the Series, though, and the Cubs did win."

Eric stopped. "You're grasping at straws because, I guess, you want to believe in the supernatural."

"Not as much as you *don't* want to believe things are happening that right now seem outside the realm of possibility. And look, you're the one who told me about these events. Was that just to mock your grandfather? All I'm saying is we have an interesting case here and we should think about having him evaluated. There are reputable universities studying this sort of thing. And what if they did find that Dhani is imagining these things and is in need of serious psychiatric help. That would also be a good result."

"Look," Eric countered, "this kid is a quiet guy, an anti-hero type, who's trying to impress a pretty girl he thinks he's in love with. I say we tell Claire not to buy into it, not to engage in conversations about this stuff with him."

"Ignore it and it will go away—seriously?"

"No. She should also report to us immediately if he gets inappropriate with her in any way. It's just a bid for attention. But we don't need to over-react. Remember—anything we write in a report goes straight to Sewell and then to this Monica Saint woman who's got something in her craw about this program. All we need to do is say we think one of the kids is psychic and you know what happens next. I'm going with my gut on this one."

Bay let out a frustrated puff of breath.

"I'm not going to let this drop, Eric. If something truly big and important is going on with Dhani, we should find out. And speaking of gut—we need to get moving again, because those jogging shorts you're wearing are getting tight in the waist."

He laughed and took off again. "I didn't say I wouldn't check this out more. Now can we lighten up? And by the way, if your spandex breaks I'll be a dead man."

"You'd better outrun me," she called after him.

Claire stopped halfway down the short path to her cabin, sounding impatient when she spoke. "What are you doing here?"

Vajra was lying at the top of the porch steps. His golden eyes had not left her as she approached and now he rose, came down the steps, and stood right in front of her.

She tried to step around him and he moved, blocking her path—then nudged her hand with his nose.

"I'm not going to pet you, so leave me alone. Go home to Sahm."

He cocked his head to one side. Then in a moment loped away down the path and left her standing there.

Watching him, she felt a sudden emptiness.

The voice of a past counselor flooded her head.

"You seem to want to get close to people. You're nice to them and attract them to you. You want to be liked. But when they do get close, you push them away."

Maybe Dhani wasn't the crazy one, the thought came to her. Maybe she was. She wondered how long it would be before Dhani got tired of her *come-close stay-away* thing, the way other people had.

Later, as dusk was settling, Claire heard Makayla call out for her from the front room of their cabin. "You gotta come see this."

Outside, the swiftly setting sun had turned the snow pink and lavender, making the charcoal black figure stand out in stark contrast. It was Vajra, curled up against a drift.

"He's watching our cabin," Makayla said.

Slipping on boots but no coat, Claire went out to drive him away.

"Go home. It's freezing out here."

Vajra stood, shaking the snow from his thick coat and staring as if studying her. Since last summer, she had caught him watching or following. Once, in November, he had driven off something that was stalking her in the forest while she was sketching.

The snow colors were rapidly leaving as the sun sank lower and the night's cold was coming down like icy rivers from every mountainside.

"Go home!" Claire shouted, then turned back to the cabin.

When she reached the porch, Makayla and Imani were standing in the open door, both smiling.

"Look behind you," said Imani, pointing.

Bring him inside, Makayla begged. "He looks cold."

Vajra was practically at Claire's heels.

"He keeps following me," Claire objected. "He won't go home."

"Maybe he thinks he is home," Makayla insisted.

All night, Vajra slept at the foot of Claire's bed.

Okay.

She would ask Kate in the morning if it was alright to let the half-wolf stay in her cabin, since that was what he seemed to want.

12TH

Sun glittered off the snow, turning it to a carpet of white with scattered diamond-points of light. Some caught the light and turned it into spectrum flashes of yellow-red and green-indigo. On the hillsides, the shadows of trees, snow folds, and drifts fell in shades of pale and deep blues.

Dhani trudged back from Mike Yazzie's Spanish class toward his cabin, shoulders slumped, feeling gray as his wool socks, which were pilling with ice as he shuffled along.

When he had walked into class an hour ago, all conversation had stopped. And when he dropped his notebook on a desk next to Tia Leesha, she quickly grabbed her things and moved—not without comment.

"I don't need some of your crazy juju jumpin' off on me."

Since their encounter in the aviary, and then at the bear cub's death, Claire had become a little distant. Again. It was getting old.

Halfway down the path now, a flicker caught his eye.

Out on the lake, a low wind set a small snow-devil spinning until it dissipated into nothingness.

I want to disappear like that, Dhani thought, and the words bore a deeper hole in the empty sense that was overtaking him. He felt hollow, as if the cold wind could whistle clean through the stark emptiness between his ribs.

Claire had said she wanted to be his "friend"—but also that she didn't believe him. Which meant she thought he was lying or stupid or. . . .

Maybe she's right. Maybe everyone's right. I'm just a lunatic.

He felt crazy. Or what he imagined crazy felt like.

More flashes of light from ice crystals on the frozen lake caught his attention.

"I am here to free you."

The words he'd imagined the eagle saying kept circling in his head. And the powerful sense that there was a wide-open place inside his mind that he could step into was becoming more frequent.

Halting, he stared out across the white expanse. All over the lake, the snow crystals winked on and off and on, the simple beauty of their prismatic colors mesmerizing.

Without thinking, Dhani turned and plodded through the sloppy, melting snow toward the lake front. When he reached it, he didn't stop but stepped out onto the ice, slipping once, catching himself, and kept trudging.

The further out he went—ten feet, twenty, thirty—the stronger the sun's glare off the icy surface felt. A hundred feet out, he was sloshing through puddles and skating his feet over the ice sheet, which was growing slicker the further out he slipped and slid. Still, the ice crystals blinked and shimmered yellow-red and blue-green. Only vaguely did it occur to Dhani that the sun's intensity might be making the ice thinner and thinner.

He felt lightheaded and light-bodied, as if his bones were made of feathers and his skin was expanding, becoming the air.

"Dhani!" someone called far behind him—a hundred feet or a thousand miles away.

"Come back!" someone else called, from the darkness beyond the moon.

Turning his head, half snow-blind, he saw the miniature figures of Ray-Ray and Claire back on the frozen ribbon of sand at the lake's edge.

A loud cracking sound thundered in his ears, like lightning striking all around him or like a tundra of ice breaking. The sight of his friends spun out of his mind.

He felt himself falling into darkness and rising into light, and for a time knew nothing. . . .

When he opened his eyes, he was suspended in a cool, soft, silvery light and felt a slight pressure in his ears. His whole body was ice cold.

Looking down, he saw ten or so feet below him shadowy rises and dips, where fields of long slender, gray blades of grass and shorter round-leafed weeds swayed together, all of it rolling away out of sight into a murky darkness that surrounded him on all sides.

A distant sound—a soft, irregular clap, clap-clap—came to him, muffled, as if through cotton.

Randomly, he moved his legs and found that even the smallest motion propelled him forward. Moving his arms and legs together, he discovered he could move faster. With a stronger thrust, his body sliced through the silver soft emptiness, the landscape below rising, falling, shifting in shades of pewter as he went.

With more maneuvering, he could rise, drop, turn, and roll with the simplest thought, the smallest shrug or twist, and a great, cool, fluid sense of freedom washed around his body and ran through him.

He was sliding along as if in the slow current of a river. Rolling to his left, his eye caught the space above him—and the gentle clap-clap came again, like small hands coming together in light rhythm.

Or like icy water lapping at the underside of a great sheet of ice.

He stopped moving his body and drifted to a standstill.

Above him was a ceiling of silver light dotted with random globes of lighter blue—air pockets caught beneath ice—and the thought occurred.

I fell through and drowned. Now I'm dead.

For a split-second, a shock of panic needled his whole body, and he felt the urge to throttle his way up and claw a hole out through the ice—to save himself.

As quickly as the urge came, it subsided. If this was death, it wasn't terrible. It was air and light rolled together. Heaven and earth as one. It was bliss running through blood and bone.

No, this wasn't death; it was a simple and pure form of life. Of just... being.

We don't die, he thought. We just change form.

That realization sent another wave of pure energy singing through every nerve, vein, and muscle.

He opened his mouth to shout with the thrill and joy of it, but nothing came out—only a great surge of energy that pulsed out and away from him in a spreading arc.

In another moment, the wave came back to him, greater, crashing into him, buzzing on his skin and tingling inside him to the marrow. In it, he felt at one with everything that could swim, flap, dart, wriggle, twist and glide through all the world's waters everywhere.

He was

an orca breaching under the sun in a far-off ocean

an eel slipping through the mesh of steel net in a
dark northern sea

a rainbow trout striking at mayflies on the glass ceiling
of a mountain stream's current

a blue fish racing with a school along the Atlantic coast

a dolphin arcing and leaping from wave to wave in a
clear-blue bay.

The dizzying mind-flight from creature to creature brought on vertigo, and he felt his stomach flipping. Clenching his hands and jaws, he brought himself back to balance and quiet, suspended in the cold, dark waters beneath the ice of Lost Lake.

The small surge of nausea subsided, and his stomach unclenched.

From far, far above him came the muffled sound of the lake gently lapping at the underside of the ice, and now only a faint silver-blue light fell through the water. He had swum far out from shore to where, Grady had told them, the lake was nearly a hundred feet deep.

Below him now, the glow cast by the upper waters faded to deep gray and then to a murky darkness. He could just make out the rise and fall of the shadowy lake bottom. Mounded sand had sifted over every gray, still form—rocks, bent branches, an angular log. Looking closer he made out the shape of a broken fishing pole, its line tangled around the reel. Lost? Thrown away in frustration?

Far out beyond the dim bluish shaft of light in which he floated, out where the light faded toward blackness, many eyes like small silver disks were fixed on him. Dozens of faint, pewter gray forms were rising and falling slightly, holding themselves steady in the dark water currents with the help of small, fanning fins and ruddering tails.

Unafraid, he let himself sink deeper, his body held in a strange kind of buoyancy, feeling heavy and light at the same time.

From the distant darkness, arrowing toward him, long thick body swaying side to side as it sped came the great fish that had jumped at him months ago as he paddled the canoe with Claire and Ray-Ray. It stopped just feet in front of his face, red gills fanning, staring at him—studying him.

The pike moved its mouth, and Dhani heard in his mind,

"Yes. He is the one we have waited for."

At this announcement, all the small silvery eyes flickered and the distant gray forms swirled like leaves in a wind, flashing silver-blue, then settled back into the concealing shadows.

For a split-second, Dhani saw an image of himself as if he were looking through these silvery eyes. He was floating, his arms and legs splayed out, his jacket open and billowed around him by the water, his mouth slung open in astonishment.

With a mighty thrash of its tail, the pike flipped around and propelled itself rapidly away into the encircling darkness. Gone were the shining-eyed watchers, too.

Words came wavering back at him through the water, like a finger tapping him just above and between his eyes, passing into his mind.

"Why do you continue to resist? Son of Humans, open your mind wider and let yourself see and hear. Tell your friends what we show you."

A kind of sickly sweet and bitter taste filled his nose and mouth, and he started to choke on the harsh tasting water.

At the same moment, a loud crack sounded in his ears.

"Dhani!" Ray-Ray called from nearby, fifty feet out on the ice and halfway from Dhani to the shore. His eyes were wide with fear.

"I don't want to come out any farther," he shouted, "but I will if you don't get back here. *Now.* Dude—I can hear the ice breaking."

"Please!" Claire begged him, from the narrow curve of wind-blown snow and sand at the lake's edge.

Dhani blinked and was standing in bright sunlight, where a sprawling white and patchy-green tableau of mountains, snow and trees spun back into clarity. He felt as if he had been in another, higher place and was coming down to a landing.

"What the hell, man!" Ray-Ray shouted in his face, when he slip-slid his way back to the frozen shore.

"Do you have a death wish?" Claire said, her voice sharp with anger. "Or do you just need attention?"

Ray-Ray grabbed the sleeve of his hoody. "Let's go inside. You're shaking."

When they reached the cabin, Dhani still had a far-away dreamy look. "It was awesome."

"What do you mean," Claire pressed, "—scaring the crap out of us? You think that was awesome?"

"I can't even tell you. I was just in this. . . *amazing place.*"

"You need to talk to somebody. Eric or Bay," Ray-Ray said, taking a step back from him.

"Promise us you'll talk to someone about what's happening to you, Dhani," Claire demanded. "We're your tribe and we care about you."

Ray-Ray was stone silent, until Claire's sharp glance prodded him. "Right. Yeah. We're with you all the way, bro."

"I don't know—," Dhani wavered.

"Promise. Me." Claire's face was stern. "Promise you'll talk to someone."

"Okay, I will," Dhani agreed, with a placid smile. "I promise."

"Why do have that weird smile?" Ray-Ray asked, stepping away a little.

"Because we don't die. We just change form."

14TH

Sahm scooped steaming, yellow *dal* into two bowls. He handed one to Dhani, who was seated beside Sahm's altar, from which a small white thread of sandalwood incense curled into the cabin's cool air.

Dhani sniffed the bowl and poked at its contents with a spoon.

"Lentils with curry and turmeric," Sahm said.

"I know what's going on with birds and animals—and now even fish," said Dhani flatly. "I hear them. Can you help me figure out what's happening to me?" He set the bowl aside.

"You are able to leave your small mind behind—the ego—and go outside yourself to feel what another living being feels. That is called empathy."

"*No*," Dhani insisted. "It's more than that. I believe an owl thanked me for taking care of his mate. I could sort of hear a flock of little birds talking and I saw myself through the eyes of a mouse. And I think the snowy owl, the eagle, and a big fish are speaking to me, Sahm. The other day, I knew something bad had just happened—it was like I got stabbed in my heart with this sad, sad feeling—and the little bear cub was dead."

Sahm blew into his bowl of *dal*.

"I think I'm just messed up, Sahm."

"No you do not," Sahm replied.

"I do not *what*?"

Sahm looked up at him with a serious expression. "You do not think you are 'messed up'."

Dhani started to object, then stopped. "Ever since that day you tapped my forehead. . . . It's that magic seer stone you gave me and the magic eagle feather Randy gave me." He sounded frustrated. "They're making me see and hear things."

Sahm's look was intense. "I have said there is no magic in *things*. All abilities are in the person. Objects can only awaken and focus the abilities you already have, Dhani."

"They make me see and hear things. But why didn't they help me save the little bear cub?

"You don't think the stone is magical?—Wait. You're saying you *do* believe what I'm telling you? That I'm not making stuff up or crazy?"

"Yes, that is what I am saying. You have empathy *and* you can hear creatures and know hidden things."

"You think an eagle and a fish are telling me stuff."

"What do they say?"

"'You are the one who is one of us.'"

Sahm's eyebrows shot up and he looked past Dhani to the altar, silent.

"Do you see?" said Dzes-Sa. "You cut one cord and he is awakening more on his own."

"What do you think that means?"

"I think someone is at the door."

"What?"

There was a sharp knock.

Eric accepted the cup of tea and seated himself next to Sahm's woodstove. "I'll tell you why I'm here, guys. Dhani, your friends are concerned about you and Sahm hanging out together."

"You mean Claire," said Dhani.

Eric paused. "Yes. Claire. Hey, this isn't a big deal. No one's getting down on you guys. I just thought I'd chat with you two and see if maybe Sahm is telling tales about yogis from Tibet, and maybe that's why you're claiming to have interesting experiences. Like knowing about the bear cub."

Dhani felt himself shrinking back, but another, stronger force inside would not let him.

"I'm not claiming anything. I suddenly felt like something bad was happening and the bear cub had just died. I don't know why that happened."

"I heard that you jumped up and went straight to the barn."

"Yeah, and it wasn't because Sahm told me some story about a bear cub dying." He felt another wave of strength and pushed back more. "It's not like I'm trying to make knowing strange stuff my *thing* or impress anyone. I don't even really like it when that happens to me. Most of the other kids already avoid me."

Eric held up one hand. "Okay, relax. Really. I'm not accusing you of anything."

"I can assure you I have not told Dhani any 'tales' from Tibet," Sahm interjected.

"I'm just trying to figure things out, guys," Eric nodded. "Because that's my job here, and a very unusual thing happened last week involving Dhani, and you guys spend time together. I thought there might be some connection."

Dhani broke eye-contact.

That's bull. You're here because my so-called friend *talked to you behind my back.*

"What a fake," Dhani said bitterly, when Eric was gone. "He's not 'looking for answers'. He already knows what he thinks."

Sahm ignored that. "You asked me 'what does it mean' that these things are happening to you. It is time for me to tell you what I have told no one else."

He lifted the *phurba* from the altar.

"I did not have this with me when I left Tibet. My grandfather sent it after me—through the *Bardo*."

"Isn't that like a different dimension? How could he do that?"

"I will tell you *how* another time. *Why* is what is important now. The *phurba* is empowered with my grandfather's intention for me. It fixes me to my path, the way a tent peg holds a tent to the ground. I was trying to leave something behind when I escaped Tibet. He was not willing for me to stray from the work I am here to do in this lifetime."

"Which is. . .what?"

"I am what is called a *Sakyong*. An 'earth protector'. I am here to do the work of the one you see on my altar—*Dzes-Sa*." He nodded toward the small, bronze statue centered among the odd-shaped stones, mottled feathers, shiny broken shells, and beautifully twisted twigs.

"He's the Buddha of the Beautiful Earth, right?"

"You remember. That is good. He embodies the energy of all things living and, as you say here in the west, inanimate. We *Bönpos* learned a great truth many ages ago—that *la*, the life force, runs through everything. An earth protector is one who knows all people and all things are connected, and everything must be honored as sacred in order for the planet to remain healthy and continue its life."

"You think that like, rocks are alive?" Dhani pondered. "That doesn't make sense."

"That is also talk for another day. What I need to tell you now is that I believed I had left behind my calling as a *Sakyong*. Just for a time. It is a heavy responsibility. It is also the kind of honored position certain powers at work in Tibet want to usurp.

"You see, Dhani, they are kidnapping people like me, and those men and women disappear and are never heard from again. Then they put their own puppets in our place. This way, they can control the people who still respect the true spiritual teachers such as *Sakyongs*."

"I thought you just came here to help with the animals and the survival stuff. From what you're saying, this is kind of beneath your dignity, isn't it? Shouldn't you really be sitting in a temple somewhere, telling people wise things?"

Sahm smiled. "It is all one and the same to me, Dhani. If I am hauling stones for a fire circle, or cleaning dung from a cage for Jo, or talking with you now. . . it is all the same. Someone on the spiritual path knows this. They do not seek the kind of honor that puts them above others. They know there is no such thing as being above others. I know this may be hard for you to understand."

"Well, what are you going to do about being a *Sakyong* while you're here?" Dhani pursued. "Is there something special you have to do?"

"There is, so it appears."

"What is it?"

"Train another *Sakyong*."

Dhani hesitated. "Are you talking about *me*?"

"Yes."

"Geez, I don't know if I want that."

A surge of frustration hit Sahm. "Yes, I am talking about you, Dhani." He breathed and regained control of himself. "And I would not worry so much about the bear cub. His spirit went through a short karmic cycle this time and will come back in another form. Perhaps as another bear. Perhaps as a human being. That is the way it is.

"What is important is the fact that more *Sakyongs* are awakening. One sits before me now. That is very auspicious." He thought of a vision he'd had during meditation, of the sky filling with young eagles. "If the portents are true, there are others. Perhaps even here."

"Who?"

"That is yet to be seen."

When Dhani left, Sahm felt pangs of deep regret. Now that the time had finally come to begin training this young man in earnest, he felt inadequate, having left off his own training before it was complete. The sense of urgency impressed on him by the portents made the duty feel even heavier. His impatience with Dhani's slow awakening made it worse.

Dzes-Sa, my Teacher, he called out, *can you help me to learn from this young teacher you have given me, who sometimes frustrates me so?*

23RD

Jalil draped the last blanket over the windows of the workout building and called to Emmalyn who was standing by the door. "Blackout is in effect. Hit the lights."

There was a *click*, and the lights revealed Dugan and Rocco sliding between ropes at opposite sides of the sparring ring.

"Who's on lookout?" Garrett asked. "We need a warning if Grady is out doing his watchdog thing tonight."

"Me," Tia Leesha answered, peeking out on the camp road through a blanket covering one of the windows. "'Cause I don't want to sit up where blood and sweat's gonna splash on me. I just wanna watch. I don't want to get AIDS."

"No one here's got AIDs.—Wait, do they?" Garrett balked.

Some of the others—Emmalyn, Makayla, Carter and Jalil—were seating themselves in folding chairs around the ring, and ignored him.

Imani stood beside the ring and summoned Rocco, who had begun to dance and jab at the air.

"You don't have to do this. I heard Dugan rag on you about being soft. This isn't just for fun. He's got somethin' else on his mind."

"You really don't get it."

"Fill me in then."

"I have to do this."

"Why?"

"You know, girls are all about, 'Hey, boys, stop being so aggressive.' But if we're not, we get our asses kicked."

"By who?"

"Come on," Dugan called, sounding impatient. "You sparring or doin' soft-soft with the ladies some more? Why'nt you come out here, and I'll show *Ih-mah-ni* who the man is when I take you down."

Carter pulled her chair close to Jalil's. "Wouldn't surprise me if half these people had a disease. Humans are like bacteria."

"That's a nice thing to say."

Imani had taken a seat beside Makayla, with Garrett on her other side. "Why're you so worried about Grady? You claim he's your boy, right? If he shows up you can just ask him for some more Jackie D and sit him down right on the other side of you."

He pretended not to hear. "Guys—you warmed up?"

Rocco was strutting around the center of the ring while Dugan was still in his corner stretching.

"Let's get this going," Rocco called out, moving closer to Dugan—who moved away from him along the ropes.

"I think Dugan's afraid," Jalil whispered to Carter. They were sitting together on the far side of the ring from the others.

In thirty seconds, Dugan met Rocco in the center of the ring, where they tapped gloves.

"Let's go, gentlemen," Garrett called.

Dugan dropped his gloves to chest level.

Rocco kept his left hand up at chin level, his right hand below it, shielding his face and torso. He started dancing to the left, forcing Dugan to circle away from him backwards, his hands still lowered.

"Aggressive," Carter whispered, her lips close to Jalil's ear. "I like aggressive."

Jalil was fixated on the match—mostly—though he kept looking across the ring, hoping Makayla was watching him and Carter.

She wasn't.

Garrett called out, "Gloves up, man."

Dugan turned his head. "I know how to figh—"

Rocco landed a solid right punch on his jaw.

Dugan swore.

"Shouldn'a looked away, buddy," said Rocco, and kept dancing around him. "You're holding your hands wrong, too. Get 'em up. Come on, let's spar."

Dugan shook it off and continued to circle backwards.

"Just for fun," Rocco said.

"Right."

Carter leaned so close to Jalil he could feel her breath on his ear again. "He looks like he knows what he's doing."

He looked at her. "Who?"

"White boy. He's making Black boy move backwards to his left."

"That's pretty grossly racist."

Dugan was trying to reverse their movement, trying to circle to his right and force Rocco to move backwards. Every time, though, Rocco jabbed with his left, forcing Dugan to keep backing away.

Carter was staring at the pair in the ring, her face eager. "See?—Black boy has to keep moving his right foot, pivot on his left. Takes away power from his right punch."

Jalil shifted uncomfortably. "Stop saying White boy, Black boy. They're just *guys*."

Dugan kept pivoting backwards, jabbing weakly with his left arm while Rocco easily dodged the glancing blows or threw his right arm up to block them.

Jalil remained fixated on the action. "Wow, you were right. You know a lot about boxing."

Carter slid a hand onto his thigh and pressed her fingers in slightly.

He looked at her, surprised.

Dugan was still jabbing with his left, letting his right hand drop down near his stomach.

Rocco jabbed with his left, and kept his right hand at chest level. "Man, get your hands up. I don't want to take you down in the first three minutes."

"Black boy is trying to get White boy to look down at his right hand," said Carter. "But he's not—he's focused on Black boy's face. And look at Black boy's stance. His legs are too far apart. White boy's are closer together. Watch when he throws a punch."

Jalil tried to slide away from Carter, but she tightened her hold on his thigh.

Rocco's right arm flashed and his glove drove into Dugan's jaw, knocking his head back.

Dugan tried to whip his face back around, but Rocco followed up with a powerful left jab that pummeled Dugan's cheek and sent his face flying the other direction and him half-staggering back.

"*Bam. Bam.* White boy jackhammers Black boy!" Carter whispered, closer to Jalil's ear.

Jalil pulled away from her. "*What's wrong with you?*"

Dugan shuffled backwards, out of Rocco's reach, and regained his footing. Then he began strutting in a wide circle out near the ropes.

It took Dugan a full minute to regroup.

Rocco stayed in the center of the ring, gloves up, turning with him, coiled, waiting. He smacked his gloves together. "Take your time, bro."

Dugan suddenly stopped circling and charged in at Rocco.

Rocco dropped his left hand, leaving himself open.

Jalil, who had slid to the far end of the bench from Carter, yelled. "What're you doing?—*Don't drop your arm!*"

"Watch this," Carter called over to him.

He turned his face away. *Leave me alone, creep-o.*

Dugan lunged, throwing his right arm out . . . Rocco dropped back. . . sending Dugan off-balance, making him stagger forward.

Rocco drove his right arm up, connecting with Dugan's chin and knocking his head back.

Imani raised her voice. "*Guys. Stop.* This was supposed to be just for fun."

Makayla called out, "Somebody's gonna get their teeth knocked out."

"The Bible says we shouldn't hurt each other," Emmalyn said, her voice solemn.

"Then why you here watching?" Imani tossed back at her, irritated. "Maybe you just like watching hot-looking boys get sweaty. What's the Bible say about that?"

Emmalyn looked hurt—until Imani turned away again. Then she flashed her a look of pure contempt.

Dugan staggered back almost to the ropes and spit blood.

Rocco dropped his gloves. "Hey man, this is getting too serious. You wanna quit?"

Dugan shook his head rapidly, also shaking off the dazed look. Then he charged back into the center, gloves up, and began swinging.

Rocco repelled them, pushing him back.

Flurries of lunging and punching broke the pivot-dance.

Jabs. Upper cuts. Solid body blows.

Dugan seemed to be weakening with every punch Rocco landed, then dropped two solid ones on Rocco's chest and a third into his gut. They hardly made him flinch.

"You wanna call it off now?" Dugan said, wiping blood from his lip on his wrist.

Rocco was smiling. "Nah. You're warmed up now. This is good."

And they began again.

"This is gonna end any second," said Jalil, in four more minutes. "They both look tired—and Rocco's crushing him. One more punch. . . ."

Carter laughed out loud.

"What's funny?"

"It's all a complete—"

Rocco rained a series of jabs and right hand pile-drivers onto Dugan—then for a split-second dropped his arms.

"Dude, I'm crushing you."

"—and total set up by Black boy," Carter finished.

Given that small opening, Dugan sprang to life, charged, and threw a powerful round-house punch with his right arm that smashed into the middle of Rocco's face.

Rocco flew backwards off his feet and crashed to the ring where his head bounced. There he lay flat on his back, chest heaving as he gasped for air.

Dugan jumped around Rocco, who was trying to get up but kept falling flat on his back. Then Dugan calmed, and looked down at him.

"You wanna keep goin'? Or you wanna quit?"

Rocco slowly pushed himself up to sitting and waved him off with a dazed smile.

"You got this one. I'm done."

Dugan kept circling around Rocco who was having trouble getting to his feet. "You okay, man? You shouldn'a looked away. Gave me an opening and I took it."

"*Black boy wins*." Carter called out. "*Smart* always wins."

"Stop. I hate that," Jalil said. He got up and started to walk to the other side of the ring. "I don't hang with racists."

She reached out and grabbed his thigh. "You don't hate me, do you? You don't hate *this*."

Jalil stopped, confused, caught between disgust with her and liking that a beautiful girl was giving out signals like this to him.

"I want to see him broken. Smashed in little pieces," Garrett raged at Dugan.

Dugan walked beside him in the dark back to their cabins. "Hey, I suckered him into believing we're buds. And tonight I crushed and embarrassed him. That wasn't good enough for you? 'Cause it sure felt good to me."

"Did you see him flaunting it in my face when Carter kissed him?"

"What about her? She was the kiss-*er*. He was try'na shake off the beating I just gave him. And why aren't you mad at Jalil? He was letting her get all over him."

"Hat Boy? He's no competition. She's just messing with him because he's a dweeb. She'll drop him like a bad habit."

"If you ask me, *you* got a bad habit of obsessing over a whack girl who loves to torture you."

Garrett was breathing hard. "I want to see Rocco screaming in pain."

"Obsessed much?"

24TH

Ray-Ray looked at the clock beside his bed again, and the glowing numbers had only changed by three minutes. His stomach was growling, he couldn't sleep, and it was two hours until breakfast.

Half of the dark morning sky was still clouded over, and in the other half a few stars shone through broken mists. His stomach growled louder. He would get his chores done in the aviary—Jo would have made her lists last night—and then get breakfast. In minutes, he was up, dressed and outside.

As he put his hand on the clinic door, a plaintive squeak—like hinges moving—came from inside. Quietly, he stuck his head into the still-dark room.

Someone was rummaging quietly in one of the wall cabinets where medicines were kept.

He reached for the wall switch, and when light flooded the room there was a small scream and the sound of something striking the floor.

Imani stood there, blinking.

"Turn off the lights," she hissed.

"What are you taking?" he asked and did what she said, so the room fell back into shadow.

"How did you get into the cabinets? They're always locked."

"Someone gave me a key."

"Someone."

"That's all you need to know."

He looked at the bottle Imani was picking up from the floor.

"Don't worry, I don't rat people out." He tried to make a joke. "You got distemper or rabies or something? That why you're lifting meds?"

"I'm getting something for pain."

"Why not ask Jo or Kate?"

"They don't need to know about this."

"Who's it for? You okay?"

"You'd know if you ever showed up at the parties or if you came to fight night."

"I didn't hear about any parties or a fight night. Guess I'm not one of the cool kids, so I'm outa the loop. I was hanging out with Claire and Dhani."

"That kid is strange."

"Half the people you meet are strange. The other half are just pretending they're not. You gonna say who that medicine is for?"

"Rocco got sucker-punched by Dugan last night. According to Dugan, it was supposed to be just for fun, but I thought something dirty was going on. Rocco was really hurting all night. He doesn't want to ask for an aspirin because people might ask questions. I'm sneaking him this—it's not a controlled substance, don't worry."

She held up the small bottle.

He leaned close and read the label. "Why does Jo keep Midol here?"

"Um—her and *six girls* work up in here every day."

"Why are you giving Midol to Rocco—he got cramps?"

She rolled her eyes. "Serious headache. He doesn't want anyone to know he got his brain knocked around inside his skull. Gotta keep up that stupid, tough-boy image."

"Why not just be honest and ask for meds?"

"Why? If the authorities here figure out what really went on, they'd tighten up the restrictions and we'd never be able to dip out at night. On the other hand, if Jo realizes a bottle of this is gone, I can tell her I took it and forgot to let her know. She'll be a little ticked off, but she'll also understand and let it go."

He rubbed his chin, looking thoughtful. "How did you know Rocco had a bad headache all night?"

"I checked on him, okay?"

"You spend the night with him?"

"*I did not*—but if I did, it would be none of your damn business."

"So, I want to get this clear. You're just *checking* on Rocco. What would your boyfriend say about that? Would he and his gang take Rocco for a long ride from which he would not return?"

Her face went red. "*Shut up.*"

He was surprised at her vehemence. "Guess I stomped on a nerve."

She calmed herself, and her voice was soft and steady again. "I'm just bringing a friend a pain reliever."

"Your boyfriend wouldn't feel jealous or threatened at all."

"No reason for him to feel threatened."

Ray-Ray shook his head, and sounded like he was reciting. "'It is only when our characters and events begin to disobey us that they begin to live.'"

"What does that even mean? Where'd you get that from?"

"It's from 'The French Lieutenant's Woman', a really good flick from the nineteen-eighties. What does it mean? It means we need to stop living the lie we're frontin' to everybody and start living the truth."

"So, did you prove what you needed to prove to yourself—that you're a big man?"

In the early half-light, Rocco rolled on his side and took the pill bottle from Imani's hand. "I never heard of this stuff—Midol. Does it work?"

"Oh, it works."

He dumped two in his hand, tossed them on his tongue and swigged a mouthful of water from the glass she handed him.

"Only thing is, it's a medicine for women, and now you're gonna grow breasts."

He choked and spit the water. "*Seriously?*"

"No, you idiot."

He gently laid a hand on hers, but she slid it away.

"Do you think I'm girlie now that Dugan almost knocked me out?"

"No, but I think you're stupid for fighting."

"Sparring."

"Didn't look like sparring to me. He wanted to knock your head off. I think all that '*let's just spar*' stuff was bull crap, and you fell for it."

Rocco was quiet.

"Do you think I'm weak because I cried when the cub died?"

"Rocco, wherever you got the idea that men shouldn't care about animals and other people—that's just wrong. Even animals protect each other. If a person doesn't care about other living things, what does that say about them?"

"What do *you* think? That's what I care about."

Imani shook a few more pills from the bottle and laid them on Rocco's bedside table.

"I gotta go before someone finds me in your room and reports us both."

26TH

The young blue jay tilted its head and watched Ray-Ray as he cleaned the bottom of its cage.

"I don't know why we put seeds and stuff in your feeder, you knock it out all over the place."

The jay squawked at him, making the noise that to him sounded like—"*Hey!*"

Suddenly, it flitted to another branch in its shelter. Then to another.

"*Hey,* yourself, you little badass. And look at you, getting strong, starting to fly again."

He stopped and laughed. "Wait—*that's* your street name. Lil Badass."

Jo had told them not to name the animals, but Rocco had nicknamed the bear cubs and Makayla and Jalil had nicknamed the box turtle with the broken shell. So, Lil Badass it was, for this feisty little bird.

He wasn't laughing now. The young blue jay had survived—the way he had survived on the streets of DC alone, attacked and almost hanged, scavenging dumpsters like a rat, arrested and accused and caged—until someone cared about him enough to get him into this program.

"Maybe we're both kinda badass, because we're stronger than we look."

The blue jay shouted "*Hey*" at him.

When he had cleaned the cage and refreshed food and water, he looked around. Others were still at breakfast and Jo, he knew, had gone into her clinic early and was working with the very sick cougar that was brought in. Good. Because what he was about to do was off-limits.

Lifting the young blue jay off its perch—carefully, not touching its wing, which was still weak but improving—he placed it gently on his shoulder.

"Come on, little guy. Let's clean up after these other jokers."

For the next hour, alone with the jay, he scoured cages, filled feeders with seed—or road-killed rodents, lizards, and frogs for the ravens—hung suet slabs on cage bars, and refreshed water dishes.

Except for Jo, who would be highly irritated with him for being too familiar with one of her patients, he really didn't care if anyone else came in or heard him singing quietly.

> *"When the night has come*
> *and the land is dark*
> *and the moon is the only light we see,*
> *no, I won't be afraid—oh, I won't be afraid*
> *just as long as you stand by me. . . ."*

Dhani and Claire were his friends, his tribe here at Lost Lake. That was true enough.

Is it strange, he wondered, feeling the small creature's soft feathers against his ear, *that I feel like my other best friend is a little blue jay, who got his wing almost wrecked for good?*

The narrow beam of Garrett's flashlight flicked on for a moment, illuminating a small segment of the midnight camp road—then switched off, leaving him and Dugan in near-pitch-blackness again.

"*You okay, man*," Garrett mocked in a high, whiny voice. "What are you—best friends with Tats now?"

Dugan's jaw was sore and he wasn't in the mood for this. Just twenty-four hours ago, he had taken some brutal punches.

"You need to shut up.—Are we nearing the road to town yet. I can barely see."

"The gate is right here," said Garrett, grabbing Dugan's coat sleeve and pulling him off the camp road and behind the prickly branches of a blue spruce.

Five miles away, the lights from Lake Placid created a dull, golden halo above the black horizon.

"They should be coming any time now." Garrett shivered, pulled up his collar against the freezing air, and pressed a button on his watch. *11:46 PM*. "They're late."

"Tell me why you made me risk breaking my ankle, stumbling down this road in the middle of the freakin' cold night?" said Dugan, shuffling his feet to keep them warm.

"First, tell me why you and Tats are suddenly all buddy-buddy."

"Ever hear of playing someone? I moved in close and friendly. Then I laid him out. I'm getting tired of your obsession with him, man. Did you notice how your girl Carter laid a wet one on him?" he goaded.

Headlights were coming up the road.

Garrett craned to see—then grabbed Dugan's sleeve and yanked him further behind the spruce. An old pickup truck rattled past, its heavy exhaust cloud and one red tail light disappearing past them around a curve in the mountain road. Probably someone going home after the bars closed.

"She's just trying to make me jealous," Garrett said, sounding smooth and confident. "She'll come crawling to me soon. They all do."

Dugan was cupping his gloved hands over his cold ears. "More like she's got the upper hand and she's torturing you. But whatever. Someone at breakfast this morning told me Rocco was in bed with a headache and throwin' up."

"Sounds like you gave him a concussion. Congrats."

Dugan grinned.

"Well done. But you should have told me sooner what you're up to with Muscle Head. We're business partners and you had me worried, son."

"Not your son. And when it's my own business, I do what I want without your permission or knowledge."

"Look who's touchy now."

"Yeah, well I'm goin' back if you don't tell me why I'm here freezing my ass. My ears are so cold they're burning."

"Shoulda worn a hat."

An engine sounded in the distance and more headlights rounded the curve. The driver slowed.

Garrett stepped out of hiding, turned on his small pocket flashlight and waved it.

A large black pickup smelling of diesel rolled to a stop beyond the gate.

"Let's go," Garrett signaled to Dugan. "We're expanding our business in a whole new direction, my friend. Sound equipment and cell phones are fine, but we have a chance to make bigger money."

"Expand how?"

Garrett had already hopped the closed gate.

"Welcome to Jeopardy. I'll go with *Things You Have to File the Serial Number Off*—for a thousand. Or two or three thousand, depending on how bad the customer wants it."

28th

Tom found Steve in the storage barn—not where he was supposed to be right now. And he only found him because he had run into Grady clearing the back terrace at Kate's.

"Saw him about a half-hour ago," Grady had said, "when I was shoveling the path to the greenhouse."

Why was Steve not out on the island when Tom had sent a message saying he wanted to meet there this morning?

When Tom entered, Steve looked up from the backpack he was rifling through.

"Good call on waiting for colder weather to come back in," Tom said, walking up to the table where Steve was examining a backpack. "Sahm told Kate the mountain trails have been really bad. Slick and dangerous with mud over ice."

"Yeah, frozen ground one day, mud the next is a bad combo." Steve looked at his watch. "Hey, sorry. We're supposed to be meeting at my place, right? I got sidetracked."

"Why are you going through that pack again? You handed out all the supplies and equipment weeks ago."

Steve didn't answer. He zipped open an inner pocket, fished his hand around inside, then zipped it closed.

"I'd like to schedule a meeting with Judge Sewell," said Tom. "It would be a nice P.R. gesture for the program. I could arrange it for March and make the trip to DC with you when you do the TV program." He laid a hand on Steve's shoulder. "I thought you could use some company."

Steve stopped looking through the pack's side pouches.

"Thanks."

"You're looking for drugs, aren't you?"

"Yeah. I am."

"Whose pack is that?" Without waiting, Tom turned over the name tag. "Dhani Jones."

"Just checking."

"No, you're not. You're singling him out, Steve."

There was a small noise from beyond the wall that divided the barn in-two—a faint scrape and thump.

Steve ignored it. "We gotta set some mouse traps in here. I don't need rodents chewing up this equipment.—And as for the Jones kid? He always acts like he's hiding something. I'm thinking drugs. I thought he might be stashing some for the trip. Three days is a long time to be without your weed or whatever else he's doing."

"But you found—?"

Steve pressed his lips together.

"You found nothing," Tom finished. Quietly, he stepped away from the table where the pack was lying.

"You can't be too careful," Steve replied.

"But you *can* be too suspicious," Tom said. He started moving quietly toward the door that separated the two halves of the barn. "And too determined to prove there's something bad about a person."

"During my training in Afghanistan, they taught us to read micro-expressions. Eye movements. Changes in what someone does with their mouth. Small hand gestures. You catch the tiniest clue, and it can determine whether the person you're with is a simple civilian or someone who's about to blow you to bits."

"Does it occur to you those same micro-expressions might be telling you something else about a person? Such as, they're not an enemy combatant but just a kid with a difficult past?"

Steve watched Tom, who was close to the door in the dividing wall—then looked away and cleared his throat.

"See, you do *that*, Steve—you turn your face and make that noise—when you don't want me to catch you smirking or rolling your eyes. You forget I've worked with people for decades longer than you have."

All at once, Tom seized the handle of the door, yanked it open and vanished beyond the wall.

Following him, Steve found Tom looking all around the great open space. The walls were lined with huge storage closets—more like small rooms. The open area was empty.

"What are *you* looking for?" Steve smiled.

"I heard something."

"I told you. I'm going to set some mousetraps. Maybe a big, live trap, too, in case something bigger like a groundhog or raccoon gets in."

"Good idea," Tom commented, letting Steve go back through the door to the main room ahead of him. Just before leaving the back area, he turned his head one more time to be sure of what he'd noticed.

"As far as it goes with the Jones kid—" Steve said, when they were back at the table with Dhani's pack.

Tom held up one hand. "Go easy, Steve. He's not the Taliban."

Steve bit his lip and hung the pack amid the row of pegs along one wall with the others.

"Now your micro-expression tells me you're irritated but holding your tongue. Good. A sign of progress."

"Snow's coming in a couple days," Steve responded, ignoring that. "Just a few inches. And the colder temperature will make the trails passable. I figure we'll go out about from the seventh to the ninth and I'll drive south on the eleventh. Thi's program is the next day."

"Interesting name—Thi. Asian?"

"It's Vietnamese. I remember hearing it means 'a poem.'"

"Beautiful."

As they locked up the storage barn, Tom decided he would not stir Steve's overactive habit of distrust by telling him what he'd seen—snowy footprints and melt water just inside the back door, which told him the faint sound they had heard was someone closing the back door as quietly as possible.

"Remember how you told me months ago you were concerned about security?" Kate replied to Tom. "Well I asked Grady to keep a better eye on the property and buildings. I thought you knew that. He goes in the barns periodically to check things out.—Mystery solved."

"But why sneak into the building?"

"You said he told you Steve was in there. Maybe he didn't want to disturb your conversation. And if it was one of the students snooping around, I don't care. There's nothing of any great value in those storage rooms. Old lamps and chairs. Jim's fishing and scuba gear. I think some extra office supplies are out there. At most, they'd get a laugh out of old wedding pictures, with me in a ridiculous looking 'designer' dress Jim forced me to buy."

"I had a sense that someone didn't want us to know they were there."

Kate gave a short, light laugh.

"A sense. And you say Steve is suspicious. Tom, you have end-of-the-month student reports due to Sewell—today—and it's already eleven-thirty."

Tia Leesha slipped inside the back door of her cabin, closed it as soundlessly as possible and quietly slipped off her boots but not her parka.

"Why do you wear that parka into your bedroom?"

Tia Leesha jumped, and spun around.

Carter was watching, grinning.

She pulled her parka tight around her body and pushed past her.

"What I do is my business, ain't it? Maybe I'm cold."

"Who were you talking to outside? Somebody bring you another delivery?"

Tia Leesha turned and charged down the hall.

"Your room is like a sweatbox. Maybe you're hiding something under that parka," Carter called after her.

"STAY OUTA MY ROOM," Tia Leesha shouted over her shoulder, so loud her voice went raspy.

Locking the door to her room, Tia Leesha dropped onto the bed, dug inside one of the parka's deep pockets and pulled out two small canisters. They had been in a certain closet in the storage barn which had been left unlocked for her today—right where she'd been told to find them. And she hadn't been seen, though it was close call.

A loud bang shook the door.

"Leave me alone, Carter. Stop watchin' me. You're a damn freak."

No response, and the cabin settled into a long silence.

She nestled back into the pillows, her nerves still rattled by Carter—and just by being in this horrible place where so much was expected of her.

A free afternoon. She would do what she liked to do most here. Escape from everything and everyone.

She stared at the beautiful patterns the frost made on her window, wishing she felt beautiful or even a little attractive not ugly and useless.

But, *why care?*—She didn't. Not anymore. She took out of her pocket a bag of free gummies that were left for her in the hiding spot in the storage barn. For a few hours, it would help her to numb out.

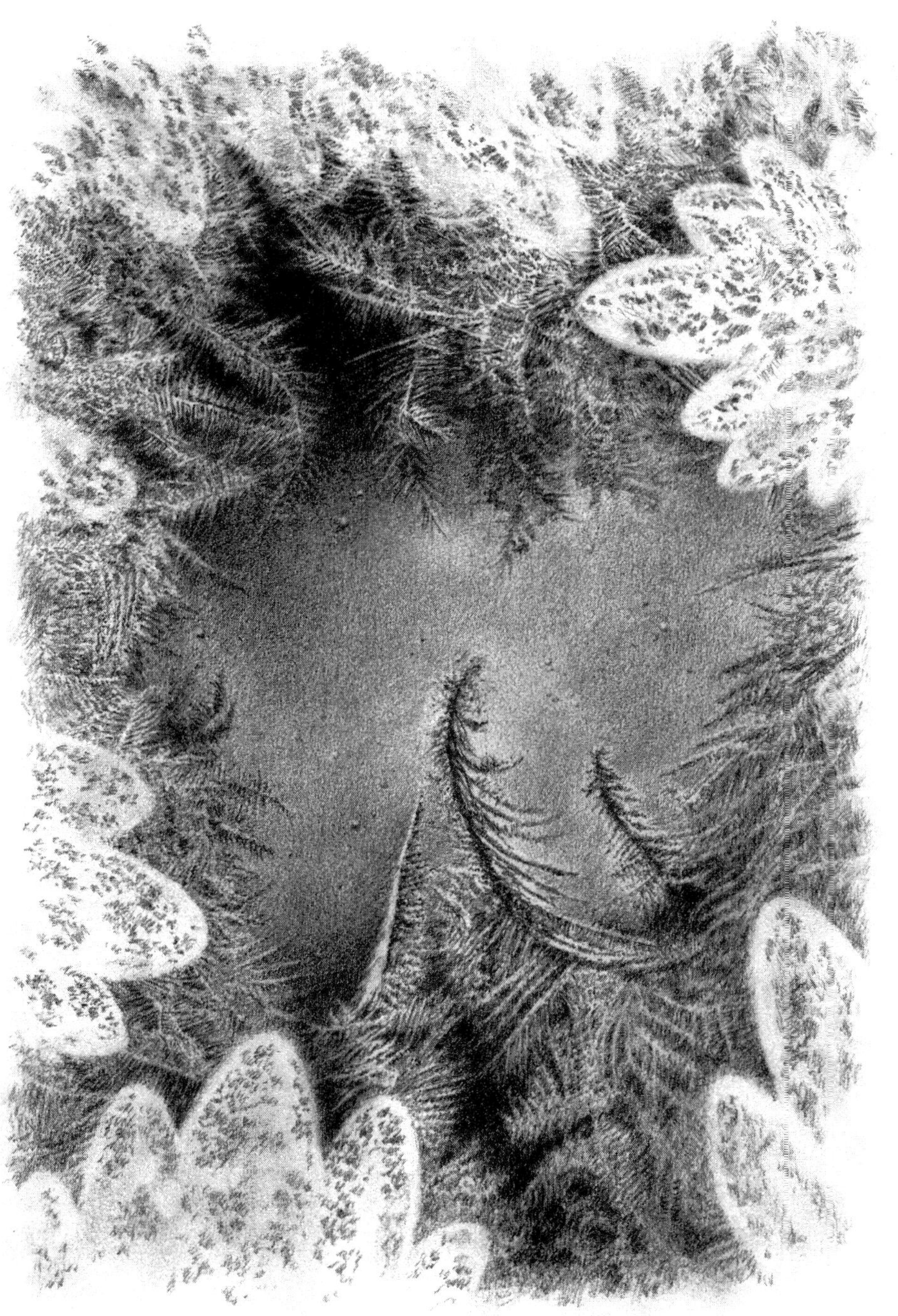

4

March

4th

Grady poured whisky shots for his three poker buddies seated around the table smoking cigars, then poured a shot for himself.

"You gonna take us up Lost Mountain and show us where those ermines are hiding?" one said, sliding the cards out of the box.

"Hell no."

Another took a sip and grimaced. "What's wrong—Holman not paying you enough to afford good bourbon? Or you just cheapin' out on us?"

"Try'na make it last through the winter in case the liquor stores run out?"

"What's you guys' problem?" Grady laughed. "You know I'm not letting you hunt or trap on Kate's property. And this is my best Jack D. Maybe you could bring some juice once in a while. Shuffle the cards and deal."

"Next time, we *will* bring our own. Yours is about half water."

Grady grabbed the handle and held it up to the light.

Even in the room's smoky haze, he could tell the liquid inside was a paler gold than it should be.

5TH

Last evening, Ron had said, "I need you at the clinic early tomorrow, Sahm. One of the Sheriff's deputies is bringing two abandoned coyote pups in the morning, and I'll need a hand prepping their enclosure. He says they're really scrawny, and Jo wants us to start them on nutritional boosters."

It was afternoon now, and work on the indoor and outdoor fenced enclosures was done and the deputy was arriving soon. On the way back to his cabin, just before the crossing the brook, Sahm saw a pile of what appeared to be large animal skins. They looked like brown, irregular-shaped carpets, and on closer examination he saw they were deer hides.

Randy Wolfmoon emerged from the woods behind Sahm's cabin, hauling onto the beach four thin saplings, stripped of branches, much longer than he was tall. Behind him was Jalil, recognizable from a distance by his knit hat, dragging four more poles, and Makayla carrying a large coil of brown twine.

"What are you building?" Sahm asked, when he reached the spot. There was a digging bar lying on the beach, and large, rough stones were laid in a circle around a shallow pit maybe four feet across and two feet deep.

"It's called a medicine lodge," said Jalil, smiling proudly, wiping his forehead. "I hauled all these big stones."

Randy's hair was matted with perspiration. "Native people made small, domed shelters with fire pits in the center—like this one I'm putting up. They used them for healing purposes and for vision quests."

Sahm stared blankly.

"You drop hot rocks into the central pit or build a small fire. The heat inside helps you sweat out impurities from your body. And in the past, our medicine men sought the help of spirits in these lodges, where they'd have visions. Men in my family used them for generations."

"You guys have anything like this in Tibet?" Jalil asked.

"Not like this, no."

Randy picked up the digging bar and began to drive it through the sand into the dirt beneath. "Kate said I could build one here to teach the students a little about First Nations' culture. I wanted it to be close to the boulder with the petroglyph. That's good medicine. I'm going to use the lodge personally for healing some joint injuries I got taking a tumble while climbing. First, I gotta sink sixteen holes in a circle, then bend these eight poles in an arc and drop the ends into them.

"While I'm doing that, these guys are going to punch holes all around the edges of the deer skins with these awls." He held up two sharp-pointed tools. "Then we use twine to lash the skins to the poles and cover the whole thing, except for a smoke hole in the center over the fire pit. If you're free, we could sure use a hand."

Sahm nodded. "This is work for many more hands."

"True that," Randy nodded, driving the bar into the ground again and again, "but these guys are the only two who volunteered."

Makayla and Jalil had moved away and seated themselves on opposite ends of a log just down the beach, where they began working on the pile of skins. The hides were pliable from tanning, soft on the fleshy side, covered with coarse hair on the outside, and smelled a little of the sharply pungent fluids used to preserve them.

Jalil was drilling holes in his third hide when he noticed Makayla was sitting perfectly still and holding a deer skin in her lap. The awl had slipped out of her hand and she stared blankly across the lake.

"These skins are tougher than I thought," he said. "Is the awl hurting your hand?"

She did not move or speak.

"Makayla?"

Nothing.

"*Makayla.* You're not still mad at me because I made that remark about Rocco and Imani, are you? That was a while ago."

She blinked, drew in a breath and turned her face toward him. "What?"

"You look zombie-d out."

She seemed to be trying to focus, then picked up her awl and began drilling it into the hide. "I just—I never thought deer skin would be this rough and scratchy."

Jalil watched her for a moment and didn't repeat his question. "I didn't picture you as the kind of girl who would be punching holes in dead animal skins."

"No. How did you picture me?" She was fully back from wherever her mind had wandered.

"Didn't you live in like, a gated community? I pictured you as a day spa and mani-pedi kind of girl."

She concentrated on the hide. "That's how my parents would like me to be. I'm more of a salamander kind of girl. There's something about them I really like. Such gentle little creatures. My parents would be horrified to know I really like working with them, and I'd love that."

"You didn't even go home for Christmas. Have you talked to them since you got here?"

"No," she said quickly, with force.

"You sound really hacked off at them."

"They're confusing. Something's going on with them and I wish they'd just tell me. But when I ask what's wrong, I get these sicky-sweet smiles. 'Nothing's wrong, dear.' 'Why would you even ask such a thing, dear?' They must think I can't see through their total fakeness."

She was jamming the sharp awl through a deer hide with the same force that was in her voice. "They keep trying to sell everyone on this 'perfect family' image. My mom's the worst. If I go home, they'll drag me to their social clubs and their rich friends' parties where they're trying to lure investors for their new medical equipment company."

"If I were you, I'd go to the parties and—"

"You're *not* me," she snapped.

"Geez, can you take it down a notch? I'm going somewhere good with this."

Makayla paused and her tense expression eased. "Oh really, and where's that?"

"I'd go to the parties, and when Mr. or Mrs. Richie Rich-Friend asked—he dropped his voice, 'How are you doing, young lady'—I'd say—," his voice went up an octave and he squeaked in a southern accent—'Whah, I've been punchin' holes in dead animal skeeyins at a school for way-wahd baws and guhls, much like mah-self. My fellow hole-puncher, Jalil, why he is a musical prodigy but he is also a ba-a-ad muthuh. Whah, Missizz Hun'red-Dollah-Bills, he sold cocaine and broke someone's jaw with a big ol' bike tool."

Makayla looked shocked. "Did you really?"

"*Shh*—yeah, I did—but I'm getting to the good part." His voice went up again. "'Puh-haps ah ought-n't to tell you this, Missizz Muh-ney, but ahh saw his wangle. Yes, ahh did."

She smiled and rolled her eyes. "Seriously—*wangle*?"

"Well," he said, still in the high squeaky drawl, "it was mo-uh of a *dangle* than a *wangle*."

She cough-laughed.

He jumped into a hip-hop rhythm.

"*Well, I can always have just what I want... I would love to take her out and flaunt... but she just likes to tease and taunt.*"

"I love this cover by SayGrace and G-Eazy. And I do not tease."

He raised one eyebrow like a conspirator and kept rapping. "*Once she seen you with your pants down... and now she thinks you're cute, hands down.*"

"I never said you're cute."

"*But nope, nope... she ain' wid it, though... all because she got her own dough.*"

She was laughing at him now—and he flipped the awl over in his hand and pushed the wooden handle in front of her face like a mic. "It's all you, Gracie girl. You know the song I'm riffin' on here."

She rolled her eyes, but went with it.

"You don't own me. I'm not just one of your many toys."

"*Ow*," he winced, slapping one hand on his chest. "Stab me in my heart, sweet girl."

"You don't tell me what to do, and don't tell me what to say. . . ."

"*When I go out with you*," he jumped in and they sang together, "*don't put me on display*."

Makayla was laughing hard and stopped singing, while Jalil mumbled his way out of rhymes.

"Dang," he said, "I got nothin'."

"You're a freak," she snorted, "and you just crashed and burned."

"I ran outa my word magic is all. But I got you to laugh—how's that make me a freak?"

Sahm finished digging the last hole, and Randy bent another sapling into an arc.

"Three poles left to set in place, then we stretch the hides. Probably need to give the kids a hand punching all those holes. The hides are tough."

Sahm nodded silently.

Randy stopped working and straightened up. "Tell me the truth, Sahm. You're a medicine man, aren't you?—or a yogi or whatever you guys call yourselves in Tibet."

"Why do you ask me that?"

"Because I heard you chanting under your breath while you were working. You were praying over this lodge weren't you—dedicating it, or calling on your spirit guides."

"That is so."

"You're still really young, though. How old were you when you started training?"

"I do not remember. Perhaps three or four years old."

"That's young. I've done a little reading about Tibetan Buddhism. But didn't I hear you're a *Bönpo*? Did they identify you as a teacher from the past?"

Sahm had liked Randy the first time he saw him interact with the students. He was kind, patient, good humored. But he was also like so many westerners. Curious and full of questions. He had been taught that the less you talk about something the more power it has. Also that to talk about yourself and your calling is to draw attention to yourself, which leads to a strengthening of ego and attachment to a label. No one was a *teacher* or a *yogi*, a *husband* or a *wife*, a *male* or a *female, nor even an earth protector*—not at the very core of their being. At that deep level, he knew, all are part of a greater Self—each one a tiny ripple on a great Ocean of eternal awareness. This view of reality was in Sahm's mind when he answered.

"I help Jo in the clinic. And when we go into the mountains, I help the students."

Randy smiled and nodded. "Okay. I get it. You can't talk about it."

Suddenly Randy's smile faded and he dropped to his knees on the sand. Leaning forward, he prostrated himself face-down, arms extended out toward Sahm.

Sahm stepped back, surprised by this gesture.

"Why are you doing this?"

Randy pushed himself up to his knees, then sat back on his heels.

"Man, I just had a sudden overwhelming urge. It was like a huge wave of awe and respect came over me. I guess the part of me that's sacred recognizes and honors the part that's sacred in you."

Sahm stepped close to him and extended his right hand, which Randy grasped, and Sahm hoisted him back to standing.

"I honor what is sacred in you, as well," Sahm responded. He bowed his head and pressed his hands together in front of his chest.

"Whenever you need to use this medicine lodge, Sahm, go for it,"

Randy said. "It just hit me that I didn't build it only for me and the students. It's for you to use, too."

As Sahm retreated to his cabin, a thought came, as if from the open air.

He is not aware of it, but he is a very old soul.

7TH

Steve was speaking, meticulously instructing him how to build the bonfire, though Sahm already knew how.

"First, you clear the fire circle and lay the kindling. . . ."

Sahm thought he had gained Tanner's respect last fall when he shared his knowledge about tracking—but apparently he was wrong. Tanner was back to treating him like a helpless child. It appeared that he hadn't taken one step outside the belief in his superiority.

Steve had delayed the winter campout during the thaw to let cold temperatures return and muddy trails harden. "All that snow up on the elevations will be perfect for cutting into blocks to make shelters," he'd said—and Randy had agreed.

At the moment, he was ignoring Steve, the campsite, and the students. Instead, he was keeping his mind wide-open to pick up more signs. On the way up the trail, a huge crow had opened its beak wide, thrusting its head forward as if it were calling, but no call came out.

"Listen for the voices beyond sound," was the message that went through Sahm's mind.

All the way up the trail to this tree-lined meadow on the south face of Eagle Rock Mountain, the crow's message had kept Sahm alert for more portents. Maybe some important event, as well.

"Randy and I will check on their progress," Steve was saying now, "and when they're done with the shelters, I'll send some of the guys to find more windfalls for the fire. Just do your best to keep it going till then."

Sahm nodded, frustrated. He had tended fires almost every day of his life, but held back saying that. He was focused on the light wind that kept shifting directions. That, and the fact that above them in the ice-blue sky the bright white low-scudding clouds were in turmoil, torn apart by stronger winds from higher up.

In the midst of all that wild energy, out of place, one lone cloud floated undisturbed—the only cloud that was turning dark, dark gray. In his head, there were whispers just out of hearing.

"What's up, Sahm?" Randy asked him after Steve stepped away. "Something's on your mind."

Sahm almost told him what he suspected, but again held back. He would use other means to see what these portents were saying—more than just the fact that spring weather was coming. As a boy, he had been trained to pay attention to the natural world and the elements. It occurred to him now that the great *Elemental* powers that adepts could sense were trying to speak to him, and he could almost hear them.

"Tanner's always got something to say. Is he annoying you?" Randy pressed—then grinned. "Or is it something bigger?"

"Why do you ask that?"

"You have the same look on your face my grandfather and great-grandfather had when they were tuned-in to the spirit world. Are you picking up something?"

"I do not know yet for sure," Sahm replied.

But it felt as if a big shift was about to take place. He could feel it in his bones. When he had time alone, he decided, he would call on his Teacher again. See if anything more would be revealed.

Ray-Ray stood up, sweating. "Dang. I think the handle of my ice axe just cracked."

This late-winter cold front had brought back bitter temperatures after the thaw, and even the strong noonday sun here on the southern face of Eagle Rock Mountain gave little warmth.

Dhani kept digging and stacking blocks of frozen snow into a large oval—the base of their shared shelter rising on the sunny side of a tall drift.

"I don't see why we couldn't just dig into this snow pile."

"Tanner says we can't count on finding an easy place to hide or sleep," Ray-Ray replied, "if we're lost out here in the winter. We need to know how to build a shelter out of snow and ice blocks."

Dhani stopped working. His face was pink with exertion, and small steam-tendrils of evaporating sweat rose from his hat and gloves into the icy air. "Speaking of Tanner—look at him over there."

Across the open mountain meadow that was swept with last night's fresh snow, they could see Tanner against a far tree line, with Claire and Makayla, swinging his arms in chopping motions. The ring of hard snow and ice blocks for their shelter was not very big yet.

"Look at what?"

"I don't know. Whenever I'm near him, I get the feeling he's trying to hide something behind all that Marine, strong-man bull crap."

"What?—you think he's like closeted maybe?"

"No, not that. But I keep thinking there's something. Like something really violent and bad."

During the hike up Eagle Rock Mountain, and now, Dhani had the unusual sense that he could see inside Tanner a thick wall—like a dark fog that would almost appear then fade, but he couldn't see what it concealed.

"Imagination's a good thing," Ray-Ray replied slowly, sounding cautious. "Always good to know where the line is between fantasy and reality, though."

Their eyes met, and except for the dim, distant sound of voices carried on the crisp air, an awkward silence hung between them.

Ray-Ray looked down, twisted the handle of his ice axe a little and there was a splitting sound. "Yep. It's broke. I'm gonna go see if Randy or Sahm brought an extra one."

"Wait—before you go."

Ray-Ray hesitated. "Hurry up, man. I been sweating, and I don't want to stop working too long and get cold."

"It's about Claire."

"Yeah, you're really into her—and?"

"Should I tell her?"

"Duh."

"How?"

"I don't know. You'll figure out and do it in your own way. That's part of it."

"I mean, do I just drop it in on her?—'What are you having for lunch there, Claire—Ivy's famous tuna melt sandwich? And by the way, I'm really into you.' What if I say something stupid or something that weirds her out?"

Ray-Ray rolled his eyes. "You haven't weirded her out by now, man. She's sticking around for some reason."

"She says we're just friends."

"A lot of people say that at first. Just work up to it, man. Maybe practice. Now I'm getting cold. I'll be right back."

Ray-Ray had only been gone ten minutes when Dhani, who had gone back to cutting snow blocks, felt a tap on his shoulder—and jumped.

"*Whoa*. Hey, Jones. Calm down."

Garrett was standing there, wearing a friendly smile.

Dhani stood, ice axe at his side. "I didn't hear you."

"Didn't hear me? Guess you were too busy cutting blocks."

Dhani said nothing. Something was happening in his head again—the snow, the meadow, Garrett, all of it was becoming transparent.

"I saw your friend. Looked like his ice axe broke. Dugan and I hauled ass and our shelter's pretty much done, so I thought I'd come and see if you guys need help."

Dhani felt as if he were floating above the whole scene and squeezed the handle of his axe to be sure he wasn't dreaming or passing out.

Garrett noticed the vague emptiness in Dhani's eyes and took a small step back. But he continued pressing.

"You alright? I'm not gonna do anything weird. Hey, I know I've been a jerk to you. But a couple weeks ago, Dugan and Rocco got over being bent up about each other. That was good. Made me feel bad about myself for ragging on you."

He pulled the glove off his right hand and extended it. "Sorry, man.—Friends?"

The strange, wide-open awareness was spreading. Deepening. He wished he could stop it. It seemed as if Garrett was speaking to him from a remote place or time, his voice echoing down through a vast empty chasm. His physical form had started to flicker, so he was there and not quite there.

What caught Dhani's attention most was what he saw inside that form.

Within the transparent mist-shape of Garrett, a gray, distorted face half-appeared, darting out from behind Garrett's smiling face like smoke out of smoke, then pulling back out of sight.

"I know you probably hate me." Garrett's mouth was moving, the echo of it sharp and jarring as metal on glass. "But come on, man. I'm serious. No more name calling. No more giving you crap.—*Friends?*" he said, louder.

Dhani was breathing hard, watching for the dark figure to appear again, sensing it was still there inside the false face.

"How about just *not enemies?*" Garrett was starting to sound impatient.

The shadow was gone. Dissipated like smoke, or maybe more deeply hidden.

Dhani felt himself settling back into his own body. He did not take off his glove, but finally reached out and shook Garrett's hand. "Yeah. Whatever."

Garrett smiled broadly. "So, need some help?" He sounded triumphant.

Ray-Ray was coming across the frozen meadow, a new ice axe in hand.

"I think we got this," Dhani said. "Thanks, though."

Garrett winked and punched him in the arm. Hard. "See ya, buddy."

When Ray-Ray reached Dhani, he watched Garrett retreat. "He come over to give you crap?"

"He came to make friends."

"Seriously?—Well, I guess it would be good if you could forgive him and let all the old mess go. My dad preaches that all the time. What do you think?"

"Sure."

"You don't sound like you really think that."

Dhani was still seeing the glimpse of shadow concealed within Garrett. It made part of his mind feel clear, while another part felt strange and off-balance.

I'm really, really losing it.

He decided not to tell Claire or Ray-Ray about the things he was imagining. Later, he would seek out Sahm.

Sahm arranged sticks of hardwood, struck a match, and touched it to the pile of pine kindling beneath. He was relieved that Tanner had stopped instructing him in how to build a fire and gone to take charge over someone else. The pine bark and chips caught immediately, sending up small flames and the sharp-sweet scent of burning evergreen pitch.

He began to recite from the *Bardo Thodol*, what westerners called the Tibetan Book of the Dead:

O child of the Enlightened One, fix your mind on he who is your Guide.

Immediately, in his mind's-eye, Sahm saw the blue diamond-flash and brilliance of *Dzes-Sa*.

"Allow the forces to arise more and more within you, Sahm, radiant as moonlight on water, stronger than every physical strength."

Radiant One, he responded, *you are the power of my power.*

His awareness was opening and his skin felt charged and electric.

"Allow me to be your peace and patience. Focus your mind, and listen."

Standing, Sahm began to walk in a circle around the growing fire, counterclockwise in the manner of *Bönpos*. His whole being felt like the skin of a drumhead that was being tightened. With each round, he picked up a stronger and stronger voice, like beats coming from everywhere—pounding in the air, the ice and trees, the huge stones, the mounting bonfire, and from the mountain cliffs and crags.

Everything was alive, and echoes resounded in the deep places of his being.

"The time has come!" voices called from all around him.

He turned in a circle, suddenly able to see through the solid forms of mountains, trees, and rocks—recognizing the voices as those of Elemental beings that quietly, secretly inhabit the whole natural world.

"The time has come—for what?" he called back. "Tell me."

Another voice spoke, louder and nearer than the others.

"He is here, and you are watching his powers slowly arise," said the voice of Dzes-Sa. "He is needed. The time of great conflict fast approaches. I am opening your mind to others, who will help you—all the Elemental forces."

He kept circling around the fire, watching the flames consume the wood. Deep in his bones, he had sensed this was coming—and he also knew he was not prepared because he had left his own training too soon.

Dzes-Sa pointed out beyond the surrounding wilderness.

Suddenly, Sahm felt as if he were climbing a circular mountain path, higher and higher until he stepped off into. . .

. . . nothingness.

He was somewhere outside and above his normal awareness, in a transcendent place. From here, he could see a far horizon, just as he had seen it in a night journey a year before and again weeks ago. Now, the dark line he saw then had gathered into an advancing force of growing thunderheads full of darkness and lightnings, threatening violence.

"This is why you and the others were born into this lifetime—to join

with the Elemental forces to care for the Earth, and also to counter the other powers that are fast arising, endangering all living things. The earth needs to be protected now—that is the Way of Bön, which has almost been lost, and which the one you train has been sent to restore."

"How will I train anyone else, if my own training is incomplete?"

Dzes-Sa reached out one hand and, with one finger, lightly tapped Sahm's forehead.

The electricity Sahm felt swirling around him shot into his mind and exploded throughout his body, making him shudder with a physical spasm that he thought would burst his skin.

"Your mind has already been partially opened by your grandfather. Now, the channel is clear. You only need to remain open and clear—free of impatience for things to happen in your sense of timing. And at the right moment you will be shown what you need to do to guide the ones I am bringing to you."

Sahm felt a residual trace of uncertainty, and asked—Can you not train me fully now, *so I am sure I know how to guide them?*

"When you were a small boy and you went by bus to your grandfather's province to live with him, when did your mother place the ticket in your hand?"

"Just before we got on the bus," he replied, "so I would not lose track of it. In that way, she made me know that the ticket was something important, something valuable that I truly needed, and so I should guard it with care."

"And all you had to do was reach out when it was needed and the important thing was given to you."

"That is so."

"The instruction you need will be given to you when it is needed."

"Why can I not be instructed right now?"

"Because your task is to walk constantly on the edge of both worlds—the world of form and the unseen world of energies that arise and create everything. To see both what is and what can be. This how what exists only as a possibility is brought fully into being."

He started to ask another question and was cut off.

"You are not instructed in everything now, because the enemy within you is your impatience and frustration. That is why you left Tibet, because you did not want to wait and trust that you had a purpose there."

Sahm flinched at the admonishment.

"Now, I school you. And you are to remain open and clear at all times, and wait—alert. That is the doorway to the greater awareness of which I speak."

Then he felt as if he were falling from a great height. . . .

. . .and when Sahm opened his eyes, he had returned from the realm of pure energies to the realm of form. All around, the winter trees looked gray and frozen, and the world appeared heavy and solid again.

Though the air was freezing, sweat was running from his forehead and temples, his body was jumpy with energy, and it took him a few minutes to settle himself down—which he did by gathering more wind-fallen branches for the fire.

What remained was the sense that a channel had been opened in his mind and deeper being. One into which, at any moment it was needed, *Dzes-Sa* or the *Elemental* spirits of the world could speak and guide and instruct him.

Though there was no wind, the bonfire leapt wildly and roared, devouring the wood, nearly out of control.

What does it mean that we have been born especially for this lifetime? What exactly are the boy and I supposed to do?

"Gnam gru 'gro yag!"—called the *Elemental* powers all around him. *"Take flight."*

As he pondered that, *Dzes-Sa* began to disappear from the vision, saying,

"More than the two of you are awakening. Others are being made ready to move beyond their small minds and old ways of being. Watch and you will see who they are."

"I see why you picked this spot," said Jalil, wiping sweat off his face.

Rocco kept chopping snow blocks and didn't respond.

"Clear view of Imani. You're like a stalker."

"Just dig."

Makayla came crunching through the ice-crust toward them across the wind- and snow-swept meadow, stopping at the edge of their campsite.

"Randy showed me and Claire how to build a shelter, but he went to help some other people and I don't think we're doing it right. One side looks like it's going to fall in. When you guys take a break or finish could you come show us how?"

Jalil smiled. "Sure. I'll come over."

"Keep digging, we're almost done," Rocco ordered him.

"Why don't you finish up?" Jalil countered. "With a few more chunks the roof'll be closed in."

"I'm not doing all the work. Get moving."

"You're not my boss. I wish Tanner hadn't stuck me with you."

"Same here, Hat Boy."

Jalil threw his ice axe down. "I told you before, don't call me that, *La Stidda* Boy?"

"I'll just leave now," said Makayla, turning away.

"You don't wanna call me that."

"*La Stidda*."

"Okay—*Jihadi*."

Jalil stared. "What does that even mean?"

Makayla was crossing back over the meadow. "I'm getting out of this war zone."

Rocco kept working in silence.

Jalil opened his mouth again to throw another insult, but for some reason that eluded him. . . he didn't.

Randy winced and straightened from a bent position, setting his ice axe down. "Daggone shoulder." His breath came in small white puffs on the cold, dry mountain air. "Anyway, *that's* how you chop a block of snow."

Imani stopped scooping blocks of ice crystals from the snowbank and wiped her face. "I thought you guys were kidding when you said we'd be sleeping in igloos for two nights.—What's wrong with your arm?"

Randy bent his right elbow and slowly rotated his arm from the shoulder. "I slipped during a long climb. Grabbed the rope and stopped the fall, but I seriously damaged the rotator cuff in my right shoulder. The pain still kicks in once in a while. No big deal."

"If I'd known you guys weren't kidding about sleepin' in a egg-loo, I woulda faked the flu," said Tia Leesha, resting against the huge boulder next to their campsite. "My idea of roughing it is a cheap hotel with no mini-bar in the room."

"It's *ig*-loo," said Imani, "and since we know they're not kidding, you need to pick up your little shovel and help me chop out a shelter from this snowbank. I don't think we can do snow-blocks—especially if you're not going to help."

"My back hurts. Why'd we hafta pick this spot? This bank is too big. I'm already exhausted."

"Why are you always exhausted?" Imani stood up, exasperated. "You sleep more than anyone I know."

Tia Leesha ignored her.

Randy dropped his arm to his side. "It's a perfect spot. Listen to me. You need to remember this if you're in a true, survival situation."

He pointed in an arc. "Sun comes up on our left and sets on our right. That means we're facing south, which gives us maximum temperature increase throughout the day. We're digging into a snowbank that formed against this huge boulder, with spruce trees on both sides. So the setting protects us from the wind.

"Now look up." He tilted his head back, scanning above them. "We're away from the snow-covered slopes. There's no risk of being buried in an avalanche. And there's no tall trees around. So the wind can't throw down a huge branch on you in your sleep."

Imani had resumed chopping into the snowbank, and a large hollow had begun to open up inside it.

"*Dig*," she said to Tia Leesha, sounding irritated. "This isn't like class, where you can just nod off."

"I gotta pee. How we supposed to do that here? The ground's too frozen to dig a latrine."

"Take a break," Randy said to Imani. "I'll show you guys. Bring your t.p. and a plastic zip-lock bag."

Some yards away, Randy chose a bare, beech sapling. "Find a tree you can get a good grip on. You don't want to slip and fall backwards. Drop trou, grab the tree at about waist-height, and squat back. When you're done cleaning up, put the t.p. in the plastic bag. What you carry into the wilderness, you carry out."

"That's gross."

"I'm good for now," said Imani, "but thanks for the bathroom tip."

She started back to the campsite.

"Why you still here?" Tia Leesha said to Randy, who had remained.

"Because I want to tell you one more thing. If you're smoking—, " he pinched a thumb and forefinger together and put them to his lips, "—or doing any other substance, that's a fast ticket out of this program."

"Why do you say that to me? And why didn't you say it to her, too?"

"It goes for everyone."

"But you just singled me out."

"The red eyes. Your slurred speech sometimes. I was a stoner for years."

"That's just—I call BS."

Randy turned and followed after Imani. "I said it goes for everyone. And anyone who has a problem should talk to a counselor. Reach out for help and you'll get it. Sneak around and get caught, and you'll probably get expelled and sit out your time in a cinderblock building back in DC.

We're all here to help you succeed in life, not to bust you. But you need to know this isn't just a vacation from juvenile detention."

"Oh, I'm sure *this*—," she swung her hand around, pointing at the frozen mountains and woods and ice-blue sky,—"ain't no vacation. You know, I may just tell Ms. Holman you're harassing me," she called after him.

Randy kept walking and called back. "If you want a warm place to sleep tonight, better pee fast and get back to work."

"I mean it," she shouted, her voice cracking with anger.

"Timing you," he shouted back. "Two minutes for a pee. That's all you got.—Remember. I file a report when we get back."

She stared at his back as he retreated, frustrated.

She would probably mess up even this simple task, she told herself, and slip and fall in her own urine. Why couldn't she be sophisticated like Imani, or sweet like Makayla, or talented like Claire? But why even try? She could never be like any of the girls her mother ruthlessly compared her to.

Looking up, she saw Randy returning.

"You know what," he said, "I was being tough on you because, truthfully, I can see you're holding back for some reason. It's like you're afraid to try. But the thing is, you've got amazing potential, if you just use it."

She snorted. "No, I don't. I'm a loser. I can't do anything right. You tell everybody they have potential, because that's just the kind of stuff you guys say."

"Who told you that negative crap about yourself? It's not true."

She sniffed and looked away into the snowy trees. "People."

"Well, they didn't tell you the truth. As I was walking away, this thought came to me—I'm not even sure where it came from, but I know it's meant for you."

She stared at him, waiting.

"I came back to tell you this. '*Think the big thought, dream the big dream, do the big task. You can.*'"

When he was gone and she was done with what she needed to do, she stood in the silence of the winter mountainscape, feeling warmth pass through her as she repeated the first words that had ever brightened her soul.

The early evening sky over Eagle Rock Mountain was bright and bitter. Brilliant white moonlight was beginning to light up the snowy mountain meadow, casting blue swaths where the shadows of trees, drifts, and stones moved slow as minute hands over the ground. The bonfire they had built earlier had amassed a huge bed of red-glowing coals and now the flame was easier to keep.

As the last light of day faded, Sahm noticed Claire seated nearby on a blanket on the snowy ground. She had a book in her lap, her hand was moving, and she kept staring at the fire and the surrounding evergreens.

"Are you making a new drawing?"

She pulled the book up to her chest and did not reply.

"Why do you hide your sketches? Are they not very good?"

She smiled a little. "You're so direct, Sahm. You just say what you're thinking. I like that. And no—they're not very good. I do them just for myself."

"What is it you have drawn? Is it me?" He smiled and posed.

She laughed. "Just a quick sketch of the bonfire and the trees. Snow on branches."

"Please, may I see? Perhaps your own eye is not clear enough to see whether the work is good or not."

She stood and gathered her blanket, her smile gone. "Don't be offended. But no."

It was well past midnight, and in an hour or so, Randy would take his turn as fire keeper. Sahm had volunteered to keep first watch, because as the evening deepened, an energy running rampant within him would not allow sleep.

Since his earlier encounter with *Dzes-Sa* and the *Elementals*, something vital had changed. At first, he had felt the presence of his Teacher nearby, as if he might turn his head any time and see this ancient, transcendent One watching him. Then, he realized, this sense of presence was not outside of himself but within him. In a kind of awareness that filled his whole body. The pure blue, healing light of *Dzes-Sa* had passed inside him, and he himself was now a bearer of that light—a living witness of the truth that this one Beautiful Earth and everything and everyone in it must be protected.

Crouching near the fire, Sahm stuck out his hands to the flame to warm them.

What did that mean for each of these people at Lost Lake? For any who had been born into this life, as *Dzes-Sa* had said, for the special purpose of protecting the planet? And what about some of these young people, like Claire who was so untrusting of anyone, or Garrett who mocked everyone, or secretive Imani, or Tia Leesha who complained about everything. . .?

Feeling an icy draft on his neck, Sahm pulled up the collar of his coat. With firelight to guide them, the young people would not be disoriented or unsettled by the mountain's vast silence if they woke to relieve themselves. But how was he to guide them?

A single line from the *Bardo Thodol* came into his mind as a reminder of what *Dzes-Sa* had told him.

O, son of the Awakened Nature, remain on the edge of alertness. Watch for the radiance you now know within yourself to arise in the ones who are awakening.

Another sense arose—that everything was watching him. In the leaping light of the bonfire, the trees and rocks all around seemed to move, as if they were alive. The water trapped in crystalline snow and ice shifted from shadowy blues to pulsing reds. The air itself seemed to circle around and breathe itself into and out of him.

The Elementals have awakened me to them, he thought, *and stood in respect.*

"A very great challenge lies ahead. You have seen the approaching darkness that is coming over the whole Earth. You and the other Earth Protectors are being called upon to fight for the life that runs through this planet."

Sahm spread his arms and said loudly to the clear cold night, "For the sake of all sentient beings and the Earth itself, show me what is needed now."

In response, the fire and air, crystalline snow and frozen ground began to shift all around him.

From behind a tree next to her snow shelter, where she'd come to pee, Emmalyn had been watching Sahm. He was speaking in some language—Chinese or Japanese or whatever. He hadn't seen or heard her, but she had watched him and just now heard him say—to something invisible—that he would do whatever they asked.

For half a moment, she had thought she should wake someone. Randy or Tanner. What if Sahm was possessed? After all, hadn't she just seen him summoning his evil spirits?—No. She didn't really believe in all the bull crap she was taught in the storefront church her mother had forced her to go to as a little girl.

Her flesh was tingling, though, not with fear but a sudden thrill of delight.

What she was witnessing would be very useful.

When Sahm slipped outside his body, he felt momentarily disoriented.

There was his own physical form beside the bonfire, the yellow light flickering across his features. And he was here, a few feet away outside himself.

Free of his body, he felt lighter than thought, invisibly joined to everything in an infinite connection. Every tree, rock, and bare shrub had become a translucent veneer, its outer form made of swirling mists. Each object carried in its depths a pale light that looked like an ignited version of itself.

He reached out to touch a small, wind-twisted mountain shrub that looked like a spiraling fog with blue fire flickering within its branches.

The faces of the students rose in his mind, and it occurred to him that since he could now see into things—see their ultimate reality—he might be able to learn something important about them. One in particular, who was holding back from trusting Sahm, guarding a deep secret, blocking his own emergence into power.

Moving away from the bonfire, passing the first snow shelter, he was able to see inside the swirling shape of it. Two forms were curled in their transparent sleeping bags, each of them a circulation of bright energies—like lights in water circling in different patterns.

Rocco and Dugan. He was aware that the syllables of their names were just noises. Useless to describe who they were in their true essence.

Passing other shelters, he came to the one he was seeking.

One of the mist-bodies, he knew to be Ray-Ray. Within him, the circling light was mostly steady, but jumped as if it was being switched off and back on.

He has suffered a stab of terrible grief. A great betrayal. It was not a guess, it was a knowing.

Dhani's shifting form was the one that held his attention, though.

At his core was a tangle of darkness. From behind this dark mass, pinpricks of brilliant light shone weakly into and through the boy's physical body. Then came a flash of light, jagged and searing.

The jolt shot out from Dhani and passed into Sahm, searing him, so that he almost cried out.

Then the surge of energy was gone, leaving behind a paralyzing *fear* that nearly made Sahm's knees buckle.

Of course. Sahm thought, when he recovered. *Fear is always the great force that blocks* lung, *the life energy.*

He remembered, too, the wounded rabbit he had rescued from the woods. The terror and traumatic shock he felt emanating from Dhani was what that small creature must have felt when it was struck by a predator and dragged off toward annihilation.

Now he knew why the creature was dropped for him to find. It was indeed a portent, the message of which he now understood.

He is mostly frozen inside, like a terrified creature shaken to its bones. Terror is the force that binds him.

And yet, Sahm could sense that behind the fear were stores of an even greater energy, one that was vibrant and potent. A force for great good.

"This is the first great work you were brought here to do."

"How am I to do that?" Sahm said out loud, into the cold night air.

"He believes that what he fears is greater than he is. Watch until he frees himself from that lie."

He remembered *Dzes-Sa's* words, that he would be shown what to do at the right moment.

"Observe the others, as well. You will witness all their powers rising. Some for good, some for ill."

Again, he had the sense that a mighty shift was about to occur—and that he himself was at the edge of it.

"Yo! What the—"

A shout in the darkness brought Sahm back into himself, where he had been standing near the bonfire. Turning, he saw Randy Wolfmoon, who had stopped in his tracks and was staring at one of the thick evergreens some twenty feet away in the darkness.

"What are you doing, hiding over there?" he called out.

Emmalyn stepped out of the darkness into the moonlight. "I had to pee," she said, in her sweet, country voice.

"But you were standing there, watching. I saw you peeking around that tree and it scared the crap outa me. We both musta scared poor Sahm here."

Emmalyn looked over at Sahm. "Sorry."

Sahm's consciousness was merging with his body again, and for a split-second as she stepped from hiding he saw inside the mist-form of Emmalyn—into her essence.

Within her, two energy patterns were twisted together—one dimmer and one stronger.

"Why is he staring at me like that?" she said to Randy. "He's scaring me."

Sahm blinked and said without thinking, "I am sorry. I am staring because there are two of you. The person that people see, and the person that you really are."

Emmalyn drew a sharp breath that sounded hurt or angry, then turned quickly and retreated through the darkness to her shelter.

She would not forget what she had seen or Sahm's evil mutterings, which would be his undoing.

8th

"Something's happening to my mind, Sahm," Dhani said quietly. "I think I'm going psycho."

Sahm heaved the last big branches on the fire, and looked up into the blue-pink sky of morning. During breakfast, they had let it burn low, so they could get close enough to heat water and cook morning meals. Now everyone was crouched near it, night-tousled, hungry—and full of grumbles.

"Oatmeal again."

"I need steak and eggs."

"I want bacon."

"Wait'll this summer," Randy teased, "when Laurel teaches you how to eat soft under-bark and weeds to stay alive."

Sahm stoked the fire until it was leaping again, then turned and stared at Dhani, not comprehending what he had said.

"I'm schizo. It means when you go crazy," said Dhani, stepping closer to warm himself. "It means your mind is. . .sick, I guess."

"Why do you say this?"

"I already told you," he said quietly, "that I think animals are saying stuff to me. And now—," he dropped his voice to a whisper, "—I think I saw something *inside* one of the other guys."

Sahm was on higher alert, as he had been instructed, and aware of a new opening into Dhani's spirit. "Your mind is not sick. Your belief about such events needs to change. That's all.—When did this happen?"

"Yesterday. Garrett came to talk to me."

"Tell me what you saw within him."

"It was like a face, but it was kinda smoky and see-through. It kept shifting and didn't have eyes or a mouth, it just had darker spaces in it in place of a mouth and eyes that made me think of a face. All the time he was talking, I wasn't looking *at* Garret—I was looking *into* him, like I said."

"What was happening when this occurred?"

"Garrett apologized and wanted me to shake his hand and be friends."

"What did you do?"

"I wasn't really paying attention to him, I was watching this shadow thing. Garrett was smiling and talking nice, but it didn't seem right. I just shook his hand and said, 'Sure'. Then the shadow, like, dissolved."

"Dhani," Sahm faced him squarely, "what you saw is the reality that lies within Garrett."

"What does that mean? What should I do now?"

"First, you should stay away from him for the time being."

Dhani looked thoughtful. "I don't know what I'd do if you weren't around for me to talk to. Probably lose it. So much is happening in my head and I feel anxious a lot."

"Yes, I know. You are jumpy as a rabbit."

"You said stay away from Garrett. I thought you spiritual guys were all about forgiveness and kindness. That's a thing in your Bön religion, right?"

"Bön is not a religion. It is a way to connect with the vital energy in all things. And yes, we believe in forgiveness but there is also something we call 'idiot compassion'. That is when you are so kind you ignore when another person has the will to harm you. If you saw a dark aspect of Garrett while he was offering you his friendship, you must continue to be mindful of that."

"Okay, but he seemed honest when he said he was sorry for saying crap to me. I did feel like I wanted to punch him in the face, though, for giving me shit."

"Stay alert. That is all I am saying. And yes, also be kind. That is always the way."

"I don't know if I can do both—watch out for him *and* be kind."

A large burning branch in the bonfire broke in half and a section fell into the bed of red coals, popping and sending up a shower of yellow sparks along with a billow of gray and white smoke.

They stepped back from the leaping flame.

"It is not easy to do both together. That is why we call our spiritual work a *practice*."

Dhani looked unhappy. "I don't want any of this, Sahm. It's too hard."

Sahm felt impatient. "Every training is hard," he snapped. "We practice until we are good at it."

Sahm moved a big piece of flaming branch that had fallen outside the stone circle back into the fire—hoping *Dzes-Sa* and the *Elementals* would quickly give him the next bit of insight he needed to guide this young man whose powers were emerging fast and who was still so resistant.

At the same time, he sensed within Dhani a power that wanted to erupt, like the flames of this bonfire. It would need to be directed or it could be destructive. Would he be able to help control it?

He wished the pace of his own progress on the path would quicken.

9TH

The final morning's wake-up was cold, but now the air temperature was rising rapidly under a surprisingly intense March morning sun. Ice and snowmelt were dripping from the trees.

"Trails are gonna get slick again by this afternoon," Steve announced, as breakfast ended. "Break up camp. Scan the area for trash. I don't want even a gum wrapper left behind. Randy and I will be checking. And then let's get down the mountain."

"This thing hurts my shoulders," Garrett said, shifting his backpack an hour later when they were on the trail.

"Steep descent," said Randy Wolfmoon. "Your knees and quads really take a pounding going downhill. With a big pack it's even tougher. Harder to keep the weight off your shoulders, and there's a lot more weight to keep balanced when you're climbing over stones and boulders and there's slick footing."

"I just want to get off this stupid mountain and be first in the hot shower."

Jalil pushed past him. "Outa the way, son. You and Tats are gonna stand in line and wait when we get back to our cabin. 'Cause I'ma take a lo-o-o-o-ng hot one."

Garrett picked up his pace, passed Jalil, and shoved him off to one side of the steep trail. "The hell you are."

Jalil skidded toward a rocky drop-off, shouting and wrapping his arms around a sapling to keep from falling.

Hauling himself back onto the trail, he started to jog, caught up to Garrett, and plunged past him down the slope almost running.

"*Guys,*" Randy called after them. "You gotta be real careful or—"

Jalil's feet shot out from under him, his legs went up in the air, and he came down on his backpack—the left side of his head glancing off the sharp edge of a boulder.

Randy had almost reached Jalil, when his feet went out from under him and he came down on his right elbow.

"Oh damn oh damn oh damn," he said, gasping. "Jammed my shoulder *again.*" He pushed himself up to standing.

Jalil had raised his left hand to his temple. When he brought them back down his fingertips were red.

Garrett had paused just below on the steep trail, looking back up at them.

Dropping his pack, Randy knelt beside Jalil. "You're lucky," he said, still wincing. "Looks like you just nicked your scalp, which bleeds a lot. That's why it's trickling down the side of your face already." He pulled a tube of something out of his first aid kit and leaned closer. "How's your vision? You dizzy?"

"I'm. . . okay. I didn't hit my head too bad. I just sorta grazed it. But damn it hurts."

"Press this to your temple," Randy instructed, handing him a square of gauze. "The bleeding should stop in a few minutes. Like I said, the scrape's not deep." Then his tone became firm. "You know what we told you guys when we started downhill. Descents can be treacherous in slick conditions. We told you to go slow."

Jalil looked at the gash of mud and ice where he'd slipped. "It's like there's booby-traps everywhere.

"The trails can be this way well into May. Hey, in my younger days, I climbed many of these rock faces in early June, and some of the ledges and handholds were still coated with ice in the most shaded areas. Untrained climbers fall here in the High Peaks almost every spring, and a few die, because they forget how long the ice lasts on these cliffs.

"So that means," he finished, "you gotta go real slow and be very careful about your footing." He was watching Jalil closely. "You sure you're gonna be okay to walk now?"

Jalil had pushed himself up to standing, still holding the gauze to his temple. "Yeah, I'm good."

"I'll be in the shower before you," Garrett smiled, "taking a nice, long, hot one."

"Dude." Randy shook his head. "Give it up with the foot race crap."

"That's okay," Jalil smirked. He said in a low voice to Randy, as Garrett trucked off down the trail, "When he's in the shower a long time, I just turn off the valve on top of the hot water tank and the water goes ice cold. He's so stupid he never catches on."

Randy shook his head. "This warfare between some of you guys can't lead to anything good."

11TH

Two years, his mind repeated.

Olivia's death was as fresh in his head as the hour it happened.

Steve had packed at daybreak for the trip back to DC and now, at seven, he was at loose ends until Tom was ready to leave after lunch. He had begun to feel unsettled and decided a walk around the lake would get his mind out of a place he didn't want it to fall into—vivid memories of that day.

It was his duty to appear on Thi's show. It was a good idea on her part. And he hated that he had to do it.

Passing the first barn, he saw Jo's Jeep and kept going. He didn't need or want conversation. At the second barn, he decided the inmates could be a good distraction. He would check on the playful antics of the young otters and the condition of the sick cougar. Maybe that would lift his mood, or at least pull his mind in a better direction.

Inside, hung on the edge of the huge tank, was a bucket of large, silver minnows that darted around inside the container when his shadow fell on them. He pulled one out and tossed it in the water, which brought both the otters torpedoing through the water—one of them snatching the minnow just ahead of the other.

"Don't worry, buddy," he said absently, "I've got more for you." He threw in ten more minnows.

Garrett charged through the door. "Hey, thanks for doing that, sir—but I'm supposed be feeding them."

"Are you late? These guys looked hungry."

"Jo had me take something up to Kate's office. A supply order. I can take over now. Great campout, sir."

Steve ignored that. Garrett had a way of trying too hard, and it grated on him—but then everything grated on him right now.

He heard a sound coming through the divide between Jo's small animal room and the bigger large animal area.

Leaving Garrett staring after him, he went to the other half of the barn and found the young cougar rubbing its face against the bars of its enclosure, pacing a little, then rubbing its face again. Its movements seemed listless, without much energy. The skin along its sides was drawn tightly over the curved ribs, and it looked half-emaciated.

The big cat had been brought in by two Environmental Conservation guys who thought she had been shot but couldn't find a bullet wound. Jo had run tests but couldn't find what was wrong with her.

Someone had left a large bucket of fresh, raw meat just inside the door of the area. Steve lifted it, walked up to the bars and tossed one red hunk into the cage.

The cougar sniffed at it, licked twice—then slunk listlessly to the back of its enclosure where it collapsed into the straw, breathing heavily.

"I'll have to make you part of the Bear Tribe." Jo had come in behind, and stood watching him. "They take care of the large mammals. I'm guessing you need a size-large tee-shirt."

He started to pull another hunk from the bucket.

"Don't," she said. "Someone else should have been here an hour ago to do that."

"Someone not carrying their weight," he responded with disgust. "Surprise, surprise."

She ignored that. "I heard from Kate that you're going back to DC to be on a TV show."

"True." Talking felt hard. A one-word answer was all he could manage.

"Promoting the Lost Lake program?"

"No."

"I didn't think so. You don't seem like a big fan of what's happening here."

"Actually, Kate and Sewell don't want any mention of it until it's proven itself in a year or so. I'm not supposed to talk about it."

"So then—does the TV gig have to do with your military experience? Reliving some victory?" There was a touch of not quite sarcasm but maybe a challenge.

Steve realized how much he had been bracing against appearing on Thi's morning program, how difficult it was to form in his mind sentences to say in response to any questions, let alone the ones he guessed Thi would ask. As well, he realized how hard it would be to keep images from flooding his mind—the ones he had fought to push out for most of the last year, not with great success.

With Jo's jab, he started to feel frayed.

"No," he said. There was a sharper edge to his voice than intended.

"Hey, sorry. Just showing interest in what you're doing. So what's the trip about? Checking out another job offer. That would make sense."

The edge was there before he could stop it. "Why do you women do that?"

Jo turned her head away from the cougar's cage slowly, her eyes flashing at him. "What is it *we women* do?"

"You got that wounded sound in your voice when you said, *'Sorry.'* You guys make everything about *the feels*."

"Oh, really. You equate an attempt at being friendly as being about 'the feels'?"

"And you push. I just need some space and quiet and you're pushing."

"And *we all* do that. All of us women. We push?"

He wanted to say, *You're doing it right now,* but didn't want to go down this road. It was confusing because he felt attracted to Jo. Maybe not to this constantly-sparring part of her personality, but to her. But he had to cut this off. Making her really angry seemed the best way to make her stop.

"Yes."

Jo was not without instincts, and as she stared at Steve there was something about him that made him seem like a wounded animal—sullen and retreating, lashing out at anyone who came near. Still. He was not an animal, he was a grown man. And in her mind there was no excuse for his superior attitude, which seemed to shout, *I don't need you or anyone, so leave me alone.*

She laughed at his reply. "Women push? Maybe that's because hiding is what *you men* do best. At least guys who think you're all alpha-male macho. Like you, for instance."

He started to turn his back on her to leave.

"Right. Turn your back to run and hide." She felt herself letting go, no longer holding back. "You've been hiding out on your little island all year. Is it like the tree fort you had when you were little boy? You could boss the weaker kids around, throw sticks and stones—and then hide so no one could 'get' you? You're not the big warrior you pretend you are. That's a convenient façade you hide behind."

She knew she was twisting the knife. After months of Steve's attitude, she didn't care.

Steve wheeled on her, fists clenched, clamping down hard on the desire to slap or shake her.

Seeing his reaction, she smirked and relaxed, hands on her hips, making a show of letting him see he didn't intimidate her.

He let his fists relax.

"I hope your TV appearance is a big hit," she called after him. "Maybe you'll get to star in your own reality show—*Angry Warriors*."

He had turned and kept walking away, an indifferent silence his only response.

"You know, if you flub up on live TV that could be the best thing for you. Then you'd be like these kids who know they've blown it. Once you realize you're not the big hero and the measure of greatness, maybe you'll come down off your pedestal and join the rest of the human race."

"You seem very calm," Tom said, looking across his truck's bench seat at Steve, who was driving. "Or absorbed."

Steve stopped his tuneless whistling. "Why wouldn't I be calm?"

"Given the fact that you're about to be on television tomorrow to talk about Olivia"—he didn't say "Olivia's death"—"I thought you might be a little on edge. If I were in your place, I would be."

Steve looked out the window at the cars and trucks blowing by them on the New Jersey Turnpike. Since the episode on Christmas Eve, he'd been methodically rebuilding the perimeter of his inner world. Garrett had tried to breach those walls, mistaking usefulness for getting close. He had stomped that idea out cold. There would not be a repeat of that dark night when he had come dangerously close to an edge from which there was no return. Too-close connections and too-strong emotions were the enemy of stability.

"You never told me why you need to go back to DC," Steve deflected.

"Strangely enough, I did. Driving out the camp road five hours ago. I knew your head was somewhere else. You looked angry. What's going on?"

Steve shrugged and smiled. "Nothing to report, General Baden."

That's a lie, Tom thought. *I know how you bury and hide things.*

"Tell me again. Why *are* you going back to DC?" Steve asked.

"Pre-emptive strike. A certain D.A. who's trying to make a name for himself is threatening for the second time to pull Claire out of the program so she can go back and testify against her parents. He's trying to get her mother and father to divulge where they may have hidden a huge sum of money. Possibly a million dollars or more. He says the dealers downline from Claire's parents have spilled how much they paid them in the months prior to the bust, and nowhere near that much money was recovered."

"Why can't he just depose her and let her stay in the program?"

"Sewell thinks the man believes that by threatening to ruin Claire's chance at a better future one of her parents will break under that pressure."

"If they didn't give a crap about her before, why would they care now?"

Tom shook his head. "That's exactly what Claire has said. That poor wounded girl."

Steve was silent for a time.

"Do you really think Kate's program is going to help and change some of these kids?" he asked. "Or any of them?"

"I take it you don't."

Steve bit his lip. "Truthfully—I can't see it. I think there are some kids who were already good when they came here and some kids who are never gonna change for the better. Not even with all the support and coddling they get there. I think that by this age their track in life is pretty well set."

Tom ignored that. "What about you then? Do you think working with these young people has been a good thing for you?"

Steve went silent again and stared at the highway ahead.

After several miles Tom broke in. "So that means *no*."

"Don't take it hard, Tom. You meant well by pushing me to give Lost Lake a shot."

Tom kept his voice steady. "That has to be the pukiest thing anyone's said to me in a long time." He repeated in a slightly mocking tone, "'*You meant well.*'"

Steve drove on, the industrial parks of northern New Jersey flashing by.

Staring at the highway, Tom felt chagrined. Why had he read some miracle into the coincidence of Kate's needing a survival instructor at the exact moment Steve needed something new to do with his life?

Maybe, he concluded, his knowledge of how miracles happened was seriously flawed. They hadn't said anything about it in seminary or pastoral training.

12TH

Tia Leesha wandered into the clinic. "Sorry I'm late. I got sleepy after breakfast and took a nap."

Jo looked up from the examining table where she appeared to be working on a small animal. "A nap. Right after breakfast. It didn't occur to you that the cougar needed breakfast, too?"

"I'll go do it now."

"You don't have to. I had Rocco do it when you didn't show up. And Tanner did it yesterday. Come over here, I want to talk with you."

Tia Leesha stepped closer, then halted when she saw the creature Jo was working on.

On the stainless steel table lay a small gray animal with a black- and gray-ringed tail, a young raccoon—or what was left of one. An irregular patch of fur was missing from its left side which looked like red, raw meat. Half its face and head looked as if they'd been scorched, leaving a muzzle of pink and black-charred muscle showing.

Tia Leesha put one hand over her mouth and the other went to her stomach. "I'm gonna throw up."

"No, you're not," said Jo. "I need you to watch. You see what I'm doing here? I'm debriding the burned skin from this young raccoon. That means I'm peeling away the charred parts, so hopefully new skin can eventually grow. If it lives. Some idiot in Lake Placid threw flammable liquid on this poor fella, probably because they thought he was being a nuisance. Then they lit him on fire. One of the town police officers brought this guy here."

"Why you makin' me see this?"

"Because you're here, like every other student, to learn that these creatures need our help to make it. Did you get your breakfast on time this morning? Do you have a comfortable bed and a good roof over your head? Do you get attention when you need it?"

Tia Leesha felt nauseous and didn't respond.

"Go get that plastic container on the counter over there. Put on rubber gloves before you pick it up. I need it as sterile as possible."

She did as she was told and handed the container to Jo. "What's in it?"

Jo lifted out a silver-gray, scaley square. "Fish skin." She sounded less angry than focused. "Believe it or not, we can use it as a natural bandage to cover the burn wounds. I'll cut it and fit it in place, and then hope it keeps some of his body fluids in while we try to grow his own skin back. He'll be a mess, but he may live and I'll keep him here and give him a decent life."

"You said Tanner fed the cougar yesterday?"

"Yeah," Jo let slip, "—Mr. Angry Man."

Tia Leesha's eyes were fixed on the fish skin, which Jo was shaping with the fine point of a scalpel.

"I guess I'd be angry like him, too, if I saw my wife shot and bleed out right in front of me on the street. I just avoid him." Then her eyes got wide.

Jo set down the scalpel and stared at her. "What did you just say?"

"Nothing."

"Where did you hear that about Tanner?"

Tia Leesha's mind flashed to images of the person listening at Kate's office door and searching Kate's computer for private information.

"I didn't. I just—I made it up."

"No one makes up something like that. Who told you he saw his wife murdered?"

Tia Leesha's eyes darted around like a cornered animal's. "Someone who overheard it from someone else." She would not betray her source—who was also her source of everything. "I'm so stupid. I wasn't supposed to tell anyone else and I haven't—till just now. God, I have a big mouth sometimes."

Jo's thoughts were not on Tia Leesha anymore.

"Who thought it was a good idea to silo this 'little' piece of hugely important information?" Jo demanded.

Kate stepped off one of the treadmills in the workout room, wiped her neck with a towel and remained calm. "It was Steve's explicit request. A condition of his taking the job. He didn't want people here to know. He thought they'd treat him like he was some poor wounded soul, and he hated that idea."

"Kate, he *is* wounded. Do the Troverts know?"

"Yes."

"And they were okay with his being here *and* agreed to keep this traumatic event he suffered a secret from other leaders in the program."

"Yes. Well, Eric thought it was acceptable. He wanted to respect another man's psyche and wishes. Bay wasn't so sure, but she was willing to see if his being here and helping with the program would help him, as well. And frankly, I was the tie breaker. The Lost Lake program should be good, even healing, for everyone involved in it."

Jo was pacing, between seething and remorseful. "Well, not knowing this little tidbit of information wasn't good for me. I can't tell you how angry I am that you kept me in the dark—*you*, Kate."

"I'm feeling my way along here, Jo. I'm not a counselor. Tom encouraged it, the Troverts signed off on it. And as I said, it's an ideal I hoped—"

"Stupid, stupid, *stupid*," Jo said, her voice sharp.

Kate moved toward her, studying Jo's face. "No excuses. I'm very sorry. An error in judgment on my part. But tell me what's happened. Why are you so upset? It's got to be something more than the fact that you just now discovered a piece of information you didn't have before. You're shaking."

Jo's eyes were filling with tears and that made her angrier. "Is he going to DC this week because of something having to do with his wife's murder?"

"Yes. A reporter there has a morning show on one of the big, network affiliates. She was close with his wife, and she's trying to get the police to move on the case or get someone to come forward with information. Because they haven't found the man who did it. Olivia was gunned down right about this time two years ago, and Steve's going to talk about the murder."

Jo put her hands over her face, struggling to regain equilibrium now that a foundation stone of information had fallen into place. Her mind was flooding with her mistaken impressions of Steve from the first time she met him.

The way she'd misread his aloofness as arrogance.

The way she'd believed he thought he was God's gift to women.

Interpreting his brittle temper as a result of entitled male ego.

There was his strong, even demanding personality, she tried to argue on her own behalf, but it was no stronger or more demanding than her own.

"I'm—I'm mortified, Kate. I said some things to him. Oh lord. I once said, when I thought he was just being a jerk, 'No wonder there's no Mrs. Tanner.' And this morning I nailed him about going to be on TV. As he was leaving, I said, 'I hope your appearance is a big hit—I hope it makes you a star because you'd like that.' Kate, can you make the ground open up and swallow me?"

Kate let out a long breath and placed a hand gently on Jo's shoulder. "If only it were that easy. Right now, I think I'd jump in with you."

In the back of her mind was the question. How had Tia Leesha come by this information about Steve.

"Oh, I asked her," Jo said. "She froze up. I doubt you'll get her to reveal her source. They're young adults, and they can be amazingly secretive about things."

"What are you doing in here?"

Carter knocked and swung open the door at the same time, giving Tia Leesha just enough time to shove a plastic bag under her pillow. The rag and container she left in plain sight.

"What's that smell?"

Tia Leesha held up a plastic bottle. "Cleaning stuff. I'm gonna clean my room."

Carter stared at her.

"You know how Ms. Holman is all about us keeping our rooms clean."

Carter laughed and backed out the door. "Just wondering who's getting you your 'cleaning stuff.' I might want some."

Locking the door behind Carter, Tia Leesha sat back on the bed, feeling angry at herself and shaken.

For the first time, she felt bad she had been so careless all year about the animals she was supposed to care for. Sometimes she had forgotten to feed them, but checked off on the tracking sheet that she did it. Seeing the suffering raccoon and getting a scathing reprimand from Jo had shaken her into seeing how self-focused she could be at someone else's expense.

And there was her big mistake. If it got back that she had slipped up with Jo about Tanner, the person who supplied her with everything—from private info to her chosen way of escape—would probably cut her off.

She pulled the plastic bag out from under her pillow, soaked the rag in cleaning fluid and stuffed it inside.

Seeing herself for that moment was uncomfortable. This would knock back the guilt.

13TH

Sahm had begun the ceremony long before the sun came over the eastern ridges. In the dim light, a white thread of smoke rose from the tiny glowing point of the incense, filling the deerskin medicine lodge with the mixed scent of cedar and juniper.

In his mind, he went carefully over the stages of the ceremony, trying to recall them all. He hoped he could.

Yesterday, he had fashioned a small deer out of the barley flour he'd purchased in town. Then placed it on the altar with chanted prayers to the Five Guests—the *Elemental* beings he needed to summon for help and guidance.

Now, he would make the arrow and empower it.

Kneeling before the small, stone altar before the central fire of wild apple and fragrant hawthorne branches, he took the small piece of turquoise he had sharpened to a point and attached it to the tapered end of a straight stick. It was not the three-jointed bamboo length that the ancients used. He had substituted a branch from a paper birch, but it would make a straight, strong shaft—and it was more flexible. His grandfather had added that as a deviation from this practice of soul retrieval, which was passed down by healers from before Tibet's recorded history. Bamboo did not bend, birch did, and before the soul clearing could be done, divination was necessary, direction must be sought.

When the arrowhead was secure, he reached for strips of white, yellow, green, blue, and red cloth to attach to the other end of the stick. These would draw energy from the *Elemental* powers—*Earth, Air, Fire, Water* and *Ether*—to awaken the arrow for freeing and healing purposes.

He tied each strip slowly, chanting long recitations of welcome to these powers, feeling the arrow start to vibrate.

He would seek help from greater forces to free Dhani from the dark entanglements of terror he had seen at the core of the boy's being, and it seemed they were heeding his respectful summons.

He was tying the last strip onto the arrow—white, to summon the power of *Ether*—when the shaft started to bend in his hands.

Steve glanced at the clock in the TV station's green room—*8:43*—then at his hands. They didn't seem to be attached to his body. The makeup technician was applying a light dusting of tan powder to his face and neck, making small talk, presumably to relax him—"You'll do fine, you'll see"—but he was a million miles away.

Focus on your hands, he thought. His face felt cold. *Keep your breathing steady. Talk about facts. Not feelings.*

Thi had nodded in agreement to his demand: "No personal questions."

"I told you, this show is about raising the public's awareness and hopefully flushing out someone who's got information. Getting the DC police more active again, too. There's been no word about any new information for over a year."

"I admire you for doing this," said the makeup tech to Steve. "It can't be easy."

It would be, not easy but doable if he kept the door inside himself that cut off his emotions shut tight and sealed.

He replied stiffly. "Thanks."

"It's 8:46, Mr. Tanner," said the floor director, leaning in through the green room door. "Thi will come out of her dressing room in a minute, and we'll mic and position you on the small sofa opposite her chair. Did she fill you in about the short breaks and progression of the interview topics?"

Steve could see through the open door, out onto the set where a young man and woman were adjusting lights and placing glasses of water on a coffee table. His breathing became shallow.

"First, I'll talk all about the great work Olivia was doing with kids," Thi had said on the phone last evening. "I'll ask you about her awards and recognitions.

"In the second segment, we'll set up that day. I'll ask you about the event at the Cathedral, and talk about being there to cover it.

"In the last segment, I'll talk about the case going cold, and close by asking if anyone has any information—if they've heard someone slip up and talk about it. I'll probably end with a personal reflection on my friend."

And all I have to do is not lose it.

The floor director drummed his fingers on the doorframe, waiting for a response, and Steve tensed all the muscles in his arms, legs, and jaws, forcing himself back to this place, this time.

"Yeah, she did," he replied, his voice bland—as if he were going to be talking about the weather. "It's all good."

The director gave a quick glance at the makeup tech, who raised her eyebrows.

"If you're not okay at any point during the interview, I want you to start tapping your right leg. I'll signal Thi, and we'll cut to a commercial."

He was starting to feel annoyed. Maybe they wanted him to choke up. That would make for better live TV.

With a final fist clench, he took full control. Just like when he led a raid in Afghanistan. He would crush the interview and get out of here.

"Right leg. Got it."

The arrow kept bending in Sahm's hands, refusing to do what he wanted it to do. He kept trying to aim it west toward Dhani's cabin, but each time it pulled and gradually twisted to point south.

What am I doing wrong?

Repositioning the little barley flour soul deer between the two butter lamps, he reviewed the fact that he had placed a tiny chip of turquoise on which he had scribed "DSJ"—for Dhani Singh Jones—in its center, as the ritual dictated. He ran through the opening of the ceremony, to be sure he had not left out any of the five *Elemental* guests—*Earth, Air, Fire, Water, Ether.*

He thought of the dark tangles he had seen months before, the ones trapping Dhani's life energies—terrors upon terrors.

From everywhere, voices erupted. "Bring to light what is hidden. Set in motion the great healing work that is needed."

Are you speaking of Dhani?

"No and yes."

Then his vision blurred, his body trembled until his teeth chattered, and he felt himself shoot out of his body.

The first ten-minute segment mostly involved Thi praising Olivia's achievements—the start of three new programs for young people in need or in detention settings, the tireless work to raise funds to support free clinics.

"She was unrelenting," Thi said, ending the segment, "She told me over and over, 'Valuable young people are falling through our society's cracks, and we can't let this happen. So long as I have breath in my body, *I* won't let it happen.' That's how dedicated Olivia Neri was, and that's why I am so honored to still call her friend, though she was taken from us."

Red lights on the three cameras turned off, and Thi reached over and squeezed Steve's arm. "This next segment could be a bit more difficult for you."

Steve was stony, barely nodding.

"What do you recall about that day?" Thi prompted, when the floor director pointed at them again. "Where were you and what did you hear?"

Steve's lips went dry and he cleared his throat. "I was getting into a Humvee beside the Cathedral."

"So you were not with Olivia."

He felt a twist in his gut. "No, I was not. We got separated."

"You were going to a reception for the Nobel Prize-winning speaker we'd all just heard—hosted by a Senator? I don't recall. Why was Olivia not with you?"

Because I trashed her that morning and she didn't even want to be there with me in the first place. Because I promised to take her to lunch and stood her up to go with the Senator instead.

He stumbled through an answer about coming back from Afghanistan, needing a viable job, hoping to talk about working for the Senator with his head of security. Such a valid reason that day. So lame sounding now. He felt hot, imagining so many thousands of people watching him on their sets at home, saying, *"Be honest, jerk. You weren't there when she needed you because you thought you had more important things to do."*

"But you never got into that Humvee. What kept you from climbing inside?"

The sound of gunshots—five rounds—*sounded in his mind.*

He must have said that. Must have said that he knew what it was—and that he'd even sensed what had happened. His face felt numb.

"How did you know?"

Again, he must have said to Thi and the cameras and the watching audience that he didn't know how he knew—that he'd had a terrible, terrible feeling in his gut and that he had sprinted across the lawn out to the sidewalk on Wisconsin Ave—"and she was just. . . lying there."

Thi was watching him closely. She said something in a low voice into her lapel mic to the floor director.

"We're going to take a short break. Please stay with us. We're going to give you, our viewers, a chance to help."

A powerful updraft pulled at Sahm, and he felt as if all his joints were being painfully yanked apart.

"No," he shouted to the *Elementals. "You are too strong. You are going to destroy me."*

A thousand loud, pounding voices shouted at him. *"That is so."*

Struggling, fighting, wrestling with the tearing energies, he tried to keep his being together—but felt his joints and bones coming apart.

Overpowered, he watched his body fly into a million pieces and scatter into the void in which he was rising—the wide openness of the ethers.

And in a moment, there was. . . only *crystal clarity,* as if his mind had found a final freedom from his body.

A new vision opened.

He was flying through crashes of thunder and blinding flashes of lightning that crackled all around him.

"Where am I?" he called out.

No answer came to his question, but he found himself standing before a door in the void, understanding that this was an entryway and he was supposed to open it.

He held back. Something of extreme importance lay beyond the door—a secret maybe, or events to be unleashed. The whole vision pulsed with a sense of urgency and hints of danger.

He held back. *"What will happen if I fail to open this door?"*

"This is the task you were brought here to do," the *Elemental* powers said in unison. *"It is for your own progress and for events that must come. It is most urgent."*

"Surely, not to release danger."

"It must be so."

"No—I will not."

"This is a door within you that has its consequences in the world of form. You must relinquish control. It is the source of your frustration. You must let it finally dissolve."

"What will happen?"

"Events will be set in motion that must occur before all can be brought to conclusion."

Gathering his strength, he breathed out—until he felt empty of all resistance.

Then he reached out to open the door in the void, but before he could touch it the door exploded—and the sight of what lay beyond overwhelmed him, and he heard himself cry out.

Steve had known the final segment would be the toughest.

Images flashed on the monitors—footage of Thi running ahead of her cameramen out across the Cathedral's front lawn, dropping to her knees. Fortunately, they'd cut off the sound, and Thi was supplying a calm-sounding voice over.

"Steve was already there, kneeling beside his wife. He was shouting to her to hold on. I could not believe what I was witnessing—what had just happened to my friend, Olivia."

A new image flashed, and he heard two members of the floor crew draw in sharp breaths. He had prepared himself for this moment, and he was going over and over in his mind the basics of a particularly detailed military drill procedure to hold it together, staring at the floor and not the monitors.

Sahm stood at the center of a great, dark expanse that sprawled in all directions. Looming around him on all sides were thick, black clouds, roiling with lightnings like coiled and lashing snakes.

He sensed toxic things, violence, and death.

"Call these terrible powers out into the light," the voices were telling him. *"Set these events in motion."*

Sahm held back.

Why—why would I do this? I am a healer. This has the feel of a terrible, destructive force.

"Only what is brought into the light can be dealt with."

"Why must I be the one to do it?"

"It is the reason why you are here in this lifetime."

His grandfather had told him many times that every person comes into this life with lessons to learn and work to accomplish that no one else can do. "To fail in our individual work means failing for the whole." And Sahm believed that to be true.

Dhani, Claire, Ray-Ray. . . Kate and Tom. . . even darkly brooding Steve flashed before his mind's-eye.

If something in this strange, powerful act would somehow help them in their lives—whatever they might have yet to face—how could he refuse to do what was being asked of him, even this?

Ten minutes into the last segment, the temperature on the set seemed to be a hundred degrees, though Thi appeared to be cool and calm.

"Steve was holding onto Olivia's left hand," she was saying into a camera, "and she reached up and put her right hand in mine. I thought she was just reaching out to us for comfort or assurance. But to my surprise she opened her hand and dropped *this* into my palm."

Steve looked up from the floor and saw Thi holding out in front of her what looked like two small rectangular pictures, each one just an inch long, connected to each other by two narrow, white ribbons about a foot long—though not pure white. Both were mottled with a copper-brown color.

"This is called a *scapular*," Thi said. "Catholics wear these around their necks. It was Olivia's, and she placed this in my hand as she lay dying, felled by five bullets to the neck and chest."

Steve was fixated on the ribbons' coppery stains.

Olivia's blood.

"I was too shaken and distracted, as you might imagine," she went on, and one camera zoomed-in on the stained scapular, "to tell my crew to shoot footage up and down Wisconsin Ave. I wish I'd had the presence of mind, because we might have filmed the murderer fleeing and gotten a description of him."

Steve was still staring at the thin white ribbons, fixated on the rusty stains, a trickle of sweat sliding under his collar.

Olivia! his mind screamed. *He was kneeling in her blood as the pool expanded out from beneath her body.*

"I keep this heartbreaking, final gift from my friend hanging on my bathroom mirror," said Thi.

The floor manager was giving her the three-minute wrap-up signal.

I am so sorry, baby. Rage and grief tore up his guts.

". . .It reminds me every morning that Olivia's killer is still at-large. So far, the DC police have no leads. That's where we need your help. If you know anything, if you've overheard someone talking who was involved in this tragic event. . . ."

Steve made a sacred vow, on his own life.

". . .please help us. Call the number on your screen."

Sahm raised his hands toward the encircling dark thunderheads, calling on the *Elemental* powers for assistance. Emptying himself of the last shreds his own small will, he called out.

"I open the way for whatever must come," Sahm roared. *"May it emerge from darkness and make itself known."*

A roar from the void shook him—and clouds split.

"You have it?"

"No." He looked around to be sure no one in the Ritz-Carlton Hotel's lobby was near. "But I know exactly where it is now."

The voice at the other end swore. "I told you that my money people—"

"To hell with them. Tell them we're taking the risks, so we call the shots. We've got too many pieces in place already. Listen to me. I *just* finished a morning meeting with a lobbyist and the television is on in the hotel breakfast lounge. I happened to turn my head at the right moment—strange, how random it was—and I saw a reporter holding it up on camera."

"So she's had it the whole time we were looking for the husband. How soon can you get it?"

"It'll take a little time to get the right guys involved. They won't come cheap. But we'll get it. This is on again."

"Remember, we have a sacred cause."

"Was that for shock value?" Steve sounded hostile.

Thi had followed him into the green room, where he'd retreated after pulling off his microphone and tossing it on the floor. "What are you talking about? Do what?"

He felt violent. "Don't play stupid. You never told me about that scapular thing. Then you just hold it up in front of me on camera. Were you hoping I'd break down crying? Did you think that would spike your ratings?"

"Steve, no. You're right, it was stupid and thoughtless. But I didn't do it to shock you. Please believe me. I've died a little every time I've looked at it. The only people I wanted to shake up was my viewing audience. I wanted to show them something concrete, something pure and good that was defiled."

She opened her right hand. The ribbon and cloth necklace lay curled in her palm.

Steve had calmed himself a little, and his racing pulse had slowed. Maybe Thi didn't deserve the blast he had just dealt her. It had been a very emotional morning for her, too. She just handled it better than he did. And maybe now someone who knew something would come forward.

He looked at the small pictures, not much bigger than postage stamps, printed on the two cloth rectangles but didn't touch the scapular.

"This one holding the sword is Michael the Archangel," Thi said, "with his foot on the neck of Satan, who looks part dragon." She turned over the second picture. "And this one is the Virgin Mary. I read this is something Catholics sometimes wear for protection."

They let the terrible irony hang there.

"I don't know where this thing came from," Steve responded. "It wasn't Olivia's. She wasn't Catholic, she didn't believe in divine protection, and I've never seen it before today."

"But she was wearing it. You were holding her left hand and leaning down talking to her—but she had pulled this off with her right hand. It had caught on a gold chain necklace she was wearing, which was broken but hooked on her sweater. I wasn't paying attention to what she was struggling with. I was freaking out at the bullet wounds. But then she put her hand in mine and. . . just let it go. That's how I got it."

Sahm knelt in the trail of morning sunlight. His mind had stopped pulsing and his head was clear again. The vision had been so crystalline, lucid—and unnerving.

The *Elemental* powers had receded again. His body, which he had seen fly into pieces, was solid and whole again.

On the floor, the ritual arrow that Sahm had fashioned, intending for it to bring a healing he had imagined, now lay broken. Instead of trying to force it to do his will, he had allowed it to fly wild to do its own untamed work.

Whatever had been released by his letting go would run its course now.

He sat in there a long time, trying to keep his breath steady—feeling as if a great, dark flood of events would soon to come upon them.

Only later, as he walked back to his cabin would he realize he felt like a new being. Someone who had died, passed through the *Bardo*, and returned.

Thi wrapped the scapular in the white silk cloth in which she'd brought it to the studio. She held it out to Steve.

"I should never have held onto this. I should have given it to you sooner."

Steve's hands remained at his sides, still shaking.

"Please. I don't feel good about keeping it any longer. It was with Olivia. It should be with you."

Reluctant, numb, Steve took the cloth and slid it in the pocket of his blazer. He would bury it in a drawer. Or maybe just bury it.

"I am truly sorry, Steve. I was so caught up in what I hope will happen because of today's show that I just didn't think it all through."

"We're good," said Steve. "No hard feelings. Let's hope this brings someone out of the woodwork."

27TH

Grady shrugged. "You sure you don't want to play poker with us tonight?"

Steve stood in the half open doorway of his cabin. "I'm good. Gotta work on some survival program plans for Kate and Tom."

"How was your trip to DC?"

"Fine."

Grady smiled. "You got a lady back there, wondering how you're doing all alone up here in the woods?"

"Nope."

All out of conversation, Grady started down the porch steps. "Come on by tonight, if you change your mind. Got a new bottle of scotch. Top shelf. You sure I can't tempt you?"

When he was gone, Steve dropped into the chair by the fire.

Pal padded up, and laid his chin on Steve's leg.

"Don't do the sad dog eyes."

Pal gave a little rusty-hinge kind of dog whimper.

"What?—the lie about the program plans? Hey, I only swore off alcohol two weeks ago and I need to get used to it and not give in to guys pushing shots on me.—You gotta give me some time to clean up the rest of my act."

Also time to get strong enough to hear Olivia's name and feel her presence without plunging into a hellhole of despair.

5

April

1st

Ron shook his head, looking unhappy. "I'm afraid Rocco's gonna really lose it this time."

Jo's voice was even. "He'll have to learn."

"Why am I gonna lose it?" Rocco had come into the clinic, to get supplies from the storage closet. "Is it The Flash?" he asked, sounding anxious. "Is it his front paw?"

"Looks like he developed an infection after his claw tore in the cage wire and I had to cut him out."

"Can we just treat it with hydrogen peroxide or the stuff you used to treat the blue jay's puncture?"

"No. I'm afraid it's started to travel up his leg." Jo showed him her clipboard. "I'm working on a treatment plan right now. We don't want gangrene setting in. We'll medicate him, but it won't be easy to stop this."

"Why?"

"Because we'll have to try to keep him from chewing it. An injured paw is one of the worst wounds to treat, because as it heals it itches, and an animal will chew through bandages to gnaw on it. We may have another uphill battle here, Rocco."

Rocco paced in a circle, running his hands through his hair. "I don't want to lose this guy, too."

Jo was trying not to sound impatient. "He's not *yours* to lose. He's not anybody's. He belongs back in the wilderness—which is why you have to stop getting attached. How can I get that through to you?"

"What are we gonna do?"

"Our best," said Ron. "That's all we can ever do."

"You're going to apply medicine, make sure his plastic cone stays on—if possible, he's rambunctious—and keep his cage as clean as possible so he doesn't pick up more bacteria."

Rocco sounded miserable. "What if it's not enough?"

Rocco pushed Jalil's book aside and banged his own math book and notepad down on the small desk. "You know I always sit here. Go find another seat."

Jalil was standing next to the desk, talking to Makayla who was seated at the desk beside it. He shrugged and picked up his book. "No problem."

Makayla glared at Rocco, who grinned in triumph.

"I don't like his kind."

"What are you even talking about? You know, I used to think you were okay."

"I'm better than okay." He cocked one eyebrow and winked—but it was clear he was unhappy and on edge.

"Ohmygod, that's *so* Seventies lounge singer."

"Seat's all yours," said Jalil, tossing his book on the desk behind Rocco's.

Mike Yazzie stepped into the room.

"Let's get going, guys. Nice day outside. We want to hit this math lesson hard, then get outdoors. Now that spring's here, Mr. Wolfmoon wants to give you a first lesson in rock climbing."

Rocco rolled back the desk chair and dropped into it.

BLAAAAAAAAAAAAAA—an airhorn blasted sharply.

He leapt from the chair, swearing and knocking the desk over, book, pad and papers scattered in a mess on the floor.

"*What the f—?*" he shouted, catching himself. Grabbing the chair by its seat, he flipped it over.

Duct-taped to the chair's central spindle, where the seat would drop and set it off when pushed down, was the air horn.

Jalil and Makayla who had been holding it in, burst into laughter and high-fived.

Rocco started to reach for Jalil, but Mike Yazzie's shout stopped him.

"*Whoa, whoa, whoa,* big fella. You keep your hands to yourself."

A slow ripple of laughter rose and spread all around the room.

"Other than the fact that I almost peed myself," said Imani, "that was really funny."

"You shoulda seen your face, man," said Garrett. He made his eyes go wide open and his mouth gape. "You looked like a scared little fish that just saw the big shark coming."

"Looked to me like he mighta shat himself," Dugan laughed.

Rocco was red-faced, clenching his fists open and closed, his eyes boring into Jalil. "He disrespected me."

Claire said calmly, "Rocco, it's April Fool's Day. It was just a joke."

"No," he said, half-growling and pointing at Dhani. "Your friend's spooky powers—*that's* a joke."

Tia Leesha had been dozing, and lifted her chin off her chest. "What spooky powers we talkin' about? He predictin' storms no one else can see again?"

Emmalyn mumbled something about demons.

"Sit down, Mr. Petronio," Mike Yazzie raised his voice. "Lesson one in martial arts, keep your wounded ego in-check and stay in control of yourself at all times. Lesson two, be courteous.—You owe Mr. Jones an apology. He did nothing to you."

Dhani's face was buried in his open math book.

Rocco took a deep breath and faced him. "I apologize."

"*Mr. Jones,*" Yazzie added.

"I apologize, Mr. Jones," Rocco repeated.

Dhani nodded.

"I accept, Mr. Petronio," Yazzie prompted.

Dhani mumbled something.

"Good. Now, no more b.s. in here. Turn to page 137."

Out in the hallway after class, Claire confronted Rocco, pushing her face up to his.

"Really?—someone pulls a little prank on you, and you use it as an excuse to trash Dhani in front of everyone?"

"We're good," Dhani said, trying to pull her back by the sleeve. "He gave me this cool thing a while ago—a bear claw on a leather thong. It's okay."

"It's *not* okay," Claire shot back.

Rocco looked bitterly remorseful.

"I'm an idiot. I reached out to you as a friend, and now I just lost it and took my anger out on the wrong person. I'm really sorry, Dhani." He stuck out his fist—and Dhani fist-bumped with him.

"I messed up. You've taken a lot of abuse this year from other people," said Rocco, "and that sucks. I suck. I'm having a really bad day, but that doesn't matter. I'm not gonna take it out on you ever again. Okay?"

Jalil and Makayla passed by, leaning their heads together, smiling and whispering.

Rocco grinned at Makayla. "I just apologized to Dhani."

"Good." She nodded at Jalil. "You should apologize to him, too."

He reached out and grabbed Jalil by one shoulder, drawing him into a bear hug.

"Sorry, man," he announced in a booming voice—then pressed his mouth to Jalil's ear to whisper.

"Wrong day to pull some stupid joke on me. Better lock your bedroom door.

"This isn't over."

2ND

Dhani switched on the bedside lamp and dropped down on the covers, then heard footsteps hurrying down the hallway and a loud knock.

"It's Claire," Ray-Ray said through the door, "she says you gotta come outside. Hurry."

Down the lake front, in the evening's failing light, Claire directed Dhani's gaze halfway up an oak tree. "There's a pair of saw-whets—*there*, on the crooked branch." Her face and voice bright with excitement.

Dhani had never seen her this animated or happy.

Ray-Ray said, "Must be a bunch of those cute little guys around here."

In the last golden rays of the spring evening, the pair of small owls stared down at them from amid buds just opening into tiny bright green leaves, and blinked their eyes. . . .

Dhani was looking down at three people who were talking excitedly—Claire, Ray-Ray, and a thin kid in a black hoody—and staring up at him. Next to him, the small, female owl called, Too-too, too-too-too—*then preened a wing feather with her tiny beak.*

He felt a deep satisfaction with the world as it was. . . and gratitude. . . .

"Dhani. . . *Dhani*. You alright, man?" Ray-Ray was shaking his arm.

"Fine. Yeah. Why?" Actually, he was feeling lightheaded—and more than that, it was as if his body had started to dissolve and then returned to solidity.

"I asked if you remembered where the binoculars were and you just stared with this empty, weird smile on your face."

Dhani turned to Claire, who was rubbing her arms to keep warm. He wanted to put an arm around her shoulders to warm her but—feeling just short of bold enough—didn't. Then with confidence he said, "That's the same female we took care of last year, with her mate."

She frowned. "It could be. But you don't know that for sure. Owls all look pretty much alike."

"It's her. I just know." Standing next to Claire, he felt a deep satisfaction and a great gratitude at feeling so fully alive in this moment.

Ray-Ray had stepped back from him a little.

"What's wrong?" Dhani asked, reading his wary expression.

"*What's wrong,*" Ray-Ray answered when they were back inside the cabin, "is the way you've gotten more and more spooky all year. *All year,* man—ever since you started hangin' around more with Sahm. I think his whole Tibetan false gods and magical altar thing did something to your mind. Like he put a spell on you. My dad would say—"

"I know what your dad would say," Dhani snapped. "But he's the same dad who kicked his own son out. So I could care less what he says." He was shocked, not only at the words he had just spewed but at the energy and irritation in his voice.

Ray-Ray's jaw clenched.

"Wow. That's my dad you're attacking." Then he stepped back, wary. "But how the hell did you know he threw me out? I never told anybody here.—See, that kind of spooky shit scares people away from you."

Dhani felt pangs of remorse. "I shouldn't have said that." He tried to change the subject quickly. "Sahm's my friend. Just like you're my friend and Claire's my friend. Without you guys, I'd be totally on my own and lost here. I think almost everyone wishes I'd blow out of this program."

Now I can't even trust whether Rocco is okay with me or not."

"Here's the thing," Ray-Ray said. "First, don't bring up my private life again. Second, you can't be zoning-out all the time. Especially next month, when we're on that big survival thing we gotta go on. We're gonna be on our own in the wilderness for a bunch of days. Tanner is gonna be watching every move we make and evaluating how well we remember everything he and Randy and Laurel taught us this whole year. It's a big, big deal. You can't be spacing out."

At the mention of Tanner's name, Dhani shrank even more inside. "Tanner hates me," he said in a small voice. "When I'm around him, I totally shut down."

"That's what I mean. You gotta stop saying stuff like that, too. Tanner's just all Marine-like, and bossy. It's not personal."

"It is. He wants to hurt me. Really. He—he wants to kill me."

"Whoa, dude. Stop. You sound paranoid and crazy now."

"Sometimes I feel paranoid and crazy. Maybe that's why I sound that way."

5TH

"The guys who found her were wrong. Her blood loss wasn't the result of a bullet wound," said Jo, sounding clinical. "And strangely enough, when I ran a battery of tests at first, nothing showed up in her blood or lymph other than mild anemia."

She shook her head.

No one in the circle of twelve students spoke, as they stared at the unconscious cougar lying on the examining table. Stretched out, the young female was maybe five feet long, her fur a blend of tan and russet with deep brown brushstrokes running through it.

"It doesn't make sense why it didn't show up before, but this poor girl has leukemia. She miscarried two tiny cubs, which makes it even sadder. They've been classified as extinct here in the Adirondacks, but rare individuals have started showing up again."

Every so often, the cougar's white muzzle and black mustache twitched, along with one black-tipped ear, and she moved a front paw as if running. She seemed to be dreaming.

Dhani saw an image flash in his mind. . . .

. . .chasing down a raccoon. . . .

Rocco broke the momentary silence. "Leukemia. That's really bad, right?"

"Yes. Cancer of the bone marrow. Fatal. In her case, the disease progressed extremely rapidly from the moment I finally discovered it till now. Some kind of agent I can't determine may be speeding it up."

"Can I touch her?" asked Makayla, quietly. "Her fur is so gorgeous."

"Sure," Jo said, her voice softening. "She's under anesthesia, with a morphine drip, so it won't agitate her, and contamination isn't a worry now. She probably only has hours—a day at most."

Dhani noticed that Claire had stepped back from the group and was using a thick, black pencil to write on a large pad.

"Are we supposed to be taking notes?" he whispered.

"I don't think so."

"Then what are you writing?" He leaned closer to look at the sheet she was writing on.

She pulled the pad up to her chest, hiding the page. "Just something I'm working on."

Makayla stepped forward, tears forming and laid one hand softly on the gently rising and falling side of the sleeping creature. In between the ribs, the cougar's skin was sunken.

"How did she get it? Can you catch it?" asked Emmalyn, who had stepped back.

"No. It's caused by exposure to too much smoke—like cigarette smoking. Also exposure to radiation or certain chemicals. Or it could have just been genetic bad luck. I'm overnighting blood and tissue samples to the lab in Albany to double-check and to see if they can detect any external, environmental factors that might have caused it. Not likely, but I'm checking."

Claire had continued scribbling on the sheet, her body turned to keep its contents secret from Dhani.

He wished she would share the secret with him, and noticed that Carter was staring across the examining table at both of them—but in particular at Claire.

Their eyes met. Carter's flashed and she bared her teeth.

He dropped his gaze to the sleeping cougar, to avoid the weird look.

"Isn't leukemia something cats just *get*, for no reason?" said Dugan. "My sister had a cat that died of it."

"It's much more common in housecats, but rare in wild species. That's why I'm having tests done."

"Speaking of the lab in Albany," Makayla said, stroking the cougar's back, "whatever happened to those golden salamander bodies you sent for testing? That was months ago."

"With everything else going on—working with my tribes and all the animal inmates here—I forgot all about the salamanders. Ron," she said, turning to him, "give them a call for me while I do another blood draw. We may find something that tells us why her disease process moved so rapidly. You guys can go knock off your chores now," she finished.

Dhani looked up and saw that Carter had already slipped out.

Beside him, Claire flipped the cover of her pad down over the top of what she'd been doing and smiled at him.

"Be cool," she said. "I'll show you. When I'm ready."

Mopping the aisle in the aviary, Dhani listened to Claire talking softly to the birds as she did the feeding rounds—delivering small road-killed rodents for the birds of prey, small seeds and suet for the songbirds. In the cage next to where he was slopping disinfectant water, a wounded raven was tearing apart a dead sparrow, small brown feathers sticking out of its curved, black beak.

He remembered the dying cougar—such a beautiful animal.

"Life passes quickly," the thought went through his mind, *"with so much happiness and so much pain and sadness existing side by side."* And he wondered where such a deep idea had come from.

Maybe, he smiled, it came just from having Claire nearby. She made him think good and important thoughts.

Near and all around him, a faint blue light shone, unnoticed.

8th

He stepped off the top step, feeling that he could become airborne.

Maybe it was the sight of three swallows, dark blue against the sunny, open-sky blue of mid-morning. Maybe it was the surge of power that flooded him, muscle and bone, when he had stepped out onto the cabin's front porch and saw the great shoulders of surrounding mountains shrugging the last white winter mantles of snowdrift from their peaks.

Or maybe it was his plan get to Ron Cambric's health class early and get a seat next to Claire—and the strange sense that she was going to let him in on a secret today.

His mind flew open, his balance shifted, and space began to roll out in all directions.

"Did you finish your essay for Cambric's class?" Ray-Ray was saying. He had turned to close the cabin door behind them. "You don't have any books or papers—"

The voice fell away, as a warm, southerly draft coming down off Trinity Mountain lifted Dhani. . . .

. . .up and into the circle of swallows swooping, turning, and acrobating out over the lake. Rising, he could see below him the irregular ribbon of light brown sand and black water at the lake's edge, where the ice had gone out maybe five feet or more feet. Higher still, and he saw the whole body of the lake, now filled with white slabs of ice floating like broken-up puzzle pieces outlined by the dark water beneath.

He felt lighter than feathers on air.

An updraft caught him and he flapped his wings, soaring even higher, lifted by sunlight, moving air, and a leaping exaltation that expanded his whole being. The sky rushed past him and into his lungs. His body felt lightning charged—like a kite let loose, or a balloon that had slipped from the fingers of a child—free and wild on the open highway of the sky.

He was wind and sunlight, carelessly happy and daring.

Turning, he dove toward two other swallows who were barrel-rolling and somersaulting just above the lake, feeling his face and wings parting the air. Knifing between the startled pair, who dodged away, he plummeted further down, feathers streaming back along his sleek body, pulling out of the dive just feet before striking the lake's ice break-up.

I wish Claire could see what I can do, he thought.

Winging across the lake, he spiraled lower and lower, down toward the entrance to Kate's lodge. . . .

. . .until his tennis shoes touched the front steps and he came out of the strange, vivid daydream.

Looking over his shoulder, he saw that somehow, inexplicably, he had gotten here ahead of Ray-Ray. In fact, his friend was not even in sight. What kind of fantasy had he been caught up in?

"Where the heck did you go?" Ray-Ray demanded, minutes later, dropping his papers on the desk next to Dhani's.

"Could you sit behind me?" Dhani responded. "I'm saving that seat for Claire."

"Ten minutes ago, you were standing on our porch with me. You were there one second. . .I turned my head. . . and the next second, you were gone."

"You should check your watch then, because it's way off," said Emmalyn, looking up with clear-eyed innocence from her yellow pad—on which she was writing fast, apparently finishing the essay that was due. "Ten minutes ago, he came in and sat down. He's just been staring into space—," and under her breath she added, "—like he was zombied-out."

"No, no, no," Ray-Ray insisted. "He was *with me*. At our *cabin*. Ten minutes ago. A person can't be in two places at one time."

Emmalyn turned back to her writing. "Whatever."

Slipping into the seat behind Dhani, Ray-Ray whispered, "Tell me, man. Where did you go? How did you get to class way ahead of me?"

"Something's going on around here," said Grady, standing before the white board on which Ron Cambric had written and underlined, QUIZ THIS FRIDAY.

Ron noticed Tia Leesha nodding off and said, very loudly, "Everyone needs to listen up. *Everyone*."

She yawned and opened her eyes. Barely.

Grady looked on-edge. "I think someone is walking around the property at night. Sometimes I go out to check on things and I've spotted someone moving *well* after your curfew. I haven't said anything before now because I don't rat on people, and you're all supposed to be here on best behavior. That's why everyone's been giving you space. So far.

"Let me say this. Sneaking out a little after you're supposed to be in your cabins for the night is not a huge deal, in my opinion. Maybe you can't sleep. Maybe you need to sneak a smoke. I don't really care what your reason is. *But*. . . ."

He made a long, dramatic pause, his gaze stopping on each face to see whose eyes would dodge away from his direct stare.

"Sneaking into my place and helping yourself to stuff is *a real big deal*. Someone's getting into my. . . refreshments. Last night I left my best cigar lighter on the table and this morning it's gone.

"Now I'm a good guy," he went on, his voice dropping low, "but if it happens again, whoever's caught doing it, I'm going straight to Ms. Holman. Stealing is a big offense and it *will* get your butt tossed from this program so fast your teeth'll fly outa your head. In case you don't remember from your orientation, there's a *zero-tolerance* rule about that."

When he was done and gone the atmosphere in the room was somber.

"Officially," said Ron, "I didn't hear anything about people breaking curfew. Unofficially, I hope you all did.—Essays?" He began collecting them.

Dhani kept looking at Claire who turned and smiled at him—and in his head he heard the words,

Will you meet me at Thunder Falls after study time this afternoon?

before she said them out loud. He stared, mouth open.

"Why are you gaping at me like that?" Claire said quietly, giving him a strange look. "*Will* you? I want to finish a. . . a project. . . and I don't feel like going up there alone."

"Why?"

"I'll tell you later." She looked up and pointed. "Ron's talking to you. Aren't you listening?"

"*Dhani*?" Ron repeated, standing right in front of him. "I said I'll need your essay by the end of the afternoon or you'll have to take an incomplete for this assignment."

Dhani smiled a vague smile—"Got it"—not looking at Ron but out the window past Claire, feeling in his body the wild, soaring sensations he had felt on the long walk over here.

Which he realized he didn't remember.

Outside, over the lake, more swallows had swooped in, a dozen maybe, cartwheeling through the sun-washed blue air on their sharp-angled wings, looking like they were doing it just for sheer joy.

He felt intensely clear—the way he always did around Claire—as if the world and everything in it were translucent crystal and he was the sunlight piercing through it all. His mind felt as open as the cloudless sky.

Ron Cambric closed his math book and stood up to leave. "Any time you fellas need another tutoring session just let me know. We gotta get your test score outa the basement."

"Thanks," Garrett replied—and Dugan nodded.

When Ron stepped out the door of Garrett's cabin, Dugan turned. "Anyone else up in here?"

"No. Hat Boy and Tats didn't come back after lunch. Why?"

"You sneak into Grady's place again to do a little shopping?"

"No, just one time for that nice liquid gold."

"You didn't snake your way in there last night and relieve him of his lighter? I got this feeling you have a distinct taste for other people's merchandise."

Garrett sounded hurt and offended. "He probably lost it somewhere, like right on his kitchen counter. You should see his place. He's a huge slob. Needs to hook up with a babe who'll clean for him."

"Assuming he's not stupid or forgetful—who else around here do you think is using the five-finger discount?"

Garrett shrugged. "Any one of these freaks. We're all junior criminals—remember? That's how we got here."

Ten minutes after Dugan was gone, the front door banged open and slammed shut.

Garrett followed sounds into the kitchen and found Rocco swigging milk from a container. He drained it, then pitched it at the garbage can and missed. . . and left it lying on the floor.

Garrett waited for him to make eye-contact. "What up?"

"Jalil. I hate that kid."

"You've been on him all year. Are you still mad about that air horn prank?"

Rocco nodded.

Garrett stared into space for a minute. "I've got an idea. You'll like this."

The morning's intense clarity was gone, and every tree and rock on the path up to Thunder Falls seemed not only solid but dense and weighty.

Something strange was happening. Again.

Dhani's mind felt thick as the clay-y mud that made his feet almost fly out from under him as he climbed. The titanic shift within his head after the daydream of flying was dragging him down.

As he neared the little bend in the trail that would turn him out onto the ledge beside the falls, he thought he heard a loud crack in the deep forest, as if a large animal—maybe a bear or a deer—was moving away quickly. But the sound of it, like everything else at the moment, seemed echo-y and distant.

What's wrong with me? he thought, slipping, lungs heaving with exertion. *I'm up, then I'm down. I think I'm hallucinating. Something's really screwed up with m—*

"Dhani!—Up here!" Claire called to him above the roar of the falls, as he stepped out onto the open ledge. "Didn't you hear me? I was calling you."

From beside her up on Thunder Rock, Vajra looked down at him and let out a deep-throated *woof.*

Squinting into the sun, which was right behind her, he called out, "Want me to come up?"

"I'll come down. I need a break from sitting on this rock."

In a moment, she had circled down the short path from above, with Vajra on her heels. The breeze coming off the falling water, the sunlight haloing her, and the fact that he was here by her special invitation started to lift his mood again. Even his body felt lighter.

"I have a surprise for you." One hand was behind her back.

"Cool."

"I hope you like it."

Her arm came around and she held up a scrolled sketch that was tied with a string. "Take a look."

Centered in the white field of paper was a picture of the sleeping cougar. It was rough at first, that's partly why I didn't want you to see it. Glynis helped me get the fur just right."

Her sketchbook had flipped open a page or two, and he saw a portrait of himself.

"Wow, you did me, too."

"I was trying to get faces right. People's eyes are usually just a little above the mid-line of their face, with the nose and mouth below. . . ."

He was basking in the sudden knowledge that she had been watching him—probably a lot—staring at and studying him.

"So, what do you think?" he beamed, standing taller.

"What do mean?" she asked, frowning. "I think it's pretty accurate. Don't you?"

"I mean, my looks. How do I look to you?"

"How do you *look*? Honestly?" She stared, thoughtful. "Most of the time you look checked-out. Kind of not there. Almost all the time, really. I tried to draw you when you looked not as spacey. That wasn't easy."

His shoulders slumped.

"I sketched Ray-Ray, too," she said, as if she didn't notice his change, sounding pleased with her work. "And Jo, and Tanner. They've got interesting faces. Glynis said I really captured how Jo's face lights up. You know that doesn't happen a lot—pretty much only when one of the injured animals recovers. She liked my portrait of her. And she liked the way I got Tanner's brooding, withdrawn look."

Dhani sank back into the slogging-through-mud feeling he had earlier. "Can I keep this picture of me?" He was hoping she would say she wanted to keep it.

"I did this picture of the cougar for you. But sure," she shrugged, "you can have both pictures if you want them."

He hid his disappointment and studied her face. He liked that her eyes, which had been flat and emotionless from the beginning, were now sparkling with happiness—but he felt sad that her happiness was all about her drawings and not about him.

Without thinking, he took a step toward her and leaned in to give her a hug.

Vajra growled.

"Geez," he said, stepping back. "I'm not trying to hurt her."

Claire had pulled back, her expression guarded again. "What were doing?"

"Just saying thank you, I guess."

She stuck out her right hand and shook his. "You're welcome."

The sound of rushing water filled the awkward moment. Dhani looked at the tops of his tennis shoes which were smeared brown with muck, wishing a little he'd worn his boots and wishing a lot that he had not tried to move in on Claire. Clearly, it had distanced her from him again.

"You're one of the things I like about being here," she said suddenly.

It sounded like a peace offering.

"Why?"

"You're a strangely interesting puzzle."

He felt like a specimen in a museum. "Wow. Thanks."

"This isn't going the way I wanted this afternoon to go at all." Claire's voice changed. "I wanted to give you the picture of the cougar—and I'm finishing a self-portrait in another sketchbook that has better paper," she said, trying to sound brighter, to shift the mood. "Glynis said with a few more touches I could submit it to a contest. An art gallery in Lake Placid is running one for student artists."

He looked down at his shoes and stamped off mud, to avoid eye-contact. "That's cool." Really, he wanted to leave before his sadness showed.

He reached out for the two pictures she had offered him.

Vajra tensed, ears perked at high alert, and let out a loud bark that echoed on the far mountainside.

Dhani pulled his hand back.

"Vajra, *sit*," Claire commanded. "Stop it. It's just Dhani. God, he follows me all the time now like a guard dog. I like having him with me, but he's so over-protective."

"Why did you come all the way up here to finish your portrait?" Dhani asked, looking up and glad the attempted hug was forgotten. "Shouldn't you be like, looking in a mirror?"

She pointed at the slope of Eagle Rock Mountain, a half-mile distant. "See how there's a dramatic opening between those pine trees—right there, that dark green gash—and it looks like a passageway into the mountain? Glynis suggested I add a dramatic backdrop, just a hint of one, to give it depth. I just finished capturing that little scene behind my image. It's called a *vignette*. Want to see? I'll go get it."

She disappeared on the little trail-bend leading up to the top of Thunder Rock, Vajra padding at her heels—and Dhani stared crestfallen at the rushing water.

Idiot, he shouted at himself inside his head as he waited for her.

Then he heard her shout—"*Dammit!*"—and another loud bark. And another.

"What's wrong?" he called up to her.

Her face appeared over the edge above him, looking distressed. "It's *gone*. My self-portrait is *gone*."

"Maybe it just blew into the bushes. Want me to come help you look?" He was already starting up the path.

"It couldn't have blown away," she shouted, sounding miserable—when he reached her side, scanning the tangle of still-leafless laurels and low-growing blueberry bushes around them where Vajra was sniffing.

"Geez, I don't see it anywhere."

"I *just* finished it. Then I closed the sketchbook and put a rock on top of it," she held up a granite chunk the size of a softball, "*—this one—* to weigh it down. The rock and pad were still in the same spot but my portrait is gone."

"Stuff doesn't disappear. How—"

"Someone *took* it. That's how it disappeared." Tears of anger rose in her eyes. "It took me hours to get it right. *Hours*. Glynis said it was excellent work. I'll never be able to do it over." She sounded despairing, and fought to blink back the tears.

Turning, she shouted at the heavily-wooded slopes all around them. *"This isn't a joke, and it's not funny! Whoever took my picture, bring it back. Now."*

Again, there was only the roar of the stream's current plunging over rocks and echoing up from the chasm below.

"Whoever did this," she shouted at the forest again, *"I hate you!"*

Dhani reached out a hand and rested it on her shoulder but she shook it off with a violent shrug. He remembered hearing something moving in the forest when he was climbing up here lost in his own head—a person? Who would have stalked Claire up here?

"I was starting, just *starting* to like this place. Back at Christmas, Sahm made me begin to feel good about being here. Like maybe good things could start to happen for me. But it's. . . it's like everywhere else.

No matter what I do, someone always comes and messes with my life. Everything here is just one more big disappointment."

The words gouged a painful pit in Dhani's stomach.

He trailed behind Claire as she marched down the mountain. "Who would have done this?"

"I know who did it," she growled. "If you think about it, so do you."

"Do you want to do something to get your mind off this." He didn't know what would do that, but maybe he could think of something—like looking for early wildflowers in the meadows with her or. . . something.

"No," she rebuffed him. "I want to be alone."

The look on Claire's face as she entered into the dining room at six o'clock, and seeing her eyes narrow and focus warned Dhani that he should intercept her—but he was too slow.

She charged past the table of savory dinner meats, trays of fresh vegetables and rolls, straight past the first round tables, where the kids in other tribes were talking and laughing.

Ray-Ray seemed to know what was coming, too, and knocked over his chair jumping up to step in.

Stepping up beside Carter, who was sitting by herself, Claire knocked her elbow with one hip—so hard the food fell off Carter's fork.

"Give it back," she demanded, loud, angry.

All conversation stopped.

Carter's face was calm, with a half-smile, and she slowly pushed back from the table. "What is rich girl's problem now? Give what back?"

"Stop playing innocent. You took it and I want it back."

Carter was sipping her water and choked on a laugh. "You're delusional."

"You stole my self-portrait, and you better not have destroyed it. Go get it. *Now.*"

"Someone would have to be desperate to want your skank picture."

"Someone like you. Stalker. *Go. Get it!*" Claire shouted.

Carter threw her head back and laughed. "What are you gonna do if I don't?"

Color flashed up Claire's neck and cheeks. She grabbed the half-gallon pitcher of ice water on Carter's table and sloshed its contents full in her face.

Carter leapt to her feet, dripping, banging her chair over onto the floor, clawing for Claire's shirt—but Claire slapped her hand away and seized Carter by the ponytail, wrenching it in a tight fist.

"*Girl fight!*" Dugan laughed.

Imani and Makayla were yelling. "Stop it!" "Don't do this."

"Dear sweet Jesus!" Emmalyn shouted.

Rocco had jumped up and was crossing the room to intervene.

Claire swung Carter's head down toward the edge of the table, but Carter pulled away, stood and started to lunge at her.

A roar from the doorway—"STOP THIS NONSENSE!"—brought every movement to a halt.

Ivy, Kate's cook, stomped across the room and shoved Claire and Carter apart. "Ms. Holman brings you here to teach you how to behave in life—and *this* is how you act?"

Claire and Carter spoke over each other. "She stole—" "She's a freak—"

Ivy shouted over them. "*I don't care!*"

Then she regained her calm. "You're in *my* dining room. You behave. That's the rule."

Claire started to object.

"*Don't care,*" Ivy repeated. "Now something's wrong between you two. I get that. After you clean up this water—," she reached for a stack of napkins and stuffed them into both girls' hands "—you can go talk it out with Ms. Holman and Tom Baden."

"So, you didn't actually *see* Carter take your picture?" Kate said.

Claire gritted her teeth and forced the words out. "No. I didn't see her do it."

Carter had the wounded look of a martyr.

"Did anyone else see her? Or hear her say she did it?"

"No."

"Well, if no one witnessed—"

Tom held up his hand and intervened. "But there's a reason why you think she did."

Claire felt a small relief that someone was willing to listen at least. "Yes."

She glared at Carter, who now stared at the floor to shield a faint smile. "She's been harassing me all year. Following me. Teasing me. Calling me 'rich girl', which I hate, even though I've told her a million times to stop."

She was looking at Kate's and Tom's faces, and knew she didn't have what they were asking for—hard evidence—but pushed ahead anyway. "I—I can't think of anyone else who would take it. She's the only one here who just wants to taunt me and make me angry."

Carter looked up suddenly at Kate and Tom. She looked remorseful. "I did pick on her. It's true."

Then she turned to Claire and said, her voice tinged with remorse, "I'm sorry. I'll stop. But I didn't take your artwork. I wouldn't do that. I hope you find it."

With all eyes on her, Claire felt suddenly off-balance and like an idiot. And outplayed. She wished she had reported Carter the day last year up at Thunder Falls, when Carter had grabbed and flaunted her drawings and performed a dramatic plunge off the cliff to scare her. She said nothing now, though, and stared hard into Carter's face and ice-blue eyes, challenging her innocent expression, willing it to collapse into an admission of guilt.

A quick glance at Tom told Claire that maybe he was trying to read Carter, too. He seemed to be looking, as she was, for the tiniest sign—the flicker of an eye, the twinge of a grin—to signal that this girl was lying.

Carter's look of sincere innocence remained firmly in place.

I know you're lying, Claire shouted silently, willing Carter to read her thoughts.

"I want you two to meet with Bay, tomorrow," said Kate, "and work out your differences.

"Resolving conflict without physical confrontation is one of the skills you're here to learn. And so, in that sense, I'm glad whatever it is you don't like about each other came to a head today. Now you can use the conflict resolution skills the Troverts have been teaching to resolve it."

Claire was looking past Kate as she spoke, at Tom—who gave her a quick wink and a look that seemed to say, *Let's talk later.*

"I don't know if Carter did this or not," said Tom, "but I want to say I'm very sorry that your picture is gone. It's a big loss, I know. And if it were mine, I'd be very upset and angry, as well."

"Is that why you wanted to talk to me," Claire asked, "—just to say how very sorry you are? I've heard that all my life."

He smiled at her directness.

"No. And what I have to say won't bring back you're lost picture—though if Carter did take it, I hope she now has the good sense to give it back."

"So you think she might have—"

He held up a hand. "I said I don't know. I can't tell about her. She's very mechanical emotionally, which seems to go along with her sharp, mathematical mind, and that makes her tricky to read. Here's what I want to say.

"Glynis Candor has high praise for your exceptional artistic talent. Kate is thinking of setting up a small studio to help you develop your skills."

She felt a small sense of uplift, until he finished his thought.

"—but the prosecutor back in Virginia is pulling some legal nonsense to force you back there to give testimony. Not a great time to break this news to you, but we learned today that he's pushing to set the date for some time next month."

"What does that have to do with getting a studio here?"

"He may maneuver to keep you back there. Kate is going to hold off on the studio till we know the outcome. However, before you let that get you down—"

Too late. Once again, the old voice was shouting in her head.

Just when you think things are going to work out. . .

"—you need to know that Judge Sewell is still fighting for you tooth and nail." Tom was trying to sound upbeat.

. . .it all crashes and burns. Every. Time.

11TH

Emmalyn softly closed the office suite door behind her, careful to keep the latch from clicking. It was past noon, Ivy was lugging trays of food from the kitchen to the dining hall, and Kate and Tom had just driven out the camp road to lunch in town.

Just to be sure, she turned the small, brass latch that locked the office door. No one could know she was here.

In a few moments, she found the number in Kate's computer and called it.

"Last month. On our campout. He was calling demon spirits out of the bonfire," Emmalyn blurted, making sure her voice sounded trembly and fearful. "And I think he's teaching about his false gods to that kid who set his mom's boyfriend on fire. How can we be safe if he's teaching Dhani how to pray to. . . to *fire demons*?" She forced a small sob.

"*Thh*-ank you, Ms. Hatfield," Monica Saint replied, tamping the anger in her voice down with thinly disguised professional calm. "I've made a note, and though I'm quite busy I will look into it."

Just get off your fat butt and do it, Emmalyn shouted in her mind and hung up.

Sahm had called her a two-face during the last campout—and it had felt as if, even in the dark of night, he was looking straight into her soul. Had he seen anything? Weird psychics and even sexual predators seemed genuinely able to look inside you, read your mind and motives for their own manipulative purposes.

Whatever. He seemed like he might know too much, and he had to go. The stupid Saint woman with her self-righteous, anti-religious ways just might succeed in keeping Sahm far away from all the students, herself included, and restrict him to shoveling animal shit out of cages in the clinic.

The clock on Kate's computer said *12:29*. One more urgent matter to take care of. Quickly.

Dropping into the seat at Tom's desk, she pulled up on his computer a half-finished office supply order form that was minimized on his desktop. He was always too busy making doctors' and dentists' appointments, and only too happy to have her take over the program's mundane, boring details.

Scanning the products on the screen, she found what was needed, added to his order twelve of one thing and six of another. . . and hit *Send.*

Time to slip back into the stream of the day. If she was too late for lunch, someone like the stupid Troverts would question where she had been.

12TH

In the dark of night, someone heavy landed on Jalil's chest, pinning him under the bedcovers. At the same moment, duct tape was slapped over his eyes, pulling and pinching the hair of his eyebrows. He tried to shout, but something—a sock?—went into his mouth and another strip of duct tape stretched over his lips, holding it in place, pinching the skin of his face.

Strong arms and hands seized him—three sets, around his chest and legs—and hauled him out of bed.

He tried to struggle as they wrestled him to the floor, but was no match. He heard the zip of more duct tape being pulled from a roll, and felt them wrapping it fast around him, starting with his ankles, painfully tearing out leg hair as they wound it up around his calves and thighs. The binding continued around his wrists, which were pinned to his sides, and up around his chest, until he was practically mummified.

Outside, the night air was cold, and because he had on only jockey shorts it raised gooseflesh on his whole body. From the jostling and bumping, he could tell they were carrying him down the dirt road and out past the greenhouse and storage barns.

Rocco, for sure, he thought. He had forgotten to lock his bedroom door and this was payback for the prank. But who else? *Dugan and Garrett*, most likely.

In minutes, the sound of their footsteps changed from scuffing over dirt and gravel to swishing through deep grass then crunching through old leaves. Dropping his feet to the ground among scratchy brush, they shoved him roughly against a tree, the bark scraping between his shoulder blades. His bare feet stung with the cold.

There was the sound of more tape being ripped from a roll, and two straps of it—one at his chest, one at his knees—bound him to the rough trunk.

His skin was starting to tingle and burn in the icy night air. When they had gone to bed the temperature was hovering just above freezing.

Someone slipped the slim handle of a pocketknife into his right hand. Of course they weren't leaving him to freeze to death, just suffer.

Then footsteps receded back through the night.

He was alone.

Swearing to himself, he struggled against his bonds, the tape pulling and pinching his skin more. He vowed some kind of revenge. At the moment, though, he was chilling rapidly, starting to shiver. His feet and fingers were burning.

He had to work quickly to peel off all this tape. *Which is going to hurt like a mother. . . .*

The pocketknife in his hand was closed. Turning it carefully in cold fingers, he tried to grip the handle with his clenched palm, pinch the blade between his thumb and forefinger and ease it open without slicing a finger or dropping it.

Four times he tried, but the blade kept closing—and on the fifth try the knife slipped out of his hand, bounced off his right ankle bone, and landed in the leaves beside his foot.

Inside his head he raged, and he began to writhe against the loops of tape that bound him tightly to the tree.

A sound caught his attention—the sound of someone walking up through the woods.

He heard Sahm say, "So this is why I was awakened from a deep sleep."

"Yeah, this was pretty bad, I guess, but it was a just a prank," Jalil grimaced, peeling off the last of the tape by the beam of Sahm's flashlight. Hair had torn out of his legs and forearms, and his skin was raw all over. "Who woke you up, though, and sent you out here?"

Sahm ignored that.

"This was very cruel. And dangerous. If I had not come, you might have frozen."

"I'm not going to report this to anyone. Don't you tell anyone either. Okay?"

Sahm, who had given his coat to Jalil to warm him, stared, confused. "If you don't tell Kate or Tom, then what will you do about this?"

"I don't know. I'll come up with something. Know any good Tibetan pranks."

"I don't understand this—*pranks*."

"When you were a kid, did you ever pull stuff on other kids? Like put vinegar in someone's drinking glass and tell them it was water? Or, I don't know, dress up in a yak skin like the abominable snowman and scare someone so they peed their pants?"

"No."

"You never tricked *anyone*?"

"No.—Wait. Yes. There was one time."

"What did you do?"

Sahm looked sheepish.

Slipping inside the cabin door, Jalil listened carefully. No one was awake to jump him again.

In bed, he smiled to himself, thinking of what Sahm had confessed with such innocent remorse.

"You never got to be a normal kid, did you?" he had challenged Sahm on the walk back here. "You should let me help you see what it's like."

Now, Jalil thought, if Sahm could find what they needed in town he would get sweet revenge—and Rocco, Dugan and Garrett would not even know he was involved.

18TH

Sahm knelt beside his altar and blew out a short, noisy blast of breath between his teeth, once again feeling mildly annoyed. What had happened to the new being he sensed himself to be after the ritual in the medicine lodge?

Dhani had come last evening, with his usual fretting about Claire, Claire, Claire. The complaint—"I like her, but she doesn't like me the same way"—was so lodged in the boy's heart-mind.

Touching a lit match to small, dried juniper twigs and purple berries on the altar, Sahm bent down and touched his forehead to the pine floorboards. His lips began to move in a silent chant, and the tendril of smoke rose.

Focusing on his breath, he slipped easily out into the open expanse of his consciousness. . . .

. . . and there was his body kneeling on the cabin floor, there was his own face—topped by a headful of hair that was standing up in places after his night's sleep like tufts of wind-torn grass.

His grandfather's voice flew up at him from the depths of memory. . . .

"There are more important things to concern yourself with than the young women down in the villages," his grandfather had scolded him.

"But you had a wife, grandfather," he teased the old man. "Surely, she did not climb up this mountain to your meditation cave, lugging a dowry on her back, and beg you to marry her. Or perhaps she did. Were you shy?"

The old man swept that aside with a reproachful grin and a wave of one hand. "If you are not pining for a girl, then why do you always stare, stare, stare far away from here down into the valleys?"

"Not into *the valleys.* Beyond *them. I wonder about the wider world. I wish to see it."*

"You have a restless spirit, Sahmdup. You believe that being somewhere else, anywhere else, will satisfy your craving. And so your mind roams. That is why I will call you Cetan—because your mind flies far away like the hawk or eagle, who goes in greater and greater circles, always hunting for something else to try to satisfy its hunger."

Sahm had smiled and liked the nickname. And kept looking at the small line of blue horizon visible between the huge V formed by two mountain slopes.

"You need to concentrate on the skills I am trying to teach you." His grandfather had been adamant. "These are very old and fine arts. Difficult to master. Few are left who know them, and you will need them one day. Sahmdup," he said sharply, "listen to me.

"No matter how free you believe you are, the world will keep trying to trap you in its illusion—calling to you with its beauty and promise of adventure. These things offer you temporary satisfaction but they are a trap because they do not ultimately feed and satisfy the spirit. If you chase after them they will keep you seeking and grasping for more outwardly beautiful places and greater adventures your whole life. You will be like the people who are the big-bellied, hungry ghosts—restless, unsatisfied creatures, whose appetite for things is so great they must keep eating but they are never able to satisfy their hunger. Because the things they crave are not the thing that will make them satisfied."

His eyes came open, and he stared out the cabin window at the lake.

As it so happened—or did anything truly happen just by chance?—a redtail hawk was circling out over the lake, which was finally freed from the grip of ice. The hawk was peering down into the waters, watching and waiting for a fish to rise for its breakfast, to make its flesh his morning meal.

To satisfy the body's hunger was a good thing, of course.

But when your inner cravings attach you to outward things too much, you will never be fully satisfied, he thought. *Attachment to outer things is what prevents you from finding your way on the soul's journey to ultimate bliss.*

He understood that part of his grandfather's lesson immediately.

"If you are not careful," his grandfather had warned, "attachment to the world of objects obscures the path completely, until it is forgotten."

He thought of Dhani, so preoccupied with Claire. He himself had always been preoccupied, not with girls primarily, but with an impatient and restless hunger to go out into the world beyond the Himalayas, beyond Tibet. He had been less-than-half-attentive to his lessons in the *Elemental* arts. Yes, there had been the real chance of being kidnapped, since it had become widely known he was training to be a spiritual leader. But that had only been one reason for fleeing Tibet, and not the most driving one.

A realization rang like a bell in clear air.

He is caught up, not only in his fears but in his attachments and desires—just as I *was.* Him, to a girl. Me, to my desire to see the world.

On the heels of that understanding, something else came to mind—the revealing of something far greater than what mere words could ever transfer.

"Look at me, Cetan," his grandfather had said, with a gentleness far more compelling than a command.

His grandfather's whole being illuminated—shining with the radiance of pure bliss.

"One day you will forget much of what I told you. My words will not matter as much as what I show you now. Look closely, Sahmdup. Look into my face."

It was his grandfather's eyes that drew him in, and it was as if a current of joyful wind lifted him into the wide open space of the old man's soul.

At once, a great force struck him—the fierce and tender heat of love and compassion. It rushed from his grandfather's spirit into his own, engulfing him fully, filling every muscle, bone, and cell.

"Remember what I am giving you now, Sahmdup."

Outside, the hungry, circling hawk was gone. He had not fully understood why his grandfather had made him look deeply into his soul that day. He had turned outward to find his satisfaction in the world.

But the vibrant, bright-flowing force he had felt on that day had returned. In fact, it had lain dormant within him until now.

As he stared out at the lake, a presence filled the room. Filled him.

"You have concerned yourself with how you would train the young man, whose mind and spirit wander," Dzes-Sa spoke into his mind. *"And now you have finally arrived at the true starting place."*

What he felt was a deep, infinite ocean of *compassion*, in which Dhani was now lifted and carried within him.

Without it, he mused, *how can a person succeed in truly helping someone else?*

23RD

The white light of a full moon shone through the midnight forest, casting the black, twisted lines of trunks and branches in a web of shadows over the entrance gate. The sound of the truck engine receded, and they headed back up the camp road.

In a few steps, the thick trunks and branches of the northern forest closed over and around them, forming a dark tunnel.

"'Sup, dude?" Garrett called in a horse whisper after Dugan, who was double-timing it ahead of him. "You gotta walk quieter."

The temperature had dropped below freezing, and Dugan's footfalls in the frozen remnants of last year's leaves crunched like boots on gravel.

"You gotta keep it down," Garrett hissed again. "I know we're two miles out, but you make noise like a... like a...."

Dugan wheeled in his tracks. "Like a *what*? First you tell me hurry up we're gonna be late. Now you tell me be quiet I'm walkin' too loud. Last time we met your connection, you told me to keep quiet I don't know how to negotiate as good as you. And tonight—*tonight,* after all the drop-offs, you tell me, by the way, my take is not gonna be thirty percent it's gonna be fifteen. *Fifteen.* That's a joke."

"Hey, I gotta give the supplier a bigger cut because they're bringing better product and the customers don't have the kinda money we hoped for."

"Right, and what's *your* percentage? It stays the same while mine gets reduced. But I'm still sharing in the risk, making the deliveries to these backward-ass dudes livin' in those remote little shacks way back in the woods. It's like *Deliverance* out there. One of these nights, some Aryan Nations guy's gonna cut my throat."

"Let me spell it out for you again, son—"

"'*Son*'.... You just called me *son*? I told you never do that. Anyone ever tell you what a dumbass you really are?"

"You. A couple times now. Don't ever say it again."

"That one dude who bought from us tonight, he's gotta have a lot of money. This was his second big purchase in two months."

"Someone broke into his cabin and stole the first item we delivered."

"Sounds like b.s. to me."

"Now you're calling me a liar," Garrett's voice rose. "To my face.

When *I* cut you in on a great little business. You're becoming a whiny little baby."

"I'm gone, man. Just when *I* had a nice big order coming in for us."

"An order of what? What're you smuggling in?"

"Never mind. Your loss." Dugan pivoted and walked rapidly up the dark road, quickly becoming a fading shadow in the night. Then he was gone from sight.

Garrett stood and called after him. "The supplier is mine. You got no connections."

Dugan's voice was receding in the darkness when he shouted back. *"I'm tired of you thinking you gotta 'train' me, like I'm your little kid or something."*

"What the hell are you talking about?" Garrett shouted back, angry and ignoring the fact that their voices were carrying in the cold, quiet night air.

When there was no reply, he called out again. *"Hey—watch out for the* crazed slasher *up ahead. You know how it works in the movies. Two guys fight, one guy goes away all mad and gets gutted like a deer."*

"I want my money—all of it," Dugan called back, his voice growing fainter in the distant darkness.

He musta really beat feet, Garrett thought, moving carefully and quietly up the pitch-dark camp road.

For a few minutes, sporadically, he heard Dugan's tromping footsteps way up ahead of him. Then, except for an occasional owl-call or the low whistle of moving air through branches—silence.

Now, ten minutes in from the town road, the whole forest crowded closer and thick stands of evergreens pressed in all around, preventing any of the dim moonlight from penetrating under the trees and helping him on his way. The road and river ran close to each other here and the sound of rushing water filled the night air, so he could not hear anything else—no nightbird calls or even his own footsteps.

Garrett was alone now in a wilderness night, cold drafts of air carrying the scent of fresh river water and forest loam. It excited him—the risk of what he was doing, the cleverness and stealth it took to pull it all off—and despite his beef with Dugan he felt in a self-congratulatory mood.

Avoiding detection was the most tricky part, but he prided himself on acing that, too.

He slowed his pace even more now, looking up so that he could follow the twisting line of deep- gray night sky above the dark chasm of trees through which he cautiously wound his way. He went slowly, counting the turns, not needing or wanting to use his small pocket flashlight. He had memorized the road's turns and curves, because they told him how far he had to go to reach the bridge across the river by Grady's cottage, and tonight he was grateful that the groundskeeper and his crew kept the road free of ruts. Maybe he would replace the Jackie D. he had swiped from Grady.

In a few minutes, he was at the curve where there was a turnaround place. Grady's crew stopped here, halfway along the road, to take breaks and smoke a butt.

Idiot, he thought, preoccupied with Dugan's stupid little mutiny—only momentarily distracted by a faint, acrid scent.

Cigarette butts.

It smelled like someone had stubbed one out not long ago. A really cheap nasty one. But the road had been re-graded a week before and it hadn't snowed, so no one had plowed.

That confused him. Who came all the way out here to smoke?

A draft of mountain air washed the smell away and he kept walking, still irritated, focused on how to hook Dugan back into the work and be satisfied with a lower cut.

Promise to up his percentage on the next *product. Control transactions with the customers so he doesn't know the actual selling price. Tell him it's way less than it really is. That way he'll think his cut is fair.*

After all his bragging about cutting and messing up people, Dugan could shut up and do the dangerous part of this job. That's why he had been cut in at all. No way in hell was Garrett going to creep out secluded dirt roads to isolated cabins that were no better than shacks.

Tell him he's actually getting more *because he does the drop-offs—and that he needs to do them because if anything goes down he's way stronger and a better fighter.*

Pure genius, Garrett congratulated himself.

He was passing the trailhead that led out to the flow lands on his left. One more turn in the road and he would be at the bridge. He would slip quietly past Grady's cottage and then Kate's lodge, and be in his warm bed in ten more minutes.

A sudden blast of bright light stabbed his eyes, catching him off guard. He jumped and almost shouted in surprise.

"*Who's there?*" he horse-whispered. Holding up one arm, he shielded his eyes and squinted into the light, dazzled and unable to see. "Grady?—I was just out for a walk because I couldn't sleep."

From the pitch darkness behind the bright beam of light, someone laughed—a half-growl that erupted roughly and subsided. The man—because it was a man's voice—sounded older, in his fifties or sixties.

"What kinda hot goods you been sellin' tonight, boy?"

This was no voice he knew, and Garrett froze, the pulse instantly pounding in his neck.

"Stop shining that stupid light in my face," he replied, trying to keep the fear from his voice and take command of the situation. His eyes were adjusting again, but the figure remained hidden behind the beam.

"Shut up, you little idiot. You do what *I* tell *you*."

The man stepped closer, keeping the beam on Garrett's face, continuing to blind him. He was huge and smelled like woodsmoke and pungent, unwashed body.

"Don't hurt me. Please." Squinting, Garrett's eyes burned now.

Again, the chuckle. "I ain't gonna hurt you. But you're gonna do exactly what I tell you or I'll make a phone call. What you're doing, they'll try you as an adult and a bunch of guys in a cell block will have some fun with you."

Garrett started to sweat, his breathing rapid and shallow.

"Or," the guy was having fun now, "I'll just grab you one dark night and sell you for cigarettes to a guy who will hurt you way more than you can even imagine. You'll be here one minute. M.I.A. the next."

Maybe the guy was lying. Just trying scare tactics. Mind racing, Garrett impulsively tried to make a move—to run—and lunged.

A fist shot out of the dark and hit him hard in the middle of his sternum, knocking him off-balance and snapping his head back.

"You try to run again and I'll drop you in your tracks. Can't outrun a buck knife."

A hand reached out into the beam, flashing the blade.

"What are you going to do to me?" Garrett choked. His chest and neck hurt and inside his shirt sweat ran down his ribs.

"Nothing, unless you fail to follow my exact orders. And I'm gonna tell you this first, boy, in case you're thinking of *not* obeying me. I know what cabin you're in and what room is yours. I know when you get up and when you go sleep and when you take a piss and how you wipe yourself. I know you have a blue toothbrush and that you wrote 'Carter' in the steam on your bathroom mirror last week."

Garrett felt a shock blow through his body.

"I know every move you make," the man was ranting now, his guttural voice like gravel grinding, "every night you and your buddy think you're sneaking up and down this road. I know the license plate number of that nice, new diesel pickup that drives you into town and back. *And. . . .*"

He paused, as if to let the situation sink into Garrett's reeling, pounding head—and Garrett remembered the stinking, cheap cigarette butt, realizing he had been watched from the darkness when he'd passed up and down this road. Realizing, too, this man had stalked and spied on him even when he shaved and took a shower, and his stomach flipped at the mental image of him creeping down the cabin's hallway into his bedroom some black night, forcing a sack over his head and dragging him away to some horrible fate. Chills of terror shot up his back.

"*And*. . .I overhear your little, *quiet* conversations with your friend. I know what you're buying and selling, and first thing I want is one of those."

"I can't do this deal unless you've got the cash—"

The man swore violently and he shuffled his boots as if highly agitated. "I don't deal in cash, you stupid little shit. I deal in *safety*. I will allow you to pass through these woods at night and do your dealings, and you will get me everything I need. Now—I'm gonna tell you what that is, and you're gonna bring it all and leave it where I tell you. Listen very closely, 'cause I ain't tellin' you twice."

A list spilled out fast, and Garrett tried to focus through the terrified pounding in his head, trying not to miss an item—starting with dried survival foods, big square six-volt batteries, small canisters of propane for a cookstove. . . .

"You got all that?" the man demanded, when he finished his instructions. "And do you know the spot I mean—that stand of aspens I'm talkin' about up beyond the waterfall?"

"Yeah," Garrett rasped, his throat and lips dry.

The man swore again. "It's yes, *sir*."

"Yes, sir."

The agitation eased from the man's voice. "You're gonna be a good mule."

Garrett forced his voice not to shake. "I'm—I'm going into town again in two weeks. I'll get you what you asked for."

"You'll go in one week and you won't take your friend. He'll ask questions about the stuff you bring back here. And you'll never tell him about this. About me."

Garrett tried to sound confident, and not as if his stomach was churning and he wanted to vomit. "He only needs to know what I want him to know."

"You're an arrogant little jerk. Just don't ever pull that attitude with me."

Garrett stood shaking before the bathroom mirror, steadying himself by holding onto the sink and staring at the linen closet reflected from behind him. The door was ajar, its opening a thin black line. . . . Inside, when he whipped it open, his face hot with fear, there was just enough room for a man to stand between the door and the shelves and peep out through the crack.

He swallowed to keep down the bile burning up into his throat. Had the crazed guy from the darkness ever hidden in here, watching him? Every inch of his skin tingled at the thought and he almost threw up.

Covers pulled tight around him, he lay awake a long time, controlling his breathing, tempted to look up over at the window, forcing himself not to look. For an hour, he fought to keep from imagining the face of a crazy wild man who had watched him—how many nights?—from out in the deep, all-surrounding darkness.

Then—relieved, feeling back in control and pleased with himself—a plan came.

28TH

"I heard your environmental police brought in a sick cougar," said Steve, standing at the door of the operating area, sounding as if he were here but not here.

"I was hoping to get a last look before you send her body away. She was a beautiful creature and I—I have a habit of overlooking beautiful creatures."

Before the revelation about Steve's terrible tragedy, Jo would have practically lunged at him for slopping the term "environmental police" on good people. Men and women who worked hard for not much pay to protect the wilderness and its creatures.

This morning, she looked past Steve's harsh, judgmental, superior-sounding exterior—because she was now seeing *inside* him, seeing the truth about his soul for the first time. And there she saw what she had seen in every severely wounded animal that was brought to her, baring fangs and claws, growling, biting—and that was a badly hurt creature, lashing out in terrible pain, fear, and anger. If she could grant an animal that kind of compassion, then surely. . . .

"I want to apologize for how badly I misjudged you," she replied.

He looked at her, eyebrows raised, questioning.

"I am so sorry about what happened to your wife. It's so, so terrible, and even worse that you witnessed it."

His lip curled in anger and he started to say something—then didn't and stared at the floor. "I guess it doesn't matter who told you."

"Steve, I—I'm an idiot. I read you wrong from the beginning and I've had a terrible attitude toward you all year. I dismissed you and I've been unbearably rude. I'm an ass."

He was silent for a long time. "I thought I'd get a new start here, but I just brought with me the one thing I can't get away from. Myself."

"I suspect your*self* is not so bad."

"Not true." He found himself letting go, wanting to let out truths that stung as he said them out loud.

"I'm the reason Olivia and I weren't together that morning. I said terrible, destructive things to my own wife, who I said I loved. And I wasn't there when someone went for her purse and unloaded his gun into her chest. If I wasn't such a bastard, I would have been there to stop it, or it wouldn't have happened at all. But. . . ." He stopped, unable to get out the last words.

Jo's hands were trembling and tears had risen. She blinked them back. Without thinking, she stepped close to Steve and put her arms around him, holding him in a long embrace. She could feel him breathing, but his body remained rigid. He did not lift his arms to embrace her.

Stepping back, she wiped her eyes with the back of one hand. "I don't know what else to say, except I'm really sorry for all of it—for what happened to her and to you and how I've acted."

"Would it have made a difference if you'd known?"

"Of course it would have. I would have seen through that shield you put up to keep everyone out. I would have understood your harshness."

"You think I'm harsh?"

"You can be, yes. Listen, it's not a criticism or an attack. I said I understand it now and I didn't before. So I was defensive and threw some verbal punches. One of them, I—." Her face flushed with embarrassment.

He waited.

"One of them I don't know how to forgive myself for."

He eased the moment, to her surprise, with a faint smile. "I wouldn't call them punches. More like kicks to the groin. Which one are you thinking of?"

"One time when I was mad at you, I said, 'No wonder there's no Mrs. Tanner.' That haunts me and I feel sick that I said it."

"Oh, I've said one or two things that will haunt me forever. Regret is a terrible thing, especially when there's no chance of taking back what you said."

"I guess we can only learn from the past and go forward from where we are."

He stuck out his hand. "Truce."

She reached out and took it. "I wish there'd never been a war."

Jo let Steve have a last look, then zipped the black plastic bag back over the cougar's head and slid the trolley it lay on into the walk-in cooler.

"She was a truly beautiful animal. Sorry you lost her," Steve said.

This time he reached out, and placed one hand on Jo's forearm.

She laid a hand on top of his. "Thanks. I'll send her downstate for a full autopsy."

He slipped his fingers out from under hers.

"Do you—want to go into town for lunch?" Jo offered.

"I need to head back out to the island. I forgot to feed Pal this morning. Can't leave the poor guy out there alone and hungry."

"Right," she responded. "Maybe another time."

She watched him out her office window as he retreated along the lake path. She still felt, if not the full depth of his anguish at least a small taste of it. His remorse was massive, for things far greater than a few insults. Anyone in that depth of pain deserved compassion.

She wished she knew how to show that, without letting attraction get tangled up in simple kindness.

He neared the bridge to the island, feeling a little relief. Someone knew about his past and didn't hold his massive failures against him. But he also found himself fighting to keep a mess of complicating emotions from flooding in.

With each footstep, he pressed them down, down—out of his head, out of the range of feeling. Jo had to remain at a distance.

Rocco, Dugan and Garrett were seated around the noontime fire, eating mounds of steaming, pellet-like noodles from paper bowls, all three shoveling hungrily. The short, vigorous day hike had brought them to a lower ridge of Eagle Rock Mountain overlooking the lake.

"What are you eating?" asked Jalil.

"I guess Tanner musta put these in our day packs. You just dump in boiling water. Doesn't taste anything like ramen, though."

"Kinda weird tasting," said Garrett. He picked up the discarded label. "The writing looks Chinese."

Dugan held up a spoonful of the brown pellets. "I hope he's not trying to get us used to this garbage for the survival week next month." He looked around. "How come no one else got these bowls? Everyone's eating stuff from pouches."

Sahm had followed on Jalil's heels, and he eyed Dugan's spoon. "This looks very familiar. May I see the package?"

Garrett handed him the wrapper and Sahm studied it, then frowned and shook his head.

"I thought so. Tanner is really making it rough on you. It seems he is training you to eat anything in order to survive. Probably because you three are stronger and braver than all the others. He knows you can take it."

Rocco scooped a spoonful into his mouth. "What do you mean?"

"He gave you a very interesting dish. One I must admit I would never eat."

Garrett and Dugan stopped shoveling.

"What is this?"

"What's the label say?"

"It's written in Chawan dialect and says this is *ngiao chu sia*. You must understand that with over one billion people in China, they waste nothing. Everything possible is used for food."

"So, what *is* this?"

"*Ngaio chu sia* means rat dung."

"*What?*" Garrett dropped his spoon into the bowl.

Rocco spat the chewed, brown glob from his mouth and swore. "*You gotta be kidding me?*"

Dugan flung his bowl into the bushes.

Rocco doubled over, retching, and Garrett grabbed his water bottle to gargle and spit over and over. Dugan leapt up, clutching his stomach, looking gray. "Imma go stick my fingers down my throat."

"I'd rather die than survive on rat crap," Rocco panted, when he was done heaving.

Sahm said calmly, "Not if you are really starving. Maybe during your survival week you'll develop a taste for it."

"Thanks for helping me get my paybacks," Jalil laughed, "and they don't even know I was involved."

"I am not sure it was the right thing. It may have incurred unfavorable *karma*. But they treated you unjustly and the act is done."

"I can't believe Ivy found that stuff for you at the Asian grocer in town."

"It is a very common dish."

"So. . . that stuff isn't really made of rat dung, is it?"

"Of course not. In the East, we are not dogs. Rat dung is just what it looks like, which is why I do not eat it. I cannot get the thought out of my mind. It is made of brown rice."

"So," Jalil smiled at him, "you pulled your little *prank* for a second time. Whaddaya think?"

"It was very mean." Sahm's look was sober, but then he broke into a wide grin. "And also very funny." He crossed his eyes and hung his tongue out of his mouth like he was gagging.

Jalil laughed and stuck out his fist, but Sahm only stared at it.

"No one taught you about fist bumping yet?" said Jalil, shaking his head. "Man, there's a lot I can teach you."

6

May

4th

"Mom? How are you?"

"How'd you get this number? My boss won't be happy you're calling me at work."

Dhani tensed. "Mom, you never call me. It's been like, more than a year."

He was glad he had found her—and also glad that, months ago, Sahm had helped him gain a little distance from her.

"You're supposed to be in that program up in the Catskills. How'd you get this number?"

Judge Sewell had passed on information to Kate. His mother had appeared in court for a D.W.I., and on her court forms were an address and this phone number.

"I'm in the Adirondack Mountains, mom, not the Catskills. You got a *D.W.I.*? That's your second one."

She swore. "Why did they tell you that?"

"Mom, I miss you. We've got finals and then a big campout kinda trip. Then we've got a break. I could come back to DC and see you."

The phone was silent.

"Dhani, that's a bad idea. He's still looking for me. For us. Also, I haven't got a place yet and I'm working terrible hours to pay my bills."

"What bills, if you haven't got a place?"

"Dhani, it's so tight for me right now." She sounded as if she were going to cry. "I—this isn't right, I know—I had to use the money in your savings account to pay for court and some other things. Don't be mad at me."

He felt confused. "I'm not mad. I don't care about the money."

"Okay, good."

"I just want to see you when this first year is over and we have a short break."

"Bad idea, baby. Please, just stay there. We'll see each other when things are good again."

"When's that gonna be? I *miss* you."

"I know you do." Her voice was softer, and she sounded on the edge of tears. "You have no idea how much I miss you. You're my hero."

Far from making him feel better, that stuck a knife in his heart. Maybe that was why the program rule was minimal contact. It seemed like parents had a way of crushing you without even knowing it.

"I gotta go," she sniffed. "I got three tables waiting to order now, and I can't lose *this* job. The last guy accused me of stuff I didn't do."

"Mom—"

"Bye, baby. You're my hero. Remember our agreement. Be good. Don't do anything bad. And don't call this number again, though. Love you. I'll write."

"Do you even have the address?"

She was gone.

In the past, he would have been totally wrecked. Now he felt—that the little bit of distance Sahm had helped him get from her might be a good thing. He was only a little wrecked.

8th

"Maybe they won't let me come back here," Claire stated. Her voice was flat, uncaring.

Dhani was carrying a dead squirrel from the freezer to feed the eagle, and his hand fell limp at his side. "Don't say that."

"A sheriff's deputy came to deliver a subpoena this morning. So it's official. I have to go back to DC."

"But you'll try to come back, right?"

She talked to the air, ignoring him.

"First my parents ruin my childhood. Then I come here and my best piece of artwork gets stolen by psycho-girl Carter, who gets away with it. Then my hideous parents' problems come back to wreck my life. *Again*. Tom said I should pack all my things in case they force me to stay in DC. Which means I'll be back in juvenile detention or foster care."

She looked miserable.

The squirrel was freezing Dhani's fingers. "I'm sorry."

"Don't be," she said, finally focusing on him. Her expression changed, and she looked cold and distant again. "I don't even care."

Dhani felt a pain in his chest, stomach and jaw. Old images and words tumbled through his head.

"Would you like that—if mommy left? Would you be happy if I just went away?"

How many times had he been tortured with that threat?

"You don't *want* to come back?" His throat was dry, and he tried not to sound pierced by the sudden, sharp loneliness he felt. "When are you leaving?"

She turned away, dumping seed in the birds' feeders, much of it falling carelessly on the floor. "In two weeks," she said. "Right before the solo survival trip. So at least I'll miss *that* pure hell."

"You sounded like you wanted to go. You said you were taking your sketchbook so you could draw the whole time."

Her voice was full of anger and misery. "I'm never going to draw again. I hate drawing."

12TH

Sahm stepped into the office suite and immediately read the look on Kate's and Tom's faces.

"Something is wrong."

Tom gestured to the sofa beside the fireplace, in which a small log spit tiny drops of hissing moisture as it burned. "You should sit down."

"This won't be easy for either of us, Sahm," said Kate, following him to the sofa.

Within his bones, Sahm had a sense of what was coming—a wordless forewarning. But he was not at all prepared for the message Kate delivered.

"I'll be brief and direct," she said, her eyes kind and a little sad. "We've had a call from Judge Sewell, the man who has to monitor and approve just about everything that goes on here. He's had a complaint—a serious complaint—from a woman named Monica Saint. She has a very strong voice in what happens to the young people who Judge Sewell approved to come here."

Sahm stared at the fire, listening, half to Kate, half to other voices.

"They do not understand our ways," the *Elementals* said to him, speaking in his mind from within the leaping flames. They had become more present since his last encounter with them.

"They have moved so far from the nature of things, they are now afraid. Always afraid."

"I have to ask you to stay away from Dhani," Kate said. "No one thinks you've done anything inappropriate."

Sahm looked across the sofa at her blankly.

"No one thinks you've—," Kate fumbled for words, "—put your hands on him in ways that are bad. You haven't touched his body."

"That is so. I would never do that."

"But this woman Monica Saint somehow has the idea that you're teaching Dhani to worship gods or demons, and she's in a fury over it. She doesn't like religions of any kind."

"Bön is not a religion. It is—"

"It doesn't matter what it is," Tom interrupted, rescuing Kate. "This woman does not want anyone teaching the students anything of a spiritual nature. She doesn't believe in such things. She thinks there is no God and thinks it poisons people's minds to teach anything but scientific facts. She can cause a lot of trouble for Kate and this program. So we need to do what she demands—which is to insist you stay away from Dhani."

Seeing Sahm's pained expression, Kate rushed on to deliver the rest.

"I know this is drastic, but I've told Steve and Randy that you are not going on the survival campout. I think Monica Saint is out of her mind, but according to Sewell she's known to be nasty and like an old dog with a bone. She won't let this go if she doesn't get her way. So, I want to report back *honestly* that we've cut all contact between you and all the students. The program's future is a bit at stake here, Sahm. We don't want some bureaucrat stepping in and telling us in detail how to run things—or deciding we can't have the program at all. She has that kind of power."

"For now," Tom finished, "stay away from all the students—especially Dhani. No contact at all, while we try to work this out. And we will."

Sahm was thinking of Dhani. What a critical point he was at—so close to realizing who he really was, how important he was, and the powers that could be directed through him.

"Peace, peace," the *Elemental* voices in the fire said to Sahm. *"It must be this way."*

This, he did not understand, but the assurance made the pain of unhappiness in his chest ease a little.

"...and Sewell thinks that if we comply with this directive from her," Kate was saying, "she'll be satisfied that her authority and power were recognized. And maybe she'll go away. He says she's not a bad person, but a vicious fighter when her will is challenged."

Sahm nodded, and stood.

"I will honor you *and* your request, Kate." He placed his hands together before his chest and bowed his head slightly. "I will do exactly as you ask, and stay away completely from the boy."

And you, he said to the *Elementals,* as he trudged back to his cabin, *must show me what to do now, if I cannot train the boy directly. He is the reason I was guided here, and he is coming to the beginning of his life's true course. We can continue to open his mind and being for the benefit of the whole Earth... or we can lose him now.*

"As we almost lost you—but did not?"

The words stung—and also reassured him that Dhani was encompassed by greater powers.

15TH

Garrett knelt beside the bridge, pretending to tie the lace of one running shoe, and stood when he saw Steve jogging past Kate's lodge toward him. He had a plan for pulling Dugan back into the business. He had a plan for handling the wild man in good time. Right now, he would set in motion a plan to use this idiot Marine and his volatile temper.

As Steve approached the bridge, Garrett began jogging, too. "Okay if I run with you, sir?"

Steve nodded, his expression ambivalent, and Garrett fell in-step feeling uncertain. If Tanner was in his usual headspace, with his unpredictable mood, this might not work.

"I've been training hard all year, sir," he began. "Pushups... going out jogging... in the morning."

"Haven't seen you out running."

"I run out past the barns," he adlibbed, amazed and pleased at how easily a lie always came to him when needed.

Steve said nothing and his face was unreadable.

"Good man," Steve replied after a minute. "You want to be in shape for this trip. You've all got a big challenge ahead."

"Yes, sir. I'm doing my best, sir." Garrett pressed ahead, his breathing quickly becoming labored, though he tried to control it. "Thing is, some of these kids aren't getting it." He went for it. "Like that Jones kid."

"Keep your head in your own game."

"Yes, sir. It's just that some of us are trying hard to do this program the right way. Earn our right to be here. I *try* to ignore Jones, even though he makes us all nervous the way he creeps around and everything."

Steve looked over at him and kept running. Garrett hoped he wouldn't notice him struggling to breathe and catch him in his lie about running.

"We never know what's going on in his mind. He hides inside that black hoody. I mean, what if the kid ever got ahold of like, drugs? or a knife?"

Steve had picked up the pace again.

Garrett was starting to suck in air.

"You're keeping an ear open for me, right?" Steve said. "You'll tell me if you pick up anything."

"Yes, sir."

"Good man."

"Thanks. *Oh geez.*" Garrett stopped dead in his tracks. "Sir, I would really like to keep running with you," he called after Steve, who kept going, "but I just remembered something I gotta do for Jo at the barns. I don't wanna let her down."

Steve said over his shoulder. "Go take care of your chores, son. Be eyes and ears for me on the trip."

"Son." Go screw yourself, idiot.

"Thanks, sir," he yelled. "Can't wait for the trip. I'll do my best, sir."

He waited till Steve was out of sight around the next curve, then bent over with his hands on his knees, panting. The genius of his plan made him grin.

Operation Smokescreen is in motion.

The next step would be to set up the decoy. Someone to use as a big distraction. Even if he got caught sneaking into town after this—say, if Dugan didn't go for the new deal and ratted on him—it would seem like a minor infraction compared to what he had in mind for the patsy.

"Tweezers," Jo said to Ron.

He handed them to her, and she carefully lifted a corner of the fish skin, checking to see if the burned raccoon's own skin was growing back.

She looked up and said through her surgical mask, "It's working."

Garrett charged into the clinic, out of breath. "One of the coyote pups is like, eating himself alive."

"Stay back," Jo cautioned, and nodded at the raccoon. "This guy is still susceptible to infection. Tell me what's going on."

"I was playing with one of them—"

"Garrett," Jo interrupted, "I've told you guys a bunch of times, you can't play with the animals."

He ignored her. "Yeah, well, he's scratching like crazy and he's chewing both front paws. They're bleeding. What do we do?"

"*Listen* to my instructions, first of all." She looked at Ron. "I can finish up here. Go take a look."

In a half-hour, Ron returned, shaking his head. "It does look pretty bad. I moved the pup to the outdoor run, to quarantine him and I put the dreaded, plastic cone around his neck. He hates it."

"They always do. I want you to keep an eye on this. Make sure Garrett keeps the run clean of feces and spilled or leftover food. We don't want to attract other wild animals. That can cause more problems."

"It doesn't look like hot spots, and the pup seems kind of skinny. What do you think it could be?"

"I need to see it, but I hope it's not mange. It's possible he ate poisoned mouse or rat."

"Wouldn't the poison have killed him? And where would he have eaten it?"

"He and his litter mate were picked up just outside of Placid, with a few homes and a couple of restaurants nearby. Someone could have been poisoning rodents. When larger animals eat poisoned rodents, it slowly destroys their immune system. That allows the parasitic mites to take over and it results in mange."

"Damn."

"Hopefully it's just something more common. Some kind of canine dermatitis. We can treat that with Cortisone."

"What do you mean hopefully?"

"All I'm saying is there are more serious possibilities. Go get Garrett's daily chart of chores and write at the top—*Do not play with or handle the animals. Dr. Rondeau's order.* Underline it."

Ron wrote on the chart, muttering, "Good luck, getting this one to obey *any* order."

16TH

Dhani stood on Sahm's front porch, feeling sick and upset. He didn't care about Yazzie's tutorial, which is where he was supposed to be right now. He didn't care about anything.

Sahm cracked the door open just a little at Dhani's fervent knock, but did not open it wider to let him inside.

"I need to talk to you about Claire," Dhani said, sounding anxious. "She hasn't talked to me in over a week."

"You have all been studying for your final exams and writing your last papers—isn't that correct? She is busy."

"Yeah, but—Sahm, just let me come inside. I need to talk."

Sahm continued to peek out through the narrow opening. "I cannot let you in now."

Kate had told him what he had to do, not how to explain it, and he groped for more words. He didn't really understand the issue involving Monica Saint—a woman who had no beliefs of her own, so she forbade others to have them—and he skipped over that. "We have spent too much time together. You must make friends with the other students."

Dhani stepped back, confused.

"It doesn't work. I've tried. Sort of. They don't like me."

"You must talk to your friend Ray-Ray."

"I think he might be afraid of me, too. He just wants to be alone all the time now."

"Then you must *try harder.* You must have friends your own age." That sounded reasonable.

"But—it's about *Claire.* She's leaving and says she doesn't want to come back. I feel terrible. I need to talk to someone. I need to talk to *you.* You're my closest friend, Sahm. You're the only one I can really rely on. *Please.*"

Sahm felt as if his heart were splitting. He felt a great ocean surge of compassion for Dhani, and wanted to throw open the door and let him in.

And at the same time, he knew he had to listen to what the *Elementals* had said—*"Peace, peace"*—and trust their enigmatic words, though in this situation that was hurting Dhani those words made no sense at all.

"I do not mean to be terrible to you or rude, but you must go away now."

Sahm shut the door firmly—and Dhani was left standing alone, floored, feeling like he'd been kicked in the gut a second time.

He wandered down the shoreline, past the footbridge to Osprey Island, in an abyss of sadness. The one true friend he thought he had left had just sent him away.

Sahm watched out a window as Dhani's form, so thin and slumped, vanished down the path toward The Arrows.

I do not understand, he silently railed at the *Elementals. Why must it be this way? What good can come of this?*

Right after lunch, Ray-Ray went back to his room, making a final check of things he wanted to pack. Extra socks. Tee-shirts. He would do his afternoon chores later, after Dhani got back from his required math tutorial, and there was not much on Jo's list today. It wasn't clear if Claire would help, since she was packing to leave for DC soon and avoiding everyone.

Outside, Grady's men were mowing, and he dug through his dresser drawers for the special things he wanted—first of all, a pocket-sized *New Testament* his father had given him years ago the day he was baptized. It made him feel protected somehow.

He also pulled out the sweatshirt he had on the day he left home. It had gotten a little stained and torn when he was sleeping on the streets, but it was his favorite one—he'd gotten it at church camp—and he had not worn it all this year.

All year. . . . No. For almost *eighteen months* he had been away from his family. Away from his mother's pan fried corn bread and the scent of her favorite vanilla-lavender perfume. Away from his church family, like Elder Silas, the holiest old man he knew who also made him laugh. Away from the sound of his brother's praise band playing his favorite worship song.

Jesus, name above all names. . . .

He felt a heaviness again. In his mind's-eye, he could see his brother, playing his drums in the praise band and on the streets feeding the homeless. Maybe one day, he would get back to DC and get back in his father's good graces.

"You're not the kind of son any man wants."

Those severing words hurt him deeply, like a gash in his soul.

His whole body suddenly felt drained of energy and, setting the socks, tee-shirts, and sweatshirt aside, he sank down on the bed. He needed to get away from these thoughts, and to rest and be ready for the survival trip. Big hike. A lot of gear to pack in. A lot of set up. A lot to remember—how to build a shelter from branches, how to scrape out a fire pit, how to locate wild edible plants to prove you could find them if necessary.

Through the slightly opened window came the scent of fresh-mown grass and the steady, white-noise hum of the mowers. Dugan was also at Yazzie's command tutorial for strugglers, so the cabin was otherwise quiet. His eyelids grew heavier still and his body sank deeper into the mattress. . . .

He had barely fallen asleep when a sound startled him awake. Just fifteen minutes had passed since he had last glanced at the clock. The mowers were more distant now, so their noise hadn't roused him.

A *thump* came from Dhani's room—but only a half-hour had passed and he must still be out.

Ray-Ray's mind cleared, and he realized it sounded as if something had bumped against the wall between Dhani's room and his.

"Dhani?" he called out.

No response.

"Dhani?" he called louder.

Faint footsteps passed his door, moving quickly down the hallway—carefully, quietly, as if the person going by did not want to be detected.

He rolled up out of bed, alert, curious.

The hallway was empty, and when he got to the main room and looked out the front door, there was no one. No one out the back door either, but by then they easily could have vanished into the surrounding woods.

Weird.

He looked in Dhani's room. The bed, the dresser, the bedside table and lamp—nothing seemed out of place.

Who would sneak into their cabin, and why?

Later, when Dhani came into the aviary, his face was clouded with signs of distress, and Ray-Ray figured it was about Claire and decided not to bring up the afternoon's curious incident.

19TH

The sounds in the supply barn were not exactly happy ones, more like the sounds of apprehension. Tom was on a mission, though, looking for one person.

"A whole ten days," Emmalyn said, as he passed. She was nervously tying back her hair with a red bandana she had been issued. "I hope I can do this."

"You'll be missed around the office, but you'll do well," Tom said. "I envy you. I used to backpack and hike all the time." A thought intruded—*Before I married a woman who turned out to strongly dislike almost everything I love.*

He was looking around for Steve, who wasn't present.

"I don't know how I'll do," Makayla said, when he walked by her. "I'm not sure I'll be okay alone most of the day and every night."

"You'll only be completely solo the last two days, and Laurel and Randy say you're prepared and that you're a strong person."

"Maybe," she said, biting her lower lip.

"They believe in you. So do I. Have you seen Mr. Tanner?"

"In there," she said, tying her bandana around her forehead and nodding at the storage area beyond the wall. "I wish Sahm was coming. He's always so happy and he helps us. But yesterday, Laurel said he isn't coming and she wouldn't say why."

"You have great chaperones. Randy, Mike Yazzie, Ron, Laurel. The Troverts will hike in tomorrow and be there most of the time. They'll all travel around to check in at your solo camping sites."

"It put everyone in a weird mood, though," Makayla responded, "because we think something's being kept from us. Is Sahm sick or did he do something wrong? Will he be here when we get back? This doesn't feel right."

"No. He did nothing wrong. Try to let it go, and finish getting ready. Is your water bottle filled?"

Steve was rechecking a large first-aid kit when Tom found him on the other side of the barn. Tubes of ointments and paper packages of gauze pads lay strewn on a table in front of him.

"I thought you'd be gone by now," he said, not looking up. "Long drive ahead."

"I wanted to find you and have a word before I go."

"You found me."

"You've been very distant since you came back from being on Thi's show, and when I've asked you how it went you just said 'Fine'. But I know that's not true. Are you going to handle this long outing alright? It will challenge everyone, even you."

A memory flashed in Steve's mind—of Olivia's blood-stained scapular, which he'd brought back and hung on his bathroom mirror. Like a scourge, the scapular reminded him of his failure, and feeling pain was somehow better than feeling nothing.

Try seeing that every day, and tell me how you'd be.

"A couple of the instructors are concerned about you and a little uneasy," Tom continued. "They say you're withdrawn and edgy. More than before. I hope you're able to handle this trip, Steve. It could challenge you as much as the students. You really need to be up for this."

Steve calmly closed the kit, stood and squared off with Tom. "You know what? I'm tired of being the focus of everyone's 'concern' and 'unease'. I'm tired of feeling watched and evaluated."

"Everyone here is under scrutiny. Including Kate and me."

"Right," Steve smiled, and replied with a sarcastic tone. "But especially the hard-ass Marine guy."

"Oh, stop acting like a martyr," Tom bridled. "In one way or another, you've kicked against this program for the last twelve months."

Steve held himself in-check. "Yeah, well, remember how I said I'd try this for *one year?* In case you're not keeping track, that year is almost up."

"Steve, I wish you could find a connection with these young people. The way Olivia did."

That pulled a plug.

"I found one." He reached across the table into a box and lifted out a spray canister. "How's this for a connection?"

Tom was confused. "It's the stuff you use to spray dust out of keyboards. Why—?"

"Why did I find it when I did a final search of backpacks this morning? Oh, maybe because they were planning to get high off it out there in the woods when no one's around."

"Whose pack was it in?"

"Someone who doesn't deserve to be in a cushy program like this one. No worries. I'm going to put this kid through their paces out there, and if they drop out, at least they won't be a waste of time and money anymore."

Tom had recovered from the surprise. "Using inhalants is dangerous. You should have come to me—"

"You got to me first. And you're leaving. And I'm tasked with pushing these kids to their limit on this trip. This kid is in less danger now because I took away their little escape. Now I'll see how they do under pressure out there—and I'll let you know my recommendation for whether they get to stay in the program or get kicked out."

"This student may need a drug rehab program."

"Or they need to be back in juvenile detention. I'll tell you what. A few of these kids are salvageable. Maybe. Most haven't changed much this whole first year and don't deserve what they're being handed for free. Simple as that. Lots of great, clean-cut kids out there who deserve a break and they don't get it. In my opinion, Kate's handouts are a big waste, the way all handouts are. I'll lay you odds this week shows that I've been right all along."

"Steve, what have you gotten out of this year?"

"Reinforcement for what I already knew. That there would be only one kid, two if I was lucky, who would really work hard and earn my respect."

Tom walked back toward the lodge. His truck was packed and he needed to find Claire. They were late getting started. He would call Kate when they got to DC and inform her of Steve's find. At the moment, he was at war within himself.

I don't understand. I believed this was the answer for Steve. The right turn on his path. Or was it just me all along, trying to force something good to happen?

He found himself at war with the heavens, too. *Why drop this opportunity in his path, if it was only going to reinforce his arrogance?—his belief that everyone should live up to his standard and earn his respect or they're utterly worthless?*

The drive to DC would be grueling. He wanted to be up, for Claire's sake, but all he felt was a grinding discouragement.

He sensed she was there before he stepped through the entrance.

From the doorway into the aviary, Dhani watched Claire walk slowly down the center aisle and stop by each enclosure. He realized she was quietly saying goodbye.

When she caught sight of him, she turned away and kept moving cage to cage.

It was now, or he would likely never have the chance again. His stomach went hollow and queasy in the way it always did—the way he hated—afraid of what she would say. . . or not say as she departed.

She turned when he came down the aisle to her and stared at him like he was a stranger. "Aren't you supposed to be at the other barn getting ready to leave?"

He wished the two of them were leaving for somewhere together—flying away like birds, over the lake and mountains, going anywhere together instead of parting.

"I just want to say," he hesitated, not knowing how to get out everything he wanted to say and feeling blocked, "I—hope the court thing won't be horrible."

"It will be. Tom said he thought it wouldn't happen, but the Sheriff showed up with a subpoena. So much for Tom and his assurances."

"And I hope you'll be back. Soon."

"Anything else?"

He felt tongue-tied. Felt his chance slipping away—but could not get the words out. A final rejection from her would scald like fire.

"Well. Bye," she said stiffly, and walked toward the door. "My stuff's in Tom's truck, and I'm sure he's looking for me."

When she had brushed passed him, anxiety and awkwardness took hold, and he made a quick gesture behind her back.

Better than nothing, he thought.

She turned fiercely and a blast of words came out.

"You just flicked me off, didn't you? Like you did once before, only you denied it then."

In all her mood swings, he had never seen her like this. So beside herself, her face bright red, her hands clenching and unclenching.

"*No!*" he stammered, but felt himself rapidly shrinking back from her hurt and anger. "I—," the rest of his words froze on his tongue.

"*You're lying.* Just like Carter is lying. Like Tom lied."

Around them, the birds became unsettled, and from the cages came shrieks and calls, growing louder, amplifying the confusion.

"All this year, I stuck up for you—and you do *that* behind my back? Now you're hiding inside that. . . that stupid hoody. No one ever knows when you're going to snap-o, but I took a chance on being your friend. What is *wrong* with you?"

Tears of rage trembled in her eyes, and her lower lip shook. "Well, I hate you like I hate everyone else. Like I hate this world. Hate it, hate it, hate it."

Every word she said was a burning knife, and Dhani recoiled deeper and deeper inside, until he was unable to move a muscle or speak. In his mind, she was both the Monster and Tanner, directing at him their will to destroy.

But no. This was *Claire!* And she had turned away—turned *against* him completely—and stalked out the aviary door. Out of his life.

Everything in him disintegrated into ashes.

Vajra stood between Claire and the truck, moving to block her when she tried to walk around him.

"Leave me alone. I have to go."

Tom came around from the driver's side. "Go on. Leave her alone."

Vajra bared his teeth at Tom, but did not advance on him.

Tom's brow furrowed. "Seems he knows you're going away, and he doesn't want you to."

Claire stared at the huge dark creature, then extended her hand.

Vajra stop bristling, lowered his ears and walked to her. He pressed against her and allowed her to stroke his broad head.

"Strange, how he's so tuned-in to you. Beautiful, really. You have a good friend," said Tom.

"One anyway."

That slid by Tom. "When you come back, this guy will be happy to see you again."

Don't lie. You know I'm not coming back.

Vajra watched as the truck vanished down the camp road in a small cloud of dust.

In an hour, Jo opened the clinic door to let out Pal, who would be in her care in Steve's absence.

Vajra was waiting, seated at the doorstep.

Pal limped to him, they sniffed at each other, and Pal wagged his tail as Vajra licked his face.

Jo shook her head. "How did you know your buddy Pal was here? Sometimes I think you guys have a sixth sense."

Immediately, she was glad Ron had the morning off and wasn't present to hear her spewing New-Agey nonsense.

7
SURVIVAL
May 19th
EVENING

We'll be totally on our own for ten days. Makayla scribbled with a thin pencil in her small backpacking journal, and bit her lower lip.

I don't know why they're making us do this. I'd be fine back in my little comfort zone just taking care of the salamanders—so sweet!—and Lightning our box turtle. (oh sorry, not supposed to call him that). But no. We have to prove we can survive out here. So stupid. They should try surviving in my toxic house.

She lay in the tent made of half-tents, which she would share for this first night, huddled now in her sleeping bag next to Imani's empty one. From the fire pit outside, at the center of this, the base camp, carefully stacked and burning cedar logs gave off a sweet-smoky scent. It filled the small shelter and clung to her clothes.

I'm afraid it's going to happen to me again, while I'm out there alone. I just hope it doesn't happen when I'm crossing a stream or building a fire. That could be really bad.

Imani was talking to Rocco right outside the tent now.

Imani is still my best girl but something's really bothering her I can tell and she won't say what. She just says it's all good which is a crap lie.

The thought of Imani suddenly sliding inside the makeshift tent made Makayla flip the page and change the subject.

Tanner is being more of a jerk than usual. If that's even possible. Why did they hire him? Just to give us all the hardest time possible? He doesn't really give a crap about any of us. Except maybe his little favorites. Garrett and Rocco and Dugan.

If Imani asked her later what she was writing about, she could read her this last part—something Imani would agree with and it would satisfy her curiosity.

Her secret was her own business.

Before closing the journal, she scratched with her pencil. *Tomorrow it's go-time. Let's see who comes out of this alive.*

20TH

He watched from the upper branches of an oak tree, sniffing the early morning air for predators from the sky, keeping a careful eye from this safe distance on the biggest one, below.

The two-legged creature's mouth was moving, lecturing at them again about the rules and his point system for rating them on what they'd learned and how well they used the knowledge.

Predator, his instincts pulsed.

When the predator's eyes scanned the circle of young people, looking sharply at each one's face, he pulled back behind a cluster of leaves. He would keep a vigilant eye on the two-legged to see if it would start to approach. If so, he would bolt then, higher up the oak tree. Tuned to danger, his muscles twitched in fear.

"*Jones*. You with me?"

Dhani dropped his gaze from the branch where a red squirrel was flicking its tail and shouting down at them. Its chattering had caught his attention and drawn him—temporarily—out of the line of Tanner's attention, which he now felt caught in. Away, too, from the feelings of loss and depression he had almost numbed.

Tanner was standing beside the fire pit, where overnight a bed of coals had formed a bright-gold, glowing carpet from which small flames licked at the cool morning air. His eyes bored into Dhani, demanding an answer.

"Yeah." Dhani's mess kit slid off his leg, and his breakfast oatmeal splattered on his hiking boot.

"What did I just say? What was my last sentence?'

Ray-Ray was staring at Dhani from the far side of the group, and Dhani fixed his attention on his friend. Or was he? Ray-Ray was becoming distant, too. Maybe he was losing his last ally.

"*Jones,*" Tanner said louder. "I'm waiting."

To keep the predator's talons from sinking any deeper, gripping him tighter, Dhani searched his memory and, just before Tanner spoke again, he threw out the first words that came to mind, hoping they were even close.

"You said, 'Randy and I—uh, meaning *you*—will be around at the end of the afternoon to check how you did."

Tanner's look of suspicion did not relax, but he moved on. "So, you were listening. I'm surprised. I thought you were more interested in watching that squirrel than hearing what your lead instructor had to say."

Tanner kept speaking, spitting out instructions.

Dhani's eyes ran back up the tree trunk again, and he wished he could leave the uncomfortable feelings in his body behind again and stay numbed out for the rest of this ordeal.

The daydream he'd just had, of leaving his body and watching from the eyes of the fitful and wary red squirrel, had evaporated, though. The connection was broken and he felt trapped inside his own miserable thoughts and anxious body again.

I'm a psycho, and I'm totally losing it.

Instinctively, though, he knew that Tanner's kind often pretended they had moved on, then circled back when you were unwary. And so he was careful to keep one ear turned to the predator—the ear in which he had the most hearing left.

"Are you Claire Chamberlayne-Pierce?"

The man in the fine suit had charged into the crowded waiting area, straight up to Claire, and looked down at her with such obviously fake sympathy on his face. She wanted to say, "Don't make me vomit."

Tom intervened, jumping to his feet from the chair beside hers, and stuck out his hand. "Tom Baden. I'm her legally-appointed guardian. You are—?"

"Jared Armistead. The prosecutor."

As Armistead gripped Tom's hand, a large man who looked like a power-lifter stuffed too tightly in a blue uniform stepped up. "Mr. Baden and Mr. Armistead, the judge wants to see you in her office."

Tom raised an eyebrow at Claire. "Not sure what this is about, but I hope I won't be long. Do you need a drink of water?"

Claire shook her head, and then watched them disappear through a heavy, dark, wooden door with a frosted-glass window. In a second, even the ghost of their images disappeared, leaving her alone in a stuffy waiting room with a dozen complete strangers who were either nodding off or nervously fidgeting.

Tom had warned her they could be here all day, and the clock next to the painting of George Washington standing in a rowboat only said *8:37.* Among other soul-numbing drudgeries, this was one thing she remembered about "the system"—all the deadening waiting. Hours of sitting in waiting areas for a twenty-minute encounter that would determine your fate for the next X years. Such a sham, because the adults usually already knew what they planned to do with you.

"You okay, Miss?"

She turned to look at the woman who had spoken to her—a very large, bulky woman in a dark blue dress with bright green palm fronds splashed all over it. It made her look like she was dressed for a vacation in the Bahamas rather than a day in judicial offices. The young man at her side, who looked to be near twenty, was of the nodding-off type.

"I'm fine."

"You look so unhappy, though. I'm a mother and I hate to see you sitting here all alone so sad."

Oh god, she thought, *the 'motherly type'. Go away.*

Claire shrugged. "This isn't my first time. I'm an old hand at this."

"Sounds serious. Care to talk?"

Claire considered getting up and sitting across the room, but decided that would be too rude. Maybe it was Sahm's influence. He was kind to everyone in a way she would like to be. Instead, she turned the tables.

"Why are *you* here?"

The woman placed a meaty hand on the knee of the young man next to her, which made him startle. "Alex was arrested for not obeying an officer when he was ordered to halt. They mistook him for someone who'd just run out of a drug store with stolen merchandise. Alex wasn't the guy they were looking for, but when he didn't comply they pushed him down on the sidewalk, hurt his face, and arrested him for disobeying an officer." She pointed at the red scrape and purple bruising on the son's cheekbone.

Maybe he should have done what they asked.

"But you didn't tell me why you look so unhappy," the woman pressed, her big face full of sweetness and concern.

8:42. Who knew how long Tom would be gone. Why not give her something. This woman was the *relentless* motherly type, but Claire was not about to go into the convolutions of her legal issue.

"I—I just lost a friend."

"Oh dear. Car accident? Cancer?"

"No. Actually, I cut him off. He was someone I befriended because almost no one else likes him. Also because he's a good kid, or that's what I thought. Then for no reason he flicked me off *behind my back*. Or he did something like that, and it wasn't the first time. Actually, he just did some weird gestures, I guess. But I was really upset and it irritated me."

The young man next to the large woman had opened his eyes and was peering closely at Claire's face, especially her mouth. When he spoke, his voice was thick and sounded as if he were talking through his nose. "That's a bad friend. Better off without him."

Claire realized he was also smiling in a way that seemed he might be interested in her.

"What do you mean, he made gestures?" the mother pursued.

She wanted to divert the son's attention away from her face, so with her right hand she tried to make the gestures she had half-seen Dhani making. "I guess he didn't flick me off." And as she said it, she knew he really hadn't. "But he was doing something weird." He was always doing something weird and making people feel afraid of him or dislike him."

The woman and her son glanced at each other. "Show us again."

She repeated the gestures.

The two looked at each other, then laughed.

"What's funny?"

"He said, 'I love you, C,'" the son intoned.

"Are you sure? How do you know that?"

"Alex is deaf," the woman answered. "He lost his hearing when he was nine. Your friend said, 'I love you,' in American Sign Language—hand gestures used to communicate with hearing impaired people. We're here because he *couldn't* hear the officers—they came up behind him—and he let them know he was deaf but they arrested him for not obeying anyway. We're appealing the charges."

Claire was aware of heat rising from her chest up her neck, probably making her face red. Memories returned, of the way Dhani had seemed aloof all year and the way his seeming inattention angered Tanner and frustrated other instructors.

But why had he kept his hearing problem a secret? How on earth did no one else pick up on it?

"Who is 'C'?" the young man asked.

"I—my name is Claire. I guess 'C' is me."

The mother smiled. "Well that's something to be happy about, isn't it? Someone told you they love you. What did you say back?"

Oh god.

Claire felt heartsick thinking of Dhani—how she had refused to listen when he had tried in his awkward way to explain. She had left him alone and probably trashed by her furious rejection.

"Time to head out. Repack your half-tents," Randy directed them.

"Yesterday was about getting all the way up here," he said. "Once we clean up from breakfast, you'll move out and choose your solo sites. Remember what we told you to look for. A high spot, so rain water can run around your shelter, not through it. A level rock nearby, where you can build your fire spot for cooking—well cleared. And access to a stream for drinking water. Also a place to bury your poo unless you plan to carry it out in the little plastic bags."

He sounded excited about the ten days ahead.

Emmalyn was staring from the border of the alpine meadow out over the steep, wooded slopes leading up to the open peak of Lost Mountain in the distance. She sounded much less excited.

"I'm glad you guys at least didn't make us do survival week up *there*.

It was cold enough last night up at this level without sleeping on the ground at an even higher elevation."

The others had begun folding tarps or cleaning mess kits in a small stream at the meadow's edge. May daytime temps had warmed the water, and in the morning cool, wisps of fog rose from the narrow, noisy current into the clear, sunny air.

"How high are we?" Emmalyn asked, coming back to the fire circle.

"Not high enough," said Tia Leesha, just loud enough to be heard and sounding serious.

This brought laughter.

"We're at about three thousand feet," Randy replied.

"How'd you know that?" Emmalyn asked. She began to help Tia Leesha, who seemed unable on her own to fold her half-tent small enough to fit back in its sack.

"Easy," said Laurel. "Look at the trees below and above us. Below—mix of hardwoods and evergreens. Above—mostly evergreens. We're at the edge of what's called the Mountain Conifer zone, also known as 'spruce slope'. Notice that above us black spruce and balsam fir trees are predominant."

"It's also called the *Krummholz*," Bay Trovert added. "That's not important. What *is* important is that if you wander below this level, you stand a great chance of getting lost. The wilderness closes in on you fast and you become disoriented. If you stay up here, which is why this area was chosen, the trees are thinner and it's much easier to find your way. You've also been given whistles in case you run into trouble. A shrill blast can be heard for a long way."

Randy and Laurel both looked at her.

"Very good."

"Spoken like a true woods woman of the north."

Tia Leesha blurted. "I don't care how many feet we're up or what it's called. Cold is cold, and to me this is cold." She had bundled herself in a knitted hat, two sweatshirts, two pairs of sweatpants, and heavy socks. She sniffed and wiped her nose on a sleeve. "I don't know how I'm gonna move around and find my own site if I gotta keep all these clothes on to stay warm."

"I can help you," Emmalyn volunteered quickly, zipping her pack.

Steve had finished cleaning his mess kit and returned from the stream.

"No, you won't. She'll do it on her own. Each one of you has to find your own spot somewhere out in this mountain now, on your own and construct your own shelter today." He checked the sky. "It's not supposed to rain. But you know how the weather changes here in the mountains. So do a good job with your survival shelter or you'll be sleeping cold and wet. Remember, you're out there ten days, all the way to the nineteenth. Then you regroup here and we head back."

"Don't worry if you have trouble." Laurel tried to intervene. "We'll be right here at base camp all morning if you need us. And we'll be around later in the day to find and check your sites. We'll give you pointers if you need them."

Steve dismissed that. "I won't be giving pointers. You've had all year to learn. I'll be around to rate you on how well you do what you were instructed. You do this on your own, with no one else's help." He stared at Emmalyn, then Tia Leesha. "If you crash and burn, it's all on you."

Bay Trovert's mouth was moving, but most of her words slid off his mind.

Steve had left his island cabin two mornings ago after touching Olivia's scapular one more time. It hung there on the mirror like a silent judgment against him. And like a mystery.

He picked up Bay's last sentence.

"Your tone made it sound like you expected them to 'crash and burn'."

Blah blah f-in' blah.

The deep agitation had returned since Thi's show and brutal surprise, and he wished Bay would get lost. He wanted to say, as he had before, *"I don't do 'every kid gets a blue ribbon',"* but that would get her going on "positive reinforcement" and more blah blah.

"Eric and I see that your tough-love, warrior approach may be working with a few of the guys. But definitely not all, and. . . ."

He was staring at the fingers of his right hand, which he had run down the woven cord stained rusty with Olivia's lifeblood. The same surge of distress he had forced down two days ago was starting to rise again, and his hands and arms were tingling. Some kind of shock response?

Just over-tired, he told himself.

Why had he let Tom pressure him into coming to Lost Lake? His head felt like a packed powder keg, overfull, and his shoulders, chest and stomach felt compacted and tight.

He made himself take a deep breath, and another, and the explosive feelings dissipated. Pain and pressure were gone again; an aloof calm returned. And control.

"You do things your way. I do them mine. We'll see whose method works."

"This isn't a win-lose situation, Steve. You're not fighting a war here."

He just nodded, comfortably, mercifully numb again.

23RD

The warm front was much warmer than expected—in the low 80s. Combined with the exertions of the last two days—lugging bigger fallen branches to extend his lean-to, climbing through the woods to forage wild edible plants—the unseasonable heat this morning made Ray-Ray's throat feel parched.

He had made a trail through the woods by snapping small twigs on the branches of saplings and shrubs and leaving them dangling. He had heard the distant sounds of a stream on the first day, and marked his way to it so he could find his way back to his site during water runs. Following it now, he felt good about the survival skills he had learned. Felt good about himself.

When had he ever had that feeling? It was new.

The only thing he didn't feel good about—and refused to think about now—was what Jo had told him earlier this week. "It's almost time to let the blue jay go free." Right now, it was physical survival. He would deal later with losing his little friend whose will and struggle to survive reminded him that he was strong, too.

As he pushed through the last stand of ferns, he saw someone squatting beside the stream. She stood and said, "Damn," just as he stepped up beside her.

"I forgot my water filter," Imani said, frustrated.

He handed her his.

"Thank you. What's with your friend?"

"Dhani? I don't know. He's been really upset. Angry-kinda upset."

"You should talk to him."

"I don't know. I got my own stuff to deal with."

"Well, I'm glad you showed up here. I need to talk to *you*—seriously."

"Oh, here we go. Girl, I can't take you seriously. I told you before when you brought up this mess, my brother's a living saint."

"Yeah well—just before we left to climb up here, I heard the gang your brother is bangin' with just took out another guy. *One of their own.* He was seen in a bar where a rival gang member was hangin' out. Just because of that, they accused him of being friendly with the enemy. Trading secrets about their plans or some such. They held him down and shot him full of fentanyl. Then they took out his girlfriend, too, just in case he'd told her anything they didn't want to get out.

"If your brother's not already in too deep, he's got to get out. Now. It's like they got a taste for killing and they really like it."

"How do you know all this?"

She dodged that. "Trust me that I just know what I know. I'm telling you this stuff because I watch you and you're a good guy. You're good to Dhani, a kid almost everyone else avoids. I think that says a lot about you. I'm trying to spare you and your family some bigtime pain. And now I'm gonna tell you one more thing, because you need to trust me on this."

He rolled his eyes. "Really—what are you gonna tell me?"

"My real name is not Imani. It's Alberta. But you can't tell anyone here. *No. One*. It cannot get out that I'm here."

"Seriously?"

"Imani is a new identity I had to take on. I was in too close with my guy's gang. And because of some really bad stuff that went down I needed to be far away from DC for a long time. To be super safe, I only have indirect contact with my family through Judge Sewell. Because the cops still suspect me, though, they're keeping close tabs on me here, even though I didn't have any serious, direct involvement with gang activities."

Ray-Ray watched her, smiling a little.

"What's funny?"

"Nothing. But I believe you now. Nobody would lie and say their real name is Alberta."

She did not crack a smile. "Nothing wrong with my name. And—seriously?—*that's* what you focus on? I just gave you something personal and secret *and* a very serious warning."

He got a sober look. "You're right. I'm stupid. Having to hide from a gang is really bad. Totally screws up your life."

She focused her eyes on his face. "Now that I told you some of my very private stuff, are you gonna trust me about your brother—at least enough to ask him if he's involved?"

"I don't know. Maybe. If I can even get in touch with him. Before we came here last year, I heard he's forbidden to have contact with me. And suppose I *did* contact him and you're wrong? He could tell my dad

I accused him of something bad. My dad has already—" he balked. "My dad basically disowned me."

"So what have you got to lose contacting your brother?"

"I don't know." He stared at the ground. "If I ask you two questions, will you tell me the truth again?"

"Depends."

"When I caught you lifting drugs from Jo's cabinet, was it really just girls' pills?"

"As opposed to heavy painkillers—narcotics? I'm not stupid and I wouldn't do that. Ron inventories that stuff every week."

"That means you're watching Jo's drug inventory. Why?"

"I already saw two people die because they overdosed."

"So. . . are you saying somebody here is using? Getting into Jo's vet drugs?"

"Maybe."

"Rocco?"

"No. Absolutely not. He's playing it clean as can be here. I told you the truth that day. I was just getting him something because he had a real bad headache."

"Then who do you think is using?"

"I'm not sure. Just a guess. But if I can find out and save someone, I will."

Ray-Ray nodded. "Second question.—If you're in deep cover, no contact with your family, how'd you find out about the gang OD-ing the guy with fentanyl and offing his girlfriend? You skipped over that part."

"That, I'm not going to tell you."

He raised an eyebrow and smiled. "So you're not *exactly* playing by the rules here, because we're not supposed to have unsupervised outside contact."

"You're not going to turn this back on me. Everyone does what they have to do to get by. Including you—am I right? And by the way, if you need a friend I'm here."

He looked away. "I don't need a friend."

"Yes, you do. You know what I mean. That *stuff* you said you're tryna deal with."

Ray-Ray kept any sign of agreement or emotion off his face. "You seem pretty wise for your age."

"So many things happened to me already in my life. A couple really bad choices can teach you a lot."

"Yeah, but some people never wise up." After a pause, he added, "Maybe I'll think about what you said."

"Please do."

25TH

Sahm gripped the edges of the heavy plastic bag and, with Ron lifting from the other side, hoisted the body of the cougar from the freezer. From there, they carried it out to Jo's Jeep. She would drive it downstate this morning, then east to a lab in western Massachusetts.

"The lab down in Albany just isn't responsive anymore to the specimens I'm sending for analysis. All I keep hearing is, 'We're backed up.' But that's bull. Maybe we're too small a clinic for them to care about. Maybe someone's dropping the ball. Bottom line is, no one's giving me answers why we can't get testing done and results back."

After, Sahm went back to the walk-in to restock the smaller freezer in the aviary. He fed the inmates their morning meal, then went to feed the bats and the one young otter Jo had not released back to the river it came from because it had developed a fungal lung infection.

Seeing the small, sleek creature sick and curled in its nest instead of acrobat-ing through the water made Sahm think of the little rabbit still nestled in its box by his fireplace. His ministrations had kept the creature from dying of its hawk-inflicted wounds, but it occurred to him now the rabbit had not regained much of its life energy. It was still listless, its *la*—its spirit—still weak many weeks after it was rescued.

Perhaps, he thought, *I should return to my healing meditations.*

Not that he was in full possession of powers that could heal right now. His own spirit needed to be strengthened again. When Kate had forbidden him to see Dhani, he had lost heart a bit. It had pained him to think others thought he might be harming someone by teaching them practices meant to give life and strength. That had shut him down.

But now—the wounded rabbit.

What harm is there in seeking the help of Elemental powers to direct healing energy to it? he thought, finishing his morning 'rounds.

Even if there were not a dramatic healing, as there had been with the black lab months ago, perhaps it would relieve some measure of suffering.

At the far end of the lakefront, before he crossed the little bridge to his cabin, he passed Randy Wolfmoon's domed medicine lodge and felt energy stir like an invisible wind. Instead of crossing the bridge, he turned and circled the deer hide structure, counter-clockwise in the manner of his *Bönpo* people.

With each circumambulation, he felt a tingle that started below his navel spread quickly down his thighs and up his torso, through his legs and feet and out his arms and hands—until his face and body were fairly burning. With the tingle came the thrill he recognized as waves of *lung*—life energy.

To his relief, he felt connected again, to himself and his purpose, and he ran a hand over the rough hides as he kept circling.

He made a vow. He would never again let these western people, who knew so little about the ancient practices handed down to him through ages and who didn't believe in their power—he would *never* again allow their disapproval or unbelief to weigh down his spirit.

Now he was resolved. He would come here to the medicine lodge one day soon, after all the extra chores at the barns and clinic, now that the young people were gone. He would call upon the *Elementals* from here.

When he finally headed across the beach to his cabin, his spirit vibrated and soared, like a bell that had just been struck and was sounding through the vast spaces within his spirit, which were opening wide again. He felt as if his ribs would burst open.

Had he looked back, he would have seen that in the sand behind him there were no footprints.

26TH

Imani pulled harder on the cord, which only tightened the snag and cinched the bear bag to the high branch. She threw down the cord. "How am I supposed to get my food down from way up there?"

Makayla stood beside her, looking up the huge, eastern white pine. "You can have some of my food. I haven't eaten much."

"Why? You should keep up your strength."

"Hey, need help?"

Rocco made his way through the trees.

"How'd you know that?"

He stood beside her and Makayla, who turned away. "Oh, I just heard somebody who sounded a lot like you, yelling, '*Dammit, dammit, dammit*'."

"I'm gonna go now," Makayla said, her tone cool.

"Better see if some squirrels got into your lunch," Imani teased.

When she was gone, Rocco smirked. "She's really angry at me."

"She says you treat Jalil like crap."

"I don't like him."

"Why?"

He ignored the question. "You seemed like you were in a garbage-y mood when we all split up to come out here."

"Oh, and you know me so well you think you can say that."

"I kinda know you. I know that when you're happy your eyes light up and look more hazel. And when you're sad or mad or worried your eyes go dark and look brown."

"Just help me get my bear bag down."

"Tell me why you're worried and I will."

"Never mind. I'll do it myself."

"Wait—I'll help you. But tell me."

"Bear bag first."

"Damn."

He jumped twice at the lowest pine branch and the second time managed to grab it. Then he pulled himself up and swung a leg over the limb. Climbing up to another branch, he lay out across it, legs wrapped, untangled the cord—and lowered Imani's bear bag to her.

"Now tell me," he called down, pausing to catch his breath. "I got all pine-sticky stuff on me for this."

She let out an irritated sound, then looked around as if needing reassurance no one else was in earshot.

"Okay. You remember that I told you I overheard things about a murder. Before we came up here, I found out that the gang is doubling-down on finding the rat. Situation's heating up, not cooling down like the police said it would."

"How do you know? Where are you getting your information?"

"The less you know about me, the better."

Tia Leesha was hanging her sleeping bag over the lower branch of a tree when Steve entered her site. He'd come on today's checking rounds without Randy Wolfmoon, to keep from becoming irritated. In his mind Randy was too easy on these kids, and he would probably blow if he had to listen to Randy praise every little thing these guys did.

"What are you doing?" he barked at Tia Leesha.

"This is wet and I froze last night," she complained at him.

"How'd it get so wet? It didn't rain." He looked at her lean-to, a fairly well-made structure, except for one thing. "You make that by yourself?"

"Yes, I did. Because you said I couldn't have help. Laurel Wysocki was here a little while ago and she said it was pretty good."

"What's up with your bag then?"

"Halfway through last night I woke up and it was wet."

He pointed at the lean-to. "You used both of your tarps to cover it. The smaller one was to use on the ground as a vapor barrier. The moisture in the soil soaked through."

"How was I supposed to know?"

"Oh, I don't know. You've only been on campouts all year. I thought some of what we taught you might have stuck. Do you see how 'pretty good' isn't good enough?"

Then he held up the canister he had removed from her backpack down at the barn. "Care to tell me why you were bringing this can of compressed air on a survival trip? It wouldn't be because you were going to get hits off it, right?"

She turned back to the sleeping bag and wouldn't look at him. "No. It wouldn't. I was going to. . . use it to spray away bugs. Someone said there might be big spiders up here. I hate spiders."

"Spiders," he repeated, and walked up beside her. "Look at me."

She composed her face and stared him in the eye.

"Do you think I'm stupid?"

"A little, yeah. Everyone's a little stupid."

"Well, I'm not stupid. I didn't have time to report this before we left, but I'm going to when we get back."

"I'm not doin' any drugs," she protested. "That's against the rules."

"But huffing aerosols is a way to get around the rules, isn't it. That's what kids like you do—figure a way around all the rules."

"Kids like me? That's sounds prejudiced."

"Don't pull that 'you're prejudiced' bullcrap on me. You're not gonna hide behind that."

"I didn't do anything wrong. You took that outa my backpack, so how could I have huffed it? You don't have anything to report."

"You know, all year I thought you were just lazy. But you're clever and lazy. Bad combination."

"You can report me all you want. I didn't do anything wrong."

"This says you were going to."

"Your word against mine. I'll say you planted it in my pack to punk me."

He started toward her, then checked his impulse. If this were the service, he would have knocked her to the ground for insubordination.

The irritation he felt was turning into anger. Maybe it would be better if Wolfmoon were with him, to buffer his reactions. He felt like hitting someone.

When he left, Tia Leesha dropped down into the wet leaves, not caring to try anymore. Whatever good Laurel's message had done, the good way she had begun to think about herself was all but extinguished by Tanner's brutal judgment.

"You said if I got your bear bag down," Rocco continued to press, "you'd tell me what's bothering you." He was still up in the pine tree, looking down at her.

"I told you."

"Not all of it."

"I gave you some information."

"You gave me a piece of it."

There was crackling in the underbrush, and Dugan emerged. "Whoa, whoa, *whoa*, who gave who a piece?" He looked up at Rocco. "What you doin' up there?"

"He was helping me. I'm not a good climber. He is."

"I'm a good climber, too. Probably better than him. I built forts way up in trees on my grandparents' farm when I was a kid. He's a city boy."

Rocco laughed. "City boy? Then how come *I'm* up here and *you're* down there?"

"Sure, you're good at—what is that, fifteen feet? But how would you do if I raced you to the top of that tree?"

"I'd crush you."

"Care to make a friendly bet? The one who gets to the top first wins the prize."

"What prize you offering?"

Dugan nodded at Imani. "Better man gets the girl. Other man backs off."

"I'm up for the challenge."

"Better man does *not* get this girl," Imani objected. "I'm not a prize in your little boy, 'who can pee farther' contest."

Dugan had already swung up on the first big branch, and was starting to scramble up one side of the tall pine, limb by limb pulling himself higher.

Rocco took off after him, gripping the trunk between his feet and pushing himself up through the layers of branches.

"That thing's gotta be sixty or seventy feet tall," Imani shouted up at them. "You fall, you break your neck."

Rocco heaved himself higher and called down. "Nah. Lotta branches below us to break a fall. Only thing gonna be hurt is his ego when I beat him to the top."

Dugan didn't respond and kept scrambling upward—looking over his shoulder at the tops of the black spruce trees dropping away below him as he pulled himself higher. At maybe forty feet up, three branches came out of the trunk just above him close together, blocking his way. He tried to swing himself to the opposite side of the trunk.

Rocco came up fast, reaching the branches on that level before him. "Hey, dude, stay in your own lane," he laughed. "I'm climbing here."

Dugan threw an elbow that caught Rocco on the jaw. "Oh, geez, sorry man."

Rocco braced his feet against the trunk, started to push himself up and let one foot slide sideways off the bark so it slammed Dugan in the chest. "Damn. Sorry. Hard to get traction."

With a few more pullups, Rocco reached the highest safe branches just ahead of Dugan. He wrapped a leg around the trunk and balanced on a branch which bent beneath his weight, raising his arms in victory.

"*You heard him*," he shouted down to Imani. "*Better man gets the girl*."

Looking down was a mistake. Rocco felt his stomach drop and his palms go sweaty.

"You such a big hero, why you shaking?" Dugan challenged.

"Hey, my muscles are tired."

"Looks like scared, to me."

"*No one 'gets the girl'*," Imani said, her voice vehement, when they dropped from the lowest branch to the ground again. "The girl has her man. Are you both stupid? Two boys climbed a tree. One of you did it faster. That doesn't mean anything *to* me or *about* me."

Dhani kept striking a piece of quartz against the flint rock, but none of the sparks landing on the tree bark fibers ignited. He felt proud of the survival fire kit he had made, remembering Randy's instructions.

"See the fibers inside?" Randy said, pulling apart a hunk of birch bark. "Works great if you roll it into kind of a nest to capture your spark. Blow on it carefully, and once it catches—*bam*, you're on your way to some heat."

At the moment, though, he couldn't start his fire. That and everything else left him frustrated.

Two days ago, he had made his way over the rocky uneven ground to his friend's campsite, but Ray-Ray had been distant and said almost nothing. Barely made eye-contact.

"What's up?" Dhani had prodded.

"Nothing," Ray-Ray mumbled, turning away—but Dhani knew he was lying.

After a long silence, Ray-Ray said, "Dude, you been washing yourself? We been out here only a couple days and you already smell bad."

"I forgot that soap they gave me."

"End of this campout you're gonna stink."

Then Ray-Ray was silent again, and distant. No offer to loan some soap. And after thirty minutes of awkwardness, Dhani said, "I'm gonna go."

Clearly, Ray-Ray did not want him around. His last friend had pulled away.

He had trucked back to his site heavy and desolate.

Now, Dhani smashed the quartz striker stone harder and harder against the piece of flint. A chip hit him on the chin, which made him angry. He struck the stones together even harder, until a strong spark leapt off it into the small bundle of birch fibers.

Far back in his mind, he sensed that someone or something was approaching behind him at a distance.

In the cottony quiet that muffled much of his ability to hear, he listened as the fire—his first one—rose into a crackling blaze. Another time, this accomplishment might have made him happy. The only thing he felt glad about was moving his site further away from Ray-Ray's.

He sat back, warming his hands, his mind expanding to take in whoever was approaching from behind—feeling a strange, mixed sense. Whoever approached was both friend and foe.

"Hi, Mr. Wolfmoon," he said, without looking over his shoulder.

"Hey, how'd you know it was me? We came to find you."

Dhani jerked his head around to see Tanner standing next to Randy, and quickly turned his face back to the fire.

Randy squatted beside him, picked up and examined the second birch bark bundle he'd made. "Nice little fire. Very well done, man." He fed a stick to the flames. "Your first site was really nice. Why'd you move way out here? We had trouble finding you."

Because if somebody doesn't want me around, I don't want to be around them.

He said nothing in reply.

Steve felt the flashfire that always ran over his skin when he was around this rude kid who, as always, didn't have the courtesy or brains to show respect and answer an instructor.

"Where's your shelter?" he asked, as much to push for a response as out of real interest.

Dhani pointed at his tarp, which lay in a folded rectangle on the ground under a lone jack pine. "Right there."

"That's not the lean-to structure you were instructed to build. This is the sixth day you have been out here, you had plenty of time."

"No, it's not the shelter you showed them," Randy intervened, looking closely at the tarp. "But it's what you'd call a 'burrito' shelter. You fold a tarp just right—in thirds, with the sides and one end folded under—just like he did it. Then you can slip yourself right inside it. Turns a tarp into a shelter in about sixty seconds. Where'd you learn how to do this?"

"I just thought it would work."

"Really, wow," Randy said, surprised, "because a 'burrito tarp shelter' is a well-known survival technique. If nobody showed you how to do this, you've got good instincts."

"Nobody showed it to me. I just... saw it in my head."

"But you were told to build a lean-to," Steve pressured. He suspected Dhani was lying and that he had read about his lazy-man's tarp shelter somewhere. "This is quick to put up, I see that—," he glanced from Randy to Dhani, "—but what it really shows me is you're not willing to put in any effort."

Randy sounded perturbed, and defended Dhani. "This trip is all about survival. Like I said, to me this shows *good instincts*."

"Maybe so" Steve's expression remained stony. "But I'm rating how well they use skills we've worked on all year *and* how well they obey orders. He's failed at both."

"A minute ago," Randy challenged him again, "it was about following instructions. Now it's also about obeying your orders."

Steve looked angry. "So why don't we just lay the bar right on the ground, then these guys would have no standards to live up to."

Randy held up both hands. "We should talk about this later."

Steve looked down at Dhani, who was staring hard into the fire. "I'm giving you demerits. You can earn honor points back by doing what you were told."

Dhani felt a strong urge to seize Tanner by the throat, but forced it down. The force of fear and anger mixed terrified him.

Burn in hell, Tanner.

He threw a small stick in the fire. "Sure thing."

Just before they left, Randy said, in his easy, friendly way, "You should build a better shelter, though. It's gonna rain tonight. Heavy."

Dhani looked up at the clear sky. "How do you know that?"

Randy smiled. "Just a sense I get sometimes. Can't explain it. Usually, it's right."

27TH

The rattle woke Sahm, and in the pale pre-dawn light falling in through the medicine lodge's entryway he opened one sleepy eye to look for its source.

Whatever it was had fallen silent.

When he'd moved his bedroll and things in here last night, the air over Lost Lake had become unsettled, with cool air pouring in to push out the warm front. The woods, the water, everything felt unsettled and restless, uneasy as the shifting elements he sensed all around him.

Rain had fallen during the early morning hours, heavily. He rolled over and looked at the flat altar stone next to the firepit in which he had laid fragrant balsam and red oak and lit a small blaze. The tuft of rabbit fur lay next to the new arrow Sahm had made, arranged as he had left them next to an eagle feather, which Randy Wolfmoon had brought here when he dedicated the lodge—one passed down from his ancestors.

Sahm had also brought another small figure made from barley flour in the shape of a deer, the object most essential. If he did the ceremony correctly, the Soul Deer could be empowered to retrieve the energy of the small rabbit's *la*—the specific combination of energies that made it a rabbit. Perhaps the eagle feather's magic would help in the effort.

Now, coming from outside the lodge, he heard soft footsteps in the sand. Not human steps, those of an animal—no, two animals—which he could tell by how rapid and light they were.

Vajra passed the entryway, the flap of which Sahm left up to allow most of the fire's heat to escape, because it had been a mild night. Behind the wolf, limping along, was Palden. After passing the opening, the black lab let out a howl, not mournful, but—wary? or jubilant?

Why were they circling?

A reply came, not from his own mind but echoing from far beyond it.

"If Dhani were here, he would know. His powers are growing and ready to burst out into the world."

Palden howled again, a warbling cry, as if in greeting, the way a dog will do when excited by the return of someone familiar.

On the stone altar by the firepit the arrow rattled, and kept rattling.

Sahm crawled on hands and knees to the fire, stirred the embers and unburnt branches into a small blaze, then knelt beside the altar. Touching and blessing the feather and tuft of fur, he started a chant.

With every word, the flames guttered and leapt, coming vibrantly to life.

Sahm fed juniper branches to the flames, their scent filling the air inside the lodge like an incense. A light breeze blew in from outside, circled around him. He set a small shell in which he had caught rainwater on the flat stone beside the feather and fur.

Earth, air, fire, water.

What was needed yet was the all-important fifth element, the one needed to draw the powers of these four together into a creative force. The knowledge of how to do that, he had only heard about but never practiced even once.

Outside, the clouds opened up and rain started to pour down.

Lightning flashed and a roar of thunder rang over Lost Lake.

Dhani lay staring up at the branches of his lean-to, which he'd thrown together quickly and not very well last evening when dark clouds had begun to cover the moon and the scent of rain was on the air.

Randy Wolfmoon had been right about the weather. It was pouring now, the wind had risen, and the woods were soaked and dripping. Rain streamed around the little rise on which he lay.

He would not admit to himself Tanner had also been right by insisting he needed a better shelter than a tarp. He liked Randy, because he was easy on him, and he hated Tanner, because he was hard—always hard—on everybody.

He also didn't want to give Tanner ammunition by not complying with his jerky "order." Then he might use his bully-power to get him kicked out of the program and sent back to juvenile hall.

That thought and the feeling it raised made him miserable.

Why was I the one who went to jail?

He banished the words from his mind.

Hunger pains gnawed at his stomach, but he didn't want to crawl out of his lean-to to retrieve his bear bag, dangling in the rain in a tree thirty feet away through the woods. He rolled over in his sleeping bag, closed his eyes, and fell into a dreamy doze. . . .

Drops of rain began to splash his face, as an updraft lifted him higher into the air and cut through his feathers. He scanned the forest below, with a raging hunger.

His mind shifted.

Beneath a thick covering of cinnamon ferns that dripped with rain, he tucked his paws up under his fur to stay concealed. He lifted his head and sniffed, then began to tremble. In the air above him, death was circling.

Dhani fought to keep from being drawn into this daydream; he didn't want to be the strange kid anymore. The kid who imagined animals talked to him or that he was an animal.

A murderous ferocity and a frozen terror fought within him.

"You are the one who is one of us."

No, I'm not, he resisted the voice.

"Help us."

Help you what?

He tried to escape the daydream, escape his own head, but could not get out of its tightening grip. His mind was falling apart, losing its hold on the present reality of the rainy woods, the thunder and lightning flashes. . . .

His stomach churned with hunger and the wild pleasure of the hunt. He tilted his wings and went into a spiral, lower. . . lower. . . entering within the forest, his wing tip nicking a leaf, eyes focusing, searching. And there—right there—*among a stand of ferns was the smallest movement. The flicker of an ear. Something crouched, hiding. . . .*

Dhani's whole body had become hot, and he had the urge to bolt from his lean-to. The scene before his eyes began to rapid-shift, images tumbling together.

Concealed beneath the fronds, he felt his heart roar and his blood race with terror, but every muscle was frozen.

The predator narrowed its eyes, extended its talons, dove and grabbed.

The Monster seized him in a strangle-hold, enraged.

Tanner stood over him, superior, lording.

Then he was airborne, choking.

The Monster lifted him with two hands by the throat, and shook him as his mother shouted, "Dhani, why do you provoke him?"

His body squirmed and lifted up out of the undergrowth, up through the under-canopy of saplings, dangling, pierced with pain, terror wrenching his guts. He kicked and sank his teeth into the predator.

"Little bastard bit me!"

His mother came at the Monster, who threw a punch that landed solidly in her face. She fell back, spitting blood.

Then the Monster dragged him twisting and screaming toward the bathroom, pulling out his lighter, flicking it. "I know how to punish you."

The terrified little creature Dhani was. . . .

. . . felt his mind going numb. . . felt himself falling, twisting. . . roots and rocks speeding up to break him. . . banging his head on the bathroom's tile floor. . . the Monster on top of him, crushing him.

He sat bolt upright in his shelter sucking in air, his head brushing branches above him, making drops of cold rainwater run down his hair and neck.

"You are one of us."

"Stop saying that!" he shouted, banging his hands against his temples.

"But which one? You cannot be the abused and the abuser, the prey and the predator."

A hard rain fell all morning and the mountainside was dark. The thunderstorm passed, and the cool, rising and falling wind made its tapping tattoo softer, louder, softer against his shelter as the tarp rucked and wrinkled noisily.

As Ray-Ray's makeshift tent swayed, he imagined the ropes straining and wondered if they would hold or if it would all collapse on him. Overhead, branches rubbed together and around him the wilderness was full of snaps, creaks, and the groans of branches straining.

Lines from the film, "Scream," went through his head.

"There are certain rules that one must abide by in order to successfully survive a horror movie. For instance, number one: you can never do it. Big no, no! Big no, no! Sex equals death, okay? Number two: you can never drink or do drugs. The sin factor! It's a sin. It's an extension of number one. And number three: never, ever, ever under any circumstances say, "I'll be right back.' Because you won't be back."

I'm alone out here in a mountain woods straight out of a slasher movie. And I'm a terrible sinner.

He curled deeper into his sleeping bag, forcing his mind to think about something else.

Maybe I'll think about what you said, he had told Imani.

He envisioned his pure, sinless brother, Ezra, seated at his drumset, leading the congregation at Ebenezer Baptist in a worship song.

As the deer panteth for the water,

so my soul longeth after Thee. . . .

He felt a stab of loneliness and want to be with his Ezra right now. He'd looked up to him as long as he could remember. He was better looking, good natured, liked by everyone. . . and more important, just a normal guy.

A crack from somewhere off in the woods startled him, and his heart raced. Was it judgment, coming for him?

His mind kept circling back to the day his father forced him to leave in the middle of a downpour. What he always remembered about that day was his father's face—at first, distorted with anger and disgust, then a wall of cold and blank, forbidding.

"The Lord Jesus warned us that 'a man's enemies will be those of his own household'. I follow the Lord, and since you have chosen to be a son of the Devil, chosen sin, I cast you out and into his hands, so that your flesh may be punished and dealt with."

With the rain falling and the wind rattling the thin tarp stretched over his lean-to, he remembered his father in the doorway, blocking his way back into his own home. He remembered how cold the rain felt that day, running down his chest and back, soaking his pants and tennis shoes. All those details flashed in his mind just before he realized that in his upset that day there was an important detail he had ignored. One that maybe he hadn't wanted to remember.

Now it surfaced vividly in his mind.

Behind his father's tall, heavy-set frame, mostly in shadow and only half visible, was his brother. On his face was a faint smile.

What if—the new thought rose suddenly—*I'm a scapegoat?*

The rain became a downpour again and the wind picked up. The sheltering branches and tarp shook but held—protection for him from the wind, rain, and cold. If nothing else, maybe it was some small proof that even totally on his own in the world he could be okay.

The rain slowed then stopped around noon. Steve crawled out of his tent at base camp and had begun to re-stoke the fire when Bay approached him.

Ah, crap.

She pulled dry kindling from beneath a protective plastic sheet, and fed it to the red-gold embers Steve was poking. "When I said you're not fighting a war here, I think I was wrong. You are fighting a war. A big one, within yourself. I should have seen it sooner."

"Spare me, please."

She smiled at him. "I wonder if you'd be willing to talk with someone after the campout. Not me or Eric, we're your colleagues here. We know someone who works with combat veterans. He's right in town."

"What's with you guys? Everyone has to have a problem. A disorder. You guys give people a diagnosis, and then they think it's an excuse for not being able to act right. Do what they have to do. It's 'Oh, I have A.D.H.D. so I can't follow instructions because my mind is too jumpy.' Or 'My parents traumatized me, so I do drugs.' And all we have now is a nation of basket cases. And kids like these guys, who won't obey."

"Sometimes people can't obey," she countered. "Sometimes they resist or just can't do it because there's a reason. Quakers and other conscientious objectors just can't make themselves go to war to kill. It goes against their beliefs and their nature."

Steve thought she could not have picked a worse example. He wanted to punch so-called conscientious objectors.

"Can't or won't. Amounts to the same thing. Some of them just won't do what they're told. How's that gonna help them in life when they get out and someone in authority gives them a set of instructions or an order?"

"Are you sure you're concerned about them not following someone else's orders—or just yours?"

Randy had challenged him the other day in front of Dhani, and he had felt an urge to deck him. He felt an urge to hit Bay now—and immediately felt ashamed of himself.

"Just think about it. You have to want help."

And I don't. I'll take care of my own mess.

He said, "I'll let you know."

28TH

The sound of someone striking two heavy pieces of wood together led Garrett to Dugan's site.

Dugan was swinging a thick tree limb into the trunk of a tree. After two or three hits, another chunk broke off.

"Great way to get firewood," Garrett said. When Dugan didn't respond, he said, "What's up? Talk to me?"

"I challenged Rocco to race me up a tree and he beat me. In front of Imani. That was humiliating."

"So? You beat him once at boxing. He beat you once climbing a tree. No big deal. Forget Imani and go for Makayla. She's hot."

"It's about way more than that." Dugan collected the wood chunks he'd broken up. "We're gonna be in this program for two more years, and only one of us can be top man here. Rocco or me."

Garrett nodded. "*Maybe* Rocco won't be here much longer."

Dugan stacked the wood beside his fire circle. "You got an idea?"

"Maybe I do and maybe I do," Garrett grinned. "First, I came to tell you about a better business deal I'm offering you."

"How are we getting rid of Rocco?"

"Let me tell this first. You're gonna like the percentage."

"Took you long enough to get back to me."

Show time, Garrett thought. "Man, I been trying to survive up here just like you. But hey—before we left it took me a *lot* of negotiating but I got the other guys to give up the percentage points I'm giving to you."

Tanner was sitting cross-legged in front of his tent, sharpening the blade of his Ka-bar on a small, gray whetstone. Each pass of the blade made a slicing, scraping sound.

"Sir," said Garrett, pausing at the edge of Tanner's site. He had just manipulated Dugan to re-up for the dicey part of the business and he forced a self-satisfied look off his face. Now he saw exactly how to finish creating the smokescreen he needed. Everyone would be zeroed-in on one person.

"What's up?" Tanner stopped sharpening, examined the blade, and carefully slid the Ka-bar in its sheath.

"You asked me to be eyes and ears on-the-ground, right?"

Tanner unzipped a narrow side-pocket on his backpack and slid the knife inside. "You have something to tell me?"

"It's about Dhani. He's wandering around the woods."

"Maybe he's taking a dump."

"No. He's checking out people's sites. Dugan saw him spying from behind a tree. I caught him staring up at my bear bag, sorta scoping out my stuff. What's he looking for?"

Tanner stared at him for a long moment, then nodded. "Thanks. Appreciate the heads-up."

"I better head back, sir. Sure hope Jones isn't at my site going through my backpack."

"The computer tech guy is in the front foyer," Ivy called from the hallway outside Kate's office.

Kate held up one hand. Tom was on the phone with an update, just finishing.

"Sewell is fighting hard to prevent them from keeping Claire here in DC. Today, he's pulling your Congressman friend into the frey."

"Jacob Isaacs?—that's good news. As it happens, he and Jim were good friends for years. He was here doing some kind of research. He and I saw eye-to-eye on environmental issues. He's very effective and I hope he can put pressure on the prosecutor. How is Claire?"

"She was sullen and indifferent at first. Then something changed and now she seems eager to return. She said to Isaacs, 'If you can help me go back to Lost Lake, I'd be very grateful."

Kate smiled. "Well, it's good to know the program is taking hold with her. I wondered. Look, Tom, I need to speak with a technician. Call me this evening, when you're back at my place in Alexandria and I'm free."

In the front foyer was a young man in a white shirt and blue tie, holding a briefcase. He stuck out his hand as she approached. She reached out to shake with him, but saw he was offering her a folded slip of paper.

"Found this stuck in your front door. Looks like it was there a few days and got rained on."

With the students away, no one was coming in the front door, but maybe one of them had stuffed a note there for her before leaving. She started to unfold the damp, wrinkled sheet, then thought of all she had to do after getting the tech started on computer clean-ups and updates, and stuck the paper in her pocket.

Two hours later, the technician found her in the atrium, talking with a pool repairman, who was saying, "The filter stopped, because there's a short in the line. You need an electrician."

"I'm almost finished servicing the computers, but I found something I thought you might want to see."

Upstairs in the computer room, he sat at the screen and keyboard in the farthest corner in the back, with Kate looking over his shoulder.

"You had me connect these twelve computers to the same web browser—but on this computer I found another browser. No icon for it on the desktop. I found it among the "Programs" files when I was updating, along with an email program that shouldn't be there. Looks like a whole bunch of emails."

Kate felt her stomach sink. Whoever had done this was clever and knew how to hide what they were doing.

"Most of the emails are to and from one address. Just dates, starting last May until just a few days ago."

"Did you look at them?"

"They're pretty cryptic. The first ones are from a year ago this month. One says, '28th. 2 a.m.,' and the next one says, '12th. Marina'. There's a whole bunch like this, dated throughout the year. None of them were replied to."

"What do they mean? They sound like appointments."

That these existed, despite program rules stipulating no unsupervised outside contact, unsettled her.

"Then there was a second exchange," he continued, "between here and a different email address—just two emails. The first one is outgoing, just a month ago. It says, 'Everything cool down yet? It's hard here.' And there was a reply the next day. 'NO. Two more hits. And now they seriously wonder if it was you. Or was it EZ? DO NOT come near DC.'—Nothing more after that."

Kate let out a long, deep breath. "We have an honor system, and I thought everyone was abiding by rules. Looks like I've been a bit naïve."

"Do you want me to check out the email recipients? Easy enough to get their IP address."

"No. This isn't a criminal investigation. But I do want you to delete the browser and email program. That will put whoever set them up on notice. I'll post a note on the computers for the students to find when they return, reminding them of the program rules."

"We could set up a program to monitor keystrokes. I can feed it to a computer in your office."

"And turn this into a surveillance situation? No. I'll deal with this head-on when they return."

Back in her office, she was glad Ivy had noticed her troubled expression and followed to ask, "What's wrong?"

"Someone set up a secret communication system on a computer. I'd thought I could trust them all by now. I keep hearing Jim's voice. 'You're too trusting, Kate. That's because you're a bleeding heart and a sucker for poor, needy people. Sometimes people are just throwaways.'"

Trust was something Jim knew little about, though, or he would not have betrayed hers over and over. She had to believe the atmosphere of trust she was establishing here would work—would cause these young people to become trustworthy. No one was a throwaway. Still It was hard to hold onto an ideal when evidence said she was foolish to do so.

"Most of them have become very helpful and hardworking, at least in my opinion," Ivy said. "They do whatever kitchen cleanup duties I give them without an argument. I overhear their conversations, too—how much they like caring for the animals and how they really like being up here in the wilderness now. A few of them, not so much, of course. Tia Leesha mostly. *That* one, dear God. Still, you're doing a very good thing, Kate. Your trust will be repaid, you'll see."

When Ivy left to pick up supplies, Kate found herself thinking about Claire, a budding artist eager to return here where her talent was being nurtured. She thought about Emmalyn, pulled from her mother's strip club and God knew what else, asking for more office responsibilities, taking lesser duties off Tom's shoulders, showing signs she could become an executive someday. She thought about Jacob Isaacs, standing up for her program.

Make a point about the computers again and let it go. That's what Tom would advise if he were here. *Don't let Jim's cynical voice in your head turn little issues into big ones.*

The wrinkled note the tech had found was still there on her desk where she had laid it. Absently, she unfolded the paper.

The printed message had streaked, but was still legible.

Search Dhani's room.

Kate closed the door to Dhani's room.

Her search of the drawers in his dresser and nightstand and in his closet revealed nothing.

Who left the note? Was it a foolish or vicious prank?

As she walked back to the lodge, she looked downhill at Grady's cottage. When he returned from a few days off, she would have him go through the room again.

Why did she have the deeply unsettled feeling now that something was very wrong?

In the glow of the low cedar wood fire, Sahm sat before the altar, staring at the small objects resting on it.

The deerskin covering of the medicine lodge had faded and the darkness inside had deepened and expanded out into distance.

He drifted among the stars.

An eagle feather floated out in front of him and the tuft of rabbit fur. Between them was the small, barley flour Soul Deer.

Sahm waited for words or directions to arise from within him, aware that he must be the vessel of powers far beyond his human abilities. He was focused on the rabbit in its safe enclosure—but a face sprang to mind.

A human face.

At that instant, a tiny patch of brown hair appeared on the deer's flank, spreading rapidly out over its sides and down its legs. At the same time, the figure expanded and grew in size. When the spreading tide of brown hair reached its neck, the twigs he had used as horns stretched out and transformed into a great crown of antlers, and out at the end of each sleek leg a sharp hoof appeared. Around its neck and down its chest spread a thick white mane, like the mantle of a great ruler.

Sahm watched, filled with a sense of awe. He had heard stories from his grandfather and other *Sakyongs* and yogis about auspicious events and signs like this one.

His vision wavered, and he was floating in the blackness of the cosmos.

The Soul Deer turned its majestic head and stared directly into Sahm's face.

Some instinct arose in Sahm, and he understood. He reached out and took the tuft of rabbit fur between his thumb and forefinger. Before him, flames in the firepit had risen.

Without a sound, the Soul Deer spoke to him. Enigmatic words.

"Who he is must die."

And now Sahm knew. He was not here for the small, injured creature in the box beside his fireplace.

"You know this dissolution of the small, limited one. You passed through it to greater power. Let us go with him into the fire. Together, we will destroy what must be destroyed, save and protect what must be protected."

Images passed rapidly before Sahm's eyes—a maelstrom of strange people and events, some peaceful and beautiful, some violent. Images of things to come? At the center of the storm was his young friend. His charge.

Dhani.

He reached out to the fire, offering the tuft of fur in his fingers... offering himself, as well, to whatever the future and fate and choice held for them both. The flames leapt up to receive both gifts.

From the fire—surprising Sahm—the ancient petroglyph eagle sprang into the air, pulsing like flame and circling, first around the soul deer figure, then in wider and wider arcs, finally soaring up and out through the lodge's smoke hole with a call of triumph.

When the walls of the medicine lodge wavered back into a single vision of solidity again, Sahm was on his knees in the near dark. Only red-gold embers pulsed within the circle of stones.

In the dim light, he saw that the eagle feather still rested on the small, stone altar where it had been. The tuft of fur was gone—as was the barley soul deer.

He crawled out through the deerskin flap, and saw that night had fallen. He stood and stretched in the cool air beneath a black sky spangled with stars. Vajra was waiting for him.

"I have done what I could," Sahm said to him, as if seeking assurance. "Perhaps there was power in it. I think so."

When they reached the cabin, the front door was open just a crack, though Sahm was sure he had closed it.

Inside, Vajra padded across the floor straight to the box where the rabbit was convalescing. Sahm followed him and peered inside.

The rabbit was gone. The healing energy of the soul deer pulsed in the air.

If the door ajar meant anything, the creature had returned to its place in the surrounding wilderness. A sure portent.

Portents were just signs, though, of what might come to pass. Sacrifices only showed the *Elemental* powers that you were willing.

Now, he thought, *it is all up to the boy.*

29TH

Dhani had lain around all day in his lean-to. He didn't care to get up, not even to stir the ashes of his fire enough to boil water and make the hot oatmeal mix. Instead, he dumped the dry packet into his mouth and swirled water from his bottle with it, until it was a lumpy paste he could swallow.

Orange light fell through the woods and it was evening of this last day of survival hell.

He felt weak, and didn't care if he had enough strength to crawl back down the mountain. He also smelled bad because he had not bathed himself in nine days, and didn't care about that either. Maybe everyone would stay away from him. They all hated him anyway.

He heard the footsteps just before he heard the loud, angry voice.

"Get up and get out of there."

Tanner was standing just outside his lean-to, arms folded across his chest.

Dhani felt his muscles tensing, freezing up, but he forced himself to crawl out. "Why?"

Tanner nodded at his backpack. "Open it. Empty all the pouches and pockets."

"I—I just got everything put back in it for the trek back tomorrow."

"Doesn't matter. Take everything out."

"I don't want to," Dhani managed to say in a hoarse whisper.

Tanner's face hardened. "Do it. *Now.*"

Dragging his pack from the lean-to, Dhani knelt, then unzipped and emptied the main pouch of everything—the clean socks and tee-shirts he had not bothered to change into, the rolled up and still-damp jeans he had exchanged for the ones he was wearing when he'd soaked the lower pant legs in a stream.

Dhani hesitated, feeling Tanner's eyes penetrating him like talons. "Why are you making me do this?"

"Side pockets, too," Steve demanded.

Dhani unzipped a side pocket and reached in—then paused when he touched something unfamiliar. He pulled out a red bandana with something hard wrapped in it.

Steve reached out and took the object from his hand, unrolling the cloth.

"Like I suspected."

In his hand was a knife—a Marine Ka-bar, with *TK* carved on the leather handle.

Tanner's jaw clenched. "I was just packing to go back tomorrow, and realized this was missing from my backpack. I always know exactly where I keep it because it's extremely valuable to me. But it was gone. How did I *know* I'd find it here?"

Dhani looked up at him from where he was kneeling. He tried to croak out the words, "I didn't take it." But what would it matter?

The Monster. . . .

Tanner. . . .

He was shaking. Unable to speak to defend himself.

"Nothing to say to me? No 'I'm sorry'? *Nothing?*—Can't even defend yourself, can you?" Tanner goaded him. "Doesn't matter anyway. You're a little thief. Tomorrow morning, we hike back. And if I can help it, by afternoon you'll be on a bus with a one-way ticket back to juvenile hall."

When night fell, Dhani's campsite fire was long dead and even the last embers had gone cold. . . .

Twisting, the small creature let loose a high-pitched scream.

"I didn't do anything," Dhani shouted in his dream. "Why do you like to hurt me?"

The predator that clutched him in its hooks looked down with hard, gloating eyes. "Because I'm strong, and you are little, weak, needy and pathetic. I do whatever I want to you because I can."

Down in the shadowy trees below, where the predator was descending with him, something dark lay in wait. . . .

Dhani woke from the dream, his throat dry from shouting.

30TH

The group quit the summit's central campsite before eleven. The trip down the mountain trail was a mixed reunion—some joking and laughter, some storytelling about events.

"I heard something big walking in the woods two nights in a row," said Jalil.

"I heard something, too," Garrett tossed in. "It was Emmalyn, at the next site over, letting some big ones. Musta been the beans."

Beside him, Dugan snickered—while, four paces ahead on the trail, Emmalyn turned just long enough to give Garrett a hateful look, then hauled herself and her pack over a wind-felled log and kept descending.

In five minutes, Carter came up behind Garrett and Dugan. "Move it, slow boys. Or just get outa my way."

"I'm gonna hang with her," Garrett said to Dugan, picking up speed to keep up with Carter as she passed them. "Me and this fine lady need to talk."

"Why have you been ignoring me all year," he said to Carter, falling in-step. "I'm your biggest fan. I think you're hot."

"So do a lot of other guys. So what?" Before he could say anything, she tossed at him—"How's it going with you and your trained dog."

"Wha—oh, you mean Dugan?"

"So you admit it."

He grinned slightly.

"You're using him in your little business."

"Don't know what you're talking about."

"That's bull. I've watched you. I even followed you one night. I watch everyone. I know what everyone here is all about."

"What am *I* about?"

"Mainly, thinking you can control and use everyone."

"I'm good at it. So are you."

In response, she made a strange sound.

"Tell me the truth," he pressed. "You were just using Jalil to piss me off, weren't you?"

"No, I'm using him to keep Rocco guessing."

Garrett's smile disappeared. "What does that mean?"

"Rocco's very hot. Amazing lover. But he's also got a thing for Imani. I'm not going to lose out to a Black girl."

Garrett felt heat go up his neck. It was her racist remark. Rocco was a problem for his boy, Dugan, and now Rocco was an even bigger problem for him than he'd been from day one—unless Carter was lying, to wreck his head.

"He's a stupid muscle head," he half-choked on the words.

Carter smiled to herself, thinking how easy it was to play this boy and, like every other boy she knew, keep him dangling. Just to do it. Just to tease and hurt them. Because she could.

Dhani hung back on the trail, feeling irritable, then angry at the whole world. He'd located his mother a month ago and talked to her just long enough for her to say she had emptied his pathetic little bank account, then tell him not to call her again. And now the jackass Tanner was going to get him sent back to detention, while whoever put the knife in his backpack would get away with it—just because Tanner *wanted* to believe he was a thief.

After an hour's descent, he caught up to the group, where Tanner had stopped everyone at a fork in the trail.

"Go left here and you'll be back to your cabins sooner."

The words were hardly out of his mouth and every one of the girls was raising a hand or talking.

"I'm done."

"I want a hot shower."

"Get me back *now*."

He looked at Bay and Laurel. "That just bought you guys a fast ticket home." To the guys he said, "Looks like we're going right on our own."

"Wait," Jalil objected. "I want a hot shower, too."

"Oh, I've got something better than that for you fellas. A surprise. Make a man outa ya."

Another half-hour down the trail, they heard the sound of water falling—not the noise made by Thunder Falls but a gentler sound. Water flowing over rocks, and splashing lightly. Around a bend in the trail, the trees parted to reveal a small spring pouring out of a sheer rock face and splashing into a large, clear pool surrounded by nodding ferns. Sunlight penetrating through the tree canopy and the pool's surface revealed it had some depth.

Steve slung the backpack off his shoulders.

"Okay, guys. This is it. Strip down and jump in. All of you smell pretty bad, and we're not going to show up back at Kate's place stinking. We're gonna show up clean and proud."

Jalil bent and stuck his hand in the water. "Holy crap, that's ice cold."

Garrett peeled off his shirt, then dropped his jeans to the ground. "Good idea, sir." He stepped one foot in the water and shouted—*"Daggone!"*

Dhani showed up then, but hung back from the pool.

Rocco and Dugan were hooting and pulling off their clothes, splashing into the pool and diving under—coming up with shouts that echoed off the rock face.

"So cold!"

"Yee-ha!"

Jalil dove in and came up shivering and shouting.*"I'm turning blue already!"*

Ray-Ray was reluctantly fingering the lower edge of his sweatshirt. "Do we have to do this?"

"Yep. Get in," Tanner responded—then added, "That's an order. Wash yourself."

Ray-Ray stripped down quickly and eased his way into the water, arms wrapped around his torso. *"Ohmygod,"* he said, through chattering teeth.

Tanner looked at Dhani, who still hung back, unmoving.

"Get in. Wash up."

Dhani didn't move.

"I know you heard me," Tanner said louder. "Get in. *That's an order.*"

Dhani pulled the hood of his black sweatshirt up and looked away.

Steve felt his mind and his temper fray. This disrespectful little thief had gotten away with ignoring or defying or dodging him all year.

A flash of rage exploded inside him, so forceful his whole body shook.

"I'm so sick of you!" he shouted. *"You don't deserve to be here. You should be back in DC, out working on a road crew."*

The shouting from the pool stopped.

He charged at Dhani, grabbing at his hoody, yanking it—hard—while Dhani tried to twist away, objecting.

"Stop! Leave me alone. . . You're hurting me!"

Steve had caught the lower part of Dhani's teeshirt in his fingers along with the hoody—both of which he continued to tear off over Dhani's head.

"Don't!"

With one more yank, the hoody and shirt came off.

Steve stepped back, his eyes wide with a stunned look.

In the pool, all the other boys stood dripping and staring.

Dhani's chin had dropped to his chest, as he stared at his own exposed torso. All across his chest and stomach and down both arms, lines of small pale spots stood out against his tan skin. Dozens of scars, some of them deep, as if whoever made them had dug and twisted something into the skin to cause the most pain.

Dugan smirked at Dhani. "What the hell are you, dude—a leopard?"

Ray-Ray slapped the back of his head. "Shut up."

"Well what the hell are those spots all over him from—AIDS?"

"I told you *shut up*. That's what happens to people of color—like you, me, and *him*—when you burn us. Can't you see that's what it is?" He gave Dugan a hard shove that sent him falling backward into the water.

Steve held the torn hoody and tee-shirt in one hand, staring, mouth open.

Dhani looked stunned.

. . . fearful woodmouse. . . wary red squirrel. . . terrified rabbit. . . all dissolved.

His face altered, his usual mild look vanishing. His eyebrows arched, his fingers curled like the talons of a bird, until his fists doubled, and he charged at Steve.

"*You jerk! You goddam jerk!*" he shouted, slamming both hands into Steve's chest.

Caught off-guard, Steve staggered backwards but kept his footing. "Dhani, I'm sorry. . . I didn't know. . . ."

"Didn't know *what*, you prick? That nobody cares about your stupid Boy Scout knife except you and whoever hid it in my stuff? You didn't know that everyone didn't have a perfect life, like I guess you had? Didn't know some little kids watch their moms get punched around by their drunk, drug addict boyfriends? Didn't you ever meet anyone who tried to save his mom from getting raped *again*. . . for the *third or fourth or fifth time?*"

"Look. No. I didn't know, and I'm trying to say—"

Dhani's whole body was shaking. He'd broken into a sweat and his face was pale.

"What *do* you know? And what the hell are you doing here with a kid like *me*? What do you think you have to say to *me*? Do you think I give a shit about your stupid buck knife tricks? What did you come here for—to have us bad kids kiss your ass and tell you what a *big man* you are?"

He looked at the others, who were still gaping at his scarred body.

"You're a bunch of kiss asses. I never needed your friendship. So you can all go to hell."

Turning back to Tanner, his voice rose and the veins stood out on his neck.

"I don't give a shit about you being a big hero in Afghanistan. I'll bet all your buddies buy you beers, and you sit around telling how many innocent villagers you blew away. How do we know you're not a war criminal?"

Steve felt a surge of anger at those last words, but he forced himself to extend a conciliatory hand and stepped toward Dhani, needing to calm him down, regain control. "Listen to me, please."

Dhani recoiled, his hands clenching and unclenching.

"NO, YOU SHUT UP AND LISTEN TO *ME!*"

Steve froze again.

"Try living your *whole life* knowing that tonight the guy who's crushing your little neck with his bare hands might just forget to stop. Try being used as an ashtray for somebody to stub out their cigarettes on—" he pointed at his body "—because you didn't look at him the right way and it pissed him off. . . . And then some jerk like you thinks it's his job to humiliate you.

"Try living your whole life," he shouted, *"feeling like shit because you were too weak to defend yourself or your mother."*

Ray-Ray was carefully, slowly moving toward Dhani. "Yo, buddy. Come on."

Dhani's eyes flared at him. "Piss off."

Steve realized the next move was crucial. He had allowed Dhani to vent enough. Whether he had made a wrong move pulling his shirt off or not, he had to regain control. If he could take Dhani down with a tackle, he could get the upper hand.

With a lunge, Steve launched himself, arms outstretched.

Dhani leaped aside, dodging him. *"Is that all you know how to do,"* he shouted,*"—force people to do what you want? You idiot. You don't get it, do you?"*

Steve landed on his chest on the stones. His right hand caught the sharp edge of a stone and began to bleed. He pushed up with his arms and positioned himself to spring at Dhani again.

In that instant, Dhani stooped and seized a stone the size of a brick.

He reared back, body coiled, arm cocked and ready to launch the stone. His eyes flashed and fixed on Steve's skull. His chest heaved.

The Monster. Tanner. The predators came together in Dhani's mind. The terror that had controlled him all his life now changed into something else, its energy rising up his spine, seizing his whole body.

Caught in this low position on one knee, Steve froze again.

The eyes he was staring up into were not those of a scared boy anymore. They were cold, expressionless eyes—a formidable foe, daring him.

"You think you can force me to do what you want? You like to push people around. Just because—why?—because everyone is supposed to listen to you because you're big Steve Afghanistan Tanner?

"Well I'm Dhani *Singh* Jones—NOT *SINGE!*" he shouted at the boys in the pool, so loud his voice frayed.

The rock stayed poised in Dhani's upraised hand.

Steve's head was still trying to rearrange, to take in the burns all over Dhani's chest, stomach, arms and back. The attempted tackle had been a bad miscalculation—but he realized now that the ways he had misjudged Dhani had been an even greater mistake.

What had he done to this kid, who now stood in front of him enraged by a lifetime of abuse and torture with a weapon in hand?

He could do it. He could smash my skull in.

In a gesture of surrender, Steve held up both hands, blood running down his right wrist, hoping this would calm and not provoke Dhani further.

But Dhani's eyes continued to bore into him, challenging, accusing, provoking.

Ray-Ray stepped between Dhani and Steve, naked, dripping, and holding up both hands.

"Dhani. Cool down."

"I didn't take his stupid, crappy little knife," Dhani shouted at him.

His hand was still raised, gripping the rock, his eyes wild. "What do you care what I do? You were my friend and you dumped me. Like everyone else."

"No, Dhani. I didn't. Really. I—I just got news of something really big going on back home that could affect my brother. My head was all up in that. I'm still here for you, man."

Dhani's eyes darted from Ray-Ray, to the guys in the pool, to Tanner—and back to Ray-Ray.

"Move!" he shouted—and he drew his arm back, his body coiling to throw.

Ray-Ray dodged to the right.

Tanner—watching from his crouch—curled his body into a ball, hands protecting his head.

When Dhani released the stone, it flew high over Tanner's head and crashed in the underbrush behind him.

A stunned silence hung in the air.

"You're *stupid,* Tanner. You've been watching me all year and still don't have a freaking clue that I would never hurt anybody. How'd you ever make it out of Afghanistan alive if you don't know *shit*? I don't 'stick' people with knives. That's what guys like you do, when you're not putting people down or blowing them up. Why'd you even come here to teach survival if you don't have a clue what kids like me had to do to survive?"

Steve rose slowly, his mind reeling. The things Dhani had just revealed about his childhood struck harder than a rock could have. He groped in his mind for words, an apology, anything, and couldn't think what to say. Every response that came sounded shallow and ridiculous.

It didn't matter.

Dhani had grabbed his backpack and started alone down the trail.

Grady held out his hand, holding a cigarette packet out to Kate.

She set her coffee cup down on the kitchen counter. "What's this?"

"Marlboro pack with three rollies.—Joints," he added when he saw her confusion.

"Oh lord."

"I went through everything in the kid's room. Even turned over the mattress and box springs. Then I turned over the nightstand and found this duct-taped underneath the lower shelf. Nice hiding place."

She took the packet from him. "This is so disappointing."

"I should tell you something else."

She raised her eyebrows.

"Someone got into my place a few weeks ago and stole liquor."

"You have liquor on the property when I made it a point that no one is to have alcohol here—for this very reason. And this happened a few weeks ago and you didn't tell me then."

"I handled it in my own way."

"You were wrong not to tell me."

"Well, it was my place and someone took—"

"Yes, I know. Going into your place and stealing is the point you want to make. Whoever did it, if we can find out who, has seriously broken rules and that's a big problem. But you went against the no-alcohol policy. Judge Sewell stipulated that. And I already have a small problem with a woman in charge of social services. I don't need a bigger one."

Grady stared at his boots, then raised his head looking unsettled. "Am I going to lose my job?"

She looked at the cigarette pack, which he'd laid beside her coffee cup.

"We're not in a good place, you and I. I've trusted and relied on you until now, Grady. I need to think about where we stand. At the moment, I have something more urgent to deal with—this student, bringing drugs here."

When Grady was gone, Kate stood staring a long time out the window at Lost Mountain. She shifted her mind from its agitated state to her spiritual practice, breathing deeply until the knot in her stomach released.

I will not give in to fear or anger. We will find the way to correct and heal what's happened here.

8

JUNE

1ST

Steve would not turn around when he heard Jo call his name. He crossed the bridge and turned down the camp road, determined to leave her and Lost Lake behind.

"Tanner," he heard her call again, then heard her quick footsteps on the gravel road jogging up from behind.

"What's with the duffel bag?" she said, falling in stride. "Where are you going?"

"Time to move on. I committed to be here for one year. Year's up."

"That's not why you're leaving. It's because you blew it with Dhani Jones. I heard Kate and Tom were all over you."

"So glad the word got out."

"Stop running and talk to me."

"I'm not running, I'm walking—but I do need to pick up my pace. The bus from Placid leaves for Albany before noon. If I can hitch a ride from the hard surface road I should make it in time."

"What did Tom and Kate say about you leaving?"

He didn't respond and walked faster.

Jo stopped in the road and let him keep walking alone. "This is really about blowing it, isn't it? So what? Like I said, stop running. Stay and face your mistakes."

He slung his duffel higher on his shoulder and kept moving quickly. Just before he disappeared around a bend in the camp road, he heard her call after him—shouting a question.

Which he forced out of his mind.

"Mom says you hit her, Dad. I just talked to her and she's crying again. You always make her cry."

Rocco looked over his shoulder to be sure no one was in Kate's library, where she'd told him to make his return call home. His face felt hot with anger and shame.

His father swore. "If she didn't make me mad, I wouldn't have to straighten her out."

"Dad, you hit my *mom*. Your *wife*. What do you think that does to her? How do you think that makes her feel?"

His father became hostile. "Is that what they're doing to you up there in that program—getting you all wrapped up in feelings? You're there for one thing. To stay out of trouble, get your record wiped clean, and come back here in a couple years to step into the business. Don't go all feely-feely snowflake on me."

"Mom's thinking about leaving you. Doesn't that bother you?"

"She's not going anywhere. She knows where she's got it good. And listen to me." His father's voice dropped, like he was taking him into some great and secret confidence. "Women like it when you're rough with them. For some, the rougher the better. If you got a girl up there, you don't let her tell you how it's gonna be. Those strong women types wanna turn you into a pussy-boy. Someone they can toy with and control. That'll make your life miserable. You got a girl you like, you treat her a little mean, then a little nice, then mean. Keep them on the string. Trust your old man."

"But mom—"

"*To hell with your mom,*" his father shouted. "What are you—a mama's boy? You do what I say. You think the way I want you to think. You got that? Anyone in that program messes with your head, I'll send a guy up there to knock some teeth out."

Rocco swallowed the words he was thinking.

"Did your mother happen to tell you I bought her the arctic blue fox coat she asked for? Very expensive. Did she tell you I'm takin' her to a ritzy resort in northern Italy? That ain't cheap, either. Did she tell you she kissed me and said I'm her 'knight in shining armor'?"

Rocco's head swam with confusion. "No. She didn't tell me any of that."

"That's women. Always twisting things. Leaving out the good things you do, to make you look bad. You just get home for your break and you'll see. Everything's good."

When he threw open the door of his cabin it banged into Jalil who was on his way out.

"Dude, what the hell?" Jalil said to Rocco, stepping back in the entryway rubbing his shoulder.

"Get out of my way."

Jalil stood his ground. "*No.* Screw you. You've been treating me like crap all year. *All year.* You left me out in the cold taped to a tree. I coulda froze. What'd I ever do to you?"

"I just don't like your kind is all."

Rocco tried to pass but Jalil met him chest to chest, glaring up into his face. "What do mean *my kind?*"

"Muslims. You people shouldn't even be in this country."

Jalil blinked. "You think I'm Muslim?"

"Jalil—that's a Muslim name, right?"

"You hated me all year because you thought I was Muslim. Just because of my name? You idiot. My family's been Coptic Christian since, I don't know, maybe the time of Christ. Centuries anyway. My dad is a scholar at Catholic University in DC. He translates old, old Christian scrolls written in ancient languages—Aramaic, Greek, Latin and a bunch of others. He made me be an altar boy when I was younger."

Rocco's mouth fell open. "I—I—"

"You're you're—I see what you are. You're a bigot. Did you just get that way on your own or are you from a family of bigots? You know Italians were hated when you guys came here on the boat, right?"

"What's Coptic mean?"

"Read a book, you moron. We're Christians."

Rocco stared at the floor, his face flushed. "I'm. . . really sorry. I don't know what else to say."

"I don't really care what else you have to say," said Jalil, pushing past him. "Just get out of my way."

"Ohmygod, he's so stupid," Makayla laughed. "Now that you set him straight, do you think you guys could be friends?"

"I don't know. I think I'll treat him like crap for a while."

"Don't do that. Then you'll be doing the same thing he did to you. Someone has to be the bigger person."

"I don't want to talk about Rocco anymore. I came to ask you something. You said you needed a guy friend who can keep secrets. Then we got busy with finals and the trip and never got to talk. What's the secret?"

She cleared her throat and looked around, even though no one else was near them on the lake front. "I lose minutes."

"What does that even mean?"

"It started about a year or so before I wound up in detention. I would like, get in the car with my mom in our driveway. And the next thing I knew we'd be at a stop sign a few blocks from our neighborhood. Like we just disappeared and reappeared there. I'd walk out of my room intending to close and lock the door behind me to keep my parents out—they're always going through my room—and when I'd go back the door would be wide open. I just sort of blank out."

"And you had no memory of what you did in those lost minutes?— Can I ask you a question?

"I overheard you tell Imani months ago on the bus ride up here that you were in detention for stealing a lot of really expensive stuff."

She shoved his shoulder. "You little sneak."

"Hey, I liked what I saw. I wanted to know more, so I listened in. Did you steal stuff when you were—what do you call it—blanked out?"

"No. That's all on me."

"I don't get that. You said your parents are doctors and run a company that sells medical equipment. I mean, you gotta be pretty rich. Why would you steal?"

"That was really stupid. But you don't know my mom. She would buy me tons of stuff. Expensive clothes. Anything I wanted, really. But there was always a string attached. A big one. 'I just bought you this, so you *have* to do that.' 'I just spent all this money on you, so you agree with me your dad is a terrible person, don't you?' It's all about trying to get me to think like her and act like her. Especially when it comes to trashing my dad."

"Is he bad to you guys?"

"No. He's not a great dad. He's all about his money, too. All about dressing us the right way. Vacationing in the right places. Sending me to the right schools. Making sure I talk and act the right way around their wealthy friends and business investors. Like I told you before, I only exist to make them look good. We're supposed to be the ideal family. Then I blew that up. I was actually relieved I was going to detention just to get away from all the pressure and fakeness."

"Is that why you didn't even go home for Christmas?"

Her face clouded. "No. There's something else going on. My mom keeps pumping me to find out if my dad did something to me."

"Do you mean like—?"

"Yeah, like did he come into my room at night and touch me or force himself on me. That's such a gross thought." She shuddered. "She just kept asking me that over and over."

"He didn't, did he?"

"No."

"Don't tweak out, but if I'm gonna be your close friend I have to ask. Is it possible he did and you're having these blank-outs because you don't *want* to remember?"

She looked unhappy. "I mean, he's a self-centered egotist, but I don't think he'd do that."

"But you're not positive."

"I know he didn't force himself on me. He couldn't have. I'd know. But did he touch me? No, I'm not sure."

Tia Leesha rolled over in bed and pulled the pillow back over her head, wishing the breeze wasn't blowing the curtain aside letting the sun fall on her face.

Someone grabbed the pillow and yanked it away, making her squint. "Who is that?—Oh god, what do you want?"

Imani was standing beside her bed, pillow in hand.

"Get up. It's a beautiful afternoon. Why are you inside in bed?"

"I'm tired. Why do you think?"

"I don't think you're tired. I think you're hungover."

"So what if I was. What're you tryna be now—my friend? You ain't bothered with me all year." She rolled over and kept grumbling unintelligible sounds.

Imani dropped heavily onto the bed to make it shake.

"You're making it pretty obvious you're using. I just think someone should give you a wakeup call. Do you want to go back to juvenile detention? Or do you want to stay here and make a different future for yourself?"

"What are you—Oprah? And why're you down on me? You're racist."

"Racist?" Imani gave her a sharp look. "I'm the same race as you."

Tia Leesha rolled back to face her. "You play both sides of the fence. Black boys and White boys. You're a light-skinned sell-out."

Imani's eyes narrowed. "If you ever say that to me again, I will beat you till you can't breathe. You know, I wouldn't be down on you if you just tried. You did for a little while during the winter campout. But now you don't again. You're just like a bucket of water somebody dumped over and you roll downhill to the lowest spot and lay there like a puddle."

Tia Leesha glared and her eyes grew intense with tears.

"My mama always had high standards," she snapped. "*Really high* standards. My bathroom wasn't spotless enough if she found a tiny tiny dab of toothpaste on the sink or a single hair on the floor. My bed was never a thousand percent wrinkle free. I don't sing good enough in church, like my cousin, Velda, who sounds like Etta James. How'm I supposed to compete with that? Nothing I do is good enough. So I gave up even trying. Then she called me a lazy n-gger."

"Your mama did that? That's horrible."

Tia Leesha sniffed and looked away.

Imani reached out and put a hand on her shoulder. "But you're mama's not here now. She's not your excuse now. You gonna prove her right or wrong?"

"I can't live up to what everyone else can do. I'm not a math genius like Carter. I'm not the sweetest girl on earth like Makayla. I'm not an amazing artist like Claire. And I'm not you."

"What does that mean? What am I?"

"You're like a beautiful model. Your skin is so light and smooth it glows like—like creamy coffee."

"You want this skin? Do you know how many people have trashed me because I'm a light-skinned Black? Do you know how many times I've been called 'mulatto girl' and how many times I've been asked if my great-great grandfather was the overseer on a tobacco plantation? Or if my great-grandmas spread their legs for money to buy grits or shoes?"

Tia Leesha was upset and shaking. "I just—I see how boys drool over you."

"My reality is not the one you imagine. A boy slobbering on you is not what you want. If he's drooling it's because he's high, drunk or stupid. That kinda boy wants to use you like a drug."

Tia Leesha seemed to be considering.

"Speaking of drugs. Who's supplying you?"

Tia Leesha rolled away from her again. "I'm not using. And if I was, I wouldn't tell you my hookup. That's private information."

"Just be careful," said Imani, turning to leave.

"Of what?"

"Of ignoring the chance to be the person you want to be, not who your mama or anyone else says you are."

The face reflected back at him from the bus window had a blank look. As if the man it belonged to were an empty soul.

And that, he knew, was because the man behind that mask did not want to deal with the painful images and feelings that kept trying to rise with greater and greater force inside his mind. For hours—months and months, really—he'd tried to crush them out. At Christmas, they had almost dragged him down into a final darkness.

"Folks," the driver announced, "we'll be pulling into the Rensselaer Station in Albany in fifteen minutes. We're running ahead of schedule, so no worries if you're hoping to catch an Amtrak train."

The blank face in the glass kept staring back at him, now barely containing the force of bitter judgment.

He was, finally, too fatigued to resist anymore.

The question Jo had shouted at him came back to sting. The same question Olivia had asked him through tears the morning he'd driven her away—the morning he failed to protect her and she was mugged and shot in the chest five times.

"What's it going to take, Steve?"

The answer was slamming itself at him now.

He saw the burn scars on Dhani's body. Heard the frustrated anguish—and the truth—in the boy's accusation.

"Why'd you even come here to teach survival if you don't have a clue what kids like me had to do to survive?"

Olivia and Dhani were right. He didn't know anything about the way some kids—maybe a lot of kids, or even adults—were forced to live, or what they had to do just to get through a day. Let alone get through the life they were handed or stuck in.

He tried to tell himself lots of people fight their way up and out of terrible situations. But did that mean they didn't carry scars for their whole lives? It had never occurred to him to wonder about that.

Other images flashed in his mind, of Dhani as a little boy, held down by some sick bastard, unable to escape, being tortured with lit cigarettes. Being a powerless kid, with no place to go and no options. What would that steal from you or destroy in you? How degraded and cowering from life would you feel by the time you were his age? How would you be able to face and deal with an angry Marine who was in your face, pushing you. . . .

. . .making it clear he hated you—even though he knew nothing about the conditions you had lived through that made it impossible to live up to his standard.

"What's it going to take, Steve?"

In the bus window, the deeper past came back—no forcing it down, no stopping it now. . . .

"Don't let me die, Tanner. You said you'd send us all back home safe. Keep me alive so I can kick these bastards' asses with you."

"I got you, TK. I promise."

"Don't let go of my hand."

"I won't drop you, man. We're the Death Hawk unit, remember? We don't let anybody fall," he said, as an ambulance driver pushed him aside.

In thirty minutes, he was shouldering his way inside the medical tent after hearing a medic say, "The chopper's not here and I gotta call it."

He gripped TK's hand until three orderlies pulled them apart, and dragged him out kicking and shouting, "You can't stop. Keep working. . . ."

Travis Konnick's leg had been blown off in Kamdesh, and the horrible conditions there were dead set against both of them. Carrying the Ka-bar with his initials kept alive the memory of a good man, a great young Marine.

But you didn't keep him *safe or alive like you promised, did you?*

The thought landed on him like mortar fire. He had made big promises, to keep all his men safe and to keep TK alive. Promises that made him sound big and which he had no realistic way to fulfill.

He looked down at the insignia sewn on his travel bag—a large, blue-gray hawk's claw clutching a small brown rabbit. He should not have let go of TK's hand. He should have stayed with him and shouted at him to fight for his life. He should not have let Olivia leave the Cathedral alone, hurt and rejected, and slip from his grasp, his life.

Why, then, had he judged someone else so brutally—especially a beaten, abused, and terrified kid like Dhani? Or struggling Tia Leesha, or any of them? Why, when he knew—he of all people *knew*—there were places and situations and moments of personal weakness and failure when you didn't live up to your own standard, let alone anyone else's?

"Aaand here we are, folks, at our destination," the driver announced.

"Signs at the train station are easy to follow. Wherever you're headed, I hope the rest of your journey is great."

2ND

The sound of Thunder Falls was not so much like thunder today as like a gentle shower. Since last week's rain, days of strong sun and an early summer heatwave had quickly dried the mountainsides and lowered the level of the streams.

"I knew I'd find you up here," said Claire. She emerged from the trees and stepped onto the ledge next to the falls, and balked when she saw him.

"You're too close to the edge. Step back."

Dhani turned his head. "You're back." He did not sound excited. "What did the prosecutor want?"

She stood behind him, back from the cliff a little, staring at the tips of his shoes which were over the edge a little.

"The man is crazy," she replied. "I told you that the D.E.A. swatted our farm the day my parents were busted. They dredged the pond and that's where they found the crates of cocaine. Also a lot of money. A couple million. I knew it was a lot, but I didn't know it was that much. I never read the news articles."

"So. . .?"

"So get this. The prosecutor and his team believe there's a lot more money hidden somewhere. They've torn up the whole farm and can't find it. And they think *I* may know where it is."

"Do you?"

"Dhani, I was seven. What on earth would I know? The juvenile court judge almost laughed out loud at the prosecutor.—And why aren't you backing away from the edge? You're making me nervous."

Dhani looked up at the sky. "I just want to step off. Fly away from here. I had a dream last night that I could fly."

"You're not serious, are you—about stepping off?"

"If they say they're sending me back, I might."

"*No*. You're not going to do that," she said forcefully. "Look at me, Dhani."

He turned to face her fully—and she lifted her hand and made signs to him.

"You're my '*west* friend'?"

"*Best* friend."

"Oh. Your fingers were spread apart a little. B is fingers together, like this." He signed the letter. "Where'd you learn that?"

"From a lady who told me I'm lucky to have a friend like you. She told me you're using sign language.—You're partly deaf aren't you? That's why you seem tuned-out all the time."

"Maybe."

"Dhani, why didn't you tell anyone? Then people would have understood what was going on with you. Or at least some of it."

"I finally told Tom after the survival thing, when he questioned me. He wouldn't let up 'til I told him about the abuse. I got punched in the head a lot when I was little. Hard. I just learned to get by. They never tested my hearing at the free clinics.

"But why didn't everyone just treat me alright the way I was—the way I am?" he said, with strength in his voice. "I try to treat everyone good. It doesn't matter what they're like. I just figure everyone's got stuff going on. Do you really have to understand someone to be good to them?"

She stepped up, took his arm to guide him away from the edge, and gave him a long hug.

He stood still, allowing her to hold him. Then he lifted his arms from his sides and wrapped them around her.

Her body began to shake and he heard soft sobs. Warm tears fell on his neck.

Then she stepped back from him, wiping her eyes.

"Dhani," she said, her voice strong again. The softer Claire receded, and she was back to the in-charge version.

"I heard about the skinny-dipping... *event*... up on the mountain. I heard about your scars. I guess *a lot* of terrible things happened to you when you were little. A lot of bad things happened to me, too, but nothing that horrible. No one burned and tortured my body."

He was smiling a little. He liked the softer side of Claire she had kept hidden all year.

"No more stupid talk about jumping off a cliff," she ordered. "I want to be here for you, but I can't if you keep everything hidden inside. Promise me you'll tell me everything that's bothering you or making you sad."

He said nothing; he couldn't make that promise.

"One of the joints was laced with PCP," said Kate. "That's what the Sheriff said. He's only keeping it quiet because we're friends and

he believes in what we're trying to do. He also said it's so common up here that it's hard to trace where it comes from. Sometimes people who can't make ends meet working two and three jobs turn to drug dealing. They make PCP on their kitchen table."

Eric and Bay Trovert had joined Kate and Tom, and Eric responded.

"It's highly unlikely Dhani's been smoking PCP or that anyone else is either. Bay and I have both worked in serious rehab situations, and no one here shows any of the classic signs. So he's not selling or giving it away either."

There was a light knock at the office door and Ivy stuck her head in. "Someone is here to see you."

"Not now," Kate said, sounding impatient.

"I said you were in a very important meeting. They said that's why they're here. I think you should hear what they have to say."

"What's funny?" Claire asked, frowning. "Why are you smiling?"

Dhani stared far below, at the Garnet River running south. "Kind of crazy-ironic that we could possibly be better friends now. They're meeting today to decide about kicking me out. I threatened Tanner with a rock and someone put drugs in my room."

"I know. But before I came up here I found Kate and Tom and told them there's no way you've been doing drugs or giving them to anybody. I told them I've known people who are on drugs, like my parents and some of my foster sisters, and you're definitely not on drugs."

She looked him in the eye, her expression serious. "You have wild stuff going on in your head that I don't understand, Dhani. But you're really a great guy."

"I know it's wild. I don't understand it either."

"Well, I'm here for you now while you figure it out. I told them if they send you away I'm not staying either."

"Hey."

Ray-Ray emerged from the trees. "Damn. We just got down from ten days on a mountain and you had to make us climb all the way up here to find you? What the hell?"

"I didn't think anyone would find me. Guess I was wrong. And that's the first time I've heard you say more than 'darn it'."

Sahm came out of the forest behind Ray-Ray.

"They just now let us interrupt the big meeting about you," said Ray-Ray. "I told them I heard someone banging around your room the day before we left, when you were out and I was kinda napping."

"I also spoke on your behalf," said Sahm. "I told them when you left my front porch that day I saw you take a long walk around the lake."

"Why wouldn't you let me in?" Dhani said to Sahm, sounding wounded.

"Someone reported that I was teaching you about demons. Kate ordered me to stay away from you. I should have explained, but I had allowed it to unsettle me. Not good practice."

"I think someone tried to get Sahm kicked out of here," said Ray-Ray. "Sahm and I think someone is trying to set you up, too."

"Wait—you guys have been talking about me?"

"To defend you, yes," said Sahm.

"What did Kate and Tom say?"

"Troverts were there, too," Ray-Ray replied. "They all said they'd take what we told them into account. Rocco, Imani, and Makayla spoke up for you too, I heard."

"But it's still possible they're kicking me out."

"I guess. I mean, you were threatening to assault Tanner in front of all of us."

"Yeah, well it's their second day meeting about me. I told them I'd take a blood test to prove I'm not on anything. If they're gonna kick me out, though, I wish they'd do it and get it over with."

"He insisted he hates drugs because his mother and her boyfriend did a lot of drugs—and that's when she let the guy hurt him. While she was doped-up. He calls the guy The Monster."

"Seems to me she's monstrous, too," Tom said, his voice grim. "Where was Monica Saint and her people when Dhani's mother was letting someone burn this boy? And before he was sent here, why didn't she order more thorough health screening tests? It would have picked up that Dhani is almost completely deaf in one ear and partially in the other."

"He insists he didn't take the knife from Steve, either," Kate pressed on. Her tone sounded like she was reaching a conclusion.

"Both Sahm and Ray-Ray have vouched for him and so has Claire and some others. Is it possible someone's trying to get Dhani sent away?"

"I have a suspicion someone was trying to get rid of Sahm, too." Kate pursed her lips. "I have to admit, I regret overreacting to Monica Saint's anti-religious hysteria. Sahm is a very good soul."

"He is," said Tom. "I see nothing but good in him."

"I should have just stuck up for him, but instead I cut him off from seeing Dhani and ordered him not to go on the survival trip. If he'd been there, he might have intervened between Dhani and Steve and kept the blow-up from happening."

Bay said, "Ray-Ray told us what Dhani said after the incident at the spring. He had no intention at all of hurting Steve. Just knocking him down a few pegs. Two males who needed to finally butt heads, is how I see it."

"Explosions aren't always a bad thing, Kate," Eric weighed-in. "There can be a mess to clean up after but they can clear the air, too."

"Yes, well, if one or both of the people involved aren't harmed in the explosion," Kate rebutted.

"No one's harmed," said Bay. "Dhani actually seemed fine yesterday when we met with him. Calm. Kind of grounded and solid. More present. Not retreating into himself the way he did all year."

"We may have to work with Steve a bit," Eric offered. "I met with him twice. The day after they got back and again yesterday. Briefly. He wouldn't talk with Bay. I can tell you that both times he was really in distress. Of course he tried not to show it, but he had this haunted look that gave him away."

Tom fished a paper out of his pocket. "Steve's gone. This morning he left this note of resignation. Never even said goodbye."

Kate put a hand to her forehead.

"That poor man. Such a hurting soul. I thought being here would help him work out his own issues, free him of some demons—as you suggested, Tom. You believed it would help, and so did I."

Tom looked from face to face. "So much for me being a spiritual director. It seems I came up with a script that God had no part in."

"You don't know that," Bay spoke up—which made Eric turn to her in surprise.

"I think we've left Dhani hanging on a hook long enough," said Kate. Unless there are objections—Bay, Eric, Tom? Do you want to give Dhani the news, or do I?"

When the Troverts were gone, Kate said to Tom, "You were trying to do a good thing by getting Steve to come here."

"You mean I 'meant well.' That makes me cringe. All I can say is it's a good thing I stepped away from the ministry to become your administrator. I can't do any damage."

"Especially since I took on Emmalyn to follow up for you."

He started at that, then noticed Kate's faint smile and relaxed a little. "Yes. Thank God for Emmalyn. She's a gem."

"Don't take yourself so seriously, Tom. I'm not sure what to believe about God. But I suspect that what he or she wants can happen with or without your help—or anyone's."

"True. But I suspect it doesn't help to get in the way by trying to play God either."

"What makes you think God can't override our mistakes?"

5th

Steve was standing outside on the porch when Dhani opened his cabin door to the knock.

He stared Tanner in the eye. "I heard you left."

"I did. I made it as far as Albany. Spent a couple nights there, facing myself. I came back because I left without facing you. I need to man up and tell you I'm sorry for the way I misjudged you and treated you this past year. Really sorry."

Dhani kept looking him in the eye, a dozen responses rushing through his head. He settled on one.

"I heard your wife was murdered. Kate and Tom called us all together and explained that. They said you didn't want anyone to know about that before you got here. You didn't want anyone to think you're this 'poor guy'." He paused, thinking. "I get that, I guess. But you know what?" His voice took on an aggressive edge. "I didn't want anyone to know what happened to me either. Now they do."

Then he shoved his hands deep into his pockets and stared at his shoe tops.

Steve cleared his throat. "Well, thanks for not kicking me off your porch."

Dhani remained silent.

When Steve was partway up the beach, heading for Jo's clinic, he heard someone call and turned to see Dhani still watching from the porch.

Dhani called. "*You staying?*"

Steve hesitated.

"*I said, are you staying?*"

Jo swiped a second swab at the nose of a pet rabbit belonging to Ivy's small grandchild. Supporting the little boy on her own, Ivy couldn't afford a vet bill. From the nasal discharge, Jo suspected the problem was non-fatal, probably *pasteurella*—the "snuffles." The boy would definitely need to stay away from the creature, though, until it was cured.

"You got a treatment plan for a really messed up former Marine?"

Jo carefully slipped the swabs in a tube and sealed it. Then she turned to face Tanner.

"'Former'? I thought it was 'once a Marine, always a Marine'?" She saw his duffel leaning against the doorframe. "How far did you get?"

"All the way to the truth about myself. Something I didn't want to see. Then I spent a couple nights in a cheap hotel before I could accept it."

"What truth is that?"

"About the way I judge people. Which is pretty black and white. If you don't earn my respect on my terms, I think you're not worth my time. If you don't live up to my standards, you're a loser—a deadbeat."

"That *is* pretty black-and-white."

"And ugly. I make snap-decisions about people without knowing anything about them. Anything. You know, making quick decisions worked in the military when I was leading guys into battle, assessing situations with just a few factors to go on. You have to read the situation fast, and I prided myself on being good at that. I kept my people alive. I only lost one—and it happened to be my best buddy—because of a miscalculation. Everyone said it wasn't my fault, we were under heavy attack and extreme duress. But I still blamed myself for Travis's death."

"The way I guess you blame yourself for your wife's death."

"Yeah. I screwed up. Really, really bad. I thought I could unload on her, say a few 'I'm sorrys', and make it right later. But there was no later.

"After that, I promised myself I wouldn't misjudge a situation again. But then I did. A third time. I misjudged that poor guy, Dhani, on-sight. The hoody, the no eye-contact, the spaced-out-ness, the half-trying. He wasn't a threat. He just didn't live up to my standards. He looked like the kind of kid I couldn't trust. That's all I saw every time I looked at him. I didn't even want to know anything about him. It aggravated me just to look at him."

Jo had led them outside to escape the confines of the clinic and take in fresh, spring air.

Pal was sleeping in a patch of sunlight in the grass. He startled when Jo called to him—"Look who's here."

The lab picked up his head, struggled to his feet yawning and stretching, and started to limp over to Steve, his tail and whole body wagging.

"Look at him," Jo said, watching Pal's approach. "He's glad you came back."

Steve was watching her. Studying her form again—he couldn't help it—but also the way her face went from so serious to so sweet at the sight of an injured dog.

Maybe it was time to let go of more than the way he judged people. Maybe it was also time to let go of the past. Move toward the future. He understood a bit more about Olivia's heart. That was the challenge Tom had thrown at him once, and he was beginning to see why she had given so much of herself to help kids like these. He'd survived war; some of them had survived impossible odds in their young lives.

He would stay, if Kate, Tom, and the Troverts agreed to it. He would stay in order to see if he could change enough to be a better trainer for these young adults. Prove to himself—and to Olivia, if she was watching him from somewhere—that maybe he could change enough to help some kids that life had beat up on. Maybe even help straighten out some who had made really bad choices that were truly all their own.

"I'm glad you came back, too," said Jo. She rested a hand on his shoulder.

He looked up from petting Pal, into her face. And he felt again what he had felt watching her step from the helicopter the day she'd scrambled out on a frozen lake to rescue the dog. What he felt on a June evening a year ago, when Pal had led her out to the island and he had seen how the late, setting sun ignited the gold highlights in her hair.

A wave of happiness started to flood in, but he checked it. Did he deserve to feel this happy? Olivia's killer had never been found. Didn't he still have a duty to her? But here was a beautiful woman who seemed strong enough to put up with him.

Maybe, the fleeting thought went through his head, *I could be a little better man for someone now.*

When he stood, Jo stepped close and kissed him—on the cheek, but her lips lingered—and then she pulled back, looking surprised and unsettled at her own action.

"Just a welcome back kiss. That's all."

"No worries," he smiled, and held back from what he wanted to do, which was to hold her.

Yes, he would stay to get closer to Jo and see what happened. It seemed to him at this moment that Lost Lake was exactly where he needed to be if he was going to let the past go. To move on.

"I just have to ask," Jo said, watching him ruffle the dog's ears and stroke his sides. "Did you find any kid here who measured up to your standards? Just curious."

"Actually, yeah. Rocco, Dugan, Imani, Jalil, Makayla. . . . They worked hard and I didn't tell them that. But I will. Some of the others were really trying."

"Anyone you'd rate as exceptional?"

Yeah, he thought. *An exceptional liar.*

Epilogue

Ganapuja / Summer Solstice

June

20th

Garrett stubbed out his early morning cigarette, and stepped from behind the barn, nearly crashing into Steve Tanner.

"Oh—hey, sir." He turned his face away. It was too late for a mint and he smelled like nicotine. "I was bummed out when they said you left. But I heard you're back. Really good to see you, sir."

"Funny. You knew I was back and it's good to see me.—So why did it take me so long catch up with you? I went to your cabin a couple times. They'd tell me you were there. But then it was, 'Oh, sorry. Guess he just stepped out the back door.' Almost like you'd run away to avoid me."

"Me, sir? No."

"Cut the 'sir' crap. I fell for that before. 'Yes sir, no sir.' 'If you need someone to be your eyes and ears and report on what these kids are doing, pick me, sir, pick me.' All your kissing up and volunteering snagged my ego and you saw that it worked. Not anymore."

"Sir. . . . Mr. Tanner—"

"You took my Ka-bar and slipped it into Dhani's backpack."

Garrett's turned to face him full-on. "I wouldn't do that. Why are you accusing me?"

"I went out to the equipment barn when I came back, and went through your pack. When I found my knife in Dhani's pack, it was wrapped in a red bandana. Yours is missing. Dhani's isn't. In fact, it's still starched and folded up and in a side pocket. He never used it."

"You issued everyone a red bandana. Did you check all the other packs?"

"I don't have to. I already figured out that I was a sucker for the wrong kid who knew how to say and do all the right things. You played me good."

Garrett was keeping his cool, his eyes holding steady with Tanner's. "You got me all wrong. My t.p. got soaked in the rain and I used my bandana. It's buried up there on the mountain."

"I don't think so. But I can't prove it. Just like no one can prove that you're the one who planted joints in Dhani's room. Grady handled the nightstand and the cigarette pack that held them without thinking, so his fingerprints are on everything. I'll bet you used gloves when you planted it."

"What if it was Grady who—"

Steve reached for Garrett's shirt collar. Then checked his anger and stopped himself.

"You're a practiced liar. In my mind, that makes you one of the most dangerous people in this program. But you know what? I can't prove what you did."

"Come on, man. Did you talk with Dhani again since he snapped? If you push him, he might tell the truth."

"What goes on between Dhani and me is not your business. I'm going with my instincts about you. All that you need to know is, I'm going to be watching every single move you make this coming year. Every. Single. Move."

Garrett had a wounded look and kept staring Steve straight in the face. "You're wrong about me, Mr. Tanner. It was someone else. You'll see."

"How many times have I told you not to name the animals?" Jo said. "You can't become attached."

"We call him Lil' Lightning because of the white scar on his shell," Makayla responded, running a finger down the back of the box turtle as Jalil held him. "When we took off the last round of duct tape, the shell was totally solid again—and he's got this killer, zig-zag, Harry Potter kinda mark."

"The scar gives him cred. Lil' Lightning is his street name now," Jalil added. "And don't worry, we read your Salamander Tribe list. We know he's gotta go back to the woods today. We're really happy about that. He needs to be back with his homies."

Jo smiled. "Okay, but don't name any more animals. I promise you, one day there'll be one you don't want to let go, and when you have to it will leave a scar. Now take him back right where we found him. You remember—it was right beside the trail out to the Flow Lands. You've got a little time to do it before breakfast."

"How come you didn't go home for the one-week break before the program kicks-in again?" Makayla asked when they were a little ways down the camp road. "Dugan, Rocco, Tia Leesha, and Emmalyn did."

"My parents want me to stay here," said Jalil. "They're afraid I'll hook up with my druggie friends if I go home."

"Would you?"

Jalil looked serious. "Probably not. But to be honest, there's a chance I would. How about you?—Going home?"

"Oh no, no, no. My mother is doing this weird thing where she wants to keep me away from my dad. On the phone she keeps pushing me to tell her if he ever hurt me or did anything perverted to me."

"Gross."

"Tell me about it. I'm a lot happier here than there."

The turtle was starting to move around, thrusting his head and neck way out of his shell.

"He's gonna be really glad to be back in the woods and streams again," Jalil smiled.

"Do you think what Jo said was strictly professional, or do you think it was from personal experience?" Makayla asked.

"About not naming anymore animals?"

"Not that. The part about not wanting to let someone go and it leaving a scar when you have to. It was weird she said it that way."

Jalil gripped the small box with the turtle hunkered inside. "I don't know. Why do women read into everything?"

"Can I ask you a question?"

He looked wary. "Oh god, is this where we go deep?"

"Depends on how you answer. If you like drumming so much, why didn't you take lessons?"

"My dad thinks drum lessons are a waste. He wants me to study engineering or technology. Stuff I hate. So I tried to learn by listening to some real kickass drummers."

"But you really love drumming, I guess." She stopped in the road, looking thoughtful. "Put down the box."

"Why?"

"Just do it."

When he set the cardboard container gently on the dirt road, she said, "Listen until you hear all the bird songs."

He frowned first, then tipped his head to one side. "What am I listening for?"

"Each one has a rhythm they repeat over and over. When you hear it, say it."

He eyed her with suspicion but in a moment, began.

"Chirr-up-up-up. . . tweet tweet. . . chirr-up-up-up-up. . . tweet. . . . I sound stupid."

"You don't. Say it and drum it." She drummed the rhythm on her thighs. "And now there's another sound."

His face brightened. "I hear it." He began to pat his hands against his jeans. "*Shhhhhhhhh. . . . chrr-up-up-up. . . .tweet tweet. . . shhhhhhhh-chrr-up-up-up. . . .tweet. . . . shhhhhhh-chrr-up-up-up. . . .*"

"Nice work," she smiled. "Maybe I can make a drummer out of you."

Jalil leaned in to give her a kiss.

"Dude." She pushed him away but smiled. "Friends—*just* friends."

"Damn."

"You should practice on your own. I bet you can get good.—Now," she said, changing it up, "let's get Lil' Lightning back where he belongs."

As they moved down the road, he studied her face. "You stopped smiling. You don't really want to let him go, do you?"

"Actually, I do. I just have something else on my mind. It's been really bothering me for a while."

"Are you going to tell me now?" Jalil asked.

He lifted the turtle out the box, set it down, and in a moment it thrust its head and legs out and trucked eagerly into the lush green undergrowth beside the road.

"Look at that boy go. Our boy Lightning knows where the ladies are.—So tell me what's bugging you."

Makayla looked at the trail leading out to the Flow Lands. "I've been thinking all spring about the spot where we found the golden salamanders."

"All spring? Why?"

"I didn't think about it at all until Jo kept trying to reach the State lab in Albany and couldn't get an answer. I keep wondering why the salamanders died. They were so beautiful."

He kicked at the dirt road. "Maybe they just. . . did. Stuff dies. There doesn't have to be a reason."

"But one was missing a whole front leg."

"Maybe a bird or a bullfrog tried to eat it, and it got away. Then the injury iced it later."

"The other one was missing a back foot."

"Same thing—predators. Everything tries to eat everything else." He grinned. "Or mate with it."

She ignored the last part. "Maybe," Makayla replied, but the troubled look did not leave her face. "I don't know why it's still bothering me. They're so beautiful and they don't hurt anything. What if it's something toxic where they live?"

"We're too far from civilization for an oil spill. Let's go back," said Jalil. "Breakfast is in fifteen minutes."

"Randy Wolfmoon told me the salamander is probably my spirit animal. That's why I like them so much and why I 'just happened' to be chosen to be the Salamander Tribe."

As they headed back up the road, Jalil began patting his thighs again. "*Shhhhhh... chrrr-up-up-up. . . .*" He looked at Makayla. "I think I got this bird-call drumbeat thing. Thanks."

"So what are they teaching you in that foo-foo program?"

"Good stuff." Rocco yawned. "Why'd you get me up so early?"

"That priest is taking you back this afternoon and I gotta show you something very important."

His father had angled his Mercedes off the interstate thirty minutes ago, onto secondary roads leading through fields of green, just-sprouting corn with red barns and white silos in the distance. It was still early morning, and they were almost two hours away from DC, in rural Pennsylvania.

"Nice ride, Dad," said Rocco, running one hand over the leather dashboard. "What's it got under the hood?"

His father's mind seemed to be elsewhere. "Five-hundred and ten horsepower.—So is it 'good stuff' they're teaching you or goody-goody stuff? You been talking about baby bears and cute little otters."

Rocco's stomach tightened a little at the memory of the runt bear cub and how he had willed with all his might for it to live. He decided that telling his father about being in the Bear Tribe and that he liked that would make him angry—and didn't. No way would he tell him he had cried when the little cub died.

"I like working with animals. They're awesome."

"Forget all that." His father reached over and patted Rocco's shirt, right over his five-star tattoo. "I told you when you fought me about getting inked that you're marked for the family business. That's your future and that's all. So I want you to avoid the useless crap and get real smart."

"Dad, stop worrying. There's a lot of classes and studying, too. I'm doing okay. A's and B's."

His father's hand shot out and this time slapped the back of his head, hard enough to sting.

"I want all A's outa you."

"Yes, sir." Rocco stared out the window and rubbed his head. They had now turned onto a narrow tar and gravel road through rough woodlands full of tangled undergrowth.

"Where are you taking me?"

His father grinned. "Takin' you to visit one of my boys. He owns a place."

"But why are we coming all the way out here in the boonies?"

"Just something we gotta check out."

Right. They were going to one of the hideouts where his father's men avoided being picked up.

"So, what else?" his father pressed. "You got some girls on the string up there? Better be more than one. One gets clingy. Two or three, you keep 'em on edge. Give 'em nice things. You stay in control. Always."

Imani's face came to mind, and he smiled faintly at the idea of someone trying to control her. She was not able to return to DC during the short break, of course, but if anyone was going to come out of the program later and be totally in-charge of their own life it would be her. He liked that. His mom would like her, too, and probably say, "There's something about her that's wise beyond her years"—because there was.

On the other hand, was she just toying with him—controlling and messing with him? Just before he left for home, he saw her on the front porch of her cabin with Makayla, listening to music, dancing, holding her arms above her lithe and slender body as she swayed. . . .

. . .She started singing—was it to him?—when she saw him watching. He found the lyrics translated from Spanish on-line.

Despacito!

You know I have been looking at you for a long time. . .
You are the magnet and I am the metal. . .
All of my senses are asking for more
But we cannot do this in a rush. . . .

Was she signaling something to him or was he just imagining that, wishing?...

. . . His head slammed into the car ceiling and his father swore.

They had turned off the gravel road onto an even narrower dirt road leading into thick woods and hit a pothole. The stands of shadowy scrub trees and thorny underbrush clotted together and looked sullen.

"Dad, this place is kinda creepy. Where are you taking me?"

"I pay Sid all this money and he can't keep the road fixed up."

In a hundred yards, the trees opened into a circular clearing with a dingy gray farmhouse at its center. To the right was a weathered barn, its metal roof half-rusted.

When they stepped from the car there was noise from beyond the barn. The arrival had set dogs barking—two of them, big ones, judging by the loud, deep-throated woofs and low growls.

"You can't afford paint? This place looks like some lazy, stupid *boombots* lives here."

Sid had stepped from the house to greet them.

Rocco watched his father throw a bear hug around the huge shoulders of a dark-haired man who looked like he could crush anyone he wanted to in a bar fight. His dad was big—six-three, built like a bull—Sid was taller, more muscular, a giant.

"I got other things to spend my money on."

"Your money?—*My* money."

"Geez, I thought I earned it."

"I don't pay you to think."

The dogs had begun to bark again.

Rocco's father turned and slapped him hard on the chest. "This is my boy. Great kid—a tough guy. He got himself in a little bit of trouble but we're fixing that. Making him look all respectable, like me." He laughed. "You need to get to know him because he's coming into the business in a couple years."

Sid's handshake crushed Rocco's knuckles together, and Rocco noticed the small, five-star tattoo on the back of the huge hand.

"Roc, you go take a look at Sid's dogs. He and I have some business to transact. We'll be out in a minute or two."

"Hammer and Lulu," Sid called after him, as they stepped into the house. "They're good dogs."

On the far side of the barn was a wire run, and when the two dogs—pitbulls, one solid tan, one a tan-and-black brindle—saw him they began to growl and bark again.

"Hey, easy," Rocco said, kneeling beside the fence. "Hammer, Lulu—it's okay. Good dogs."

He focused on the dogs, but smiled to himself. The reason they were here was waiting for him in the barn—he knew it. A vintage muscle car? A motorcycle?

The two pitbulls sniffed at him, then snorted, their whole bodies wagging as they pushed up against the wire, licking the hand Rocco stuck through the mesh to pet them.

"Yeah, you guys sound all tough but you're just a couple big babies. And whoa—" he said, seeing Lulu's thick girth and teats, "—looks like you're gonna be a mama soon."

Lulu kept licking his hand, her liquid brown eyes fixed on his face. Hammer pawed at him, all high energy and jumpy.

"*Ouch*, dude! Those claws. I'll pet you next. Calm down."

"Rocco."

His father and Sid were watching him from behind.

"Geez, you startled me," he said.

"Come here. Sid's got something for you."

His father had a faint smile.

Rocco looked at Sid, and stood. "I guess Lulu's gonna drop her litter any day. Right?"

Sid nodded.

He decided to play along, teasing, knowing his father hated dogs. "Dad—a puppy? You brought me here about a puppy? She hasn't had them yet."

"Come here," his father ordered again. "Stand next to me."

The mood was off, and Rocco was suddenly uneasy. "You told me to come see the dogs. They're nice."

"They're just bags of meat."

Rocco looked at Sid again, who turned his face away.

"Give it to him," his father ordered Sid.

Hesitating, Sid pulled from his belt a black metal handgun, a small Ruger. He cocked it and held it out to Rocco.

Rocco's brow furrowed. "Are we gonna practice today?" He looked around. "Where's the range?"

His father pointed at the brindle.

"That's your target."

Rocco stepped back. "*Lulu*? She's carrying puppies. I'm not going to shoot a *dog*. Dad—are you crazy?"

His father's arm lashed out, fist doubled, and struck him on the side of his head.

"Don't ever disrespect me. Especially in front of my men," he growled. "Take the gun and shoot the bitch. Then shoot the other one."

Rocco's heart was pounding. He looked back at Sid, whose face was now grim, his jaw set.

"You're gonna let him make me shoot your dogs?"

"Don't talk to him," his father growled. Both fists were doubled. "He just got a pocketful of green for this. They're my dogs now and I said shoot them."

Rocco rubbed the side of his head, his breathing shallow. "Dad—don't hit me—but why are trying to make me do this?"

"Because you been away in that program with all those faggy people trying make you soft like them. I came to check you out and see what kinda damage they done. Now shoot the damn dogs and prove to me they're not turning you into some kind of liberal-minded, animal-loving pussy."

Hammer pawed at the fence and barked. Lulu was sitting on her haunches, yawning, looking at him with a doggy grin.

Rocco's pulse pounded in his neck. He clenched his teeth.

"No. I'm not doing it." He glared at Sid, and turned for the car. "You're a chump."

"You disgrace yourself and me," his father roared after him.

Halfway to the Mercedes, the sound made him jump—one shot and a sharp yelp, like a scream of pain or terror. Then a second shot and silence.

Inside the car, he punched himself in the thigh, hard, so the physical pain would keep him from crying.

Bumping back down the dirt road, Rocco wished his father would shut up. In the pit of his stomach, he felt a sharp pain, while his father acted as if nothing had happened. He had loosened his collar and his face was just losing its angry red color.

"When you're back, I'm gonna undo whatever garbage they're pumping into your head about cute little animals. The world isn't about nicey-nicey, let's take care of furry creatures."

"The female was carrying puppies," Rocco shot back.

His father's hand launched out and fingers dug into the back of his neck.

"Listen to me." His tone was tough. "The real world is competition and who eats who first. That dumbbell was smart to take money for those two useless sacks of meat. There's a lot you need to learn, kid. A lot I gotta teach you when you get back."

Then he released his pincer grip.

Rocco stared at the road ahead. His neck hurt, but not as bad as the pain inside his chest—two gunshots, two beautiful creatures. Dead. For nothing. Less than nothing.

"Snap out of it," his father said in a minute, his tone now brighter. "Forget what just happened."

When they were back on the road through corn fields in full morning sunlight, his father was fully relaxed—smiling. Completely changed. He turned on the radio.

"You like this hip-hop stuff, right?"

His dad could be such a bastard.

"When you get back here, we get you a ride like this one—or no, a muscle car. The 1965 Mustang Shelby GT-350. Serious high-performance machine. I always wanted one. Red. I'll get it for you. The women will be all over you."

Rocco nodded just to prevent another slap in the head.

"Hey, you love waffles, right?" His father rolled on. "Remember when you were a little guy and your mother said 'no' but I was the one who let you have all the waffles and syrup you wanted? There's a nice little place up ahead. All-day breakfast. I'm gonna treat you. Best homemade sausage you ever had."

His dad could be such a great guy.

So confusing.

In Rocco's head. . . .

. . .his dad pointed and fired the Ruger at Hammer and Lulu. . . "those two useless sacks of meat". . .

. . .and offered to buy him a car and his favorite breakfast. . . .

In the very back of his mind, Jo's voice sounded, too.

"Rocco, I know you try to hide it, but you have a big heart. That's a good thing. A gift. Don't waste it."

But she was a woman. She was supposed to be soft.

So many other images and thoughts scrambled his mind. So many feelings tangled up his guts.

"Something's different about you now," Claire said to Dhani, as they approached Sahm's cabin along with Ray-Ray.

"I'm thinking the same thing," said Ray-Ray. "Can't put my finger on it. But it's like, whoa, dude, who's this new person?"

Sahm was not in his cabin when they knocked, and they found him outside, up on the boulder beneath the white pine. It was mid-afternoon, and the sun fell on the rust carpet of needles all around the huge stone. His eyes were closed, his legs crossed and his hands were palms-up in his lap.

Dhani cleared his throat.

Sahm's lips kept moving silently—then he finished his chant, opened his eyes, and slid down to join them.

"What's the cool design for?" Claire said, pointing to a large, circular picture made of brightly-dyed red, blue, green, yellow, and white powders. "It's beautiful."

The pattern Sahm had made on the ground near the boulder looked like a huge, opening flower maybe ten feet across, with geometric shapes inside it. At the flower's center was another large circle, and at the center of that was a small Buddha figure in bright blue surrounded by a green halo.

"Today the sun reaches the highest point in the sky," Sahm began.

"Summer solstice," said Ray-Ray.

"I am celebrating *Ganapuja* and I am glad you have come. I'm about to eat the ritual meal, and you can join me."

Ray-Ray looked uneasy.

"Don't worry," Sahm said, winking at him. "Ritual meal of dried meat for them. For you—hotdogs, hamburgs, potato salad, chips." He laughed and winked. "I was careful not to let any demons get into the salad."

Ray-Ray swallowed hard, and Claire laughed at him. "You gotta get out of your subculture."

"Are you gonna tell us what *Ganapuja* is about?" Dhani asked when they were seated in the center of the design.

Sahm had directed them how to carefully step inside the sacred mandala made of brightly-dyed barley flour, arrange themselves in its central circle, and not to touch the figure at its heart.

"It is, as Ray-Ray said, the summer solstice. Look how brilliant the light is. It is also the night of the new moon. Tonight, no light at all."

"Who is the Buddha guy in the middle here," Claire asked. "He reminds me of the little figure you have on your altar."

"Very good," Sahm smiled. "He is indeed *Dzes-Sa,* the Awakened One, a most compassionate protector. He is my greatest Teacher and the source of my greatest strength and wisdom."

"He is so beautiful. I'm going to sketch him later."

"I honor *Dzes-Sa* on this day, which is very, very auspicious."

"Why?" asked Dhani.

"It is a day that balances between the greatest light and greatest darkness."

"So—that's just a nature thing," Ray-Ray said. "It doesn't mean any special powers are at work."

Claire seemed to intuit what was about to come out of his mouth and shot him a look that stopped him from saying, "That's superstitious."

"That is the problem with many of you here in the west. Do not dismiss this day so blindly. It is a day when the power and *karma* of every action is increased. The good that is done will have best consequences. The bad that is done will have terrible, terrible consequences. It is a day to be very mindful about all that you say and do. Every thought. Every word and action."

"Guys."

Ron had come around the corner of the cabin at a jog. He glanced at the mandala but ignored it. "Glad I found you. Jo and I know you wanna come see this. *Hurry.*"

The eagle was high up on the branches in the outdoor part of its enclosure. Jo was standing beside the wire barrier.

The bird shook out its wings and all its feathers, then let out loud, intermittent shrieks as they came up to the cage.

"What's happening to his head?" Ray-Ray asked.

"This is his first molt," Dhani said. "He's changing. Starting to get his first white feathers. Becoming mature."

"That's exactly right," Jo replied, staring at him. "But how did you know? I never taught you guys about that."

"I just—it just came to me."

"You brought him outside," said Claire. "That's cool."

"No, we didn't," said Jo, with the same tone of wonder in her voice.

"I looked in on him after you guys did your rounds this morning," Ron said, "and he wasn't inside. I found him out here. *He flew On his own.*"

Claire and Ray-Ray sounded amazed. "How?" "I thought you said he'd probably never fly."

"I don't know how to call this one," Jo said, looking mystified.

Ron replied. "I think he just suddenly made up his mind, and felt free to fly."

Dhani stared into the eagle's eyes, which bore into him.

I get it. You were right. I am the One. I just wish I knew 'the one' what.

Then he wondered why that thought had arisen and what it meant—as Sahm had said, on this day of power.

Jo had turned to Ron. "Oh lord, Ron. Animals don't 'make up their minds', like, 'Oh hey, I think I'll fly today.' Don't anthropomorphize."

Dhani, Claire and Ray-Ray were looking to Sahm.

"Auspicious," he said simply.

"I don't know what happened here," Jo finished. "I don't know what to say."

Of course you do not, Sahm thought, *but you would not believe the truth if I told you.*

"Ron, there's something we need to talk about," Jo said, when the two of them were alone back in the clinic's examining room.

"Sounds serious," he smiled, leaning casually against the stainless steel table.

She did not smile back, and folded her arms across her chest.

"It is.—Just before we went outside, I was going over the last two packing slips that came with pharmaceutical deliveries. Tom asked me to double-check them in case Kate's paying for items left out of the orders."

Ron cleared his throat.

"You seem to know where this is going."

"Let's see if I'm right."

"Normally, I have one of my teams unpack drug shipments and

check what's in the box against the packing sheets. But since some of them have gone back to DC, I did it myself this time. You know what's missing from the cabinets?—the four bottles of Dexedrine I ordered. They're listed on the sheet, but there's the same number of bottles in the cabinet as there were before this shipment arrived. I checked it against my inventory list."

"What about the other drugs and supplies? Anything else left out."

"No. Just the Dex."

Ron's eyes flashed anger. "Four bottles of doggie meth are missing and you're confronting me about. . . what?"

"I ran into one of the Sheriff's deputies at yoga this week. He says your brother has been back in town since last November." She let that hang in the air.

"He did his time—eight years—and he's clean, Jo. But the reason you're cornering me about this is because you want to know if I am."

"Are you? Or maybe you're supplying someone?"

He started to reply, and she cut him off, her tone harsh.

"Ron, you've 'lost' equipment—like expensive GPS's. You can make good money reselling those. Do you have the third one I requisitioned for you or is that one 'lost', too? Now pharmaceuticals are missing."

He looked irritated. "I'm not stealing stuff, Jo."

Her voice was louder. "I went out on a limb for a good, long-time friend—*you*—when I hired you to work with me here. In a program for troubled minors. I did it because you told me over and over that the only thing you're addicted to now is distance running. But you and I both know that training for marathons and halfs takes a lot of physical stamina. A boost sure would help, wouldn't it, Ron?"

He answered through gritted teeth. "I've been clean for over five years, Jo."

"We both know opioid addiction can be hard to kick long-term."

Then she searched his face for a long moment and dropped her arms to her sides. The confrontational tone was gone.

"I hope you're clean and have nothing to do with this. I really do. You're good at what you do. The kids like you a lot. But," the cautionary note was back, "if I find out you're using again, you'll be fired on the spot. I told you I'd give you a chance. And I meant *a* chance. One."

"I'm not using or stealing. I swear. I love this job and I wouldn't jeopardize it."

"One more thing. The deputy saw you talking with your brother behind a dumpster next to the grocery store. Why the secret meeting?"

Ron went silent and his eyes slowly reddened.

"He's eating out of dumpsters, Jo. He has no money. No one in town will hire a former crack addict."

Her face softened. "I'm sorry, Ron. That's gotta be tough on you. On him."

Then her troubled look returned. "It's good news, bad news then."

He looked at her, questioning.

"You're clean—but someone *here* could either be using or dealing."

"Can I make a suggestion?" Ron countered. "Can you have Tom check with the supplier before you jump to that conclusion? It could still be a mistake at the packing end. Someone would have to have a lot of guts to walk off with four bottles of Dex. What if the supplier's guys are stealing?"

"Maybe. But these kids weren't in juvenile detention for nothing, Ron."

"I know, but come on. They're still just young kids. Dealing speed is pretty sophisticated."

The sun had long before disappeared behind Peregrine Mountain, and the dark blue bowl of sky above Lost Lake slowly filled with budding stars.

Sahm began to sweep away the intricate mandala, which now lay in the lengthening shadows. Out of sight now, the sun was about to cross the celestial equator, *Ganapuja* was ending, and it felt as if a subtle hum was running through the earth and air.

He let the image of *Dzes-Sa* rise in his mind.

When should I tell the boy about his true purpose and the struggle that is ahead. He knows he is a Sakyong, but that is all.

He had almost done so when they had returned here after the surprise of seeing the eagle. Truly, that was the greatest portent of the day, perhaps the year—but still he felt hesitant. *Ganapuja* was not a day to set in motion something that would have powerful and lasting *karmic* effects, unless you were certain the timing was exactly right. It would be like opening a chrysalis before the butterfly was fully developed, and ever after it would spread wings that were twisted.

An answer sounded, with bell-like clarity.

"Watch for the final sign. It will tell you when he is ready to know."

Sahm stared at the only part of the colorful mandala left to sweep away. *Dzes-Sa*. The Buddha of the Beautiful Earth.

He did not want to scatter this image into the ferns and pine needles. He had drawn it with special care. Sometimes he did not like what he had been taught—that everything is impermanent.

But it is, he resolved.

With reverence, he used his small, pine bough whisk on the green and blue barley flour image, until the likeness of *Dzes-Sa*, his Guide and Teacher, was wiped away. What was not swept away was his small cloud of doubt that Dhani would be ready to embrace or act on the full truth any time soon. As best he could tell—*The boy is still so much about Claire, Claire, Claire.*

He smiled, allowing the longing that sometimes came over him to have its moment. *And maybe he should be.* Intimate companionship was something Sahm knew he must never let himself enjoy.

Once Dhani understood his work in the world everything would change for him.

Maybe I should just allow him be a normal young man. . . for now. Before the difficult work begins.

Near eleven that night, he emerged from his cabin and hoisted himself to the top of the boulder again. He wanted to watch the fully blossomed stars wheel across the black sky until midnight, when this day of auspicious events would end.

The portent of the eagle was still on his mind. It had also arrived here on an auspicious day over a year ago. Now, on another one, after being flightless, it had taken wing.

Surely, some kind of great events were about to take place. Would they be benevolent events—or harmful ones?

He began a chant of protection for every person at Lost Lake, knowing that actions and even plans set in motion today would have powerful consequences in their lives for a long, long time.

Indistinct in the late evening shadows, two figures stepped out from behind a parked car on the narrow, cobblestone street. She glanced over her shoulder, feeling her heartbeat quicken.

She was always uncomfortable, walking the streets of Washington alone at night. Even here in tony Georgetown. Now, when the two figures fell in-step behind her she felt afraid. The sound of their heels on the sidewalk picked up and her mind raced.

Do I stay calm? Or run?

When she got to the end of the short, uneven stone walk leading to the townhouse steps, the small path-lights between the boxwoods were out. But they had been left on this morning in anticipation of a late evening return.

The footsteps came faster, closer, and her heart sped up as she tried to stumble quickly up the dark walk.

A hand clamped over her mouth and a forearm closed tightly around her throat.

"Thi Martin," a hostile voice said in her ear. "Make a sound, you're dead."

Garrett took a drag from the glass pipe. In the pitch-dark he sucked in and watched the contents of this, his second bowl of the night, glow bright red. He had been pacing and anxious for days, and Rocco and Jalil told him to chill the hell out and tossed him from the cabin.

"I can't stand you walking in circles in here."

"Take it outside."

He held the smoke for almost thirty seconds, tapping his leg, watching the sliding glass door that led from the greenhouse into the potting room where he was slouched.

11: 41 his watch read.

Late as usual. I said be here at 11.

"Great business partners are hard to come by," his father had taught him. "A good one keeps his mouth shut and does what he's told. Bad ones get bossy and demanding. You eliminate those."

The sliding door opened quietly.

"Don't even ask again if anyone saw me," a voice whispered from the shadows. "I never once let that happen all year."

He had not taken his father's advice. He had negotiated with Dugan, hoping that didn't give him the idea he could become more demanding. He had enough pressure on him now. From Tanner. From the wild man, who had left yet another list.

Now—*this* irritation.

"That's because you're smart," Garrett said, in a flattering tone, his voice dry and croaky from smoking. "That's why I made you my business partner."

"You wouldn't be smoking the best herb if I didn't bring it in.—Give me a hit of that."

He reached out with the pipe.

From the shadows, the figure stepped forward to take it, and the red glow of a long drag briefly illuminated Emmalyn's face and hair.

She held the puff, then let it out. "What happened to your hand? Did that ugly little coyote thing scratch you again?"

"Yeah, I was messing with it and it kind of attacked me."

"Didn't Jo tell you to stay away from it? What if you get mange or something?"

He swore. "I do what I want."

"It's a good thing you wised up about one thing. We make good business partners."

"Yeah, right."

She took another long drag, held it, and let it go. "Didn't I get Kate and Tom totally distracted and off our butts worrying about Sahm messing up Dhani's head?"

"Yeah, well I did the Ka-bar thing."

Then she laughed a dry laugh. "Don't you think it's funny how all these imbeciles believe we hate each other? You were totally right not to tell Dugan about me. The fewer people who know about our business the better."

Our business.

Those words, made him mad every time she used them. It was *his* business. She had blackmailed him into a partnership after he made the mistake of telling her what he was up to. *He* was bringing in most of the cash. She didn't earn the split she extorted from him.

"Hey, I got things rolling," he said, sounding peevish. "You're making some good green."

"Maybe so. But Tanner's onto you. If he takes you down, someone's gotta step up and take over."

He silently wished evil on Tanner. Wanted to see him crushed. Something really bad needed to happen, either to get him gone or take him out.

"Now listen up," Emmalyn said, with no trace of the sweet, country girl she had sold everyone else all year. "I'm going to get revenge on Carter. I know you think she's your babe, but she doesn't have any interest in you. I know she killed the otter pup back in the winter, the little guy I loved, and I need you to stay out of it because she's going to pay."

He wasn't listening. He was remembering items on the wild man's latest list of demands. More dried foods. Boxes of ammo. Also some weird or kinky requests that had caught his attention: *ponytail ties, tampons, a bottle of women's cologne.*

Did he have a woman out there in his wilderness hideout? Or was he lonely and planning to find one?

"And don't get too stoned," Emmalyn bossed him, when he reached to take the pipe back. "I'm gonna tell you what our next moves are and you need to *pay attention*."

It crossed his mind exactly how to resolve one of his big problems. Not right now, when everything needed to settle down for a while. But sometime. She was right about one thing. No one did know they had anything to do with each other, so no one would look his way when it happened.

If he helped satisfy the wild man's primal urges, that might make two problems disappear.

The ride back from DC had been tough, with angst about the two executed dogs making it hard to breathe. Rocco slipped into the large mammal room, knowing no one would be here this late at night.

Opening the cage door, he let the cub out—though it could hardly be called a cub now that it was nearing a year old. He rubbed the shoulder with the blond blaze.

"What am I gonna do?" he said to the young bear. "We fought for the last couple months to get you better, and now you are. And Jo says it's time to reintroduce you to the wilderness. How are you going to make it?"

By which he meant, *How am I going to make it?*

And he wished they had never rescued the two bear cubs from the site of their mother's senseless death at the hands of idiots. And he was glad they had, though the painful loss of the small cub—like his father shooting the pit bulls – had cut him to the core.

He thought about how rotten he'd been to Jalil all year and how he'd trashed Dhani after saying he'd be his friend. The anger he saw in his father was in him, too, and he wished he could wash it out of himself.

He hugged the bear cub—hearing his father's voice calling him a freakin' sissy—and his throat constricted and his chest ached.

Just before midnight, Dhani and Claire sat on the porch of her cabin in the dark, watching bats flutter into the halo of the porch light, snatching mosquitoes and moths. Curfew had relaxed, and there were things Dhani wanted to say to Claire, now that he was secure in their friendship.

For the moment, though, he focused on her.

"So, you're back for good? All the court crap is over?"

"Maybe. Maybe not. The judge said I convinced him I don't know anything that's of interest to the prosecutor. He's going to stonewall the guy if he tries to *yoink* me back to DC again. He thinks he did it this time just to harass my parents. As if they'd care. But the guy is still sure there's money somewhere."

"You're still ragingly pissed at them aren't you?"

She opened her mouth, then hesitated. "Not ragingly."

In a moment, she said, "What about you and Tanner? Did you guys kiss and make nice?"

"Don't joke about that," he said, annoyed.

She noticed the tone. "I like that."

"What?"

"That you were pissed at me just now and let me know it."

"Why?"

"Because all year you were kind of like a puppy dog. Just all sweet and ga-ga around me. Like a little boy. Now you're being more real. More like an average guy. It's a good thing."

"Oh. Thanks."

She snapped her fingers. "I know what's different about you now."

"What?"

"You don't act like a scared little rabbit anymore."

"So what was I, a puppy dog or a scared rabbit?"

She ignored that. "It's like the fear is gone. Maybe you blowing up at Tanner was the best thing. You let the fear and anger out."

The eagle had said, *"This frightened boy—this is the person you must shed."*

He shrugged. "I'm not afraid now. But is the anger gone? Not all of it."

She reached under the collar of her sweatshirt, and pulled out the shell pendant he had made for her last fall. "Look what I'm wearing, Dhani. For friendship."

He nodded, with not much enthusiasm. "Cool."

"So," she changed the subject, "you said Bay wants to have you tested for psychic abilities. I think that's cool."

"Maybe. Psychic or psycho. Who knows."

"Stop. I said I think Bay's right. You should find out the extent of your abilities. And I'm with you in this. Dhani, who knows what you could do if you let yourself open up and learn who you really are?"

He was silent—and the eagle's message came back.

"Who were you before you let other people twist you into who you have become? You must meet that person."

"So what *about* you and Tanner?"

"I really don't want to be anywhere near him. If he's staying, I'll just avoid him."

"Got that. But—you know—the Troverts filled us all in on how his wife was murdered, after Tanner gave them permission. He didn't want it known before."

"That doesn't mean you get to be a jerk to everyone. I had a lot of bad things happen to me, too. So did you."

"Yeah, but we're gonna be here a long time and I heard Tanner *is* staying on."

He blew out a long breath. "I have a right to be angry."

"You know what Sahm would say."

He looked at her, surprised. "You're listening to Sahm now? I thought he kind of weirded you out."

"He would say—," she was recalling Christmas Eve "—'You can walk in any direction you choose. Make a new path'."

"I don't know."

Alone in his room, Dhani picked at the small cotton-pills on his sheets, thinking about the great change in Claire. They were *friends*. Not what he wanted. But he liked that she was way less hard and angry than before and that she was listening to Sahm's wisdom.

"You can walk a new path."

Right.

A cool night breeze slipped in through the cracked-open window, feeling good on his bare torso. He crossed his arms behind his head, sleepless.

He wished she hadn't pushed him to change his mind about Tanner. Rather than calming him, as she intended, it brought back a restlessness and angst.

"You really should listen to what Sahm's telling us," were her last words to him tonight. *"What we think and say and do has big consequences. I thought you were trashing me behind my back, and because I had that idea I was bad to you. When someone straightened out my head, it changed everything."*

He was still pissed about Tanner tearing his shirt off, exposing his hundred burn scars. The memory made him dig his fingers into the sheets, and his stomach tensed. Tanner was a jerk. He wanted to punch and kick him. Wanted to stab at him with a lit cigarette, watch him squirm and hear him scream and cry, and in his mind images arose. . . .

. . .He was the big man standing over Tanner's cowering little form, slipping a Marlboro between his lips, flicking his lighter, taking a long

drag, moving closer. "You little shit. . . . I'm gonna make you wish you were never born."

"Please—no," Tanner, the little boy, begged and cried.

The angst became anger—and Dhani let pure meanness take hold.

"I heard you tell your mother to call me 'The Monster'," he told the little man."So from now on, that's who I'm going to be—The Monster."

Tanner curled into a ball, shaking, peeing on the floor.

He took the cigarette from his lips, listening to the begging and screams of terror as he moved closer, grinning.

He roused himself from this brutal fantasy. What the hell was he thinking? It made his stomach uneasy to imagine hurting anyone the way he had been hurt.

"Do you now see how fear turns to anger, and anger leads to harm?"

Dhani sat bolt upright in bed. "Who said that?" he asked out loud, though the voice had spoken in his head.

Immediately, in his mind's-eye, he was back in the small mountain village, surrounded by snow-capped Himalayan peaks near *Danzeng-cuo,* the Five Color Lake. He had seen this place in some kind of vision back in January when he had stepped out of Sahm's cabin.

The old man in the robe covered in symbols was staring him in the eye, connecting with his mind.

"Feel the gifts and energies that have for so long been weak within you."

The old man reached out his hand again, as he had done then, and this time Dhani did not pull away. Touching Dhani's chest, he said, *"Your power is now awakened. Use it, and the world will start to rise again from its dark spiral."*

The old man began to fade from Dhani's mind, but not before Dhani noticed one last detail.

"The symbols on your robe. What do they mean?" He had forgotten to ask when he had seen them in Sahm's mandala earlier. Without thinking, he reached out and touched the man's robe.

"I will show you their meaning."

A cataclysmic energy shook the cabin and the walls dissolved. . . .

He was standing outside, but nothing at all about Lost Lake was as it had been. All the cabins, Kate's lodge, and every other structure looked like mists, insubstantial, shifting and glowing in the moonlight. All around him, the whole great bowl of the valley was changed utterly. Every tree, rock, mountain crag and the lake itself flickered as if hidden fire burned within everything.

Deep voices filled with strength and laughter called out to him from the lake, the mountains, the sky, and distant fire of the stars. "This is the meaning of the symbols."

"Fire friend."

"Sage of the waters."

"Voice of the wind and air."

"Earth protector."

Dhani looked down and saw that he was wearing the robe the old man had worn. All the symbols were ablaze, showing the titles the Elemental energies had just called out.

"Why—?" he started to ask.

"You are the old one who has returned. You are the one we have waited for—Earth Protector, first of the Lineage. You are needed now in this time."

"Needed to do what?"

Like a huge scroll rolling back, the whole sky parted, revealing all around a devouring darkness—a blackness void of any kindness or care, a hungry maw—bringing destruction to all life.

At the horrible sight, Dhani felt the blood drain from his face and hands and his leg muscles turn to rubber. All his strength left, and he fell down. . . and down. . . .

. . .waking in his bed, sweating, breathing hard, everything solid again–knowing that what he had seen was not in his imagination, but real.

The eagle's question came to him yet again. *"Who were you before . . .?"*

"I am the old man," he said to the moonlit dark in his room, filled with a sense of wonder—then dread, given what he had just seen. "I was him lifetimes ago. And I have to help stop whatever is coming."

"Yes!" voices all around him called out. "First of the lineage of Earth Protectors. Come back to raise up others—now, now, now!"

In a few seconds, Ray-Ray knocked on his door, then opened it and stuck his head in.

"Dhani—you okay? I thought I heard voices shouting."

"I can't understand you, Thi," Steve said into the phone. "Stop crying, get ahold of yourself and talk clearly."

Tom stood near him in Kate's office, where they had rushed after Tom delivered Thi's urgent late-night message: "Call me. Now. I'm at the E.R."

"A cousin from Chicago was visiting, staying at my place. I was at the studio late and my producer and cameraman drove me home. When we pulled up at the curb, we could see my front door was open. We all heard the scream. It was horrible.

"When we got inside, we heard someone crash out the back door. Binh was lying on the kitchen floor with her forehead split open. She said it was two guys. They smashed her head on the granite counter top over and over. The three of us had scared them off when we charged in the front door yelling."

Steve's mind raced to take in the details—to understand why Thi had called him. He was five hundred miles away, after all, and she had two men there to help and protect her until the police arrived.

"We're at Georgetown Hospital, in the emergency center," she raced on, her voice breaking. "Binh's skull is badly fractured and she slipped into a coma. But on the way here in the ambulance I was holding her hand—God, it was like a flashback."

"Do you think this was an anti-Asian attack by White supremacists?"

"No. Steve, listen. She managed to tell me something before she blacked out. The men kept shouting at her, 'Give us the necklace.' She told them, 'I don't know what necklace.' They said, 'The one you showed everyone on TV.' Good lord, because she's also Vietnamese they mistook her for me."

Steve's mouth went dry.

"Did you hear me? They smashed her head in because they wanted the scapular Olivia was wearing when she died. They didn't know I gave it to you. Someone wants it bad enough to kill for it."

Steve's mind was reeling. "Who would gun someone down in cold blood for two holy pictures printed on cloth—then viciously assault another woman?"

When the call was over, he stood staring out the windows of Kate's office at the blackness of the midnight forests where moonlight failed to reach.

"All this time, we thought it was a random hold up that went bad. But Olivia was killed because someone wants what she had around her neck."

He slammed his fist on Kate's desk. *"It's a stupid, damn cloth necklace that's probably not worth ten bucks.* That doesn't make sense. It's gotta be something else."

He ran his hands wildly through his hair. Why this—now? He had thought he could put the past aside, find some peace, move on, but the past was dragging him back.

Tom sounded like he was fighting to stay level headed. "What did the police tell Thi—anything?"

Kate had come in, looking distressed. "What's happened?"

Steve paced, then punched an office chair so hard it flew over backwards.

"Tonight, another woman has been violently attacked by the same people who killed Olivia in cold blood. And the police haven't told me they have a single, freakin' lead in two years. . . . *TWO YEARS,*" he roared.

"How is that possible?" Kate sounded incredulous.

"No, they haven't found a clue or said a word, have they?" Tom replied to Steve. "Something's not right. It was broad daylight."

Then he gripped Steve's shoulder to steady him.

"We're going to get them back in the game. *Now*. Because whoever wanted that scapular hasn't let it go and they're willing to kill to get it."

After 1 a.m., a sense of urgency would not let Sahm sleep.

Quitting the cabin, he went barefoot to the dark shore of Lost Lake, its obsidian waters dappled with stars, remembering what *Dzes-Sa* had told him during the winter campout back in March.

"*Watch for the final sign*" of Dhani's awakening—one that, according to the ancient teachings, must come from Dhani himself.

Sahm felt an intense pull and draw behind the night air, as if he were being sucked down under the riptide waves of a greater darkness. How long before that sign appeared? From the vision of a fast approaching tumult he had seen, and this new sense of danger, the One who began the *Sakyong* lineage far back in mists of time could not begin his work in this world soon enough.

"*His power and gifts will begin to leap forth like a roaring fire.*"

Sahm called into the air. "How will I know?"

The *Elementals* laughed. "*He will tell you himself—look.*"

Turning his head, Sahm saw a figure coming rapidly toward him along the moonlit lakefront. At once, he could see there was something different about the one approaching.

"Sahm, it's me," said Dhani. "There's something I've gotta tell you."

"Yes, I know."

"Really?"

Sahm knelt and bowed his head down till his forehead touched the sand.

"Don't do that. It's—it's just me."

Sahm stood and brushed the sand from his brow. "We both know that is not true."

"Will you help me know what I'm supposed to do?"

"That is why I was sent here."

"By that *Dzes-Sa* guy?"

"Yes. The One who awakened the first of our lineage—who has now come to us through you."

ACKNOWLEDGEMENTS

A big thank you to readers of very early drafts:

Jeanne Selander Miller—you reinforced that a path to freedom from ourselves lies in caring for other living creatures. To Sarah Hazard, who encouraged me that readers of all ages appreciate intelligent conversation in fiction. To Dan Sheehan and David Hubbard for checking my facts about Marine life and the Corps. To Maria Dampman for veterinary knowledge. To Marcia Keene and Joe Straka for listening to drafts and offering great suggestions. And great thanks to Robin Pennington for extraordinary proofreading skills.

Thank you, to Susan Rimato Hazard and to Dean and Mary Gordon for allowing me to write in such beautiful, lakeside places in the Adirondack wilderness.

Mark Ivan Cole has an extraordinary artistic gift and guides Claire's pencil beautifully. Many, many thanks.

Peter Gloege is a wizard of design. Grateful for the decades we've worked together on other people's books, and very grateful for your artistry in designing the Lost Lake Series look and each volume—not to mention the beautiful website: lostlakeseries.com

ABOUT THE AUTHOR

At the end of book one in this series, *Time of the Broken Eagle,* I introduced my deep connection to the natural world and my hope and drive to protect it from ongoing misuse and destruction.

Those idyllic aspects of my growing-up years I mentioned—tromping through marshes, catching pollywogs—finding my spiritual home in the Adirondack Mountains of upstate New York—are brighter facts of my life and energies that come to life (I hope) in my writing.

I have another important connection to the *Lost Lake* saga—the human factor. Not as bright a story to tell.

In my early teenage years, and even a little before, I was headed for big trouble on several fronts. Couple that with serious depression, and things were going downhill fast. I was only 14.

Fortunately, I encountered a high school group led by caring adults, who helped to angle my life onto a better path. Becoming part of this organization gave me a healthy perspective and good alternatives. A few dedicated, available adults slowly built my self-esteem and helped me to start focusing on worthy, contributive goals for my life. Change wasn't easy and a few of my mentors said later that I was their greatest challenge. Understandable, since I was jonesing for love and attention in so many ways. I didn't even want to be around me much of the time.

A few years later, in college, on much better footing and wanting to give back, I started to work with youth organizations and continued to do so into my early career years, co-founding a youth organization in northern Virginia.

And here's where the view broadens and my connection to the *Lost Lake* saga deepens.

During those years of working with young people, I was shocked over and over. Not shocked about the things young people get into—I knew about that only too well. I was shocked at the unhealthy contexts in which many of them had grown up and still lived.

I encountered teenaged girls who, trembling and in tears, begged for help because their fathers were abusing them. These young women were from "good," upper class homes and whose fathers were respected professionals. Because these girls were withdrawn, shy-acting, or secretive, they were labeled as snobs, backward, or troubled. No one knew their secret story.

I met teenaged guys who wanted to commit suicide—and two did—because their sexual orientation stamped them as unworthy and rejectable, and targets for horrendous abuse. So they retreated into themselves, fell into depression, escaped into drugs, avoided eye contact, sometimes lashing out in anger, hating life every day. Like the young women mentioned above, no one knew their secret story either.

There were the young people struggling with depressions, anxiety disorders, or just existential angst because life seemed to them to have no meaning at all. It seemed that nothing could motivate them, to the frustration of their parents and teachers. Most of them tried to hide their inner struggle, which meant—no one knew their secret story.

Here's my point:

There was always someone who would judge and dismiss these young people *without knowing anything about their life or their very real, painful struggles.* "Just a spoiled rich girl—what does she have to complain about?" "If he was my son, I'd kick his tail." "He's a weird-o." "She just needs a job." "Hard work will knock all that nonsense out of him."

Perhaps the reason I *got* why they were the way they were was because I had survived anger, depression, acting out, and what it's like to come so close to the final edge, hanging on by your fingernails over a chasm of despair.

In any case, I came to realize, vividly, how much and how quickly we judge each other, without really knowing a thing about each other.

Every young adult character I write about in *Lost Lake* tells a story of some hidden factor, a secret story. Most of the adult characters do, too. I give them voice to say:

You have no idea what someone else's life may be like or the painful weight they're carrying.

That's what you really need to know about me. My motivation. The rest—schooling, publishing history, personal data—isn't irrelevant. It's just not what I want to focus on here.

We have one earth to protect and one human family to support, strengthen and, whenever necessary, help to heal. Please help.

Namaste.

—David Hazard
Fall 2021

A SHOCKING AND POWERFUL signal goes out to the whole animal realm, from a dying blue whale, that worldwide disaster is imminent—and Dhani is witness to her dire warning. The forces that have been growing and threatening the natural world and all humankind are reaching peak.

From this bombastic opening, all the story lines of the Lost Lake saga explode with fiery new energy.

At Lost Lake, Dhani's confidence in himself grows—but Sahm must now reveal to him the great responsibilities and tasks that are his to fulfill. But he is still young and in search of his best life now, free of cares he has carried for too many years already. How will he accept new burdens placed on him by a past identity?

The investigation to find Steve Tanner's wife Olivia's killer is reignited when her case is taken up by a new detective on the DC Metro Police force—also a Marine combat veteran. What he learns immediately is terrible news. Olivia's case files are missing.

A trespasser who has been stalking one of the program's young women for months plans to set trap in a secluded forest grove, and it may soon bring terror upon everyone at Lost Lake.

Throughout, more of the young men and women in Kate Holman's program start of awaken to their true life callings. . .

. . .if lingering challenges from the past don't eclipse their just-forming visions of a greater future as protectors of the earth and all its living creatures

Made in the USA
Middletown, DE
09 November 2022